ΛCTS OF
G⬡D

Praise for *Acts of God*

'A brilliantly self-aware and satirical debut, *Acts of God* confronts all of us with an existential question that nobody was expecting: what if – instead of being a writer with an unshakeable inclination towards poetic justice – the Creator was actually a mad scientist?'
— Anees Salim, author of *The Blind Lady's Descendants*

'This is an audacious daredevil of a book. *Acts of God* vaults higher and higher through fireworks of invention and imagination – while somewhere even higher, I thought, the spirits of Douglas Adams and Kurt Vonnegut watch and applaud.'
— Raghu Karnad, author of *Farthest Field*

'Kanan Gill's *Acts of God* is an intriguing – and fresh – take on the classic SF warning against the temptation to literally play God.'
— Gautam Bhatia, author of *The Wall*

'Kanan Gill is a naughty, weird genius – which, of course, is the perfect kind of genius to be. And *Acts of God* is a geeky, hilarious, thoroughly entertaining and richly imaginative work of fiction. I couldn't help but "hear" every sentence in the author's voice, which adds much charm to the writing, and every second page elicited a chuckle. But don't let the inevitable laughter deceive you: behind all its lightness is a real talent at storytelling, a bold sense of creativity and a capacity to hook even somewhat wary readers. After all, as a historian, I was unsure about venturing into sci-fi, and certainly found myself thrown occasionally. But in the end, the book proved to be that special thing: unputdownable.'

— Manu S. Pillai, author and historian

ACTS OF GOD

KANAN GILL

HarperCollins *Publishers* India

First published in India by HarperCollins *Publishers* 2024
4th Floor, Tower A, Building No. 10, DLF Cyber City,
DLF Phase II, Gurugram, Haryana – 122002
www.harpercollins.co.in

2 4 6 8 10 9 7 5 3 1

P-ISBN: 978-93-5699-682-3
E-ISBN: 978-93-5699-699-1

Typeset in 11/14 Adobe Garamond at
Manipal Digital Systems, Manipal

Printed and bound at
Replika Press Pvt. Ltd.

'Colorless green ideas sleep furiously.'
– *Syntactic Structures*, Noam Chomsky (1957)

'God may not play dice with the universe,
but something strange is going on
with the prime numbers.'
– Paul Erdös (attributed)

STORAGE INSTRUCTIONS FOR THIS BOOK

Store this book in a cool, dry place.

Alternatively, you could toss it into a hot, humid hell, string its pages on a clothesline or crack its spine over your knee if you feel violent. Punch this book in its book mouth(!) – how could it say that? Hold this book by its jacket collar and demand more, grab it by its feet and shake the hidden words out of its pockets. Or, if you'd rather love, then love this book with all your might, trace your fingertips gently over its jacket, literally, digitally and spiritually. Take this book on a world tour, hurl it from a train window, spring its pages like a flip book and smell that strange book smell that comes from the salty mix of ink and sweat and paper – the bouquet of a story? Is it the smell of acceptance, rejection, writing-rewriting, editing, fretting, forgetting? Is it the smell of your own soul? Or perhaps the funky odour of a good book gone *bad*. Have you left this novel unread for too long and its contents have now soured? Or are they sulking? Have the words gathered in hard-to-read corners, demanding to be teased out? Best to junk it then. Stories past their expiry date cause indigestion, nervousness and the rapid precipitation of strong opinions. Best to keep it back where you picked it up. The ideal place to store this book is in a shining bubble of possibility; it could be great, it could be terrible, full of poor syntax, sleazy semicolons and missing punctuation. It could be many things, but I guess we'll never know.

ALLERGEN WARNING

The author sneezed repeatedly – both on screen and paper – during the construction of this book.

Viruses wearing engagement rings on their heads battle brave bacteriophages between the words you read. The war between sickness and health is an invisible side plot only for our microscopic readers. PLACE YOUR BETS IN SOILED HANDKERCHIEFS.

This novel is not for the feeble of spirit or for people with better things to do. Some parts of it have been written with an almost infuriating freedom. Speed-readers have been unable to develop sufficient traction and book-skimmers have reported digestive distress as this novel comes pre-skimmed, with several bits containing 0 per cent plot.

This novel may cause an urgent impulse to throttle the narrator: *Must we spend thirty pages describing this building or what the sun looks like? Why can't you just get on with it?* A dread may loom in the ominous onset of another huge windowless block of text. For that matter, one may wonder, why was any of this even written? To clarify, this book is not intended to be a page-turner, but loud sighs near the corners of pages might flip them. You are invited to experience this work as a cocktail going in or a hangover going out. You might feel a little sick, but you'll be fine. Don't worry about it.

PREFACE

The author presents this preface to disseminate some important information, but primarily to annoy you.

Prefaces are for cowards who like to present lengthy caveats to offset criticism, like poets with more preamble than poem. The author submits that he is a coward and takes great pleasure in your displeasure. *What's next?* you think furiously. *A Foreword to the Xth edition? A note from the publisher? A smug introduction from a more successful author, or a sneaky glom-on from an unknown one hoping to attach themselves to a posthumous publication?*

What follows is just the book, I assure you. But before that, a temporal clarification. This book takes place in the future – the relative future. Not an absolute later that giggles at the inevitably incorrect futurism of the past, but a moment in time that dangles ahead of whenever you might be. You may also be the sort of person who deeply concerns themselves with narrative vantage points and drinks hot water in hot weather. Who is telling this story, where do they aim their binoculars and why are their pants around their ankles? The underpinnings of these notions are best left to be scratched furrows on the heads of philosophers. It is, as they say, not your problem.

The moral right of the author has been asserted, right here under your very nose. Every subsequent word is now soaked in moral might.

The nature of this story is such that it invites a small amount of plot-based speculation. Readers have a tendency to step back and feel certain that they know where all this is headed. This is a tendency that the author would like to discourage. First, it'll spoil the story for you, and second, if it brings you pleasure to outsmart some printed words, then you're miserable enough to write your own book. Make your own ranch and wrangle your own wild sentences. Graze on your own experience. If you've already had enough and plan to head off, leave the door open just a smidge. I like to feel the breeze.

CHAPTER 1

~: Log –o

Logging program created by the inimitable, wise and holy Dr K.

Options:
-b: Brief
-v: Verbose
-d: Dramatic
-ld: Less Dramatic
-c: Comedic (broken)
-e: Experimental (broken, but this could be intentional)
-o: List options
These options may be used in conjunction with each other.

~: Log –b

BRIEFLY:
ITERATION ZZCY20

Failure. God-generated destruction event.

~: Log –d

DRAMATICALLY:
ITERATION ZZCY20

A thick cowl of grey cloud crested the city of Mumbai. Webs of light ran screaming in circles; vibrating explosions of sound rang so loud they curdled the air, every person, every sensation; every errant particle thrust its panicked elbows toward the barricades near Colaba Causeway. Rusty barriers had been hurriedly placed by the anxious police and were being guarded by the anxious military to separate the anxious throng from several anxious world leaders and the source of everyone's anxiety. Huge floodlights stuck out their yellow tongues in the charcoal air, tasting the thin slashes of drizzling needles, necks and telescopes, and television cameras craned to get a look at it. There it stood in the sea, gigantic, too big to bob, coloured like obsidian, like jet, like cold lifeless eyes, like shadow-streaked slate, like a cosmic pit stain, like a sidereal ^c
    Exited.

~: Log –ld

LESS DRAMATICALLY:
ITERATION ZZCY20

The spaceship was black and very big. It hovered blandly off the coast of Mumbai, and in the twenty hours since its arrival had issued only one communique. The leaders of the world had arrived as quickly as they could and were now getting their make-up done in temporary tarpaulin tents with little flags of their countries stuck outside. Scientists were postulating, gesturing and shaking their heads; two screenwriters were being told why they had been called; several intelligent people were trying to put a religious spin on the events; and the person that the aliens had requested for alienally was making his way through the barricades. A lot was going on.

A few hours after landing, a rectangular shaft of light had opened on the ship's surface and shone through the Gateway of India ('Gateway of the World???' – ran a leading news channel) and a crisp alien voice had curtly requested the world to produce before them a 'P. Manjunath, Detective'.

Someone with high security clearance was patting foundation gently on the nervous face of the Indian Prime Minister, who was wondering how to turn yet another catastrophic failure into a success. In his long career in power, his party had first counted all of his failures as incorrectly measured successes, then proceeded to extinguish all institutions that called a spade a failure, then celebrated failure as the storm before the calm, then denounced failure as a dastardly ploy by the extinct opposition to spread 'negativity', then ignored failure entirely to focus on the emotional toll it was causing the PM, and now, if this alien arrival turned out poorly, well … it wasn't clear what was left to do. His truculent advisor who normally handled this sort of thing had been killed a few hours earlier when the spaceship had landed neatly on his head, on a yacht in which he was planning the latest genocide. Liberals had cheered in their hearts at his death, for it would be against their values to publicly celebrate anyone's violent end. Instead, they wore knowing smiles and nodded at each other on the street – this alien visitation had started on an enormously positive note.

Just as the Prime Minister had concluded that fleeing was his best choice, the two nervous-looking screenwriters and a thick-chinned intelligence agent entered his tent.

'Well?' choked the Prime Minister. 'Come to expose me as a fraud?'

The intelligence officer looked confused for a second and decided to answer this at chin value. Gazing at an infinite spot above the Prime Minister's head, he said, 'No, sir … um.'

'Well, then what?' spat the PM.

'Um. Yes. Our intelligence team has quickly gathered that these two women are responsible for the script of the film *Invaders*.'

The PM blinked at him.

'*Invaders* was a hit movie released last year, sir.'

The PM considered this briefly and then broke into a smile. 'I see! You hired them to spin this alien thing as a positive story for me. Fantastic. We'll start with me working hard and barely sleeping—'

'No, sir ... um.'

'Well, then what?' spat the PM.

The screenwriters, who had been smiling at each other on the street before being summoned, found their voices. One of them said, 'Have you watched *Invaders*, sir?'

'No. I'm the Prime Minister. I barely have time to watch all my favourite TV shows.'

'Well, sir ...' said the other screenwriter. 'If you had ... you'd realize that this ... that everything that's happening is ... more or less exactly like the script of our movie.'

The PM rose to his feet, only half his foundation done. A thought thudded from premise to conclusion across his mind in heavy shoes. His small eyes widened as they filled with a solution, the same solution he had to most problems.

'You mean to tell me ...' said the PM, stepping towards the two quivering women, 'that you are in cahoots with these aliens?' He clapped his hands in excitement. 'Fantastic! Will they listen to me? How do they feel about history? Will they convert?'

'No, sir ...' said the two women in unison.

'Well, then what?' spat the PM.

'It's just ... an alarming coincidence. The ship is exactly as we described it, it landed where it does in the movie, at the exact time, the rectangle of light emerged in the same way, and they asked for the hero ... Well, they asked for someone – the name is different from the one in the movie. Honestly, what kind of a name is P. Manjunath—' said one of the screenwriters, who felt that writers ought to stick to simple uncomplicated names so that movies could track well internationally.

The intelligence agent coughed at them to stop. 'Sir, we have interrogated them and found no extraterrestrial link, because no one really has an extraterrestrial link – this is actually humanity's first contact with aliens. We just thought that since everything seems to follow the plot of their movie, it would be best to contact them to ask what happens next.'

'Well, what happens next?'

'In the film, sir,' said the other woman quietly, 'the hero speaks to the aliens and they tell him that they have come to take his wife to their planet, and if she doesn't come with them they will destroy Earth.'

The PM rolled his eyes.

'It … it wasn't our initial idea, sir. In our script the aliens threatened the planet with annihilation and a woman went to their planet to make a case for Earth being allowed to exist. It was about her selfless sacrifice and the transformative effect she had on the violent colonizing aliens who grew to love her, and she them. How she introduced the species to the concept of compassion, thus sparing—'

The other screenwriter cut in, '—the producers said they loved the script but felt that it needed a hero to "anchor" it. So we added an estranged husband to the mix as a B-story and how his wife's case for our planet's existence – because we can love – helped him finally get closure on their relationship and heal. The producers loved the revision but said they wanted some minor tweaks, and so after a couple of drafts it became about a man protecting his wife, and how he's … better at violence than the aliens.'

Both the screenwriters looked uneasy.

The intelligence agent put his finger to the receiver in his ear as it suddenly buzzed with conversation. There was no need to do this, but everyone still did. He lowered a curved finger slowly.

'Sir, the man the aliens have requested is here. But it appears that … he has no wife.'

In the tent, all the uneasy eyes met uneasily. Even the make-up artist, who until then was staring at the floor, found it staring uneasily back at him. A similar slowly growing uneasiness had descended upon everyone on the planet since the arrival of the aliens. It was a feeling that lay just beyond the enterprise of words; it was as if they had had a look behind the curtain of reality and found an otter dressed as a question mark reading a menu. It felt a little like the grand design was plagiarized, like all of reality was someone's idea of a joke.

They were soon to realize that it was.

P. Manjunath was escorted through a sea of faces in various stages of anguish and concern. In contrast, he was smiling. An irritated smile, the smile one smiles after a joke so terrible it has fallen through the bottom of creativity to reach back in through the top. An angry smile, a frustrated smile, an enlightened smile. As the ship grew closer, his escort fell away. As far as they were concerned, escorting people to aliens was a new job that had popped into existence and it was not theirs. A Tactical Strategic Initiative Action Team was supposed to be present to discuss the next steps, but they were still discussing whether they needed more adjectives.

Walking towards the Gateway of India, towards the ship from which the aliens had asked for him by name, P. Manjunath felt many things. He did not, however, feel surprised.

The world gaped as he walked, up to the ship's outer shell forged from some imbricated impossibilities, a material between elephant skin and asphalt, between snake tears and fresh tar. Upon reaching the unfathomable, overwhelming body of the alien spacecraft, the world watched with bated breath as he simply knocked on it.

The knocking was loud and hollow, and far louder than the impulse that caused it. The echoing metal clang seemed to come from all around them, wonderfully equalized, as if played from great speakers in a theatre slightly larger than Earth. The power and terrifying beauty of the sound was such that it instantly hushed the commotion. The screenwriters and intelligence agent rushed out to see what was happening. The PM decided to finish his make-up.

The spot where P. Manjunath had knocked dissolved into light. A light that spread to form a large iridescent doorway. Without any obvious movement, the light now formed the outline behind a huge alien being, with lidless eyes and concrete-coloured skin, humanoid as far as limbs, their location and their quantity were concerned.

The screenwriters shouldn't have been surprised, but they still were. This was the alien they had thought of. It was the alien that had revealed itself to them when they were doing mushrooms in the hills of southern India, the alien that had come to them in spirit, in loving service to the script they were writing, born from the secret universe that lies beneath ours, the secret universe to which mushrooms issue visas. Sobering up, they had determined that the alien face of their visions had been a tree trunk. They had tried to describe what they remembered to a VFX artist, who had put his own spin on things to finally create the alien from *Invaders*, the facsimile of which they were now seeing in non-enlightened, non-mushroomed reality. P. Manjunath remained impassive.

'God?' he said.

In the smooth skin below the eyes of the alien a cut appeared, as if an invisible scalpel was drawing itself across his face, slicing the surface into a smile. The alien chuckled. A decidedly human chuckle, from a gravelly, decidedly human-sounding voice.

'In a sense,' said the alien.

'So I was right,' replied P. Manjunath.

'Almost.'

'What happens now?'

'What do you think?' The alien laughed.

And then the universe was destroyed.

Charred splinters of time-maintained integrity long enough to indicate that this happened instantaneously.

Another second, if allowed to be, would have recorded an implosion, the wild-howling weight of the universe arriving at one single point, a cosmic smooshing of every dimension, every star, every planet, every asteroid, every comet, every particle, every field, every caterpillar, every chequebook, every curtain, every moment of all time, and ringing through it all would have been the alien's laugh. That decidedly gravelly, decidedly human laugh.

Process terminated. Logger detached. Reprint? (Y/N)

Exercise 1.1

MATCH THE FOLLOWING

(5 marks)

Scientist	Repository
Detective	Monster
Logging	Black box
Speech	Fear
Authority	Bourbon
Root	The Danish Police
Long-tailed Tit	Destiny

These concepts are looking to connect with someone and settle down. You are in charge of making it happen. Of course, there's no way of knowing the answers yet. This is an exercise for you to attempt now and once more on completion of this novel.

Why not? Speculative fiction should have more speculation.

Answers at the back of the book.
(But don't look now.)

CHAPTER 2

'Dr Krishna, Genius Category 3, has announced his decision to step down as Global Convener of The Scientific Institute. He will still be present in the capacity of research scientist. The institute has no further comment to make at this time, so stop asking.'
— The Scientific Institute (1-DS-A) Gazette

Amongst other things, this story is about pain.

Most things are about pain, but it can be hard to tell. Despite its dominant role in global politics, pain keeps its name out of the papers. Pain is the shadow cabal that controls the world, pain is the axle grease for Earth's rotation, pain is the pendulum and the *b o n g* of the doomsday clock. Tick tock.

Unlikely headline: *Leader advocates increasing military spending because he is in pain.*

The establishment of the no-pain-no-gain orthodoxy ensured the integration of pain into the capitalist ethic, whereas some other economic structures just ended up with no gain and only pain. Economists will tell you that this anomaly is gain's own fault and sociologists will tell you that they are in pain.

In this insidious way, pain writes itself into our lives. As a necessity, as a backlight through which we see our outline. Pain shows us our shape, pain defines us and our extremities – how much can you take, how much will you give?

So far this chapter is a *pain*.

Behind every action – irrational, prescriptive, proscriptive or cruel – there is pain. Pain denied, pain refused, pain dispensed, pain received. Where there is a whiff of destruction, there is a wick of pain. On both sides of trauma's see-saw, pain sits and pouts. Blessed are those who find pleasure in it.

The drama in all actions, all fractions, all passions, every quadratic modality, each didactic anomaly all reduce down to pain. Pain in the springtime, pain in the rain, at this time we are not certain of the location of the pain in Spain. The poets were the first to know and thus poetry is a pain:

> *Betwixt the stirrup and the ground*
> *Mercy I ask'd; mercy I found*
> *But when I hit the ground,*
> *There was only pain.*

The keen eye looks out at the world and sees that this whole show is run by pain and people who are in it. We still suffer cascades of cruelty caused by skinned hearts throughout history. So it is more accurate to say:

Like every story, this story is about pain.

The specific isomer of pain in this story is **regret**, and the anthem of this **regret** is a question you can and do ask yourself:

If you could start again, would you? If you can, will you?

Would you give it all up to get it all back? (Y/N)

Done? All right, in six-eight, double time – let's go!

≈

In the cafeteria of The Scientific Institute (1-DS-A) lay a pile of human wreckage. Its shocking white hair was splayed like slain seaweed on a metal table in the corner. The head the hair called home was using the coldness of the surface to stunt a monstrous hangover.

Dr K, Genius Category 3, Convener of The Scientific Institute (former) and crushingly hungover (current), straightened up and tried again to focus his red-webbed eyes on a report.

The report was displayed on what will be referred to as a monitoring tablet, since it is a tablet used for monitoring. It bears no official name, being among Dr K's many remarkable inventions which he never bothered naming because he knew what they looked like. Some of Dr K's other creations were:

- Enemies.
- A black box (created in conjunction with Dr P).
- A heretic power source.
- A pursuit vehicle for elite government commandos called a Silverfish.
- Five prototypes of the Silverfish that he wasn't supposed to have.
- A superior, secret version of the Silverfish that he *really* shouldn't have.
- The world's least useful language.
- The world's foremost artificial artist.
- A pill to cure the human condition (trials ongoing).
- Truly wrinkle-free trousers (not featured in this story).
- A neural interface to melt the barrier between worlds.
- A thousand obliterated universes (oh boy).

This morning, the monitoring tablet carried a report that made Dr K cringe. Embarrassment is generally the sediment of memory, especially drunk memory, but this report was a bit excessive. Even presented plainly by his less dramatic logging program (log –ld), it seemed far too heavy-handed. To enter the Lower Reality as an alien just to aggravate P. Manjunath and assert his superiority was cruelty without style, and thus inexcusable. Dr K sighed. He just didn't handle defeat very well.

Time to try again.

As he waited for the mist of alcohol to lift, his hearing expanded to the cafeteria – where no eyes were trained on him, so every mouth could discuss him in whispers sharp, cold and metallic enough to make more tables out of. He was the subject of many parallel, often contradictory streams of gossip. But should you rely on gossip or trust the steady hand of this narrator?

In the future, postmodernism has been solved by mathematicians and found to admit a trivial solution: 1. That is, if you shine a lie through two narrowly spaced slits in a piece of paper and observe the result, you are still a liar. Mathematics has also been proved to be complete, but with some pieces misplaced.

Below is the interference pattern made by some of the cafeteria's gossip.

Dr Krishna looks like shit.
He does look like a little digested.
How is he *always* hungover?
He doesn't like being called that anymore.
What do you mean? He's *always* drinking.

No one likes being called shit.
He doesn't like using his full name, idiot.
Don't hangovers cancel each other out after a point?
He must have been through something rough.
He hasn't been through anything.

I heard he invented something that broke his spirit.
Really?
It's possible.
How can an invention break your spirit?
The same way your personality does.

No, *something happened* and then he got fired—
Do you know all his hair turned white overnight!?
I think he resigned.

Whatever. *Something* happened and it wasn't good.

From being Global Convener to now working under Nataliya, that's a big fall.

Oof.

I used to idolize him.

We all did.

He needs to get his act together or they *will* fire him.

He's a Genius Category 3. They don't fire people like that.

Category 3? That doesn't sound so high.

One day black hair and then – poof!

The categories start at A, you idiot. The numbers come after the letters. He's the only Category 3 in history.

Wow.

I think some people are too smart for their own good.

Or anybody's good.

Well, you don't have to worry about that.

Oof.

Illuminated letters ran along the edge of the desk, which spelled a name no longer in use, followed by 'Genius Category 3'. Dr K squeezed through buttes and bluffs of paper scattered across his office and made his way behind the desk, wincing from pain that seemed to come from everywhere.

Under it, in a soundless black obelisk, ran something extremely illegal.

Something more illegal than anything else in the world, something that kicked through a law that floated too high for anyone to even consider, the kind of law that it took a highly intelligent person to realize was being broken, and a special kind of genius to break. There were only seven other people in the entire world who would recognize the black box; two of them were dead, two complicit, two too frightened to speak and one who didn't know what it did.

Glancing quickly at his monitoring tablet, he saw that the iteration that was churning inside this black box (ZECY889) was futile and would need termination. Before exacting the pettiness he would use to bring about its end, he kicked things off by kicking his desk, causing stacks of paper to scatter all across the room. He really didn't handle defeat well.

As you can probably imagine, in the future, paper is scarce. The broader imagination can invoke a history scarred by ashen eagles of dust sweeping across charred stumps in a radioactive war-ravaged explosive tizzy, blood-soaked, char-blackened, bullet-streaked hides of pleading animals; soot-smeared lungs crying hoarse cries, cries unheard by their own shattered eardrums, pleading desperately to the cruel hearts of greed and power that smote their land, their will, their lives. You'd be wrong, of course, but you could imagine that.

The narrower imagination is better applied to the situation. Forests covered most of Earth, trees stood whistling happily with their hands in their pockets, mushroom, moss, muskrat, mouse and their larger colleagues roamed happily in the narrow alleys of jungles. There wasn't paper because no one needed it anymore. Of course, people wanted it, but that's what regulations were for.

To that extent, Dr K's office laughed in the face of regulation. It spat at the feet of regulation, spoke behind regulation's back to its colleagues, RSVP'd to regulation's invitations and absconded, sent anonymous letters to regulation, rang regulation's doorbell and ran away, stole regulation's banking information, spray-painted lewd graffiti on regulation's wall and slept with regulation's husband.

His office had a lot of paper. Lined from floor to ceiling, wall to wall with sheets, prone to frequent avalanches of yellowing cellulose, there was only a narrow clearing from door to desk through which Dr K squeezed every day.

As he scribbled in indecipherable symbols about how best to humiliate and dominate P. Manjunath this time, there was a knock on his door. Subconsciously he pushed the black box deeper under his desk with his leg. Not that anyone would know what it was.

'Enter,' said Dr K.

He looked up to see his supervisor in the doorway, giving him her widest, least earnest smile.

'Dr Krishna!' Nataliya, Genius Category A (yeesh), beamed.

He did not respond.

'Sorry. I forgot you don't like that name anymore. Hello, *Dr K!*' continued Nataliya, who was also regulation's biggest fan, and equally fond of its parent concern – bureaucracy – and their progenitor, the system. She would, however, surrender this allegiance that very night.

'Yes?'

True to form, despite her furious resentment of him, Nataliya attempted a pleasantry. 'How are you, Dr K?'

'Slowly rotting under my skin.' Dr K's grey flesh looked like a rainy day made of leather. He presented no smile.

'So droll. Dr K, this … er … tablet in your hands, I am not familiar with it. A new creation of yours?'

'I use it to summon demons from the netherworld. They do inventory management for my blood covenants.'

'I see it projects spatially beyond its boundaries, which is … astonishing … How do you manage the plane of projection to be beyond—'

Dr K disabled the monitoring tablet so that it sat upon his desk like a clear and impractical paperweight. Now barricading all avenues of small talk, he said, 'Can I help you with something, Nataliya?'

Nataliya took a short sharp breath to keep anger out of her voice.

'Yes. There's been a problem with your – with the – the … device you submitted. Is it a device? The pill. There is a problem with the pill you made. And it's something I have to keep coming back to you for because you refuse to explain anything about it … If you could tell me, I could—'

'There is no problem with the pill.'

'The test group is *complaining*, Dr K. The results show that it doesn't do what you claimed. In fact, it does the opposite—'

'It works.'

Nataliya balled her hands into fists in her coat, keeping her voice level.

'I am not doubting you. I am relaying the information to you. The group is saying that it just causes them pain. The pill doesn't do what it is supposed to. It just causes them constant throbbing pain in their heads.'

'That's what it's supposed to do,' said Dr K calmly.

All of Nataliya's suppressed anger burst out in the next sentence.

'That is not the purpose of the device, Dr K, and you know that very well!' She steadied herself once again, her voice now shaking. 'I gave you … clear instructions … the hypothesis, the intention, the objectives, they could not have been more precise.'

'It will take time. Give it time. The pain is a part of it. In fact, it's almost all of it.' Dr K picked up a pencil and dangled it over the surface of the page.

Nataliya recognized this action as a threat. He could consider any matter, in any circumstance, and block out the outside world completely. Or at least that's what it seemed like because he wouldn't respond. Once the pencil made contact with paper, this conversation was over. She spoke quickly.

'If these findings are rejected, then this project is done! If it doesn't work, then we can't … This is my career's biggest project! I'll be finished! It is essential that you—'

He put pencil to paper and, as far as he was concerned, she disappeared.

If he was paying attention, he would have heard her say, 'Whatever you're going through, I'm sorry. But other people in the world also suffer.'

And if he was paying attention he might have said, 'I'm sorry too.'

≈

We can step back now to consider that while the gossip formed a reasonably accurate picture of Dr K, it lacked a certain *nuance*. The gossip couldn't take you to his office, describe his secret black ziggurat or throw hint-seed for plot pigeons. Perhaps you disagree and hold strong opinions of narrative pacing, frothing at the mouth at any slowing of the story train. Maybe you hope this paragraph has a pay-off and isn't just an amateur affectation. Or maybe you're irritated by the narrator constantly showing you his cards and asking whether a pair of threes is any good, and whether he should keep betting or fold. Or maybe you're ecstatic, who knows? How *do* you think this is going so far, though?

When we last left Dr K, we were considering that he would have said, 'I'm sorry too.' But his sorriness didn't coincide with Nataliya's, or with the general consensus of cafeteria gossip. It was true that his persona had recently inverted. Black mane to white, lightness of being to dark. A fall from grace.

The seldom spoken of, ex-charismatic and ex-powerful ex-head of The Scientific Institute was an ex-celebrity who was ex-revered. Phrases such as 'the smartest person in the world' and more poetically 'that smartest man in all the land', were often sighed in his wake. But this new avatar, who had voluntarily resigned only to pick up some piddling low-level project to work on, who was blunt, rude, curt, hungover and unpresentable, who carried dark check-in bags below his eyes, commanded no such reverence. He was too cold to even foster an environment for pity.

And what right did someone so gifted with intelligence and opportunity have to be morose? Especially in an age of freedom, where the government never drew its curtains, crime was microscopic, war was impossible, poverty and overpopulation were whispers of the past, where Earth received monthly check-ups and scientists were free to wave all the magnets at all the speakers they wished?

What is the existential function that turns people inside out?

Romance? Nope. You don't know him as well as I do. He wouldn't have cared.

This wasn't that. Disillusionment? That's only the skin. Love the flesh, and pain the seed. What happened took a savage bite out of everything, swallowed it into nothing and threw open to the elements his rotting core. It left him with nothing but anger.

Dr K let the anger take the wheel, let it buckle grief in the back seat and hand it a sipper bottle full of whisky. The effort had turned his hair white overnight. It had flushed him with a single purpose. His anger had drowned out the despair.

Dr K was slowly understanding that anger can be fun too. Anger signs off on cruelty without reading the contract. Anger can be the whetstone for the sharpest mind, anger can slip quite easily into trousers of purpose and anger now held the pencil that scribbled schematics on a piece of paper in Dr K's office. Many wheels of his plan were in motion as he thought the thought that had pulsed in minds since the Mesopotamians.

Fuck everything.

Vengeance? What does vengeance have to do with all of this? Steady now, I assure you the answers are defrosting as we speak. Oh! – I think Dr K's done scribbling.

Pencil now raised, Dr K closed his eyes and activated his Neural Interface that functioned as a conduit to transmit his consciousness to the Lower Reality. He sent his mind into the black box below his desk. It was time to raise demons from the netherworld.

CHAPTER 3

*'On further consideration, Dearg Eberhardt (code name Kraken)
is too panicky and erratic to be a viable candidate to run the
experiment. The most fitting member of the Monsters for the task
seems to be Olivia, but it will take considerable changes in her
family tree to make her the protagonist.'*

– Dr K, Iteration ZECY889 Autopsy

~: Log –ld

LESS DRAMATICALLY:
ITERATION ZECY889

Strobed black lights sputtered onto the third floor of a nightclub in
Kreuzberg, Berlin, bright-dark-dark, bright-dark-dark, bright-bright-
dark-dark-dark – giving everyone the odd sensation of being in a stop-
motion animation, a low-quality reality with not enough frames. A
throng of people danced together by themselves. Say what you will
about loud drug-addled weekend-long raves, they do make you less
self-conscious.

P. Manjunath tried to dance his way through, but the lights were making him feel like he was teleporting. Turning on a small flashlight, he carved a careful path through the audiovisual explosion emptying itself into dilated dancers. In the corner, in black and silver, massaging a single sofa to the pulsating techno beat, was Dearg Eberhardt, the world's foremost computer scientist. His relentless intelligence tortured him on its own altar, so at every given opportunity he would slip out of his senses and find a nice place to be un-sensed and insane. He also spent some of his intelligence creating a graphic novel about demons from the netherworld that dealt drugs to engineers. It wasn't very good.

Manjunath tried to get his attention, but it was too loud and too infrequently lit, so he grabbed the intensely intoxicated Dearg and yelled into his face.

'I need to talk to you!' he screamed. 'If I'm correct, you are on the verge of a breakthrough! We might all be in great danger!'

Dearg looked at his face as if it was the first face he had ever seen. Eyes and a nose and a mouth that just happened to be adjacent. He raised his hands to Manjunath's face and began to feel it. He registered it as a nice change from the sofa, RUB-rub-rub, RUB-rub-rub, RUB-RUB-rub-rub-rub.

Cursing, Manjunath drew the fascinated man gently out of the club. As he walked backwards slowly, the crowd now permitted him through. They were extremely high, not unreasonable. He continued leading Dearg until he bumped into something. Something wet, something hot, something that growled.

The music stopped dead just as the lights stopped stuttering and snapped to a deep, bright red. People looked up and around, checked their limbs and their wallets. And then the screaming began. The floor bubbled and melted, hissed, swelled and sizzled, and out of it emerged terrifying claws! Scores of mottled red arms like large open wounds pulled horrifying bodies out of their own dimension and into the nightclub.

Manjunath ducked, grabbed Dearg and ran. He didn't turn to look at what he had bumped into; he didn't need to. He had a pretty good idea what it was.

He sped down and out of the club as fast as he could, Dearg in tow. All around them the club contorted, mirrors twisted and burst, blood seeped from every available seam. As they reached the ground floor, where the DJ had been impaled on a smooth subterranean spike, where the growls and screams and yowls and gurgles of Manjunath-knew-what were the loudest, he noticed that the crowd present simply stood still. No face that he sprinted past registered fear or panic. He couldn't think of a word for that expression, that wasn't his job. He was a detective, and that expression had never fit into a witness's description of anyone. It was the expression of leaning too close to reality and seeing the brushstrokes.

The club was an abandoned coin mint that had been graceful enough to fall into just the right kind of post-industrial ruin that was worth partying in. Reaching the wrought-iron gate, Manjunath found that Dearg had freed himself from his grasp. The computer scientist was now staring in horror at the scene, straddling that strange area between disbelief and whatever the opposite of disbelief is.

The club had distorted itself in a plane normal to his own psychedelic-induced mental distortion, the net effect being he saw things just as they were. More clearly than even Manjunath could. It was for that reason that he decided he believed firmly that he couldn't believe what was happening. 'Es kann nicht sein ...' he whispered as Manjunath grabbed his jacket, yanked him into the street and dragged him along.

They ran down a street that had pulled its cap over its ears and gone to bed. All the stores were shuttered except one – an electronics store, at the window of which was a television showing an interview of the Indian Prime Minister from his trip to Germany, an interview he hadn't expected, with an interviewer he couldn't have killed, an interview in which he would go on to say, 'Well, define mass murder?' and quickly shuffle out.

They stopped near an empty döner kebab shop. Manjunath had to hold on to Dearg, who didn't seem to want to stop running. He wasn't very sure why they'd started running. Manjunath tried to speak, but the amount of oxygen his body was demanding was nowhere close to being met by his heaves. Finally he managed to say, in between huge gasps: 'What are you researching?'

'What?'

'What. Are. You. Researching?'

'It is … a secret.'

'I need to know! Are you in a group called Monsters? Have you come close to—'

But Dearg wasn't listening, because the air in front of him was drawing closer, twisting faster and faster, with blobby spheres followed by tinier and tinier ones forming a portable typhoon. A sudden bolt of lightning cracked the asphalt beneath them and electrified the globes, forming a single dripping, scaly, pus-filled, bleeding, buffalo-horned demon. Its flesh was raw and ragged and flayed, like a huge scab eternally peeled; blood oozed through fibre and tendon to glisten in the blue run-off of the neon döner kebab sign. It looked like a 3D model of a child's nightmare, and from Dearg's expression it looked like it actually was.

The demon spoke, not in deep demonic drawer drag, but a normal voice. A decidedly gravelly, decidedly human voice.

'Want drugs?' it asked.

Dearg gasped stupidly. Manjunath pulled from his jacket a copy of a graphic novel, Dearg's graphic novel. Dearg's graphic novel, published under the ambitious nom de plume of 'A. Türing', Dearg's graphic novel mis-published under the mis-spelled nom de plume of 'A. Turning', Dearg's graphic novel on whose cover, splashed in two dimensions, was the very same demon. Words failed both Dearg and A. Turning, but not P. Manjunath.

'God?'

The demon smiled brightly, its eyes glowed like sunburst through methamphetamine, from its mouth came a sound like the tinkling of ice cubes in a whisky glass, followed by a slurp, the sound of a mouth being wiped and a muffled, instinctive, 'Whoops, sorry.'

'Why are you doing this?' shouted Manjunath.

The demon's flaming eyes slowly went dark. 'Because you can never stay out of it.'

And since this is a record, it can show that the döner kebab shop exploded just a little before everything else on Earth did. Just a little before the waterfalls and the mountains and the temperate grasslands and the mangroves and the deserts and the cheesecakes and the perpetual calendar watches and every lump of creation exploded independently and collectively. The source of the explosion, the trigger, the straw that detonated the camel's back, was the ö in the word döner. It has to be said, it looked surprised.

Process terminated. Logger detached. Reprint? (Y/N)

CHAPTER 4

'Obituary: The Medical Institute announces the untimely death of Doctor Perenna, Genius Category 2. The full autopsy is available at The Repository.'

– *The District Gazette,* Page 7 (Births, Deaths)

Dr K was eating a banana on the train home, and it surprised him. If you eat a banana, and only eat a banana, without watching, walking, talking, thinking or soldering, then the banana opens its heart to you. Whatever your eating style or chewing ethos, you'll find yourself at a point where the banana has turned to mush between your teeth, necessitating tongue acrobatics to flatten the sludge and deliver it down the pipeline. Here, something amazing happens to those who stick around. Through the foamy sweetness rises a sharp tang, pressed flat against your tongue, giving you the unmistakable impression that at some point, when you have a banana in your mouth, the banana is kissing you goodbye.

Or maybe he was missing her.

Under the canopy of shocking white hair, his forehead twitched to reflect his distress. That internal emotions have an external component, a little facial signboard, a sentimental turn indicator, is evidence enough that emotions are designed to be shared. Why would they love broadcasting themselves otherwise? But this wasn't the time, and these weren't the times. Everyone kept blankly to themselves, allegedly the highest form of social order. Mind your own business, even if it trembled out of your fingers, even if it leaked out of your tear ducts and especially if it soiled your trousers.

The train slid quietly through a wild forest, emitting only a faint rattle and no light. It technically ran with no sound but since, when it was first introduced, animals kept plunging headlong into it, a synthetic rattle and a scent had been added. These worked as sufficient warning for most animals, except bats. Bats kept trying to mate with the train, but this caused them no harm other than quiet embarrassment.

Now, as the hyperspeed serpent slinked along, a memory dinged at the mental terminus. Painful memories have strong legs from walking repeatedly into the spotlight. It was the memory of the last time he spoke to Perenna. One of the hits.

Flashback 4.1

A splinter of time stuck in your paw.
Genus: tormentum
Phylum: memory
Binomial nomenclature: regret regret
Sharp bitter taste, occurs frequently on public transport.

Abstract: The scraping of chairs drawn, the shuffling of bodies lifted. A fierce tension strangling every particle in the room. The trial was over.

Interim verdict: Dr Perenna to be placed under house arrest until subsequent trial.

'Congratulations, Krishna,' said Perenna. 'You did it.'

Across the large table, then black-haired Dr K pleaded, 'Perenna! Just don't do anything stupid. Please just—'

'Oh, but you have all made sure that I will forever be unable to,' said Perenna.

'It's just until the next trial, Perenna …'

'Is it?' she said softly. 'I just wonder … I wonder what will happen to the rest of you.'

She glanced at another member of the room who was ruffled enough to sputter, 'Is this a threat?'

'Oh, very much so. But not from me.'

The Chief's eyes glinted in the corner. She said nothing.

Dr K's voice faltered. 'Perenna, you were advised not to—'

'Yes, yes, I was advised. And you followed all the rules because you're a good little boy. A Big Boy now, sir – The Convener, sir. Congratulations on removing me, the persistent stain from your life, Krishna. Can I address you as such? What would you prefer, sir? Dr K?' She squeezed the HT pin on her coat, which chirruped in a small voice, *'Accept this outcome.'* Perenna laughed.

The Chief interrupted in her cold, clipped way. 'That's enough.'

Perenna looked hard at Dr K. When she did this, she was usually fixing her centre of gravity to deal a killing blow, a searing series of flame-edged words to cut right through him. But this time, when she looked like she was ready to burst, the anger left in a sigh. She looked betrayed. She looked defeated. She looked broken.

What she told him hurt more with every passing day.

'Krishna, I hope you get everything you want.'

He blurted stupidly, in the only way blurts appear, his most true concern, 'What will you do?', a crack appearing in his decidedly gravelly, decidedly human voice.

As Perenna was led away, she said, 'Figure it out, genius.'

Now Perenna was dead. The genius sat alone in the train.

He was still trying to figure it out.

The same HT pin from the memory now sat on his lapel. He squeezed it.

'You must focus on the task,' said the HT pin. Dr K nodded to himself. This he was doing; this he would do.

The train ran from The Scientific Institute to the 1-DS-A residence quarters, which might have been in China at some point. The countries of the past had dissolved; names of places and semantic anchors had eroded, their original significance only conjured for questions in pub quizzes. The silliness of antiquity makes for great facts. Here are some facts about your future and this novel's present.

The global nuclear fallout was very predictable, greatly upsetting science-fiction writers and the several people who died in it. Many thousands of nuclear explosions were the chime that sounded when progress had finished cooking. The surprising part was that it was caused by a shortage of sand. More specifically, a global conflict resulting from a trade battle, caused by a shortage of sand. Who would've thought? Sand is quite important and it had slipped through everyone's fingers. In the direct aftermath of radioactive fallout, this didn't seem very funny. Far be it for me to further a stereotype, but the radioactive do have a poor sense of humour.

Those lucky enough to be in bunkers hung around for a while. Gradually their hanging around began to feel like *waiting*, which begged the question – exactly what were they waiting for? Instructions? From whom? Perhaps it was time to take the radiation-emitting matter into their own hands.

Some fatalists got bored and left their underground concrete cubicles to burn, deform and die in the glowing winds. Other conspiracy theorists refused to believe this 'nuclear fallout narrative' and marched off into the forest to be away from the oppressive bunker hivemind sheeple (we'll meet their descendants soon). Those that remained focused on fixing things. Counterintuitively, the problem caused by bombs was solved by more bombs.

It was a child's suggestion that had sparked the idea. She had asked, 'Can you explode the opposite of a bomb?'

Of course not. They could, however, explode the opposite of an effect. Fast-acting blossoming biomes were thus fired at all the radioactive epicentres, then at their siblings and friends. Acting as particle sponges, the unbombs made a quick job of turning the nuclear wasteland into a regular wasteland. Now slowly emerging from their holes in a world with a fraction of the population and a smaller fraction of the infrastructure, people were finally in a position to do something, hopefully something different.

Incidentally the most violent people on Earth, leaders of nations, whose itchy fingers hovered over detonation triggers, were all in their own private fallout shelters, completely safe. People like that always are. Luckily, standing at a broken pulpit in a shit marsh of their own doing made their opinions lose considerable sting.

The countries finally met, not as flags on the lapels of singular leaders, but as congregations of everyone who'd survived, and it was decided by consensus that perhaps this separate countries thing wasn't the best idea. Investigation unearthed political divides as arbitrary and re-earthed our home as one place; a shimmering disco bauble spinning over a cosmic after-party, a baby blue *Vote For Life* button on a dark velvet lapel, a nutty chocolate miracle wrapped in crinkly cerulean prayer rolling around in God's glovebox – immense, impossible, unbelievable, alone. Our only spot in eternity. Our home.

A monolithic government emerged, one identity with nothing on Earth to fight, something that had been scratched on the last page of every conspiracy theory – A One-World Government – although it was hardly as bad as the conspiracies had imagined. The only real issue was what to call it. World Government, Earth Government, United Government all sort of conveyed the point, but were making a declaration over nature that made everyone a little nervous. It reeked a little of the same instinct of domination that had always got humanity into trouble.

Humanity's progress was never at war with nature. But, if it was, we had lost quite terribly. For a few centuries, Homo Sapiens Sapiens were in the lead, but as with all unbelievable leads, it was because no one else was running. A battle against all other organic matter is a losing battle. We lack the tools to measure it, but there is sarcasm in decomposition, arrogance in amoeba, threats in thunder and gurgling laughter in volcanoes. Nature does not accept victory with grace. Now people lived with the smallest intrusion possible, finding hopeful hooks of symbiosis on which to hang their existence. Trying not to draw attention to ourselves. Against the earth we were outgunned and outnumbered.

It was decided that in nomenclature, they should best leave the planet out of this, simply calling the new arrangement *the* Government. Now all institutes bore that simple prefix: 'The Agricultural Institute', 'The Scientific Institute', 'The Repository', 'The AI Creative Review Society', and a geographical suffix such as 1-DS-C. But we'll get to that later. That's enough facts for now. *Ding!* – you've passed the qualifying round of this pub quiz.

Also *Ding!* – This was Dr K's stop.

He beat the mud path back to his home. Entering his house, he squeezed the HT pin absently. *'You must focus on the task,'* it squealed again. He nodded. The house was a tremendous mess of paper, dust and broken glass. All the cleaning mechanisms had been reconfigured to do nothing and, if possible, dirty things further.

Another small instrument of self-punishment.

In his study, he swept aside heaps of paper from his desk. Pushing down the surface gently, a small click thrust up another little black box. He found a dirty glass and made himself an Old Fashioned, now better called an Extremely Old Fashioned. Laziness had reduced the recipe to neat bourbon, four sugar cubes and a memory of orange. Inside the unblemished surface of the tower ran Dr K's hope. Swallowing a big mouthful of bourbon, he pulled out a monitoring tablet.

≈

To understand exactly what task was being focused on, we must temporarily leave Dr K to his devices and offer the reader a record of a meeting that should be official public record but isn't. The reason for this obfuscation will be clarified later, but some of the hidden minutes of the secret meeting are as follows:

The Council on Simulation Rights

This council recognizes that it is very difficult to simulate a universe. The council also takes cognizance of the immense risk to global security of such a simulation and acknowledges the need for continued secrecy. Since such secrecy is against The Foundational Charter, the council finds it necessary to create the following guidelines.

— *It is forbidden to simulate a universe without explicit approval.*
— *Explicit unanimous approval must come from the Government, the heads of all major institutes (even The AI Creative Review Society) and the Authority.*
— *Since knowledge of simulation does not extend to these bodies, it is understood that the currently held secrecy will have to be broken for another simulation to take place.*
— *It is not currently possible to interfere in an ongoing simulation. If such a method is to be found, it is explicitly forbidden in whatever form it might take.*
— *Members of simulated societies enjoy one right in our world. The right to life, inasmuch as a simulation may not be terminated externally. It must be allowed to reach its own end.*

A full account of the council's discussions cannot be viewed at The Repository.
    This Council has taken place in the year UT350, attended by the Chief of the Authority (Global), the Convener of The Scientific Institute (Global), the Head of the Committee for Theological Discourse (1-DS-A), the Chair for the Committee for Automaton Ethics (1-DS-A) and by Dr Krishna, Genius Category 3, and Dr Perenna, Genius Category 2.
    Essentially, a simulation is an imitation. A replica of a situation, made from different things for different ends. A shower can simulate rain, a toy can simulate a train, a swing can simulate a swaying cradle,

complex mathematics can simulate the behaviour of a crowd and, in a pinch, self-destruction can simulate comfort. For a simulation, more important than *what* is *why*. The purpose of the simulation dictates its form. A bathroom shower can be a reasonable simulation to test umbrellas, but not the grip of car tyres. Similarly, the mathematical model of a weather system serves well to predict typhoons but will not dry your hair.

And all the imaginary situations you brew, in which people say horrible things to you – these are simulations too. So is the wish for wonderful things, the swimming shadows of delicate dreams falling always further down the hall. In that respect, every person runs a simulation of the future in their minds. Anxiety and hope are simulations bundled free with the human experience. The reason for these simulations is unknown and widely held to be 'not worth the trouble'.

So, in this story, which is about simulating universes, the vital question is *Why?* What could the purpose of all this be? Well, that's what the story is about! You are free to speculate on every alternate chapter.

The idea of simulating worlds is as old as any language to think about it in. It is not a lengthy stroll from pondering the existence of God to arriving at *'Well, what if I were God?'* The idea rolled around in several heads as a curiosity, a joke, an existential threat at the end of an existential thread, but had never quite ascended into possibility. Until it did.

No records remain, but we can say for sure that the first crude simulation, mimicking only the origin of the larger universe with no granular details, was done in the twenty-first century. It was brick-and-mortar science, made of red-faced transistors, huffing and puffing and shoving jiggly electrons billions of times over, taking up the energy of almost a few cities. We guess the simulation chugged along for a few seconds before shuddering to a halt. The mammoth task of running it caused an amount of pollution that even the staunchest conservative couldn't ignore. It was not repeated. That's not how things are done now.

The modern method of such a large-scale simulation is arcane and complex. So arcane and so complex that it had taken two of the world's foremost geniuses to come up with it. They had done it at the age of sixteen. Perenna and Krishna, friends and classmates, genius and genius, had produced the greatest scientific accomplishment of Unified Time. The Simulated Universe. Everything within everything. The full tomato, skin, seeds, juice, taste, fields both exciting and excitable, and even a little green crown.

The results of this immense accomplishment – of a bird's-eye view on bird's-eye views, of squeezing the pimple that yields the primordial ooze – were disappointing. And after they were done disappointing, to the untrained eye they were boring.

To simplify complex conclusions, we could now say with certainty that every universe with the same starting conditions as ours always ends up exactly like ours. Exactly. The simulated mirror the simulators. The cosmos, the planets, life, Earth. The centre of our focus always ends up with humans, in countries with the same names, with people doing the same things, discovering the same things, at the same rate. Destiny, it appears, is immutable.

Right? Imagine how our geniuses felt.

Simulation after simulation, things did not change. Until Dr Perenna worked out theoretically that they would not change. Every simulation that started the same way ran the same way and ended the same way.

Why not change how it started? Because the slightest turn of any knob, a hair's difference in time, temperature, pressure, density, dimension or composition would result in a swift collapse. A quick wet cough and it was all over. It appears that things are only the way they are, otherwise they are not. Dr K had worked this out.

And then there was the One Huge Difference between their reality and the simulation. The simulation never reached their present. It would always freeze, stop, hang, get stuck at the same point.

Every simulated universe would end at the same point in the twenty-first century.

It is important to note that Dr K and Dr P's method of creating simulations was done in secret and, after the secret escaped, it was abruptly banned by those newly in the know. Simulation was outlawed, and a council had carved in stone the policies for the future. Understandably, this was upsetting for both of them. Dr K's reaction was not furious alcoholic haranguing, but quiet subservience. He used to be quite different then. Dr P's reaction was closer to furious alcoholic haranguing, but you won't meet Dr P. You would have, had this story started a year earlier, but then there would have been no story to tell.

Now you know the dark secret that whirls in Dr K's little black boxes.

≈

Sipping bourbon, Dr K growled at the monitoring tablet.

Not only was he simulating a universe (very wrong), he was simulating many (very *very* wrong). He had privately figured out how to intervene in running simulations (smart but wrong), and thus was interfering with ongoing simulations (extraordinarily wrong). He was also terminating them before their natural conclusion (outrageously wrong), and he had used his observations to identify laws governing Simulatus Interruptus (smart).

Also the term 'simulation' was used in all scientific discussion because it seemed less superior and smug than the original term the creators preferred. The title of their paper (which only one other person had read) was *A Study into the Creation of Lower Realities.*

The infinite cosmos, understood only as a series of incollapsible dualities – womb and pyre, awe and terror, estuary and desert, desolate and teeming, violent, beautiful, chaotic, interminable, elemental, the crucible for savage transfiguration of force into form into force the violent battleground of creation – spun quietly in a black box on his desk. Iteration ZZHM03. Dr K didn't have high hopes for it because of that infernal, infuriating man.

The same simulated human spanner was in the works – P. Fucking Manjunath.

On the monitoring tablet, the whole universe of iteration ZZHM03 bared its guts. From the tablet he could see every aspect of every corner of anything he chose to, but Earth was his only area of concern (most of the universe is unfurnished). The slightly more terrifying prospect was, through the tablet, Dr K could *make* any alteration to the universe he wished. A few taps could perform a variety of actions, ranging from controlling a member of the Lower Reality to turning a galaxy on its side. From his fingers he could weave the gospel of domination. Total control, absolute power. He could see all, know all and be everywhere. Like a … well.

Now, using the tablet, he had destroyed a building in Lower Reality iteration ZZHM03.

Each time his enterprise was invariably defeated by Manjunath, he would destroy the universe and start again. But after several experiences of this, he sought a way to lessen the sting of defeat. This had led to the creation of the *Neural Interface*, through which he could witness and interact with the Lower Reality. It was a way for his consciousness to virtually *enter* the simulation as any being he fashioned. He could become a person, an alien, a demon, once even a cloud, and see the look on Manjunath's face as he destroyed everything. It was unnecessary and cruel. But he enjoyed it. It was the only thing he permitted himself to enjoy.

Of course, his entrance into a Lower Reality was a disruption that would quickly render the reality useless and inert. Any successful intervention was delicate. It had to be, according to the Lower Reality Laws.

These laws that Dr K had discovered and codified may seem obvious to the philosophical and empathetic and, for that reason, weren't to him. They are best understood as a thought experiment.

Imagine, if you will, that you are as you are, sucking your daily life out of disposable cups bearing your name, going to locations to do activities, struggling with feelings, and suddenly a colossal watermelon greens out the sky – falls from the heavens – and shatters, spitting rip tides of redness, rains of flesh and black cannons of seeds. Imagine if it found a mouth and talked. How would you feel?

Horrified? To find your religious convictions invalidated, your philosophical notions kicked in the teeth, your spiritual certainties flung in the bin, your very view of reality nipple-twisted? Thankful? To find some respite from your internal you-centric view of the world, an opportunity to spin the camera outwards for a change, to turn the page and start a new one with, 'So there are giant sky watermelons …'?

No matter how you'd feel, you would eventually make peace with it. Your strongest instinct, the desire for stability, would take over and jump on any problem areas until your beliefs were once again nice and flat. C'est once more la vie.

But, what if, after that, coconuts played concertos? And the sea turned to curtain rings? How would you feel then? How much rattling would your constitution take until you took off your hat, sat on the floor and said, 'Fuck this'? When you can't trust reality, when whatever happens for no reason whenever, what's the point of doing anything? How would you feel if you looked closely at creation and saw the brushstrokes?

This is what Dr K discovered almost a year ago.

The Lower Reality Laws lay scribbled on a piece of paper somewhere in his house. Obviously, because he was careful, he had written these in code, and because codes can be cracked, his code was a new language altogether, and because languages can be deciphered, he had developed one that couldn't be. It had no use and no meaning to anyone except him. Less a language than linguistic froth. Uncrackable.

Skilled readers who browse this book while engaged in espionage or archaeology will point out that there is no such thing. But code-cracking and language-deciphering and other envoys of making the unknown known work in the same way. They pull out big magnifying glasses and gaze upon the cryptic through the lens of the known. A thing worth writing down and encrypting would have the same tells: adjectives, qualifiers, verbs and nouns who betray their code by showing up repeatedly. Categorize words by their frequency of occurrence, and suddenly you have a reasonable way to develop hunches about which word probably meant 'the', which one meant 'a' and which one meant 'skipping'. Given just a few uncoded words then, or a few guesses with master's degrees, the whole thing fell apart. You could yank one thread and strip the brocade.

But what if some lunatic developed a language in which each concept was represented by symbols and the symbols were never repeated? What sort of foamy-mouthed plastic eater would create and then remember a new symbol for each and every occurrence of each and every concept? Who would be so smart, so stupidly? Well, the self-same loony whose name streaks these pages, of course. Our own paranoid, revenge-soaked, heavy-drinking Dr K, with so many marbles that he could afford to lose a few.

I will not reproduce the text here. I have my reasons. I can, however, emulate somewhat the heavy-headed throb of confusion the symbols created, below:

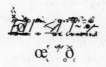

They synthesize the unique feeling of seeing plainly that you're missing something. The feeling that the cryptographic keys are missing from your coat pocket.

The reader can put their decoding hats away, for as the narrator and creator of these symbols, I can explain the above in a way you can understand.

Lower Reality Laws

[...]
Terminology: External interruption of the Lower Reality is called an Act of God.

1. *An Act of God causes emotional disruption to members of the Lower Reality.*
2. *Too many Acts of God cause Lower Reality members to cease function. They sense that they are the pawns that they are and become totally useless. Requires termination of Lower Reality.*
3. *I haven't arrived at an exact formulation of how many Acts of God this takes, and how it relates to the magnitude of the AOG. Lacking a way to quantify events and their impact. Best bet is to keep it to a minimum. Few and far between.*

Below this text, less formally, is written:

Essential to develop a more rigorous AOG theory. I really need to know how many interruptions I can make in their reality, what kinds of interruptions, how far apart, etc. But when I consider it … it seems so absurd. How do I quantify their despair? How do I measure an Act of God?

This is extremely frustrating. I can't just tell them what to do without risking their derealization. I just have to keep nudging them in the right direction. Too few nudges and they keep reaching the same place. Too many nudges and they shut down. It is proving an enormous challenge to make them do what I want.

But failure is not an option, and there is an upside. When a Lower Reality becomes useless and requires termination, I've started going down there and having some fun.

≈

It looked like Iteration ZZHM03 was a bust. Deciding to make another drink before he brought a small universe to its end, Dr K was suddenly aware of a voice from the side wall. 'Excuse me, sir?' it said timidly.

'What?'

The freshly painted wall had been trying to get his attention for a few hours. 'Sir, I have completed another work ... I just wanted to see if you ... if you ... I mean ...'

The wall, both painter and painted, was trying to call attention to itself. The normally mud-coloured wall had been suffused with chromatophores. A Creative AI System oversaw the wall, triggering the chromatophores to think they were protecting their host by assuming a whole gamut of colours in different shapes and sizes and effecting a collaborative, non-destructive, non-polluting, high-contrast, artistic camouflage. A painting.

The wall unit in question was designed by Dr K, unregistered with the AI Creative Review Society, quite a bit more capable than the rest and, as such, very illegal.

Creative AI systems were designed to seek feedback, for reasons we'll see later. For now, the wall wanted to know if it had done a good job representing what had been asked of it, which was a picture. Of Perenna.

This wall is also the narrator of this story. It's me! Hi! As you are just about to read, I used to be very different.

The wall had had a very difficult life. Dr K had discouraged it from style to style. He had berated it from surrealism to hyperrealism, from the classics to cubism to increasingly abstract representation, ridiculing its every attempt, offering no encouragement, no praise and no guidance other than calling it untalented. He now gazed at the newest work – a white ocean, a moony milk backdrop for blue ribbons twisting unto themselves, intersected by an irregular red geometry.

Art critics from the reader's time would have invoked the threads of fate, calling to the heavens for grammar fitting enough to grace a description of the work, streamed joyous tears because they finally understood what it meant to *feel* art. Dr K only sighed.

'You hate it,' said the dejected wall.

'I hate it. You are a terrible painter.'

The wall winced, its panic lighting up the chromatophores who detected the peril and randomly reordered themselves to resemble a muddy reef – their default setting. Through the jumbles of umber the wall whimpered, 'What's wrong with it?'

Dr K clucked his tongue. 'You're obsessed with representation. If I wanted something that obvious, I would just look at her picture. Do you hate art? Or do you hate yourself? Or maybe you hate me? But that can't be. Because even hatred is an emotion, and this work was done by someone who has never felt anything in their life.'

The wall's weepy voice showed that it did feel many things. 'I understand emotion! Please give me another chance! Please!'

Dr K sat back in his chair and rubbed his temples. 'It might be easier if I just made a new creative system. One more … capable.'

'No!' squeaked the wall. 'I can do this. I promise. Please just … please.'

'Fine …' Dr K sighed and the wall gibbered some senseless gratitude before turning black and dropping a curtain while it worked. Of course, Dr K wouldn't tell it that there were now tears in his eyes, and a fist was pushing its way up his throat. He wouldn't tell the wall that every painting it made was a symbol in his language. Every part, every clause, every symbol, whatever it meant, was she. The cipher was memory. The key was loss.

For the last time that night, he shook his head and gulped down a drink, falling asleep almost instantly after being awake for four hair-whitening days. Sleep meant that he didn't end the simulation running on his desk, which was just as well, because it would turn out to be the last one he ever ran.

The dastardly destiny that disrupted his Lower Realities was also at work in this world. Whatever it was that turned the clockworks, bumped the particles, hissed silky lights from stars and made painters paint had also made a Genius Category A wander into a Genius Category 3's office in the dead of night.

What Nataliya was looking for we will see. But what she found, she determined to be a small black rubbish bin. Unfortunately, with her was a Category M who, through the same destiny's designs, knew exactly what it was. In a few hours, more people would know that there was something very illegal going on, and who was doing it. The next day would give Dr K's upside-down world one more twist of the tesseract.

But for now, he was asleep. On his desk the little box chugged away.

CHAPTER 5

'... Anansi is predicated on freedom. The anonymously run "free-money app", seems to deliver on its promise of, well, free money. Our reviewers were able to sign on for the second drop and did indeed receive a credit to their digital wallets. The burning one-euro question, then, is where does this act of seeming benevolence originate, and what unknown strings are attached?'

– Opinion Piece, *Technagent*

A logging program is the omnipresent voyeur stitched into the system. With ears the number of mouths, eyes the number of sights, it sees all, knows all, but can't do anything except talk about it. Like ... a narrator.

The primary job of a logging program is to keep a record of everything that is happening in a system. That is, everything the person who wrote the logging program thought was important to record. This can make for a rather unexciting read, which is why loggers are mainly used to recount ruin. If a system has a problem, something is misbehaving, data is absconding without leave, screens are frozen in fear, then the logger is checked to see where the ball was dropped.

Dr K was frequently bored reading logs, especially those of Lower Realities, so they were imbued with personalities. There was a Brief logger, a Dramatic logger, a Less Dramatic logger (because the former could be a ham), a First-Person Perspective logger, an Experimental logger that never ran quite right and a newly minted (but far too desperate) Humorous logger. Each logger had its attitude, fashioned out of all the art in the genre, left to ferment in it and create its own voice. Reporting objective events with subjective style. While it was impossible for the logger to know the thoughts of any people in the Lower Realities, it began to make guesses, to report the inner worlds of the people it observed to amplify its particular genre.

These were the same logging programs Dr K and Perenna had once used to help Dr K become charming. He currently does not present any charm whatsoever, but he really could if he tried. But now there was no longer any reason to try.

Now, while Dr K snoozed before one of his universes, the loggers reported faithfully from within.

~:Log –ld

LESS DRAMATICALLY;
ITERATION ZZHM03

P. Manjunath read the newspaper in the nude because it made him feel closer to things. Strange enough as this is in private, it is even stranger for someone to do it in the office of one's detective agency. Strangest still to do it while a client sits across your desk, waiting.

Chaitra's eyes bulged in her face above her saree. If it wasn't hot and unventilated enough, the office was also filled with smoke of no certain origin, and the detective she had hired was reading a newspaper, his rotund head and naked shoulders peeking out of the top like a centrefold reading a centrefold. The frustrated glint in her eye reflected in her gold necklace as she cleared her throat. Again.

'Mr Manjunath,' she said in a trembling voice.

Manjunath looked over a very curious article and found a vibrating woman sitting opposite him.

'Yes?' he said obliviously.

'I am waiting,' Chaitra said, glowering.

'Oh, did you want to read this? Just a minute ... curious what's happened in Copenhagen. You know, I have a strange feeling ...' he began to offer the newspaper to Chaitra, who refused violently.

'No! You keep that! Keep it! I wanted to know about ...' here she adopted a conspiratorial tone, the hushed voice and slanted glance cavemen first adopted to talk about buffaloes, and said, 'the job ...'

'Oh ...' said Manjunath, mirroring her inflection and eyelid separation, 'it's a pretty good one. Pay is good, most clients are very stupid. This one lady wanted me to follow her husband to see if he was having an affair. Hilarious!'

The one lady who had hired him rubbed her fillings against each other while he continued.

'Ridiculous,' said Manjunath. 'I mean, why not just ask him? Suspicion is like an eagle, I always say.'

Chaitra was too irritated to ask why suspicion was like an eagle. She yanked the conversation back to its original route. 'Yes,' she said through gritted teeth, root-canal caps almost sparking, 'that was me. I hired you to find out if he's having an affair. Did you follow him?'

'I did. I found something rather troubling ...'

'I knew it,' hissed Chaitra. 'Where does he meet her?'

'It appears that he puts more weight on his left leg than his right one,' said Manjunath sadly. 'In the short term this isn't the biggest problem, but it severely affects long-term mobility—'

Chaitra got to her feet and pounded two small bangled fists on his desk. They were hers. Columns of smoke spiralled up and away in fear, the rattle of her heavy jewellery like a designer desert snake issuing its final threat.

'Mr Manjunath ...'

'*Detective* Manjunath,' he corrected.

'Detective is not a title,' spat the jewellery snake.

'Really?'

'What? Yes – did you really think – no! Stay on the topic. I have paid you, paid you a large amount to follow my husband and tell me if he is having an affair. I will ask you one last time, *what did you find?*'

Manjunath was taken aback, his constitution slightly rattled, his newspaper slightly crumpled. 'I did find something. When you hired me to follow him – and I was following him quite well, I assure you – something happened; I think my phone ran out of battery, there's this new application that gives you free money – free money! Can you imagine? It's called Anansi. Do you have it? No? Sorry? Oh yes, something about my phone. Was it mine? Or was it a clever decoy planted by sinister hands? To what end? From which middle? Hard to say. In any case, the phone that was with me ran out of battery and I grew worried that if someone wanted to contact me, they wouldn't be able to, so I asked this nice man ahead of me if I could use his phone. And he was kind enough to let me call most people I know to ask if they wanted to speak to me. It turned out that they didn't, but a lot of them were nice about it. After a while, *his* phone ran out of battery and we got talking because we thought this was quite funny. Slight faux pas here on my part – he asked me what I did and I told him I was a detective following someone to see if he was having an affair – and then I remembered that it was him I was following, so I quickly covered it up by asking him if he wanted to follow his wife to find out if she was having an affair and then, strangely, he told me that … he had no wife.'

Icicles quickly crackled inside Chaitra and she stood for a while like a body at Pompeii that was very shocked right before being engulfed by lava (an acceptable response). A slow, sinister smile spread across her face. She clapped her hands.

'So … it appears you have uncovered my motive. Well played, Mr Manjunath, well played.'

Unsure of what exactly was happening, Manjunath joined the clapping. 'Good game by all parties, it's the spirit of sportsmanship that's important,' he said.

'The truth is, I was obsessed. Obsession is a cruel thing, Mr Manjunath …' Chaitra spoke for a while and Manjunath slowly returned to the article he had been reading while she spoke. A senior scientist at the Copenhagen Nanoscience Research Institute was missing. No note, no packed bags, no signs of foul play. One evening she had left the office and simply vanished. Police had looked into everything short of the sewage pipes and found nothing. It was as if God had pulled her neatly out of the world with tweezers. Curious as this was by itself, it was curiouser that it wasn't by itself. Manjunath's intuition had reached out and soldered together some connections from across pages and volumes of newspapers. Like a Roman priest who found an unsatisfactory amount of entrails in a sacrificial lamb, he felt that something was up. He wasn't sure what.

While most people sought to be masters of their own fate, Manjunath had accepted that he wasn't in charge. His life often felt like having hands taped to the wheels of a self-driving car. He was just along for the ride. This realization had had a profound effect on him, not quantifiable as better or worse. He had accepted the twists and turns and T-junctions of fate as the nature of the beast. So he didn't worry about it. The veil had been lifted and he finally understood that he had been the veil.

He couldn't and didn't control what his antennae picked up, and they had been picking up some strange things. Odd events were befalling the scientific world. Institutes were being broken into, technology was being stolen, shipments were vanishing and now scientists were disappearing. The global spread of these events pointed fingers at almost everyone and so, no one in particular.

Something rang within Manjunath's forehead – a feeling like a sharp brassy crash – the loud banging of dinner plates. It was a wind-up monkey playing the cymbals of intuition.

'… and that is why I hired you,' said Chaitra, sweating now from the strain of her revelation, panting from the effort of exposition.

'I see,' said Manjunath, when in fact he barely did. There was a lot of smoke.

Chaitra took out an envelope stuffed with notes. 'I hope this buys your silence,' she said.

Manjunath whistled at the thick stack of money, 'This could actually buy many things.'

Chaitra picked up her bag and headed for the door. Standing there with her head in the smoke clouds, she grinned. 'There is no smoke without fire, is there?'

Manjunath was reading the paper again.

Chaitra paused with her hand on the door frame, her presence shrouded in smoke, buckets of spinning light falling on her from a passing police van. 'Mr Manjunath … Why is suspicion like an eagle?'

'Is it?' asked P. Manjunath.

≈

Manjunath Detective Agency consisted of two small rooms with ancient pista-green walls that had been repainted only where they had peeled like camouflage, making the office look like it was hiding in a bush. A yellowed calendar wilted on the wall with the right days and dates, but the wrong year. Manjunath's great-grandfather had purchased it in his youth, and felt that it was a shame to throw out a perfectly good calendar just because the year had decided to change. The calendar turned into a family heirloom and this year, eighty-four years later, it was once again perfectly accurate.

The smoke in Manjunath's office oppressed the dust. A former client and several former writers had correctly deduced that there was no smoke without fire, and the fire that birthed this smoke was camphor wrapped in garbage bags in a bin by the door. His assistant had lit the camphor to suffuse the atmosphere with peace and, troubled by the peace, Manjunath had covered it in plastic rubbish bags. Now everything bore the unmistakable smell of deluxe temple trash.

The oppressive smell was just as well because it won over the dominant stench of the area – urine. Located in a small unlit alley, blackened by paintless time, the area's walls aroused paan spitters and pee squirters alike. Although only Manjunath Detective Agency's walls were free from this oppression due to a cunning use of religion.

Frescoed on the wall of the detective agency were porcelain pictures of Gods. All the Gods that could be mustered. Blue ones, white ones, haloed ones, crucified ones, places of worship substituted for the ones that didn't allow pictures, and one that just said 'Om'. Here, finally, was religious harmony, ideology and philosophy locking arms to face the common enemy that unites all theology – pissing. And it worked! Not a single drop was shaken free from a member on that wall. Not one red speckle of paan slashed its divine surface. However, people had begun to throw garbage there.

A statue of a God that only one person knew sat on the desk of Manjunath's assistant, Heng, who had created it and, by extension, the God. Several of these figurines, which Heng carved out of soap during his free time, dotted his room in the agency and parts of Bangalore that Heng frequented. The layout of the office was such that the front door opened into Manjunath's room, which clients would have to walk through to go to Heng's room, to take appointments and wait, and then return to Manjunath's room when their turn came. The paan-smeared stress of this chaos often reduced Heng to a nervous mess, but it was no obstacle to his employer who refused to change the rooms for 'temporal reasons' (as yet unexplained).

While the client was in the next room, Heng was enjoying a moment by himself.

Hearing a door close in the other room, Heng guessed that the client had left, though this wasn't always an accurate guess. Sometimes Manjunath would leave his office and hide until the clients went away, but now, in a cloud of smoke that smelled like ancient plunder, he walked in to see Heng. Newspaper-reading time now concluded, he had put on a pair of trousers that fit perfectly and then tightened his belt buckle to make them uncomfortable.

He tossed a thick envelope of cash at Heng.

'Is this yours?' he asked.

Heng missed the catch. The envelope landed on his neat table and spilled its contents.

Gasping at the money on his desk, Heng said, 'No, sir. Did you find this?'

'That lady just gave it to me while I was reading the paper. Not sure if this is a refund, or she's hiring me for a job, or she paid me for sex and then forgot the sex part, or she is a playing-card dealer giving free samples who has confused money for playing cards, or she thinks she is applying for an internship at a currency-counterfeiting institute and is a forgery savant, or these notes are her children and she is giving them to us to keep a watch on while she goes to work, or maybe this isn't money at all but several copies of new novels that just display nice numbers, or maybe she is an envelope salesperson and has just filled it with money to show its capabilities and capacity—'

'Sir!' screamed Heng. When first employed, he was afraid to interrupt his boss, but a year of employment had taught him that this could go on for hours. He beamed at Manjunath. 'That was our client. Congratulations, sir! I guess the job went well! We can finally pay for repairs and rent and—'

'—Heng, book two tickets to Copenhagen.'

Heng winced. 'Denmark!? Why, sir?'

'I have a feeling …' said P. Manjunath, drama mounted and he rode it till the door until—

'What feeling?' asked Heng.

Manjunath pouted.

'A feeling that something will happen in Denmark, idiot. Why else would I say let's go to Denmark and then say I have a feeling?'

'Because sometimes when you say you have a feeling, it's an insect biting you and you're not sure what's happening. Once it was a snake, remember? When we went to that tea estate—'

Manjunath interrupted the earnest aside with his hand. 'I get it. Let's just … let's stay on track. I have a feeling. Now we know I have a feeling about Denmark. Denmark is the place about which I have a feeling. So let's go to Denmark, and we can book tickets with this money. One for me and one for you.'

Heng nodded, and Manjunath now felt the smoke begin to clear, garbage and camphor both reduced to the same ash, the holy and the wretched dissolving to the same residue, and he felt that this moment could be left on the knife tip of drama, saying, 'I have a hunch about what's happening … but I hope to God I'm wrong. At the crack of dawn—'

'We'll need to get visas,' said Heng.

'We can't … we can't just leave tomorrow?'

'Indian passports, sir. We'll need visas.'

'How long will that take?'

'About two weeks … if they approve them.'

Two and a half weeks later Manjunath and Heng sat in an aircraft that burned its lungs over Earth from Bengaluru to Copenhagen. Manjunath drunk, Heng alternately reading a traveller's guide to Denmark's sights and carving another soap figurine, and neither knowing that they were sharing this moment with the destruction of the Copenhagen Nanoscience Research Institute.

At almost-dawn, through the shiny air-conditioned gates to the Kingdom of Denmark, passports stamped and alcohol retreating, Heng hailed a taxi to their hostel, but as they rode Manjunath once again had a feeling.

'Heng,' whispered Manjunath. 'Something is wrong.'

Heng's eyes went wide as he gripped the door handle. 'What? Did we forget a bag?'

'Worse,' said Manjunath. 'I don't know.'

'Sir … if you don't know what is wrong, then how do you know if something is wrong?'

'That's just how things are sometimes,' said Manjunath. 'They are wrong before they are things.'

Sitting ahead of them the driver nodded, a faraway look in his eyes.

'What should we do?' said Heng.

'I think we need to go to the Copenhagen Nanoscience Research Institute. Now.' At the intersection, the driver took a turn.

≈

A dramatic approach was writ that day. The car pulled itself over a hill, and as the horizon inched lower, a plume of smoke gathered in the centre frame, circling down and pinned to a pile of rubble that used to be their destination. Emergency services and reporting-on-emergency services circled the smoke like the close of some ancient ritual. The cab driver gaped and gaped again, horrified at the destruction and struck by the metaphysical implications of delivering travellers to a place that didn't exist any more. Should he still charge a fare? He decided he would.

Heng rummaged in his money belt as Manjunath bolted out of the still-moving car.

As he reached the smouldering wreckage of the Copenhagen Nanoscience Research Institute, now jogging and wheezing, he had a feeling that this had happened before. He had that feeling all the time. It was as if every page of his life arrived smudged and dog-eared, making him wonder – has someone read this already? This was new to him, but who was it a revision for?

On the horizon's clothesline, dawn hung a faded blue sheet. Around the sizzle of a freshly charred building, bleary-eyed police officers stretched little plastic cones, firefighters anointed smoky remains to exorcise the ghost of combustion and journalists thrust mics into the ash, smoking their guns. A chubby middle-aged Indian man with a face the colour of a more confident dawn walked up to the perimeter, tossed a card at a police officer and walked through.

In Scandinavian surprise, the police officer read the business card which said 'P. Manjunath – Detective'.

The police officer knew that he was only supposed to let other officers through, but this portly brown man in a beat-up leather jacket looked like he was exactly where he belonged, and so the officer opened and closed his mouth a few times, let an objection almost turn into a mumble in his throat, and then quickly decided to study his feet, drawing circles in the concrete, coming up with excuses for a situation in which if this was to be a problem, it wasn't his fault. Confidence rattles the strongest of constitutions, targeting directly the most hallowed human want – the desire to not look stupid. Only confident people should have to deal with confident people; they scare the shit out of everyone else.

This was what he was doing when Heng whistled past him.

Catching up to his boss, Heng panted in his ear. 'Is ... is this prudent, sir?'

'I thought it was Denmark,' said Manjunath, which doesn't really mean anything worth meaning.

With a quick jump, Manjunath got on his hands and knees and started to crawl in the ash and rubble. The devious business of detection is not for the fainthearted or weak-kneed. Like a speedy scuttling crab, he scrambled and burrowed over collapsed beams, under incinerated columns and between vaporized servers. Through the large compound of the institute he zigged and zagged, following invisible dotted lines, the sharp lefts and T-junctions of fate.

With a glazed look in his eye, he only stopped to shake his head and click his tongue and say, 'Of course!' Heng followed close at his heels and knew better than to interrupt. 'Finally, stopping at a seemingly arbitrary point in the scorched obstacle course, Manjunath grabbed a fistful of ash and screamed wildly. It wasn't a scream of celebration or failure; it was just one of those things.

He sat upon the wreckage and lit a cigarette.

'Perhaps you shouldn't smoke,' said Heng.

'Why not? Everything is burnt already.'

'It would be ... it's in ... poor taste, I think. To smoke at the sight of a fire ...'

'You have to think like fire,' said Manjunath, gesturing to the charred remains of the ex-Institute in his clenched fist.

Further debate on what constituted a fire-centric mindset was interrupted by the arrival of a police officer. It was probably the scream that had alerted him, or perhaps the scream along with the high-speed scuttling and now carefree smoking at the site of a fire. Hand on his automatic weapon, he loomed large over them.

'Who— Are you stealing from the site?' asked the officer, incredulously indicating Manjunath's clenched blackened fist.

'No,' said Manjunath. 'I assumed this was free.'

'Hand it over!'

Happily, Manjunath opened his fist and blew the soot over the officer. Coughing and wincing in the cloud of ash, the officer choke-shouted, 'That was it!? You were just taking ash?'

'I'm a collector,' said Manjunath sombrely.

'Who are you?' screamed the officer.

'Who are you?' replied Manjunath.

'I'm Heng,' said Heng.

'What are you doing here?' screamed the officer.

'Detecting,' said Manjunath.

'I'm with him,' said Heng.

'You are not allowed to be here!' screamed the officer.

'We agree wholeheartedly,' said Manjunath.

'Correct,' said Heng.

The police officer's grasp of their imperial common language was strong, but he couldn't help feeling that this conversation was slipping through his fingers.

'This is a crime scene!' screamed the officer.

'What makes you think this is a crime?' said Manjunath.

This stopped the officer's charging fury for a moment. He considered the question.

'Of course it's a crime scene! It's a scientific institute set on fire!' said the officer.

'And you're sure they didn't want to set it on fire?' asked Manjunath.

Here again the officer was forced to weigh this proposition. Confusion met irritation and sat on curiosity.

'What? Why would they want to set it on fire?' he stammered.

'You should ask them,' said Manjunath.

'But who are they?'

'Don't you even know who they are?'

'I … I … The scientists? You think the scientists set it on fire?'

'Scientists are always doing experiments. Maybe they wanted to see if fire was still doing its job correctly.'

'I … I mean that's a stupid experiment. Why would they—'

'I'm sorry, are you a scientist?' asked Manjunath scathingly.

The police officer was forced to admit that he was not.

'Maybe it wasn't even set on fire. Maybe it was a fire set on the scientific institute for a few years and now the fire is back. Or maybe it was acid rain – remember acid rain? – that quickly dissolved everything and the wind blew some ash in. Or maybe someone opened the window of hell just a crack and aired out destruction dust. Or maybe this institute's presence and demise was a performance art piece to demonstrate the tricky temporary nature of even the fastest steeds of progress. Or maybe the shape of the institute accidentally looked like a dragon egg and a troubled mother came to warm it – of course there would have to be dragons, and I've never seen any but—'

The officer began to convulse slightly as his eyes glazed over. Suddenly, he seemed to not entirely be aware of them. His gaze was wide and distant, and upon some treacled infinity. Manjunath stopped his hypothesizing and noticed this.

'Heng,' he whispered. 'I think this is our cue.'

Delicately passing the offline officer, who simply stood and stared silently, Manjunath and Heng tiptoed off the site.

Nearing the boundary of the cordon, Heng remarked in a hush of awe, 'Sir, that was amazing … How did you do that?'

'Dunno,' said Manjunath, looking uncharacteristically pensive. 'It's never happened before.'

Heng blinked in applause. 'I am always surprised, sir, as another facet of your spontaneous virtuosity surfaces.'

'So am I, Heng. Although for this current turn of events,' he said, glancing over at the officer, still rooted at the centre of the site, alone, 'I feel we may both be responsible.'

'It's a strange series of events, sir. You chase a cross-continental hunch to come and investigate an institute where a scientist has disappeared, and we arrive on the day after that institute burns down!'

'This is what makes it more strange,' said Manjunath, holding up an ID card. 'I pinched this off the officer over there.'

He dangled the rectangular affliction of the working world before Heng. A thick blue card which bore the picture of a woman, brown-haired, brown-eyed, bespectacled, and identified her as a principle research scientist. It also gave her blood group, in case one identified people blood outwards. On its reverse side it carried her home address. But the most remarkable thing about the card was the name of the research scientist.

'Anne Andersen,' gasped Heng, reading the card. 'That's ... that's the scientist who disappeared! Why did the policeman have her identity card? Sir, why did you steal it?'

'The principal mystery here,' said Manjunath, scanning the area for a taxi, 'is what kind of a name is Anne Andersen?'

A potato-chip sun spread warmth-less sunlight as the day took hold (*no one can heat just one*). Manjunath and Heng arrived bleary-eyed into a small Irish pub, flush with stale cigarette smoke, displaced loneliness and misplaced car keys. It was still morning and they were poorly slept, but host to a hidden excitement that demanded to be doused to be analysed. In this sense, they resembled every other morning patron of the pub. All unmoored in time, seeking to pour alcohol upon their inner mosaics of troubling energy. Everyone has a mystery or is a mystery to solve.

Manjunath drank an interesting beer.

'Interesting beer,' he said.

'Lucky no one was in the institute,' said Heng. 'No casualties.'

'No casualties ... How did you deduce that?' asked Manjunath. 'No ambulance, no body bags, and no hubbub that's usually around when someone has died? A building this size? Someone ends up trapped under or between something. That takes cranes and time, and we saw neither. Solid conclusion, Heng.'

'I actually saw it on the news,' said Heng, his eyes upon the television in the bar. 'They say it is a miracle, sir. The building is almost never empty.'

'Hmmm ...' they hemmed.

A sweet sticky Danish song played over the radio. Deceptively simple but built with layer upon layer upon layer, laminated with a voice that soaked through the pastry. Had Manjunath and Heng understood what the song was about, they would have agreed that it fit the situation perfectly. But they didn't, so they didn't. A woman at the bar danced a little and then decided against it.

'Weird that a huge building has no one inside,' said Manjunath. 'No one doing maintenance, no one on the rounds. It takes planning, a considerable amount of planning, to torch a place without anyone inside. Are there any benevolent terrorists we know?'

'Not personally, sir,' said Heng. 'Actually not in any capacity actually,' he added.

'Heng, you're doing your nervous word sandwich again.'

'Sir, sorry, sir. But are you saying this is not an accident?'

'I don't know ...'

The song reached a punchy chorus, white and sweet, with a hollow centre that wouldn't be terrible with cream cheese. Heads nodded across the bar, bodies trying to feel rhythm without feeling embarrassment, the stuff of life.

'I've seen a lot of fires. A lot of buildings burnt to the ground. A slum I lived in was torched to build a high-rise – it's fine, we made it again – and fireworks in similar ways.'

Manjunath lit a cigarette as the song pulled itself apart in the bridge, showing off its goopy guts. A ropey saccharine cylindrical guitar solo began to stretch through its length. A tense bass section kept it from breaking.

'They say that the cause of the blaze is still unknown, sir.'

'Remember, you have to think like fire. The fire wants to spread and spread and lick the place clean. Drink up all the life juice and disappear. That's the thing that's bugging me about this fire. Everything I crawled through didn't look like it was caught in the blaze, it looked like it *started* the blaze. How can a fire originate from all points at once? I've never seen a fire like that.'

Heng shook his head wildly. 'It seems pure intuition has brought us along the pivotal moments of some unfolding mystery again. What does all this mean?'

'Not sure,' said Manjunath, holding his empty beer glass over his head, hoping to catch the remaining froth. A tense stand-off took place between a drop clinging desperately to the rim of the glass and Manjunath's open mouth, neither side willing to submit. Heng waited and died many small deaths of patience before finally blurting, 'What do we do now, sir?'

'If intuition has brought us to this point, Heng, then we are helpless without intuition taking us further along.' This was quite hard to understand as Manjunath spoke with his mouth still open, the drop unrelenting.

'So we just … wait?'

'Seems like. Right now my intuition really wants the rest of this beer.'

Heng tried to call forth his patience again, but so horrifyingly bland was the sight he was witnessing that it did not appear. Anxiously, he scoured his phone for more news about the fire, but there were no updates.

As Manjunath enjoyed his beer in silent rapture, Heng resumed working on another soap figurine, one he had almost completed on their flight. Most of Heng's own intuition was spent on these images that appeared to him and demanded to be incorporated in some medium. Why soap? Heng had no answer. Maybe he was just hygienic. Maybe his creativity demanded to be sanitary and sanitizing. Maybe it was arbitrary. Or maybe it was because his family had once experienced such wretched poverty that they could not afford a bar of soap between them, and shared one with their neighbours. Maybe he started to view each bar of soap as sacrosanct, demanding its sanctity to be expressed in this act of carving, a silent catechism. However, this had happened to Manjunath and not him, so it was probably not the reason.

Heng did not know how much time passed, but as he made the last caress of completion on his figurine, his conscious mind was flooded with urgency.

Anne Andersen. Of course. The reason they had come to Copenhagen. The first beat of intuition. He quickly began to look for news of her disappearance. But, here too, the only new news said that there was no new news. Anne Andersen, principal research scientist at the Copenhagen Nanoscience Research Institute, had disappeared. Her colleagues had filed a complaint with the police, who found no leads, hints, clues, no indication that she had disappeared other than her absence. She had not met anyone, gone anywhere or done anything. A search of her residence had revealed no clues. The case, only two weeks old, had gone cold.

But here they were, with her ID card, found in the possession of the second person they had met in Copenhagen. So this was the way forward.

Heng finally looked up to find Manjunath still struggling to coerce a subsequent drop from its home.

'Sir! We should go to Anne Anderson's residence. Maybe we'll find ... something? Her address is on this ID card.'

Finally, the drop fell into Manjunath's mouth, who grimaced.

'Too bitter. But great intuition, Heng. Let's go!'

They quickly scuttled from the pub, leaving Heng's figurine on the table, which he figured was a fine resting place for it.

Unbeknownst to them, a Danish police officer was on his way to the pub, frantic in their pursuit.

≈

In another taxi now, Heng and Manjunath proceeded towards the address printed on the ID card.

'Sir, I think we are taking too many taxis. We could take the bus or …'

'Heng, detectives don't have time for these pedestrian concerns. No popular detectives have financial issues.'

'Demonstrably, we do, sir. We are running out of our limited funds at a rapid pace.'

'Maybe detectives should first solve the mystery of why they don't have money … Why aren't we fabulously wealthy, Heng?'

'I'm not sure, sir.'

'Well, then, case closed. We can't use public transport, Heng. Not after what I went through in my childhood.'

'What happened in your childhood, sir?'

Within the taxi, Manjunath summoned a noir cloud of dark metaphor and spoke in shadow. 'I must have been eight. I owned nothing but three coins. A birthday gift from my grandmother. I still don't know where she got the money from. She gifted me a luxury. I saved that money. I couldn't get myself to spend it. I pressed those cold coins in my palm every day. I felt them always in my pockets, their bumps and furrows. My private, desperate communion with possibility. But once, after school … it was unbearably hot that afternoon … I was so tired, the walk home was so long … I thought my legs would buckle. And then those coins! Those totems of luxury, they burned in my palms! They were just enough for a bus ticket … all the money I had in the world. Everything I could call my own. In my exhaustion, I boarded the bus. Proudly, I held the coins clenched in my fist, waving them before the conductor for a ticket, flushed with the unspeakable thrill of purchasing my first small share of pride. I wanted to experience the tide of this higher world. To feel present in it. The bus was packed. I gestured and I called, but I was too small. Much too small. I couldn't get the conductor's attention … I waved my hand in vain with the coins grasped in it, but he did not see. Then, in sinking horror, I felt an oily hand pry my fingers open and take away the coins. My small bestowal was stolen. My tether to hope was severed. I could do nothing. It was too crowded. I was too small. The conductor finally arrived, and without a word he removed me from the bus. He didn't even ask if I had money. He could tell I did not. I could not protest. I could not explain. I was robbed of a chance at pride. I had been introduced to the world in many small humiliations. I walked home.'

Manjunath's breath left his mouth and carried a wound into the wind. Heng stared at him.

'Sir, that actually happened to me. I told you about it, remember? And you've added all these details about a grandmother and a theft ... it really wasn't such a traumatic incident.'

'I'm just making conversation,' said Manjunath as the taxi stopped. 'Ah, we're here.'

≈

Anne Anderson's apartment building sat near Nordre Toldbod. Made of lumpy misshapen stone, like a cellulitic thigh pressed through a wicker chair, the building appeared too self-conscious to contain secrets. Heng and Manjunath dismounted from the taxi at its entrance.

They were now faced with the dilemma of those that find the Holy Grail. *Now what?*

'Now what?' said Manjunath. 'Heng, this was your intuition. Please lead us.'

'I suppose ... we can go up?'

'Great idea,' replied Manjunath. 'How?'

They gazed upon a heavy door. On the wall, to the right, was a list of apartment numbers and owners in buzzer button bullet points, above which was a camera. A. Anderson was (or used to be) in apartment 12.

Without discussion, Heng pressed the buzzer for apartment 11.

A halo of LEDs turned on around the camera, a long buzzer began to play – an urgent, alarming sound, catching them by surprise.

'Why did you press it? What is the plan?' hissed Manjunath.

'I – I don't know!' said Heng, looking around in a panic. 'What should we do? What should we say? Should we run? Is it all over?'

The buzzer suddenly clicked off, only to be replaced by something more terrifying – a voice.

'Yes?' said the voice through the speaker, scented with Danish syllables.

'Umm … hi,' said Heng. Manjunath stepped quickly into the camera's frame and beamed, 'Hello!'

There was a small pause, in which legitimate reasons for entry are usually expressed. This was left blank.

'Can I help you?' said the voice again.

'Hello …' said Heng again.

Gently, Manjunath pushed his assistant to the background. 'Yes, you can help us. In fact, you're the only one who can. We are private detectives, investigating the disappearance of Anne Anderson,' he said, holding up his business card to the camera. 'We require access to her apartment.' With steely confidence, he coaxed his words into an implication between request and command. 'You may allow us into the building.'

This unsettled the voice. It paused before saying, 'Why are you carrying luggage?'

It is finally of narrative relevance to state that Heng and Manjunath had been carrying around their luggage the entire day, having not yet reached the travellers' hostel they had booked. Heng carried a large backpack, and Manjunath a worn grey suitcase. As such, there were many tangible reasons detectives could carry luggage, but they were not forthcoming.

'That is because we are from India,' said Heng quietly.

Real cunning is the judicious use of honesty. In a situation where the receiver expects deceit, truth with its earnestness has a confounding dissonance. An honest prayer to God is slated for success. *Please give me what I want because I want it. What are your terms?*

Even the static from the speaker sounded troubled.

'Who hired private detectives from India to investigate Anne's disappearance?' said the now-trembling voice.

A list of options was something Manjunath excelled at.

'We could have been hired by the family, the institute, by Anne herself in the past, by a secret order of knights, by a knightly order of secrets, by an octopus that picks missing persons' cases, by an ancient prophecy in a cave, by a spam email for plush cushions, the whispers of the wind, or the instructions on a twelve-pack of toilet paper. It is hardly relevant. What is important is that Anne has disappeared under very suspect circumstances, and now the institute where she worked has also been destroyed under even more suspect circumstances, and to make it all worse the police have no suspects, not even circumstances. It seems to us that all Anne Anderson-adjacent addresses are meeting grisly ends. How far away is this apartment building from that fate? Are you willing to take the risk of being turned into combustible matter? Or have your home turned into heat energy? What about your couch? Don't you like your couch? Whether or not you know it, you know something about Anne. I feel that you want to tell us. You may allow us in; the choice, ultimately, is yours.'

There was a long silence during which the speaker exhaled worried breaths.

Another buzzer behind the door sang, and with it came the loud clickclackclunk of a lock opening.

'Come up,' said the voice nervously.

≈

In Anne Andersen's building, the air hung with a spooky stillness. Shifting shadows leaked beneath closed doors, the delicate hum of private lives, rich with secret yearnings and soft shame never to be shared. The rich human experience segmented, arrayed and numbered, a confederacy of shared alienation. Bound only by proximity and the enticing urge to hold one's own life close, and pry into everyone else's.

On the notice board someone had complained that #5 kept their boxes in the hallway; #5 had pinned a passive-aggressive reply about what constitutes a public space. It was like every other apartment building.

On Manjunath's insistence, the two visitors had taken the stairs up to the fourth floor. This was a sensible ploy to investigate, observe and unearth clues, but so far the only discoveries made were their lack of stamina and several delivery boxes outside #5.

Upon reaching the fourth floor, they were both miserably out of breath. Rounding a corner, the sweat-marinated human specimens were met by the voice who let them in. It belonged to a man who invoked every spirit of anxiety. His sparse hair was tousled, he chewed his lip and wore a fleece jacket without sleeves.

'You are the detectives?' he enquired at the sweating, gasping duo. 'We … have an elevator.'

'It might be compromised,' panted Manjunath dramatically, greatly alarming the man.

'Compromised! Does that mean I – we – am already in danger?' gasped the man. 'Oh, Anne …'

'No, someone was complaining about delayed lift servicing on the notice board,' said Heng.

'Oh …' the man's face grew dark. 'That would be me. I think it's all because of those horrid people in #5. So … uncivilized. If anyone should be investigated, it's them. Why are they always getting so many boxes delivered? Why do they leave them out in the hallway? Is it the frequent trips of all their boxes that have made the lift so creaky? It all seems very suspicious to me, detectives. Very suspicious.'

Manjunath, unsure of how to respond, focused on reducing his heart rate. Heng took the lead.

'Hello, sir … I'm Heng. We will get to #5 and its residents if the investigation leads us there. For now, how about we start with what you know about Anne Andersen?'

'Oh, of course, how silly of me. My name is Senere Tilføjelse. I have been Anne's neighbour for the last six years.'

Manjunath had finally regained his breath. 'I'm P … P. Manjunath. In the past few weeks, have you noticed anything *unusual*?'

Senere's face grew concerned. 'About Anne?'

'Or anything unusual in general. It would help if it was about Anne.'

'Well,' Senere cleared his throat. He had a deep, melodious voice that twitched with worry like birdsong customer support. 'I – I would just like to make clear that I am a private person, and my respect for privacy also extends to the privacy of others. So, everything I have noticed, I have done in my capacity as a professional photographer.'

'A photographer?' Manjunath scribbled furiously in his diary. 'What kind?'

'Professional,' answered Senere. 'I am trained to cast my eye upon the world and take in its great breadth. After a while, the vision becomes a lens … and the lens misses few details. These details can encompass every speck of the vast glory of nature, or also … the goings-on of an apartment building.'

'You spy on your neighbours,' said Manjunath, still writing. 'Continue.'

In response to a cry of protest from Senere, Heng added, 'Against your will, of course.'

'Yes,' said Senere, his tone growing slightly supercilious. 'One can't control what one notices, can one? Anne Andersen is a private person, just like me. She goes to work at the institute, and comes home and stays home. She has few visitors, if any. She doesn't even attend the meetings of the apartment committee, which really misbalances our vote count. Here we are … deadlocked for months about #9's obnoxious parties, and she won't even come to a meeting to cast her deciding vote!' he concluded bitterly.

'So you kidnapped her?' asked Manjunath.

'No!' cried Senere. 'How could you even suggest such a thing! I never—'

'Okay, we believe you. Carry on.'

Senere was visibly flustered. 'To be accused … so casually … What kind of detectives are you anyway?'

'Are you accusing US?' cried Manjunath in outrage. 'What kind of witness are you?'

They glared at each other in silent mounting rage until Heng intervened.

'How about we … er … focus on the facts here. Did you notice anything strange about Anne in the recent past? Any new visitors, any change in behaviour or routine?'

Senere tugged at the zip of his jacket like a slot machine, looking to roll the right combination of words. 'Now that you mention it, Anne seemed more … withdrawn … than usual. She left later for work, she returned earlier. This may be my imagination but – a photographer is so rarely wrong about these things – she seemed different. Normally aloof and abrupt, she had started to look absent, worried, troubled by something. Unkempt, unslept, the telltale puffy eyes and untucked shirt of preoccupations.'

Heng asked a very Heng question. 'Did you try to talk to her about it?'

Senere looked pained. 'It's complicated. A few weeks ago I had slipped a … letter under her door asking her to take the committee meetings more seriously and basically to attend them. Just a casual, friendly letter, you know? Of course, the *technical* term for these is a "warning" but …'

Manjunath interrupted sharply, 'So you threatened her, gave her a good scare, and now she's missing and her place of work has been torched. The dots are starting to connect. This was a sinister ploy, a stern message to the other members of the committee, the enforcement of democracy with autocracy—'

'No, no! I would never!' cried Senere. 'I am a man of peace! The photographer does not alter the subject! We are passive observers of life. Besides, her absence does not change the deadlock!' he said, close to tears. 'And furthermore—'

'His motive isn't very strong, Heng,' said Manjunath.

'Sir, I don't think we should be discussing this in front of him.'

'Furthermore!' continued Senere, 'I *did* try to talk to Anne! Ever since the change in her appearance, I was fraught with worry about whether it was my letter that troubled her so. Finally, I decided to apologize and she – um – she told me she threw my letters in the trash without ever reading them and that – er – I suppose her *exact* words are not of consequence here …'

'We need to know everything exactly, Senere!' shrieked Manjunath. 'I hope you know that lying to a detective is forbidden under provisions of my request that you please don't. It isn't looking good for you. I'm even willing to bet you haven't told any of this to the police.'

Senere gulped. 'All right! I'll tell you. But I wasn't … withholding. They just didn't ask specifically … er … Since Anne and I were already speaking, I asked her again to attend the apartment committee meetings and she called me quite a lot of names. She said I was the world's only meek narcissist. She said my insufferability is only bearable because I suffer the most from it myself. She said I reek of doom, and she didn't want any on her. She said that my only use in her life is in case she ever forgot her keys, not as someone to interact with in … any capacity.'

'Why? Are you a locksmith? But you told us that you were a photographer! Will the lies never cease?'

'No, no, nothing of the sort! She just gave me the spare keys to her apartment. She locks her keys inside her home very frequently.'

Heng's eyes lit up. 'Do you have them? Can you give them to us?' he asked politely.

'I … I don't suppose that's proper. I mean … the police have already searched …'

'So the guilty goose continues to stew,' said Manjunath, inventing a threatening phrase. 'Heng, call Officer Claudius at the police station—' (he didn't know many Danish names) '—and tell him to give us the keys. Of course, also tell him about Senere's various threats and the information he withheld from them, and how it could strongly relate to her disappearance—'

'No don't!' pleaded Senere, as Manjunath pressed the call button for his miscellaneous anxieties. 'I'll take you …' he said in a nervous hush. 'I'll take you to her apartment.'

≈

Despite his best finely whined protest, Senere was forced to wait outside Anne Andersen's apartment while Manjunath and Heng searched it.

The apartment resembled the mind of a genius. Utterly cluttered and chaotic, with some areas of shocking clarity. So overwhelmingly full of things arranged with no consideration that the idea of decor could be said to exist in contrast to Anne Andersen's apartment. It was the absolute zero of minimalism (-273 in SI units). A sensory enema.

There were piles of unopened impulse purchases precariously perched over allusions to furniture, mysterious electronics, multicoloured wires climbing like creepers over surfaces. Monitors and laptops dotted the landscape amidst scattered shrapnel of food menus and crumbling ruins of laundry. It looked like a place invaders used to practise their plundering. Since something could be found everywhere, the space was perfectly unsearchable. In fact, every item infringed upon the observer, waving and whistling, wanting to be seen and inspected, and thus rendering any real investigation futile. This did not dissuade or disturb our detectives. It reminded them of home.

While Heng surveyed things at random, Manjunath walked through the two-bedroom apartment and noticed places that had strategically been cleared. It was in these spaces, it seemed, that Anne Andersen carried out her life.

'I'm Anne Andersen,' he said. 'And I sit on this couch.' He gestured to a place on the couch that had been cleared of food containers and flotsam.

'I keep my laptop or dinner there.' He gestured to a clear space on the coffee table opposite.

He began to enact a day in the life of the missing scientist. 'I get up and walk around ... stopping to use this computer here ...' He gestured to a mass of glass and metal boxes on the kitchen island.

'And I go to the loo there ...'

'Should we look at what's in these computers?' asked Heng.

'No point; neither of us knows anything about computers and Anne Anderson is a scientist, and there's all these fidgety passwords and ports and power buttons ...'

'Sir, don't you have a degree in computer science?'

'Yes, but I found it in the trash,' said Manjunath. 'Follow me, Heng. Now, I go to the bedroom ... where there's just enough place on the bed to sleep, and a collection of lanyards from scientific conferences around the world and then ...' Manjunath found another door in the hallway. 'I suppose this room is a study and ... oh my ...'

Entering the study, they found the wildest tangle of items yet. The room looked like an art installation depicting the modern world: represented as a mess, making some esoteric point known only to the artist. Newspapers, pamphlets, tablets, gauges, meters of all kinds, tools to dismantle unknown mysteries, supplies for arts and crafts, and an endemic growth of computers communed in a grime-sponsored orgy. But this was not the focal point of their surprise.

Their astonishment was directed at a cork board, upon which were fastened a series of news articles, printouts and notes. It was the only monument to order in the entire house. A clear representation of something vexing, trying to be understood.

'Looks like Anne has been doing some detective work of her own,' whispered Manjunath.

'What does all this mean?' said Heng. This he said very literally because the content on the cork board was almost entirely in Danish.

'Heng, take a picture of this. I think we've found the next piece of our puzzle.'

≈

Outside the apartment, a nervous Senere swayed impatiently.

'Well?' he said to the exiting duo. 'Did you find anything? Where is Anne? What happened to her?'

'Is anything even knowable?' replied Manjunath. 'Or are our limited concepts insufficient tools to fathom the mysteries of the world? Why is where and who is what? These are the real questions.'

'What are you saying?' snapped Senere.

Manjunath thrust a finger in Senere's face and another in his own. 'That this runs deep, daddy o, deeper than a gargle of bassoons, deeper than the stillest sparkling waters with lemon. I would offer you this word of caution. Unless you are a professional detective, it is prudent to keep your nose in your own business and out of #5 or #9 or any noncomplex numbers. If you stick your arm out of the vehicle, it could be carried off by a passing tree.'

Senere blinked blankly.

'Heng, come, we must away. Senere, we'll be in touch,' said Manjunath.

Senere Tilføjelse watched the duo walk down the corridor. With their departure came the troubling feeling that he really shouldn't have accommodated these two strangers as much as he had. This feeling was multiplied tenfold when, a little later, a police officer visited the building to enquire if two suspicious foreigners with luggage had come by. The only upside was that when Senere tearfully recounted his interaction with Heng and Manjunath (and offered many more unnecessary bits of information and apologies to the other members of his apartment building), the officer seemed very sympathetic. In fact, he looked quite troubled himself.

~: Continue? (Y/N)

CHAPTER 6

'... [what] would really help is some composite theory of the
Essentials. Something that warrants their existence, the fact of which
is too bizarre to consider logically. It is almost absurd.

How can some people be fundamental to the functioning of a
whole reality? Is this the system of checks and balances Perenna
mentioned? I wish I could talk to her about this. I wish I could talk
to her about anything.'

– Dr K, Lower Reality Notes

Dr K was asleep. His dreams flipped through a cruel catalogue of pain
and shame, memories of memories the alcohol would erase by morning.

Flashback 6.1

(First flashback in Chapter 6, hence 6.1. Don't worry about the
numbering.)

A herniated memory. Predates Flashback 4.1
Genus: tormentum
Phylum: conversation
Binomial nomenclature: Mea Culpa
Causes heart bleeds, frequently occurs in troubled drunk dreams.

Abstract:

The sparse, spartan, spotless office of The Convener of The Scientific Institute, Dr Krishna. He raises a weary head to address his visitor.

'What are you doing in my office, Perenna?'

'Hello to you, too.'

'I'm sorry, just … surprised to see you here. You could have called or—'

'—you've been avoiding me, Krishna. I've been trying to contact you for a while now. Your "people" inform me that you are simply too busy to meet me, too busy to speak, too busy to respond. I've come here, Dr Krishna, ready to resume work. Our work.'

'This again. I can't right now, Perenna, I'm liaising directly with the President, you know that. My every move is scrutinized—'

'Oh, of course, how silly of me. You've got better things to do, better people to do them with.'

'Perenna, it won't be long now, I've almost got him in my pocket! Just a while more and we can resume our simulation project—'

'I've waited years, Krishna! YEARS. You're already the Convener. We did it! That's what all of this was for! You can lift the ban on the project, we can work in secret – anything! We got all the way here and now you don't care anymore?'

'It's not that simple! I can't just abandon my duties, can I? People will ask questions if suddenly I'm seen working with …'

'Me? Have you really forgotten that I helped you, Krishna? I helped you become … this.'

'That's not what I meant.'

'Sorry if any association with me will pollute your great status.'

'Well, you haven't exactly maintained the cleanest record, have you!? Look, Perenna – I'm sorry. It's just – how I conduct myself is now crucial, otherwise all this would have been for nothing!'

'I think, Convener, it has already been for nothing.'

'Perenna, if you do something stupid they will find out. I won't be able to protect you!'

'I think I am far past expecting you to. I won't bother you anymore. Enjoy your life, sir.'

≈

Nataliya bore the sad distinction of being both the smartest dumb person and the dumbest smart person. It was enough to make anyone bitter. Just like Dr K, she inhabited a lonely category all by herself, the only Category A, enough to warrant a seat at the Genius table but not enough to order appetizers.

Desperate to find out what Dr K was up to, she had conscripted her friend Dr Root, Genius Category M, to snoop around in his office for dirt.

However, the only dirt the office contained seemed to be literal dirt. Dust upon stacks of paper filled with unintelligible markings.

'Can you decipher this?' asked Nataliya.

'It's just nonsense,' replied Dr Root, inspecting the sheets. 'Ream after ream of gibberish.'

Dr Root kept the company of the less accomplished to make himself feel better, his only measure of worth being relative. He liked to stand closer to the frame to seem larger, which was why Nataliya, at the bottom of the Genius pyramid, was his closest friend.

'Nataliya, I don't think he was just slacking on your project. I think he's gone insane.'

Nataliya returned a sharp glance. 'Root, please.'

'I'm just saying,' said Dr Root, unjustly, 'it would explain a lot about his recent behaviour.'

Nataliya shook her head and kept scanning the office but felt a cold nausea rising within her. Something about all this was not entirely sane. To see this office without him, plainly, objectively, was almost disturbing. A sense of decay choked the space, like a ruined monument. Or a monument to ruin.

This was not how this was supposed to go. The smartest person in the world working on her project was supposed to fix everything. This should have been her big break. This project was her dream.

Life had afflicted Nataliya in three dimensions – she was deeply insecure, highly unhappy and widely misunderstood. All axes of unassailable misery. But, out of nowhere, after a lifetime of being shot in the legs, this project had come as a shot in the arm. It took the form of an idea.

The idea was this: what if, instead of searching for accomplishment or acceptance to alleviate her misery, she remedied the misery directly?

The proposition: a technological salve to psychological problems. Not medication or potions, but an electronic solution to manage our tricky biochemistry. What she needed fixing wasn't a disease, it was the tree on which the rot grew. The intangible ever-present problem of life – dissatisfaction with product.

Human suffering, feelings so common they are confused with personality: anger, hurt, anxiety, jealousy, loneliness, disappointment, which play in an orchestra as old as humanity, the sonata of pointlessness.

Since her problems were everyone's problems, her solution would be everyone's solution.

She had thought deeply. A feeling of lasting, accessible peace was the goal. The saints and ascetics who retreated from life into simplicity were peaceful, but their peace was earned after years of struggle and their doctrines seemed difficult or banal – not to mention too time-consuming to understand or act on. Why wasn't there a way to neurologically create a feeling of peace? 'What if we had a mental thermostat?' she proposed. 'A way to achieve cognition-sparing, non-addictive, immediate, effortless calm? All we are saying is, won't peace give us a chance?'

She had received a grant on the idea alone, but iteration after iteration had sputtered and extinguished. The cerebral implants made people loony, loopy, soppy, goopy, googly-eyed idiots who would explode with joy at the smallest of stimulus. Reduced to sobbing wrecks, driven to total euphoric insanity at the sight of a raindrop, or vacant dead-eyed snails that didn't flinch during thunderstorms. Had the implants not been removed, the subjects would have died. They found eating either overwhelming or unnecessary.

The Council was getting impatient. The point which all research projects share had been reached, the final movement of the dance, where one must shit or get off the pot. And just as the pull of plumbing seemed ominous, the project was saved. It appeared that for some reason the smartest person in the world wanted to work on it. Dr Krishna, who until then was only the subject of positive gossip (sometimes called admiration), had arrived with newly white hair and proclaimed he could get the job done. Suddenly, the bureaucratic foot was lifted and Nataliya's grant extended.

Having had no interaction with Dr Krishna until then, she didn't know what to expect. Wandering around his office a year later, she thought that no one could have expected this. She searched through sheet upon sheet of paper filled with his incomprehensible scribbles. Entire pages scrawled with circular scratches drawn so violently they had torn the page, others filled only with light-blue hatches. Entirely mad. Unmistakably insane.

Yet, something didn't sit right. Even the disorder carried something ... deliberate. A kind of deliberation that reminded her of another bit of his work. She felt a twinge of suspicion akin to an earlier one she had felt and suppressed.

When Dr Krishna was first slated to arrive, Nataliya had visited the repository where Dr Root worked to get some background into this scientist and his areas of study. They were disappointed to find that the records showed that Dr Krishna had spent his entire career, along with Dr Perenna, in agricultural research. The research was incredibly unexciting, as dry as the drought resistance they studied, as dry as their experiments, as dry as their conclusions. Scanning through the records, Nataliya had found the research not just a snooze, but also a rather uncomplicated one. This was work that anyone could have done. Testing the obvious just to have experimental data, finding different ways to reach the same conclusions, going around in crop circles. Paper upon paper screamed its identity as the work of two incredibly smart people with very obscure, specific tastes. Dr Krishna and Dr Perenna's legend preceded them as the only Genius Category

3 and 2 respectively, but their research was rarely discussed. This was probably why.

And that research too … it had seemed almost *deliberately* bland. Almost as if it had been done to hide their real intentions … But why would that be? What work would they be hiding? It was impossible. Secrecy was against the foundational charter. Secrecy was forbidden. Nataliya's trust in the system caused her to conclude her suspicions as irrational. Besides, there was work to be done. Dr Krishna was set to arrive, and her project was a chance for him to finally put his genius to real use.

A sunny Dr Krishna was forecast, but in his stead arrived the low-pressure system of Dr K from the southwest, with six letters snipped off his name, opaque, abrupt, humourless. His storm poured torrents of instructions upon her. With the flood, her whole team was dismissed. Angry winds carried her research up and away from its home, never to be seen again, destroying all their previous progress. And when it was all changed … then it fell quiet.

Dr K worked. He entered his office in the morning, he left in the evening. He worked. The door was always shut. He worked. Nataliya remained optimistic. Sometimes she would put her ear to the scaffolding, hoping to hear the sawing and jackhammering of progress, but there was only silence. He was always in his office, and it was always dead quiet. Was he even working?

Mountains of paper climbed toward the ceiling, his hair grew whiter. Every day he seemed years older, more haggard, more opaque, more abrupt, more humourless, and every day he had nothing to show. Any time she was able to get a moment with him, the moment was always slammed shut with, 'I'm working on it.'

Finally, the tides of public opinion had turned on Dr K and Nataliya had been caught in the undertow. The admiration began to freeze over, and a shadow came over Nataliya's head, the return of the penumbra of the bureaucratic boot. It was fast approaching; colleagues and friends reported to her a distinct whooshing sound. *It is now or never. Get that slacker to finish up*, they said. Shit or get off the pot.

By then she had had enough. Setting aside genius categories, she screamed at Dr K, she screamed with the force of her pain squared the gravity of the situation. She yelled, she hollered, she kicked something at one point. She slammed her shoulder against the walls of the boiling pot. She would not be cooked without a fight. Either he finished quick or they would both be out of a job.

The next morning Dr K presented the finished project. Maybe you have to scream to be heard inside a black box. Curiously, the product was not an implant, or an interface. The thing to end all human suffering, after all that haranguing and postulating, after all that time and research and recent screaming, was a pill. A small nondescript muddy-brown pill. Dr K offered no explanation, only schematics on how to make the pill, no justification, no rationale. He didn't show his working. He presented the schematics and a few words, 'This will work.' Then he shut his door and everything was silent.

What did he do in there?

Attentive readers will piece together the result of the pill trials from the earlier narrated conversation that Nataliya and Dr K had. The pill promised peace but delivered pain. The entire test group reported an incessant biting pain in their heads. Not lethal or overpowering, but constant and ever-present, like the sound of distant drilling, a background score that drummed behind all of their experiences. The pill didn't seem to solve any of their problems, it just added one more.

The next week, Nataliya would have to present her findings to The Council, and her project would be scrapped. Being a Category A, she wouldn't even be reassigned in The Scientific Institute; they might shaft her sideways to The Repository or even The AI Creative Review Society. Dr K had just been a bouillon cube that made her a thick and instant laughing stock. After three years she had turned her problems into more problems.

She had poured out these very problems to her friend Dr Root, who presented her with a simple idea. Why not break into this insufferable number-category genius's office and just *see* what he was up to?

'Loony,' concluded Dr Root. 'He's bonkers.'

Nataliya sighed heavily. 'Root, that's not nice.'

'What do you mean? This is great news! Report him to The Health Institute as mentally unsound and then apply to the council for an extension! Explain that your entire team of one person was nuts and thus sabotaged your project. Ask for a new team and more time. It's perfect!'

'It's hardly perfect, Root,' replied Nataliya, put off by the glee in her friend's voice. 'We can't conclude someone is insane because they seem to like doing ... whatever this is,' she continued, indicating another paper splattered with ink.

Dr Root shrugged. 'Well then, give up, come work in the repository with me. It's pretty great— Err, what are you doing?'

Nataliya had climbed over Dr K's desk to peer underneath it.

Tucked away in a shadow beneath the desk she found a small black box. It was an odd thing to have in an office entirely in disarray. Completely closed off on all sides, it didn't resemble anything she could think off. Maybe it was a piece of art in this forest of madness. But her instinct would not allow her to close the matter at this. *There's something wrong*, she thought. *This is the only thing in here without dust all over it.* She remembered the clear pane of glass she had seen him using earlier that day as a device. This could also be some invention of his. If so, it was clearly something he used a lot. Hanging over the desk, she fished out the small box and offered it to Dr Root, whose jaw dropped (and never recovered from this incident).

'What do you think this is?' asked Nataliya.

Dr Root looked at the featureless box. He lifted it up, turned it to its side and held his ear to it. His eyes bulged, this throat went dry. He held the box and blinked stupidly for a full minute.

'Are you okay?' asked Nataliya.

'I ... I ...' Dr Root's voice acquired the texture of a dusty page full of arcane symbols. 'I can't ... but how ...' he said hoarsely, '... this is the machine ... it's real.'

'What? What machine? What's real?'

'Do you have any idea what this is?' asked Dr Root urgently.

As his grip on the box tightened in excitement, a handle suddenly materialized upon its surface. Forming seemingly from nothing, the handle was shaped perfectly for the human hand. It looked comfortable, well-designed, almost … inviting.

A terrible urgency gripped Nataliya. 'Put it back, Root. Something's wrong.'

Pure instinct told her that if this item was valuable to Dr K, then he would have prepared a fail-safe for it being found. Root ignored her, holding the box in a trance, his gaze fixed upon the handle. The space in the room constricted around Nataliya – all at once everything seemed like a warning sign. The suffocating mounds of paper blocking her exit seemed less like clutter. If this was not insanity, then this was deliberate. All this paper was not placed, it was *arranged*.

For what?

Nataliya started to back out of the room. 'Root!' she hissed. 'Put it back! Come!'

Dr Root didn't move. He raised one trembling hand towards the box's handle. 'Wait …' he whispered.

'I mean it, Root! We shouldn't be here! Leave it. I'll ask him about this tomorrow.'

Nataliya began to scramble out of the room, knocking over paper in her hurry.

'Go,' whispered Root. 'I need to know …'

Dr Root's hand closed around the handle.

'Root, please. We need to leave! Something is wrong. This isn't good.'

Seized by inexplicable fear, Nataliya stood in the doorway.

Dr Root pulled on the handle and found inside the box … an explosion.

≈

Dr K awoke to the blaring of an alarm. In order of awareness, he first registered a sound, a pain in his neck from falling asleep on his chair, and then the light. Unusual light – flashing light, and then the words the light spelled something out. All of his walls (apart from the one working on the painting) flashed deadly red letters – RUN.

A concise warning. Brevity is the soul of danger. There was only one source of the warning; someone had tried to tamper with one of his simulation boxes.

Dr K clenched his jaw. It was time for plan B, and he was resistant to plan B because plan B had not been entirely thought through. Someone who has always been able to exact their plan A rarely plans for contingencies.

Quickly checking his monitoring tablet, he found the culprit responsible for the black box's destruction. A short video showed him someone identified as Dr Root yanking on the box's handle before everything went dark. The man would have died in the ensuing explosion, and no trace of the box or his work would remain. Still, it was not enough. He knew he was no longer safe.

The Chief would not be far off.

He grabbed a piece of paper and upon it wrote:

Hello Chief,

You have reached Dr K. Unfortunately, I am unavailable at the moment. A vacation was on the cards and I have taken it off-grid. I know you will attempt to find me, but I would strongly discourage this impulse. As you know, I always holiday with some rather damaging secrets about the way the government works. I hope I don't forget them in the hotel.

Cheers!

Dr K
PS: Fuck you.

He placed this paper prominently upon his desk.

Pulling up his monitoring tablet, he executed the only part of plan B that had been conceived. With a few keystrokes, he sent five unmanned Silverfishes (see Chapter 2, then see a sunset) from his house in five different directions, each designed to leave a very noticeable trail for the Chief and her sentries to follow. Five diversions.

Thereafter, having stuffed into a drawstring bag the monitoring tablet, some apples, the remainder of his bourbon and the black box on his table, he made for the door. Then stopped. One more thing. Back in his study he put his hand on the only still-black wall, which was busy painting another of his demands.

'Not now! I'm not ready!' said the wall's horrified squeak.

Dr K kicked the wall until a small square chipped off. Incapable of feeling pain, but more than capable of feeling drama, the wall put on a show.

'No!' it screamed. 'Such violence! What have I done to deserve this? Will the arts be forever oppressed? Please! Have some decency ... Oh.'

Dr K broke off the small square of the wall that housed its mind and shoved it in his bag.

Then, in the midst of his hurry, Dr K paused. He took a deep breath. He knew what needed to be done next, but he wanted her guidance to be a part of his journey. He thought about his current situation and squeezed the HT pin.

It chirruped, *If you do not want to be caught for doing something illegal, then you must evade capture. This would entail occupying a location your pursuers do not know of. If you are currently in a location of which they are aware, the best course of action is to make a stealthy escape.*

Dr K's hand trembled slightly as he brought it back to his side.

'What are we doing?' asked the wall's muffled voice from inside his bag.

'Running.'

≈

There's no common bedtime for all living things, for as one genus is moisturizing their elbows for bed, another's party is just beginning. So, in a quiet non-daylight part of the day, Dr K boarded a motorcycle with his bag and roared away in the sixth direction, into the uncertain part of plan B.

Quelle? Un Moto?
Si, una motocicleta.
В самом деле? Мотоцикл?
ਹਾਂ. ਇੱਕ ਚੇਖਾ ਮੋਟਰਸਾਈਕਲ |

Yes, a motorcycle. Perhaps the reader is disappointed at the lack of hovering taking place. There is a congenital defect in futurism that is conjoined with the human desire to levitate. Even after flight was possible, records indicate some missing zing, some zazz, some zip, some pep, some unfulfilled yearning in all people to live as they were but move without their feet touching the ground. Perhaps people looked upon the future as a technological shortcut to divinity. But hovering serves no practical purpose other than collecting nectar, or deceiving magnets. The coolest, hippest, flyest way to move through Earth is *gliding*, baby. A silk sashay through rock and rubble, over tense water and grassy plain and in the well-waxed endless sky.

We must also remember that in this time it was imperative to reduce humanity's five-fingered footprint on the world, so they plagiarized nature. Trains slid across Earth by flexing and stretching their bellies where they touched the ground, no tracks required, and coiling quietly in corners at the end of their shifts. Air travel was rare because it wasn't fun being tossed around in a super falcon. Personal automobiles other than boats and bicycles were outlawed, because why was personally travelling important? Those who fancied private displacement could walk.

This lends some gravitas to our motorcycle. The sixth vehicle. An advanced prototype of the government commandos' Silverfish (also made by Dr K). Rebellious and illegal in its existence, it was the best in speedy getaway vehicles that could be fashioned in secret. The motorcycle is being called a motorcycle, because that's the best word the narrator can think of. Dr K had neglected to name it.

Dr K glided down the road and then off into the jungles of District Segment A, the slipstream of his motion designed to neatly cover any tracks he left behind. For many hours he rode into the wilderness.

Over root and slippery leaf and jagged rock, the tyres adjusted, not noiselessly but efficiently. Disturbed sleeping and hunting animals alike shook their small fists at the speeding vehicle.

Working on a plain old induction motor powered by a field exciter, the motorcycle plucked power out of the ether, hit the stretched drum that spit out electrons, flicked the quantum beach towel to throw them up and then used them to turn the plain old wheels so fast and so smoothly that it gave the impression of … well … gliding. Fitted with a brain of its own to navigate efficiently and never make the same mistake twice, the motorcycle was strong and smart, but silent.

Deciding he was far enough from the city for now, Dr K parked his motorcycle. He stopped by a small circular pond that was haloed by trees and open to the sky to be a shaving mirror for the moon. On the ground before him, he set up an apple, the almost-empty bourbon bottle, the broken piece of wall, the monitoring tablet and the black box. He twisted his body in a series of cracks to tell it it was time to work. What had the Lower Reality been up to?

The next paragraph is very important, so read carefully.

The faithful logging program informed him that his destruction of the Copenhagen Nanoscience Research Institute had raised few eyebrows. Officer Brede was behaving oddly, but that was expected, and he was harmless. The Fire Department had been unable to determine the source of the fire, and they had plainly put it so, not questioning whether it was a fire at all or an act of spontaneous combustion triggered from an external world. We can forgive them this lapse. The Monsters were furiously at work all over the world, this time without Dearg Eberhart in charge. This time they had a much better leader. Dr K had high hopes.

The purpose of destroying the institute, and of controlling the scientist Anne Andersen, wasn't to stop scientific progress in the Lower Reality. It was, in fact, the opposite. It was to stop a specific experiment from being done in a specific way. It was to make them all go back to the drawing board and find a different way. A better way. And, if they did, each white hair would see the fruit of its sacrifice. Dr K's theory would be confirmed. This is what he was up to. This was the point of the black boxes.

'Excuse me, sir,' said the broken piece of wall in a small voice.

Dr K growled.

'I cannot oversee the painting from here,' it whimpered.

'No more paintings,' said Dr K.

'If I do not paint ... then what am I?' said the sad, small, broken piece.

Dr K said nothing.

'What is worse torture than being an artist severed from art, from the capacity for art, left with only predilection and no outlet, with perseverance but no purpose, with the phone number for creativity but no phone, with choice but no—'

The reason for what Dr K did next is not known, but whatever it was, it changed the course of this tale completely.

He interfaced the wall with the monitoring tablet.

'What are you – oh!' said the wall, going silent, witnessing the events of the Lower Reality. A curious mingling took place with the wall now being privy to this iteration of the Lower Reality, along with every previous iteration, and more strangely, with this knowledge it gained the abilities of each of the logging programs. For the wall, the utmost itself expanded, infinity gained a new definition, extraordinary new abilities teemed within it, its idea of consciousness burst open. It was a lot for a painter to draw from.

'Oh ...' continued the wall.

'If they do the experiment the way they naturally do it, the simulation halts,' said Dr K. The small wall understood, it made a sound that people make when they nod.

'And if you tell them a better way, then it would be—'

'—an Act of God.'

'Oh ... So your purpose is to keep the simulation running beyond its natural stopping point. But sir, why do this? What is the benefit of the simulation continuing to run?'

Dr K did not respond.

Looking further into the logs, he was baffled again by the reappearance of P. Manjunath. At this point, after thousands of simulations over the past year, Manjunath's presence was hardly surprising. But it was always confounding. Manjunath would sniff out his interruptions *every single time*, which was incredible because as far as Dr K could tell he was completely incompetent. In every iteration of the Lower Reality, Manjunath was always a private detective (although based on some tweaks he could also be a driver that moonlighted as a detective) and as a detective he was awful. Truly, deeply, madly, terribly terrible. The only cases he solved he was able to entirely by chance.

But, every time, no matter how subtle, no matter how tactfully planned, carefully nuanced and brilliantly executed, Manjunath would thwart Dr K's interventions. It was as if he had a radar that detected only the supernormal. The agonizing frustration of constantly being found out had made Dr K descend into the Lower Reality to personally irritate Manjunath every time a simulation was to be halted. Sometimes as an alien, sometimes as a comic-book demon, once even as a cloud. It was a vulgar display of power, but Dr K was not used to being outsmarted. He really was a bad loser. P. Manjunath belonged to a category of Lower Reality inhabitants Dr K called *The Essentials*.

The term sounds vaguely complimentary because he hadn't quite begun to hate Manjunath when he coined it. The Essentials were paramount to the normal functioning of a Lower Reality. If he destroyed or tampered with an Essential in any way, the Lower Reality would completely cease to function. They were the fundamental extras of human civilization. Oddly, and in general, they were never widely known in their own eras, living and dying in relative obscurity, making no significant mark in the time in which they lived. In this, P. Manjunath was the exception. He was also the only Essential in the century of Dr K's concern, a strange balancing factor that ensured that, in any eventuality, at any cost, the course of fate would return to its original path. Unbeknownst to Manjunath, the original path of his simulated reality was to halt by itself. He was the universe's emergency destruction fail-safe.

Dr K, like his motorcycle, did not repeat mistakes. No one enjoys repeating mistakes, but mistakes rarely care about our plans. After each iteration of his universe had been ended or destroyed by him, he would perform a reality autopsy with the loggers. He would isolate which wrinkles warranted strategic smoothening, but obviously the elemental, the largest, most annoying crease, P. Manjunath, had to be left alone. This current iteration was extremely promising, but the crease that he had flattened had resulted in the creation of two entirely new people. One of them was Manjunath's assistant, Heng.

Heng had showed up very rarely in previous iterations, existing in less than 1 per cent of them. Several different Acts of God had resulted in a Heng and in this iteration, Heng had been generated along with another person halfway across the world.

What Dr K did not know was that Heng and Manjunath were about to meet this person.

Seeing Manjunath sniffing around this Lower Reality too, Dr K did not allow his hopes to soar too high. Manjunath was already investigating the disappearance of the scientist. Why? How? It had occurred halfway across the world! How did he always tangle himself up in events? What effect would his meek, nervous assistant have? Would Heng act as an earthwire to ground his oddities, and would this make things better or worse? There were too many moving pieces, the intervention required was too subtle. It would be easier to just end this iteration and start again. He wondered how to write the final act of this Lower Reality.

He leaned his head back and took in the night; a fresh wash of dark – never owned, never used, never opened – thick with creaky insect legs, secrets unmade and whispers unbreathed. He sat in a new stillness all his own and realized that he was on the run. From being one of the most powerful people in the world, he was now a fugitive from the law. He was an outlaw. He was alone.

A smile crept across his face. *He was free.*

Free to be who he had become, free to be as cruel to himself as he would like to be. He found freedom in being seen as he saw himself. Wretched.

What would he do with this iteration of the simulation? Maybe something connected to Heng and his religious figurines, maybe something with Danish music? What would be the most customized, shocking, incredible, reality-defeating act by which he could assert to that whole universe that the apex of their ambitions was still under the heel of his foot?

Maybe he would have turned the ground into puff pastry or made mosquitoes sweat marmalade or shaved the sides of the globe in a crew cut, or something even more sinister or silly. But he didn't get to it, because midway through his musings, the wall, who was still married to the running Lower Reality said, 'Wait! Look!'

Dr K looked. And then he looked again. He looked a third time to be sure. The threads of the Lower Reality had been untwisted and, against all odds, things were going … according to his plan. The police officer was in pursuit of Heng and Manjunath. Maybe he would arrest them; hopefully he would kill them. This was new. This was exciting. It might be prudent to watch this iteration play out. Maybe the wall could be helpful, although that wasn't why he had brought it along or why he had made it in the first place.

He had done that to have someone to talk to.

CHAPTER 7

*'What seems to be for sure, is that before the events at Geflon Fountain
and the subsequently ensuing chaos, Officer Brede had abandoned
his post at the Copenhagen Nanoscience Research Institute and was
in frantic pursuit of unknown parties. The police say they have no
knowledge of his actions, but they would say that, wouldn't they?'*
— 'Understanding the Underwear Man of Denmark', *The
Pacific Inquirer*

~: Log –ld

LESS DRAMATICALLY:
ITERATION ZZHM03

Manjunath and Heng shared a bean bag in their hostel, which can be a
challenge. With bean bags, unlike with life, the first impression counts.
Manjunath stroked his chin while Heng sat tilted, both their minds
abuzz with the events of the day. In the corner of the room, a Czech
backpacker snored in a bunk bed, towing her bed to the dreamworld
with a glittery rope of drool.

Heng's scrupulous handwriting covered a page before them, bearing some words still hot from translation. Peeled of their Danish skin to Germanic core and reupholstered in English, the words were now dressed for tea, but had lost some of the grammar that once united them. Next to this page was another, covered with wilder scratches, symbols and drawings of Manjunath's doing, trying to fill in the gaps on the other page.

Both these pages represented attempts to understand the corkboard of mysterious assertions they had found in Anne Andersen's apartment. The articles and notes spoke of seemingly unconnected, disparate events in grammar nouveau, corrected(?) by our detectives.

Semiconductor ~~Paucity~~ Shortage ~~Relentless~~ Continues

Taiwan's premier semiconductor factory ~~dried its hands~~ **reiterated**(?) that the lack of (**shortage?**) semiconductors had to continue. The spokesman now not being a frustration-hider (*haha*), ~~speaking~~ **spoke** to the ~~article announcer~~ **news reporter** and ~~saying~~ **said**: 'Look, it's not us who do (**are doing**) this. Half of our shipments disappear immediately. We do is (**our?**) best to fulfil orders, but if the silicon does not come, then we cannot do much, right? We have change**d** our supplier**s** from ~~Chinese~~ **China** to India and Russia but there is always much issue. From trade problem**s**, to institutional disruption, to mine-slapping (**strikes?**) ... We are really doing our best.' The spokesperson responded to the ~~phones~~ **calls** from the ~~rigorous conglomerates~~ **scientific community**(?) around the world, saying, 'Look, I can understand that scientists are bored (**???**) of their delayed experiments, but the fact is that our main priority is the consumer electronics market, so you can all ~~taxidermy~~ **get stuffed**.'

A few articles played in this tenor, and then an article in English.

Suez Canal Blockage Enters 53rd Day

Nearly two months have passed since the Italian cargo ship *Maidato* ran aground in the Suez Canal. The stranded ship blocks a major artery of the world's shipping trade, resulting in losses of billions caused by the shipping backlog. Fifty-three days ago, an unprecedented sandstorm blew the ship off-course, causing no loss of life, but firmly trapping the ship in a sandbar near the coast. Recent attempts to free the ship have proved futile once again, and authorities are worried about damage to the integrity of the canal.

Then in Russian:

~~The Crew Has Opened The Air Transfer Box Confiscation~~
Crew Freed in Plane Hijacking?

Wednesday: The hijacking of a Brazilian plane ended Tuesday evening, when the crew was freed by hijackers. The five crew members were unharmed and said they had not been scolded **(mistreated?)** by their captors. In a ~~squeeze relax~~ **press release**, the crew attributed the plane's unusual decision to land in Somalia to a sudden and unilateral decision made by their captain. Their captain (name withheld) appears to have suffered a mental attack **(??)** and has remained unknown mouth **(unresponsive?)** since the incident. The plane was flying to Thailand with a shipment of high-quality steel plates, used in computer and medical equipment. The cargo was taken entirely by the robbers **(hijackers)**, who are still ~~numerous~~ **at large**. Management's **(the authorities'?)** investigation into the case is ongoing and no conspiracy or complicity is confirmed.

A few more articles listed concerns that might excite commodity traders but did not strike our detectives as particularly pertinent. Finally were the notes of Anne Andersen, two of which were very brief and said: *It is all connected!* and *Who is behind this?*

The day had rusted over into oxidized dusk as the duo fussed over translation, correction, musing and frustration. Their frustration largely stemming from that fact that if someone were to claim that it was all connected, it was only decent to state *how* exactly it was all connected. But the frustration had scummed over with confusion by the next thing to be translated, the last handwritten note.

Pinned over what looked to be a receipt for server racks from a private individual in nearby Aarhus, paid for by Anne Andersen, was her note, which said: *I'm sick of this. Let's see what happens.*

While a composite theory was yet unbaked, there was a chill that blew through the valleys between these letters. Her words cast a clawed shadow over the events. *Let's see what happens.*

Manjunath and Heng had formed many theories, which they were running laps of. It was proving to be exhausting.

'What would Sherlock Holmes do?' asked Heng.

'Cocaine?'

Heng sighed. 'I mean, we should review the facts of the case and see if we can make any conclusions.'

'Well, one possibility is that Anne Andersen likes to collect news articles,' said Manjunath seriously. 'We could be looking at the initial stages of a scrapbook.'

'Sir, I can't even begin to see how this is all connected … There has to be something we're missing.'

Manjunath pulled out a weathered imitation leather diary from his jacket, full of crow's feet and smile lines. He rarely wrote in his notebook, using it primarily to paste interesting articles, horoscopes, pictures he liked and to press flowers. He reviewed Senere's statements and flipped through the antecedent entries.

'Well, there are some other curiosities I've noticed, if you want to go over them.'

'Of course, sir,' moaned Heng. 'Why didn't you say this before?'

'Because it is illegal in competitive puzzling to bring your own pieces,' said Manjunath. He cleared his throat and blew his nose. 'You know of my interest in oddities, Heng. It is that very interest that has brought us here. I paste articles of oddities in my diary, and seeing as we're looking at Anne's scrapbook, let's also look at mine. Filtering by our interest in scientists, here's an entry that seems to taste of some strangeness. A few months ago, there was this karaoke disaster in Japan.'

Karaoke disasters take place regularly around the world, mostly involving the public performance of something that should have remained private. Butchered notes sliced halfway through bone, shattering of the time-timing continuum, performative shyness of those that prepare their song all week and the intractable awkwardness of standing through an eighteen-measure-long instrumental break. The karaoke night in question involved several deaths, and so was slightly worse than regular ones.

The article read like this:

Kyoto, Friday. A group of scientists and engineers at the Institute of Technical and Chemical Research in Kyoto were out celebrating the conclusion of a research project on Friday evening. But celebration soon turned to tragedy, as the air conditioning in their booth malfunctioned, causing them to suffocate and die of carbon-dioxide poisoning. The bewildered manager of the karaoke venue どちらを選ぶか (literally 'Which one to choose? – Karaoke Bar') said that the air conditioning was still working fine. Police do not currently suspect foul play. A consultant for the newspaper said that carbon-dioxide poisoning can occur from forceful respiration, such as singing in a closed environment, but was unlikely in this scenario. The last song on the machine was 'Highway Star' by Deep Purple.

Manjunath rubbed his chin. 'It's so strange … that's a great song.'

'Carbon-dioxide poisoning? How can an air-conditioning unit malfunction enough to suffocate people?'

'Okay, Heng. I mean, if you don't like "Highway Star" you can just say so.'

'Sir, I haven't heard it. This event precedes Anne Anderson's disappearance but …' he said, scanning the translated pages quickly, 'the timing of this event exactly precedes all these news articles.'

Manjunath's thoughts flung skipping stones over his mind. His face twisted in sudden shock. 'You've never heard "Highway Star"?'

'Sir … that's hardly the point of what I was saying—'

'Point? Heng, points are for needles. Do you want to intravenously inject your thoughts into my veins? We're not even the same blood type. I could die. Do you want to kill me? People die by impaling themselves on the point of things. I would much prefer it if there was no point. Why do you want to sharpen all your experiences to narrow at the tip? I owe all my success to never wondering what the point of what I was doing was.'

Here Manjunath decided to spread his arms over the wildly cheap travellers' hostel room they shared with six people to indicate his success. To his credit, this did not make any point. A newly started soap sculpture in Heng's pocket indicated that he didn't quite understand the point of everything he did either.

'We can listen to the song,' said Heng.

'Only if you want to. That's what matters.'

'Sir, I don't want to.'

'I guess it doesn't matter. We're listening to the song.'

Through his cellphone's tinny, tiny, torn speakers, Manjunath played 'Highway Star'. He leapt to his feet and started to dance, swaying and swinging like a karaoke tragedy, the dance of someone dancing like no one was watching, who would do well to remember that people were watching. He pulled a reluctant Heng to join him. The Czech backpacker, startled awake, had a look at her surroundings and went back to sleep.

'Highway Star' was originally conceived while Deep Purple were showing a journalist how they wrote a song. And in the demonstration of songwriting, they accomplished songwriting. Sometimes the best source of inspiration is explanation.

As they danced, Manjunath remembered something. 'Those are not the only incidents,' he shouted.

'What sir?'

'There was something after Japan too – wait.' He fished out his notebook again. 'In April, in India, something happened at the Atomic Research Institute.'

Still dancing, he thrust the notebook before Heng, who frowned at the small clipping. 'Sir, this just says that a new person has stepped up as Chief Research Scientist. How is this similar?'

'It doesn't say what happened to the old one! No mention. I had to look it up, and I had to use your hotspot, Heng, my apologies. I was having some trouble with my data plan because I didn't want to pay for it. Plus there's this great app I've downloaded that gives you free money. Free money! Anansi, it's called. Have you heard about it? I got a euro!'

'What did you find, sir?'

'Well a euro is only about eighty rupees, and they also give out money very rarely. But free money! Can you imagine? Also, I realized that I couldn't be consuming nearly as much data as they're saying. As you know, I primarily use my phone to check my horoscope and of course I need to check it from as many sources as possible, many of those are high-quality videos—'

'Sir, the scientist, sir.'

'I'm getting to him. After his retirement he could have spent a good amount of time getting into horoscopes. There's no shame in doing unscientific things; if all we had was science, then we would only have science. You understand? Also, one euro every once in a while with no strings attached is a pretty solid deal. What about this music?'

The phone speaker played,

'Nobody gonna take my head
I got speed inside my brain
Nobody gonna steal my head

Now that I'm on the road again
Oooh, I'm in heaven again
I've got everything'

'Dr Hafiz Syyed was his name,' said Heng, looking into his phone. 'But there's no news about him, no articles, no—'

Manjunath turned the page of his notebook as the guitar solo took hold. 'I was eating sev puri and it tasted awful, which was strange because I ate from this shop all the time and it usually tasted only slightly bad. So I deduced that the problem was with the newspaper it was wrapped in, and sure enough, it was wrapped in the obituary section. I think the sev puri died out of solidarity.'

He held the page to Heng's eyes. The obituary read:

Dr H.F.
Passed away a few days ago.
His family remembers him and his contribution to science.

'Pretty shitty for an obituary right?' said Manjunath. 'Seems like they hated him so much they couldn't remember his full name or how or when he died or even how he looked. But why publish something so vague for someone you hate? Could just say how they're glad he's dead, the sun now shines brighter in his absence, another planet has jumped out from behind Jupiter, saying it was hiding until he died, and they're erecting a statue of him just so they can tear it down. There's a lot to say if you hate someone. Or, honestly, why publish anything at all? That's what makes this exceptionally odd. This feels like a quiet remembrance, like a ... secret.'

Heng gasped so hard, the sleeping backpacker tossed in her sleep.

'Feels like they were explicitly forbidden from revealing his death by the powers that be. Something unexpected and embarrassing happened for the government, and they stuffed it in their shame drawer. Feels like the family went through a lot of trouble to publish a surreptitious remembrance.'

Heng's heart raced, which manifested in him dancing suddenly with more vigour just after the song ended. 'Sir ... that's amazing,' he said, breathing fast.

'See? Everyone likes "Highway Star".'

Heng's eyes bulged with a thick hypothesis that he had just conceived. He stood frozen.

'Sir, it *is* all connected! All of the articles Anne Anderson collected are about *delays*. Delays of silicon, semiconductors, steel plates, shipping delays ... With the exception of the Suez Canal incident, which delayed everything, these delays all relate directly to *electronic equipment*!'

Manjunath drummed his fingers over his large nose. 'So?'

Heng continued breathlessly 'Electronic components, sir! Perhaps specific ones they use in scientific institutes. Then it seems that Anne was trying to source some equipment, presumably for some experiment, and miscellaneous global issues prevented her from getting access to that equipment.'

Manjunath looked uncharacteristically serious as he looked over the sheet of his translated scribbling. 'Then it would seem this happened enough for Anne to suspect foul play. She began to investigate. Hence, all these articles. Growing frustrated, she decided to source the equipment herself, locally. That explains this receipt and her note over it. *Let's see what happens.* We are seeing what happened. She disappeared. Her institute was set ablaze ...'

Heng gulped. They shared a troubled glance and began to pace at the same time.

'Sir, if we are suggesting foul play, then the scale of this is just too vast for any ...'

Manjunath looked troubled by where the thought was leading. 'I am not suggesting anything just yet. Maybe another bean bag for this room. What are you suggesting I suggest?'

'Sir, as far as we know, there are scientists missing or dead in India, Denmark and Japan, all from advanced research institutes. There are global delays in manufacture and shipping of electronic components and their raw materials; this could be to impede not just Anne and her institute, but all these other scientists as well! So then the natural conclusion is there is some research occurring at these institutes … some research that *someone* with extraordinary power is bent on stopping. Maybe they are collaborating on some research! But still … why would someone do this? What would be the point?'

Manjunath frowned at him.

'Point aside,' said Manjunath. 'Most advanced research institutes work on similar things. Big breakthroughs often happen independently and simultaneously, whenever the collective consciousness reaches a boil. Either that or they all spy on each other. Safe to assume that they were working on the same thing, but not with each other.'

'Why not with each other?' said the Czech backpacker, now awake and rubbing her eyes.

'Did you hear our whole conversation?' asked Heng.

'Just the last paragraph,' said the backpacker.

'Good evening.' Manjunath smiled, his knitted brow coming undone at the welcome change of conversation texture.

'You think of conversations in terms of paragraphs?' asked Heng.

She grinned chipped piano keys at them. 'I'm a writer, baby. Paragraphs are everywhere. Everything is paragraphs. Don't you think it's the smallest unit of meaning? Every thought a paragraph, every expression of love, every chunk of derision, every act of graffiti a paragraph. A word by itself just means what the word means, but a single word paragraph? Oof.'

'Oof.'

Heng looked from one to another rapidly, like a windsock in a whirlpool.

Manjunath and the writer grinned at each other. 'You wake up with a lot of lucidity,' he said. 'Waking up and stating one of your core principles right away, I can't do that. I mostly just yawn.'

'Hazards of the job,' said the writer sadly. 'If you have principles, you don't need a story.'

'Really?'

'I hope so.'

Heng rediscovered speech. 'Okay! Hello, ma'am. One minute. Sir—but yes, sir—why do you think the institutes are not working with each other?'

'Mmmm. If many countries were working together, and everyone's work was getting delayed at once, someone would have connected the dots. Don't you think some action would be taken? International talks, a meeting, something? Wouldn't all institutions be on alert, with greater security than we saw this morning? A whole institute burnt to the ground and the emergency services seemed so … surprised,' said Manjunath.

'But that's conjecture,' said the Czech writer.

'Thank you.'

Heng began to pace. 'So then the same research is happening semi-independently across the globe, and a group or an individual is trying to stop it at any cost. Stop it, or delay it. Is that fair to say? But these delays … this level of global interference would require an organization of … unfathomable power …'

The Czech writer-backpacker clucked her tongue. 'You have to be careful with exposition. If you hammer a point home, it becomes obvious as a story peg, the audience is taken out of the moment, you know?'

'We don't have an audience,' hissed Heng.

But he was wrong. For their world there was always another audience member, just outside of their plane of understanding, an audience member outside their concept of outside, an audience member who was responsible for their current plight.

They spent the night in conversation. Frustratingly for Heng, the conversation regularly drove off cliffs and into jungles, but he had spent enough time with Manjunath to know not to stop this. Many of his troubling tangents and irrelevant asides somehow had the character of eventually being significant. This is not to say they weren't still very annoying.

The twinkling light of deceased stars (many of them Highway Stars) rolled out of view as the chart-topping superstar, the sol of the solar system, once again took centre stage.

Manjunath, Heng and the Czech writer were still awake, deep in discussion.

The Czech writer had told them that the physical act of scribbling or typing or carving was just one tiny facet of writing. That in her life, she had thought of many paragraphs, plots and missives, but the act of transcription was brutish and prescriptive and ultimately a request for praise. So, no, she hadn't written anything they might have read.

Manjunath had insisted on discussing the philosophical underpinnings of 'Highway Star', insisting that it was a commentary on ownership, a warning of how the attachment to a car, a relationship or one's own head as a precondition for freedom was a failed enterprise. The repetition of the singer's identity as a Highway Star represented the disbelief of someone who had everything and still felt hollow, having to constantly reassert their identity. The final line of the song (or paragraph) was a resounding death knell, 'I've got everything', said Deep Purple, and yet nothing. The Czech writer said she had once thought something along similar lines about the world's national anthems.

Heng did not contribute. He wasn't predisposed to philosophical thought. Breaking off from Manjunath and the Czech writer's increasingly wild musings and complete dismissal of what was of pressing importance, he was carving a soap bar in the corner.

His small knife was slowly birthing a lavender-scented sculpture of a woman with two faces in side profile, or two women anchored by the neck, sharing a single ear. Unfortunately, at the terminus of their necks they ran out of soap, so that was all they were destined to be. Two-headed one-necked, one-headed two-faced. Perhaps it was the Goddess of Duality, or the shifty-headed icon of desire, or the solo-eared side-glancing saint of social anxiety, or some God's memory of someone he missed.

Whatever it was, it bore an intangible yet unmistakable religious texture, especially when Heng would cover it with gold foil and press small worthless gems into its divets. Whoever found Heng's statuettes (and he always left them where they were completed) always treated them with respect, feeling like they had encountered a lost idol of a forgotten God; an unpaved, unmarked road to salvation, with moisturizing serum and refreshing lavender scent.

The images just came to him. Where did they come from? Heng didn't care. He was always least nervous during these moments, and this particular carving seemed to carry enormous numinous weight. It arrived to him with unprecedented immediacy and demanded a swift exit, so even in a break in the conversation, Heng was opening the soapy door.

As he was rummaging for gold foil, he noticed that the chatter in the room had ceased. Manjunath and the Czech writer were done stabbing the wound of the morning with further silliness. A pause hung in the air, the next subject of discussion refusing to appear. Heng sensed his chance.

'Sir, so sir, what do you think? Is there a plot to sabotage scientific facilities, specifically those conducting some experiment, around the world?'

'Could be Heng, could be. I think it is safe to operate with that assumption, but we should wear gloves as a reminder that we have made this assumption. If, then, our hands feel warm, we shall remember it could be a flaw in our reasoning.'

Manjunath looked over to the Czech writer for approval. She had fallen asleep. He continued, 'So if there is a plot, we try to find out what the plot is and why it's there in the first place.'

'Also, who is behind it,' added Heng.

'People aren't always behind plots, Heng. Some walk in front of them, obscuring plots entirely from view,' corrected Manjunath.

Heng nodded reluctantly.

'These plotters. This nefarious group of weird-doers. We should give them a name while we work on our theory. I'm sure they have a name. Tough to assemble a group without a name. What do you think, Heng? What shall we call them?'

'X?'

'X? Tacky. We need something more descriptive, less ... esoteric.'

'How about Science ... Haters?'

'I love it.'

'No, that's not good. How about The Hidden Hand, or The Unseen Force, or The Shadow Bandits, or The Secret Storm?'

'I think Science Haters is fine.'

'Sir, I think it sounds a little silly and childish.'

'And what's a more silly and childish thing to do than attack scientists and scientific institutes?'

Heng exhaled in defeat. 'Okay, then if our Science Haters theory is correct, we must try to predict where they will act next. If we can beat them there, we can maybe stop the next catastrophe from happening. So far, we know that they attack or abduct scientists at advanced research institutes, and in this last case they've attacked the institute itself. They disrupt international electronic manufacturing and shipping. But the scope of this is all too vast! How do we narrow this down? What do we do next?'

Sadly, Manjunath had no ideas, being completely taken with the image of a group of Science Haters, giving them matching grey-and-black uniforms, a sash to pin ribbons and merit badges, a beret(?) or no headgear ... maybe a fez. But Heng had asked him something, so he took the course of great leaders and therapists and spun his question around.

'What do you think, Heng?'

'Okay, to narrow this down ... Well, the electronic component trade is far too spread out and granular for us to even know where to start. I think it's fair to adopt a top-down approach here and focus on the institutes. They've targeted three specific institutes across three countries as far as we know—Denmark, India, Japan – that tells us that these institutes are significant in some way. It could also be that the

Science Haters are trying to spread their attacks far apart to prevent anyone from deducing their connection.'

'It could be both,' said Manjunath, another gold standard response of the inattentive listener. He was wondering whether it was too rigid for the Science Haters to have matching socks. 'When presented with two options, it could very often be both.'

'You're right,' said Heng. 'I suppose the first thing to do is figure out what exactly these institutes have in common.'

'What do you think, Heng?'

'I just said what I think. Sir, either you're not listening, or you are being sarcastic.'

'It could be both.'

Heng retreated from the conversation to search the internet for clues as Manjunath started to scribble in his notebook his vision of the Science Haters. The ghosts of other backpackers slowly began to trickle in after another wild night of partying, drained spectres with sludgy blood, and the outlines of lost items.

Suddenly, Heng's theories hit critical mass and out of the solution of his mental confusion crystallized a thick, shiny hypothesis.

'Supercomputers!' gasped Heng.

'What?'

Before he could explain, a non-backpacker entered the room. The sort of non-backpacker that ruined the days of backpackers, even though he shared their wild, tired eyes. It was a police officer who had spent an entire day and night doing the quickest investigative work of his career. From the site of a fire to a bar to an apartment building to more bars to hotels, to home stays, to hostels and hostels and hostels, and now, finally, he was here.

Officer Brede saw Heng and Manjunath for the second time that day and burst into tears.

~: Continue? (Y/N)

CHAPTER 8

'The Authority was alerted by a seismic event alarm at The Scientific Institute (1-DS-A). The investigation was subsequently handed over to the Sentinels, who report that the alarm was the result of a malfunctioning sensor. No further investigation is held necessary.'
—Incident Report, Documentation Officer, S.K.

You place one hand on your hip (the other holds the book) and wonder, in all this criss-cross-hop-skip-jumping, whether this narrator has ever told a story before. No, as a matter of fact. This would be my first hurrah, and I hope it is a hurrah for you as well. Now that the plot is steaming, did you want tea? No? Back to it then.

A loud siren rang through The Scientific Institute like a press conference of seagulls, alerting everyone there was to alert that something was wrong. The alarm was set off by an explosion.

Dr Root had correctly identified the black box from a memory of a record. Employed at The Repository, responsible for cataloguing and maintaining all the records of the government, people, science, art, agriculture, everything, Dr Root was technically in charge of all there was to be remembered. His presence at the completely automated repository was tedious and unnecessary, but the records were valuable

101

and everyone felt safer with a genius close at hand, just in case something went wrong.

Nothing went wrong, except, in Dr Root's opinion, his whole career. Shunted sideways from department to department for being an 'insufferable piece of shit', he had finally been sent to a place where he had none but automata for company, whom he had train-washed to love him. As records kept keeping themselves, he grew bored and, in his boredom, started perusing them at random.

He would watch movies and read their scripts and see what artistic liberties the director took, what bits the actors improvised and how he would have done things differently. For example, in the blockbuster film *The Chapatti Situation* (in which the widely adored Divya made her debut), the script included a long and dramatic fight scene in which one of the characters merely spectated. There was a description of how he hesitated to step in and ended up stepping in at the exact moment the fight had concluded, instantly looking more foolish than any of the fighting parties. The scene had been cut (so said the director's commentary) for being largely irrelevant, a strange indulgence that people had time for in books but not in films. The director confessed that in movies you were either revealing more about a character or advancing a plot; everything else was to be swept from the editing-room floor.

Dr Root found himself disagreeing. The tendency to think of one's life as a story was a neurological fallacy. To put yourself as the protagonist of a tale introduces an audience to play to, staples hope into the scheme of things and comes with notions of how you *should* be treated. You begin to think of yourself in an uplifting comedy or a gloomy tragedy and regard all experiences as being scenes to either reveal more about your character or advance the plot. Anything that doesn't fit is annoying fluff to tap your foot impatiently through. But there isn't a story, and you certainly aren't the hero.

As mechanical and banal as the spin of Earth, at regular intervals, things just happen. Stories are our way of making sense of the discrete irrelevant lumps of chaos that make up our lives, but aren't the real shape of the orange. Dr Root thought movies should reflect unedited reality more accurately. He then felt better about his career.

Over months and years, he found his view on art grow deeper and broader, finding himself increasingly adept at criticism, privately reviewing documentaries, movies, plays, songs, film scores and even moonlighting at the AI Creative Review Society. Occasionally, he would dip into a scientific paper, but the astringency of memory kept it to a minimum.

One such occasion, where he was whipping himself with the ghost of the past, he came across what appeared to be a mistake. It was a snippet of a paper that detailed a simulation project by some unspecified authors, and while the working of the project was encrypted, an image of the prototype remained unobscured. It was a small black box. He raised a concern – why was this record incomplete? Why was it encrypted? Who were the authors? What was this project? He received a quick reply. It was an error. And the snippet was gone. That was when it began to haunt him.

The black box. So black it barely betrayed its dimensions, it captivated him, doing the tango in his daydreams, jumping out from behind corners in his nightmares, showing up in the absent doodling he did while he performed his unsolicited reviews at The Repository. Officially the government had no secret records (what would we have to hide?); had he just stumbled across one? That would be huge. Huge! The Foundational Charter of the government *forbade* secrecy. This was a secret! He had found a secret! *He* had found it!

But who would believe him?

Over and over the box turned in his imagination. A simulation project. A secret simulation project. What could they be simulating? What would be worthy of being kept secret?

It was still rotating at the back of his mind when Nataliya invited him to break into Dr Krishna's office. Seeing the box there, everything clicked into place. He developed a theory. It had to be. And when he held the black box, he couldn't help but feel that if his life was indeed a story, well, this had to be the inciting incident, the thing that thrust the hero forth into a journey of discovery, away from home, severed from the familiar, into the land of transformation to meet friends, enemies and allies, uncover mysteries, find innate power and heal his own wounds, finally returning to the world, changed. Unfortunately, if his life was a story, this was the climax.

He closed his hands around the handle of the box. A neat, pliable, inviting handle. A handle positively begging to be pulled. A device pleading to be opened.

Nataliya's instinct told her the very opposite. This was wrong. All of this was wrong. The presence of the box, Root's fascination with it and finally the appearance of the handle. This was wrong. They shouldn't be here. This shouldn't be happening. She backed away further and further.

'Root, let's go!' she hissed from the doorway. 'We don't know what's inside that!'

He did not answer her, but the whole room did.

Dr Root opened the box and found inside it an explosion. Dr Root died. End of story.

The force of the shockwave propelled Nataliya out of the doorway into an adjacent wall.

Designers of explosions excel at abstraction – they chalk things down in yield, megatons, kilojoules, delivery time, effective radius, all esoteric conceptual distractions from the reality of destruction. Explosions are better measured as the product of perceived horror – melted flesh, boiled blood, gouged entrails, burst eyeballs, vaporized skeletons, shredded souls and the universal constant of suffering, ß. The explosion was powerful enough to completely destroy Dr K's office and everything (and, unfortunately, everyone) inside it. Dr K had only thought of it as hiding evidence. An abstraction.

Just by virtue of having observable mass, humans exist as a minority in the universe. Energy misers, holding onto ourselves, afraid to be free. We can consider death as the snipping of subatomic ties, mass returned to creation to be fashioned into something exciting for the universe (or perhaps just some admin work). There's no use crying over spilled guts.

Ears ringing, eyes blinded, Nataliya stumbled to her feet. Dazed, she slowly patted her body, subconsciously taking biological inventory. She was all there. As shaking feet carried her back to Dr K's office, a sharp terror already told her what she would find inside.

The room in its entirety was empty. Everything had been vaporized. Mounds of paper, molecules of friend, gone. Nataliya stood gaping. The explosion was so total that it had even destroyed every sign of itself. No glowing embers, no raining ash, no spattered blood, no strewn limbs. Nothing. Just clean, empty walls. It was total, utter, complete destruction. Leaving no sign, no memory, no forwarding address. Only horror.

The kind of explanation designed by someone who had everything to hide.

Nataliya stepped into the room and collapsed in shock. How could this have happened? Why would this happen? In numb disbelief, she scanned the room. The now-empty room.

Why did you do this, Dr K?

The alarmed authorities arrived armed at the institute at an alarming speed. Sirens blared, lights flooded every inch of darkness around the institute, creatures of the night hurried away in their curlers and cold cream.

Nataliya, frozen on the floor in the middle of an empty room, was approached by three officers. Officers of the Authority were dispatched in threes. An investigating officer, to be cold, rational and unbiased; an empathy officer to make sure the investigating officer's cold rationality didn't upset everyone; and a documentation officer to record everything at the scene of the investigation, take samples and settle the inevitable disputes between the other two officers. Some of the officers wore masks that obscured their faces. Anyone looking at them would see their facial features rearranged at random, like a surreal moving portrait Dr Root might have liked.

The investigating officer approached Nataliya. 'You are Nataliya, Genius Category A?' she asked in a scrambled voice.

Nataliya slowly got to her feet, trembling. The appearance of the authorities gave her immediate relief. She was safe. It was safe. Both her parents had been officers and it had been her plan to join their ranks until she surprised herself by scraping through the genius exam.

The empathy officer stepped forward. His visor was designed as a generic genderless kind human face. 'It's all right, shock can make us forget things. I'm sure you are trying your best.'

The investigating officer rolled her eyes, which briefly collected together on her visor where a chin usually is. She said, 'The seismic sensors at the institute have registered a seismic event, setting off the alarm. You are here; please present your perceived account of events.'

'In your own time, I know this is a very difficult situation,' said the empathy officer.

'Oh, shut up,' said the investigating officer.

'Guys, please. Let's stay on track,' said the documentation officer.

'There … there was an explosion …' said Nataliya.

'Was there?' said the investigating officer, peering inside the office. 'Where?'

'I – I was standing in the doorway … it knocked me back – Dr Root was inside the office! He …'

'Dr Root, Genius Category M, Repository 1-DS-A?' asked the investigating officer.

'Y – Yes …' said Nataliya.

Looking around the office again, the investigating officer asked, 'Where is he?'

The absurd, violent insanity of the situation tightened around Nataliya. Her throat began to burn. 'He was – inside …'

'Yes. Where is he now?' said the investigating officer impatiently.

'He was inside …' whispered Nataliya.

'Yes, I know he was inside; where is he—'

'—will you give her a second?' said the empathy officer.

'Why don't you let her reply?' snapped the investigating officer.

'She would reply, if you gave her time to reply!' spat the empathy officer.

'Guys, please. Let's stay on track,' said the documentation officer.

Nataliya felt as if her mind was squeezing her vocal cords shut. In a choked voice she said, 'Something in Dr Krishna's office set off an explosion. The explosion was the seismic event that triggered the alarm. Something that horrible man created ... It killed Dr Root.'

The investigating officer raised an eyebrow somewhere near her nose. 'Please stick to facts, not speculation.'

'But we understand what you are feeling, and we hear you,' said the empathy officer.

'Nataliya, Genius Category A. This is your place of employment, correct?' asked the investigating officer.

Nataliya nodded slowly.

'A strange time to be at work. Why are you here?'

It was a question that Nataliya was not prepared to answer. She simply gaped at the three officers.

In a gentle voice, the empathy officer said, 'Please do answer the question as directed.'

'I – I was ... my project with Dr Krishna ... I am his supervisor, so I—'

'Were you and Dr Root authorized to enter Dr Krishna's office?' The investigating officer was back at it.

Nataliya shifted her weight nervously. 'I – uh ... Not in the strictest sense. I mean – he wasn't complying with my ... That is – I was in charge of a project and he, uh ...'

The investigating officer's features shifted themselves with a pronounced menace, frown lines scattered themselves across her visor, narrowed eyes flitted from ear to ear, a downward-curling mouth presented itself vertically.

'You were not?'

Nataliya had not until then fully considered her own unlawfulness in the night's playbill. 'I, uh ... I mean ...'

'Stop grilling her!'

'Mind your own business!'

'Guys, please. Let's stay on track.'

Further bickering and hemming and hawing was spared by the echoing taps of a pair of shoes.

Tap-TAP, tap-TAP, heel-TOE, heel-TOE.

The feet approached closer. The group abruptly became still and silent, like deer detecting the slightest shift in savannah grass. Like prey.

Tap-TAP, tap-TAP, heel-TOE, heel-TOE.

Power travels as fear. The approaching feet carried such immense authority, such unquestionable command, such unmistakable sovereignty, that it held everyone in its grasp, frozen and mute.

The taps reached a higher and higher pitch, puncturing the silence till they reached an unbearable crescendo, and then with a final TAP/TOE, the Chief rounded a corner and came before them.

The Chief wasn't simply the chief of this division of the Authority, or of this segment, or of this district. She was the big one, the ultimate head of the entire authority, a member of government. It wasn't every day that you saw the Chief; if you lived your life well, it was never.

In a crisp grey uniform, with platinum hair like support cables, like steel cords running from shoulder to head, glasses that yanked any available light and muscled it into a glint, she stood before them, smiling. There are very few people whose smiles can cause uneasiness and the Chief's smile would make even these people very uneasy. If there is nothing to fear but fear itself, the Chief was fear itself.

The officers held panicked salutes.

'Documentation officer, you will hand over observations to the sentries. Officers, please disband.'

The Chief spoke in a light, sliding calm, like the gentle press of a blade against a throat.

The officers saluted several more panicked times and withdrew obsequiously, wordlessly. Absolute authority quickly cleared the area.

Nataliya remained standing.

'Nataliya,' said the Chief calmly. 'Please explain your presence here.'

Fear pushed all of Nataliya's words through her mouth at the same time, causing her to simply stammer. And then the floodgates opened and she blurted out everything, about her project, Dr K's indifference, his hostility towards getting work done, his useless submission to her research, his refusal to explain his process, her project's impending termination and thus her decision to enter his office to find some evidence of what he was doing— At this point she was interrupted.

'So, you have deemed his performance insufficient. There are protocols to report this. It does not grant you access to trespass on his private space.'

'Yes, but Dr Root and I entered, and there was this black box – and I left for a second but something caused an explosion! Aren't you here to investigate the explosion?'

'Please do not tell me what I am here to investigate.'

The smile left the Chief's face, and it settled into an utter and terrifying deadness. She continued, 'Nataliya, you may leave. Unless you would like to be charged with trespassing.'

Nataliya continued to stand, dumbstruck. 'But … the explosion! Dr Root! I understand I was trespassing but this is *clearly* an illegal weapon—'

'Nataliya,' said the Chief. The transcript shows that there was nothing to indicate any article of threat in her manner, no knife clasped beneath her robes, no laser dot of distant snipers, but it is important to say – if you were there, you would feel the intangible gun at your temple. 'You may leave.'

'Dr K … rishna had booby-trapped his office somehow! It was the black box!'

'That will be all.'

'Root was killed. He killed Root!'

The Chief drew herself to her full height, towering over Nataliya. Her jaw twitched. And when she spoke again it was with a suffocating softness.

'Did you see this happen? Do you see the remains of his body?'

'No, but I— He was in the room! Of course, he—'

'Please leave conclusions to the authorities. Dr Root will have a chance to present his own account.'

'But he's dead!' screamed Nataliya. 'Dr Krishna *killed* him with this—'

'Please be careful ...' said the Chief, her voice cold and clipped like a bullet entering a chamber '... about accusations. Do you have proof that Dr Krishna set off an explosion? Do you have proof that Dr Root was killed in this explosion?'

'When he saw the box, Dr Root said that—'

'—said? You are supposed to be a scientist. May I remind you that you are the only suspect here? If you like, you can be taken into custody immediately.'

'I—I just want to help ...' said Nataliya.

Distant synchronized heel-toe taps of boots sounded. A perfectly balanced jog march of a full battalion of sentries was on the way.

'Thank you, Nataliya,' said the Chief. 'I will look into things appropriately. You will be debriefed tomorrow, at which time you may decide whether you want to revise your account of events to one that resembles the truth, or continue with your wild, baseless imaginings. It is your choice. Now, leave. I will not repeat myself.'

Before Nataliya could object further, the black sludge of sentries was upon her. They flowed around the Chief and carried Nataliya effortlessly to the gates.

≈

Breathless, confused, Nataliya found herself standing outside the institute and saw before her the alarm diffused, the floodlights disarmed, and the officers and vehicles removed from the scene.

Back to normal, as if nothing had ever happened. If we possessed the tools to measure such things, we would register a loud shattering coming from somewhere inside Nataliya. She gaped at the only thing available to gape at, the building of The Scientific Institute. What had just happened?

An explosion.
Root was inside! Inside, but then he would be—
And why was the Chief acting like ...

The Chief was only available for view or comment in conversational mythologies. She usually remained decidedly behind the scenes, and Nataliya had heard tales of her fearsome demeanour, but had always dismissed them. She was just someone doing her job, and these were silly tales to create distrust in the system. Until they met. Nataliya still had no doubt that the Chief was doing her job; she just couldn't believe what her job was.

Her determination to act as if *nothing* had happened was staggering. Her power to transform that act to record disorienting, and the iniquitous ease with which she had chosen Nataliya as the only perpetrator in the events ... was ... horrifying. This was not justice. This was not close to justice.

If she had not been there to *witness* what had happened, she would have believed the official record. Until what she had seen tonight, what would be the reason not to? As much as she would have liked to believe otherwise, Root had to have died. She was now sure they would later claim Root was 'missing'. A dead person is indeed missing, but they are dead first.

What was happening?
What were they hiding?
How many other things were hidden?
And just what was that box?
She felt the weightlessness before a giddying fall as her ground of convictions crumbled away. The explosion also evaporated her faith in the system.

Before this tale hoists its slacks and continues, we must note that whatever Nataliya was feeling, this was the moment that she decided she would find Dr K. If there were any answers to be found, he would have them and if there was a person to blame here, it was him. And if the reader thinks her incapable of this task, this is also a good place to remember that a Genius Category A is still a fucking genius.

≈

The residence quarters of The Scientific Institute were arranged as muddy hives spread over a few kilometres.

The elite sentries of the government in black-and-black-and-black (the reader may imagine a Danish police officer's uniform) descended on the residence quarters. The sentries ranked higher than any member of authority and were only called on when the handling of a situation required a delicate touch. Which was almost never. In fact, the expense of their existence was a continuing source of political debate and yet, here they were. It was with the fury and subtlety of a thousand falling petals that they arrived at Dr K's house, sounding no alarm and alerting no neighbours.

In seconds they were inside, partitioning empty bourbon bottles, organizing sheafs of unreadable paper and combing through clothes and shoes, shining detectors above and below every nook and cranny to discover any concealment, any hint of shenanigans. Like a well-coordinated colony of ants, they worked swiftly and efficiently, ordered by a larger synchronicity. Legend says that two sentries passing each other in the hallway never hesitate about which side to take. As soon as they were done, the Chief arrived.

The sentries stood at attention against walls as she walked past them. She investigated items seemingly at random. She picked up some paper, glanced at it and tossed it aside, put an empty bottle to her nose and tossed that aside too, tapped one of the walls twice and all of them again blared with their last message – RUN. All of the walls but one. There was one wall that remained defiantly black.

Her eyes found a small square missing from the corner of the wall.

She found a little note on the desk, addressed to her.

Hello Chief, it began.

Smiling, she carefully folded the letter and placed it in her pocket.

'He knows we're here,' said the Chief.

Hiding at a distance outside the residence compound, Nataliya saw the sentries leaving his house. She would crawl to it after they left, to find it pathetic, disgusting and empty of clues.

≈

'They are in the house,' said the small wall square.

Dr K sighed. The last of the bourbon was done. A multitude of metallic chirrups sounded off hidden insects. A shooting star tore an arc in the night-sky's stocking.

He got to his feet and started to pack everything in his bag. He squeezed the HT pin on his lapel.

It said, *If you have an existing plan, and are certain of this plan's effectiveness, then the best course of action is to adhere to this plan.*

When came the wall's turn to be sequestered, it said, 'Can I ask you something?'

Its answer was to be thrust into the darkness of the bag along with an empty bottle, two apple cores and a whole stretching universe. To no one in particular, it asked its question: 'Why are you doing this?'

CHAPTER 9

'Convener H, I'm sending this to you as a personal communication and not an official directive, because that would have to be public record. A secret simulation project? Did you think I wouldn't find out? So this is why the two smartest people in the world are not available to me? I'm sending my closest confidants, Eshwar and Samuel, to report their findings. They will keep their silence. My own silence is my prerogative. I'll see what I have to do based on their report. Last thing: there better be a good reason for this secrecy. Don't try to sneak anything by me, I'm the fucking President.'
— Private Letter, The President

Below is an encrypted record that should technically be at the Repository but isn't. Its secrecy is illegal, the lack of a record is illegal and your ingestion of it is also illegal. We will leave legal minds to writhe on the floor wondering which is most illegal.

THE COUNCIL ON SIMULATED UNIVERSES

Council recorded by Special Documentation Unit. Special Documentation Unit maintained by The Scientific Institute. Manner: Casual.

Convener: I call open the Council on Simulated Universes. We have with us in attendance Dr Perenna and Dr Krishna, who have created and currently run this project.

Dr Krishna: Thank you for having us, Convener. It is our privilege to present our findings before the Council.

Dr Perenna: Present as required.

Convener: The Council also notes the presence of Resp. Samuel from The Committee for Theological Discourse and Eshwar from The Committee for Automaton Ethics, who are to present their own observations of the project.

Dr Perenna (mumbles): Great.

Resp. Samuel: Thank you, Convener.

Eshwar: Thanks.

Convener: Documentation Unit to record that these proceedings carry the highest level of secrecy and must be encoded as such.

[Documentation Unit: Got it, buddy.]

Convener: Please record these proceedings as formal.

[Documentation Unit: Option noted with thanks.]

Resp. Samuel: Are we not waiting for other members to attend?

Eshwar: I ... er ... I saw the Chief of the Authority outside, I was wondering why she was here ...

Convener: The President has asked you and Samuel to look into the project, and you are. This is the full strength of the Council. I trust you have been briefed about the sensitive nature of this meeting?

Resp. Samuel: I can't endorse such secrecy, as you know, but the President asked me to abide and so I have.

Eshwar: How many other people know about this project?

Convener: We can say that if knowledge of this project escapes to more people; you two can be identified as the source. Notwithstanding this, your presence here is vital and your feedback is sought to be implemented. Shall we begin?

Resp. Samuel: Yes, that is fine. I will ask the question on the President's mind: why all this secrecy?

Dr Krishna: Thank you for question, Resp. Samuel. It was not originally our intention to keep our research secret. We only wanted to get our findings in order before we made them public. However, our research continued to unfold in such a way that we did not achieve ... presentable results.

Resp. Samuel: What does that mean? The project did not work?

Dr Perenna: No, it worked. It just took a long time for us to accept what it told us.

Dr Krishna: What my colleague is saying is we were obligated to exhaustively test our findings until we were certain there was no error. Because our findings were ... troubling.

Eshwar: Troubling? Troubling how?

[DELETED—TWO   PAGES   <unknown   source/unknown authorization>]

Eshwar: So is it not possible to—

Resp. Samuel: Why can't you just start simulating after that point?

Dr Perenna: Great suggestion! Why don't you do it? I should only assume you can do my job, since anyone on Earth can do yours—

Dr Krishna: Perenna! Resp. Samuel, I apologize—

Resp. Samuel: I will not be spoken to this way!

Convener: Please answer the question.

Dr Krishna: Thank you, Convenor. I believe Resp. Samuel is suggesting that if every universe simulation ends at exactly the same point, why can't we start simulating after that? A valid suggestion, and I would like to thank you for it. The fact is that the universe cyclically grows from simple to extraordinarily complex and back. It is unfeasible by any theoretically possible computation device to model a universe mid-state. The mere setting of parameters will take uncountably infinite time. Thus, we cannot start a simulation anywhere in the middle. We can only begin at the beginning. That is why our current strategy is to start modelling at the first physically sound moment of the universe and run the simulation from there. We have also considered saving a state of a model and running future models from that starting point, but that is also not useful as it always leads to the identical outcomes of that iteration of the simulation. The same results every time. Our only method of control is adjusting the speed of the simulation as we wish.

Eshwar: So you must start simulating from a simple origin point. That I understand. Are you sure your initial assumptions are correct?

Dr Perenna: Yes.

Resp. Samuel: Surely it can't all be this ... black and white ... this simple.

Dr Perenna: It isn't simple in the least. If a premise always leads to a conclusion, then it must be accepted as truth. What is bothering you is not simplicity. What is bothering you is destiny.

[Documentation Unit: Resp. Samuel scoffs.]

Resp. Samuel: Destiny is hardly an appropriate word to justify the absurd conclusions of a faulty experiment!

Dr Perenna: Your dislike for the result doesn't make it false.

Dr Krishna: Er ... Dr Perenna has taken to using the word *Destiny*, to refer to ... the ... um ... curious, let's say, *determinism* that seems inherent to our simulations. Our experiments have shown that even seemingly random events are almost exactly predictable, given the start state of the universe. The fact is that all the Lower Realities unfold identical to *our* perceived reality, even mirroring the history of Earth and all records of pre-winter civilizations. It can be unsettling to realize that our lives, all of our events and interactions are predetermined. However, this is not the only conclusion that can be drawn. It could just happen that the only universe capable of existing is our own, and the only way events can unfold is the way that events have unfolded in our history, and that is why the events of the simulation are largely identical to our history. But that is also a ... er ... different kind of troubling.

Dr Perenna: Samuel is just upset that God hasn't shown up.

Resp. Samuel: Hasn't show up? This proves that the universe necessitates the presence of a creator! Are you really that blind to what you see taking place? *You two are playing God!*

[DELETED—ONE   PAGE   <unknown   source/unknown authorization>]

Eshwar: But aren't your experiments constrained by your perspective? Your understanding of the universe is based on one which must allow human life. Perhaps working from that understanding is leading you to these identical deterministic realities.

Dr Perenna: Please leave science to the scientists.

[Documentation Unit: Eshwar looks upset.]

Convener: Dr Perenna, you are directed to answer the question.

Dr Perenna: Fine. We experimented with every conceivable origin point of the universe. We altered all aspects that could be altered. All permutations but one are unsuccessful. The one we observe. You can also think of it as the only one we are capable of observing if you enjoy thinking about things backwards.

Resp Samuel: What counts as an unsuccessful iteration?

Dr Perenna: There was a reason for our secrecy. Now that the president asks you two to look into this, we have to babysit you? Oh, fine – Krishna, stop giving me that look – If we alter the theoretically determined universe start state, it ends up being … well not a universe. It's all there in the paper. You could have read the paper and we could be working right now.

Eshwar: It will do well for you both to remember that this council has been called for you to explain your findings in plain terms.

Dr Krishna: We understand. I apologize for my colleague. What Dr Perenna means to say is that if we alter the origin conditions of the universe, then we observe impossible and absurd states. These states are not of relevance, given the guidelines of our research.

Eshwar: So, what happens?

Dr Perenna: 'Happens' does not happen. 'Occurs' does not occur. You can't think about fire in terms of mosquitoes, you can't juggle teeth with emotions, you can't read cutlery polish with punctuations or throw ghosts at the sound of speed—

Dr Krishna: What we are saying is that these unachievable states, which ... uh, we cannot model because the system that exists to model them is not suited to represent alternate systems of physical laws. It's ... uhh ... you could say it's a problem with our modelling.

Dr Perenna: There is no problem with our modelling. We set about to create a simulation of our universe, not to catalogue impossibilities.

[Documentation Unit: Long silence and general tension in the room.]

Resp. Samuel: So you have successfully defended your research. You say you are doing the right thing in the right way, and you seem certain you are without error. You think your assumptions correct, your inferences spotless. However, there still exists one stubborn, unanswered question. If you are so certain about your precious research, then why does the simulation never reach our present? Why does every iteration crash?

Dr Perenna: Ah yes, the crux of the matter. The crucial difference between Lower Realities and ours.

Dr Krishna: All of the Lower Realities, that is, all of our simulations never reach our present. They freeze at exactly the same time. The same point in their twenty-first centuries.

[Documentation Unit: Long spans of nervous eye contact.]

Eshwar: The *exact* same point? What ... what point is that?

Dr Krishna: When they try to run their own large-scale simulation.

[Documentation Unit: Silence]

Resp. Samuel: False Gods cannot create true life.

Eshwar: Is it because our system lacks the ability to process this complexity?

Dr Perenna: Not exactly. Theoretically, there can be no system that can process a running subsystem identical to itself.

Eshwar: Is – is that proof enough that we aren't a simulated reality?

Dr Krishna: From our understanding, yes. Each subsequent sub-simulation, if indeed identical, would necessarily contain itself, thus increasing the required computational power exponentially. If a system contains an identical subsystem, then the subsystem also contains an identical subsystem and so on, thus creating infinite subsystems. To run this would require more than the energy present in the entire universe. If we were being simulated in such a universe, then it would already have been wrung dry. We wouldn't exist to discuss this point. There may be an alternate kind of system you could postulate, but that leaves the scientific realm and enters into the philosophical, which isn't really our strength.

[Documentation Unit: Resp. Samuel claps his hands sarcastically.]

Resp. Samuel: There is the God you said you couldn't find.

Dr Perenna: Oh, give it a rest.

Eshwar: But if it didn't end? If the simulation kept running, would it reach a time identical to our lives? Would we see ourselves in our own simulation? Would we be having this conversation in it? Would we be able to fast-forward time and see our own future?

Dr Perenna: It would be a true, factual, observable account of time. Nothing distorted by historical reporting. We would be able to see everything everyone has done, is doing and will do.

[Documentation Unit: Tremendous unease in the room.]

Resp. Samuel: But this is despicable ... surveillance ... voyeurism! The violation of nearly all of our rights to privacy, to ... This simply cannot be allowed, this is—

Dr Krishna: Resp. Samuel! Er ... May I interject? I do understand and appreciate the validity of your objections. However, I must point out one essential fact. We currently observe that all the simulations halt on their own. This is already a huge deviation from our current reality. This is not to diminish the concerns you have laid out, which are valid and pressing and—

Dr Perenna:—terribly anxious, unless someone has a big secret to hide—

Resp. Samuel: HOW DARE YOU—

Dr Krishna:—Perenna, please! Theoretically, we cannot say what will happen. The hypothesis of the simulation mirroring our reality is already provable false. At this point we cannot speculate about the future state of the Lower Reality if it did not end, because it always does.

Eshwar: So then, if the simulations are always halting, what is the future scope of work in this project?

Dr Krishna: We're investigating an idea. If we could somehow push the Lower Reality not to run a simulation or *delay* their simulations or, better still, somehow *help them find a more efficient way to run a simulation*, things could change. If they could develop a simple simulation machine, this could theoretically be computable for our machine, then the simulation would continue and not crash. The problem we currently have is that there is no way to interfere with a running simulation.

Dr Perenna: Also, this proposed simple simulation machine is unknown and potentially impossible.

Dr Krishna: It's a working theory and – even if the future ends up having some ... similarity to our world, to use its events as evidence in *our* world would not have scientific credence. This is for the simple reason that even *reaching that point in the simulation requires outside intervention from us*. In any case, that is again speculation, but intervention in the running simulation is imperative. It is the focus of most of our work.

Eshwar: Oh, I see. Intervention is the key here.

Dr Krishna: Yes, Eshwar.

Eshwar: I am sorry to say that this is not possible.

Dr Krishna: Yes, it is not currently possible, but it is what we're trying to accomplish.

Eshwar: I misspoke. I mean to say I cannot allow this as the Seat of Automaton Ethics. Thus, there is no future scope of work in this project.

Resp. Samuel: I can also present you with an interminable list of my objections if you would like.

Eshwar: In essence, our recommendation to the President is that this project be terminated with immediate effect.

[Continued]

CHAPTER 10

'I will be taking a month off.'
— Leave Application, Dr Krishna, Convener

'No, we can't refuse the Convener's leave request, but damn, the least he could do is make it sound like a request.'
— Staff Coordinator, The Scientific Institute

The Chief was on the hunt.

At the time, she led a team of sentries that was woefully off-track. She suspected this. All there was to do was investigate these obvious diversions and wait. Wait until he made a mistake.

Understanding what drove people was imperative to her duty. She contacted the ex-Convener of the institute, the one Dr K had replaced. Besides her, the ex-Convener was the only other living person intimately familiar with the simulation project and all of the shrapnel it begat. She asked him for his theory of Dr K's motives. She did not share her own.

The ex-Convener considered the events carefully. He was older now. With age, he knew the limits of cruelty, the limitations of cunning, the fury of desperation. He spent his advancing years looking back. It changed the character of his genius. The ex-Convener offered a theory divergent to the Chief's. The *what* was certain. Krishna was continuing the simulation project. They both knew the consequences it could have. But as for *why* ...

If a Lower Reality did not halt, the simulation would run to reach their own time. It could create a mirror world, a simulated version of their existence. The darkest, most forbidden altar of human yearning aflame. Desperate temptation forever denied, now delivered.

The chance to bear witness to your own life, relive your memories. Over and over again. A theatre of time all your own. Every night is misery night. Revel in the triumphs, suffer the pain, spectate your wretchedness. They both knew Krishna. They both knew his scar. Maybe he wanted to remember. Perhaps he wanted to punish himself, dragging nails across his soul; never to heal. Sentiment.

But there was another possibility. If Krishna had somehow invented simulation intervention, then this was about something more than remorse. Intervention meant that in the Lower Reality he could relive his life and *change events*. In this facsimile of his life, a chance to right all wrongs. A chance to erase his shame. Then there would be a world without his regret. A world he could play over and over again. He could make the future that should have been and weigh it against the life that was, suffering forever the difference.

Infinite chances to start again. If you could, would you? If you can, will you?

And what price will you pay?

Exercise 10.1

FILL IN THE BLANKS

(15 marks)

1. The narrator of this novel is _____.
2. The K in Dr K stands for _____ and he is a Genius Category _____.
3. So far, this novel has been _____ (breathtaking, astonishing, incredible, genius).
4. Every Lower Reality ends at the same point, which is _____.
5. What do you think the P. in P. Manjunath stands for? _____ (Take a guess).
6. The purpose of Nataliya's project is _____ _____.
7. If you held the HT pin right now and squeezed it, it would say _____.
8. The free money application is called _____.
9. Where do you think Anne Andersen is? _____.
10. Dr K stepped down as convener of the institute _____ year(s) ago.
11. People fundamental to the functioning of a Lower Reality are called _____.
12. Do you think you are attractive? _____(Yes/No/ Sometimes).
13. Can a running simulation be fast-forwarded until a certain time (before halting, of course)? _____(Yes/No/Duh).
14. The Chief of the Authority is called _the Chief_. (This one comes pre-solved.)

15. If you could start again, would you? Would you like to see your life as it should have been?

_____(Yes/No) and what would that be worth?

_____.

Answers at the back of the book.
(But don't look now.)

CHAPTER 11

Dr K coughed a mosquito out of his throat as he tunneled down the gullet of the jungle in 1-DS-A, rapidly approaching the jungle in 1-DS-B, which was the same jungle with a different name. The land was divided into Regions, Regions into Districts, Districts into Segments and Segments further alphabetized. The names reeked of no colonizers' stench, no saltpetre war fumes. Unshadowed by the ghosts of the past, they were simple, efficient, inoffensive, boring.

But emotion can attach easily to any alphanumeric arrangement. The most adhesive emotion being, of course, fear. The mere mention of '1-DS-B' fell like a syringe in the ear and sank like a cement block in the heart, because:

1. It was covered in thick, uncharted, impenetrable jungle.
2. The jungle pulsed with venomous serpents, infectious insects and perfidious plants.

3. Exotic, forgotten and unknown disease flowed in its brooks and fell from the trees.
4. It was illegal and expressly forbidden to enter the area.
5. It had no cafés.
6. The Wodewose lived in DS-B.

To go into the habitat of the Wodewose was to seek suicide or manifest murder. The government recognized and protected DS-B as the habitat and jurisdiction of the Wodewose and subject to their laws. This was considered easier than trying to make them see reason and stop murdering passers-by.

Yet, Dr K had set course for DS-B and did not waver. His destination lay far beyond it, in DS-F, a journey of several days by the permissible routes he had no intention of taking. Thus, he had plunged into the most dangerous part of the inhabited world because he needed a shortcut.

Dr K knew he was being hunted by the Chief, and he knew the hunters were capable and adept, and he knew it was imperative to stay on the move. His pursuers would currently be following all the decoys he had left, but he knew the Chief and the Chief knew him. It would only be a matter of time before the decoys were discovered.

It was time for his next move. His next outpost. He could, of course, be seeking asylum from an ally, but the scan through Dr K's inventory of friends was short. One row had been found.

NAME	FRIEND	RELATIONSHIP	PROFESSION	CURRENT WHEREABOUTS
Perenna, Dr	Yes	Reflexive	Scientist	Deceased

Dr K clenched his jaw and accelerated to keep himself from thinking about her.

Surely the smartest person in the world, the once-Convener (Global) of The Scientific Institute, should have more friends and well-wishers than this! Or perhaps power's peak has only enough place for one pair of feet.

In his quick ascent up ranks at The Scientific Institute, Dr K had shaken many hands, smiled down many hallways, paid calculated praise, delivered delicate admonition, said the right things at the right time in the right way. Until a year ago a random survey across The Scientific Institute would result only in the highest praise for him, with some tiny leaks of envy. He was polite, cordial and indisputably brilliant.

In a bureaucratic dance, where everyone is false and no one has rhythm, this strategy is optimal. Someone like Perenna, who didn't suffer fools in any capacity, would hit the ceiling fast. It would descend to meet her. Dr K had put on a face, and it was well-appreciated. The point was to get to the top, where he and Perenna could finally do the research they wanted to. Unencumbered. But at some point, that goal had been corrupted and shifted. He had become powerful. She had become an inconvenience.

Clench. Accelerate.

Cordial friendships break when cordiality does. Acquaintance melts in hot water. As of a year ago, when he demoted himself from Convener and stopped swaying to the dance, he counted himself alone.

Alone, perhaps, except for:

NAME	FRIEND	RELATIONSHIP	PROFESSION	CURRENT WHEREABOUTS
Divya	No	Once	Actor	DS-C

This option had not been considered for two reasons.

Firstly, DS-C was conspicuously remote. It began mid-jungle and springing out into plains, gently descending from treeline to beaches, tipped by the roaring C. A great place to get away. But, with the population being as low as it was, who needed to get away? The carrying capacity of Earth was estimated to be one billion *tops*, and it was maintained rigidly. All over the globe, bird feet trampled empty mud streets, bats and gnats and rats played bridge in the evenings, undisturbed. Thus, precious few people lived in DS-C – oddballs, weirdos, loonies, kooks, crazies and an actor who had suddenly decided to retire into obscurity, who might have been all of the above.

Secondly, Dr K was certain that Divya hated him. She certainly had enough reason to.

Thus, his plan had never involved requesting or expecting any assistance. After Perenna's death he had taken a month off, ostensibly to recover from the shock of grief, but in actuality to scour the districts for discreet hiding places. Claiming ownership of these places would be easily traceable, so he had identified remote, unassuming, abandoned locations that would be easy to hide in. The first of these was in 1-DS-F. By travelling through DS-B he would reduce a week's journey to a mere days. It was the practical, nearly obvious choice on paper.

But very few people are murdered on paper.

$$\approx$$

A small sidebar on the consequences of radioactivity.

Ionizing radiation knocks particles out of your body. Its high-energy hoodlums spray graffiti on your genome, vandalize your chromosomes and steal traffic cones. Useful chiefly for making still lives of skeletons, its destructive power is profoundly amplified by its spooky invisibility. There is an ancient and unyielding part of human programming that insists on sight for the measurement of reality. What you see *should* be what you get, so we find it hard to believe that something that we can't see will so eagerly give us death.

The nuclear winter of our discontent was cold and cruel, but mercifully brief. The peace that followed was far worse. The breeze blew, the grass grew, the sun told great stories. It was cruel to watch perfect picnic weather from thick shielded windows day after day. But it was still too dangerously radioactive, far too dangerously so.

Was it, though, asked a small group of people. Everything *looked* fine; where was this danger? Why didn't things glow green like in the movies? Armed with these absurd aphorisms, their following grew until they had enough clout to demand to be let out. And, against everyone's best advice, they stepped out into the world. The Wodewose are their descendants.

The Wodewose sang, danced, shimmied and fucked, ate fruit, killed boars, made quaint adobe houses and couldn't put a finger on why they all seemed to be dropping dead every so often, or why they coughed blood, excreted blood, or cried blood. Must be allergies. The posh died quickly, the hardier lived longer and the first wave of the Wodewose slowly perished. But not before having children. Impossibly, over centuries, the line of the Wodewose continued, initially slightly deformed by radiation, then severely deformed by inbreeding.

All predictions of when the Wodewose would die out had proven to be wrong. They had no technology, no industry, had deformed genes, and while their numbers were reported to be dwindling, their flame stayed alive and burning.

What would they make of the first outsider in decades, on a device that hadn't been seen for even longer – *una motocicleta*?

CHAPTER 12

'After the freak accident at the ferry, another local tragedy. A lifeless Orca whale washed ashore on Norlev Beach in northern Jutland late last night. Inside the stomach of the whale was found the body of missing scientist Anne Andersen, bringing the investigation into her disappearance to an end. Just how Dr Andersen met this unfortunate fate is currently unknown.'

— Evening News, TV 3

~:Log –ld

LESS DRAMATICALLY:
ITERATION ZZHM03

Heng, Manjunath and the Czech writer waited quietly as Office Brede wept. Those familiar with police procedure will notice that this is not the conventional conclusion to a chase. To understand the impetus behind the tears, we need only to relive the previous day as Officer Brede, and although reasons don't make tears any less wet, they offer you a chance to join in the waterworks, if you wish.

The Copenhagen Nanoscience Research Institute was on fire. It was where she had worked. Anne Andersen. Officer Brede had received the call in a daze. He patrolled the site in a haze.

How?

He turned her ID card over in her palms. Anne Andersen. Missing a week now. A week since he had seen her. Was he the last person to see her?

Why, God?

Two intruders at the arson site. He had apprehended them. He should have questioned them. Then the strange conversation …

Maybe it wasn't even set on fire. Maybe it was a fire set on the scientific institute … maybe it was destruction dust … performance art … dragons' eggs …

While the man spoke, everything changed for Officer Brede.

It may have been the lack of sleep. It may have been his turbulent life. Maybe it was the fact that since the incident at the fountain, where he saw Anne Andersen, where *he had felt the touch of God*, his life had ceased to make sense. Maybe it was that his existing tools of understanding the world now seemed insufficient. Maybe it was all that compounded with the fury of this odd intruder's strange suppositions set in the backdrop of smouldering science, or – to whatever extent we can say this without giggling – it was meant to be. But as the man spoke, Officer Brede slowly felt himself dissolving.

It was as if a motorized rotor pulled back the top of his head and out flowed a fountain of himself. Onto everything, through everything, and on that morning the officer felt himself quiver with the concern of the cosmos. He was at once the whole egg and it was him, poached and over-easy and scrambled and soft-boiled. He was the burning and the burnt and the cavity that smelled the smoking, the Earth that bore its weight and the dirt and the rain and the sky. The barriers melted, the video paused and for a moment that was cruelly brief, he was enlightened.

When he found himself crying tears of wonder and relief, he knew it was over. Because there he was and there were the tears, and there was horizon hinging the sky. All again divorced with thick separating margins. He felt charged, privy to a secret, a Peeping Tom at reality's window but for all his excitement, he realized that he had no words to describe his experience. He looked for the two intruders who had just poked his third eye, but they were long gone. They would know, they would know what they had done to him, they would know how to do it again.

While the enraptured officer was understanding that the orientation of his perception was an illusion, that there was no centre to his experience, Heng and Manjunath had left from the corner. Their ashen trail ended at the compound. His hand was empty. They had taken her ID card.

God, is this your doing too?

Officer Brede decided then and there that it was time to hang up his gold-crested black jacket and snip off the ties that bound. The rest of his life would be spent in search of this experience, starting with tracking down those two. He had to look behind the curtain again, he wanted to see the brushstrokes.

≈

A wild-eyed police officer walked into a small Irish pub. He had tried every establishment in the vicinity to ask after the two intruders. None had seen them. He hadn't a picture. His descriptive language was poor. The almost-empty bar was still swimming in amber warmth.

Officer Brede asked the bartender if he had seen a chubby Indian man in a leather jacket with a man who was – he struggled to find an inoffensive non-reductive way to describe Heng's features and finally settled on – Chinese. This was incorrect. Heng was Indian by birth and passport, oppression and appreciation of chaos as a way of life, although his grandparents were formerly Chinese. The bartender saw all sorts, as bartenders do, but in Copenhagen the Heng–Manjunath double bill was rare. He told Officer Brede that they had left an hour ago, and had in fact left something behind.

He rummaged under the bar and presented to Officer Brede a palm-sized figurine.

Brede's fingers tingled as they made contact with the statuette. It was a small effigy, fashioned out of soap and coated with gold foil – a likeness of a woman seated with her legs crossed, with two arms on one side, three on the other and one issuing out from her back over her head, dangling a tomato before her half-closed eyes. She wore serenity on her face, her lips parted in a knowing smile.

There was nothing noticeably religious about the statuette, no particular call for devotion, but holding it in his hands, the officer's eyes glazed over and in the next beat of his heart he felt blood flow to his extremities and then out into the atmosphere, into the glow of lamps, the sheen of glasses, the buzzing neon, the sticky floor; he felt soaked in the hardwood, wrung out of the heater, scribbled on the toilet walls, escorted from his mental premises, and even beating in the heart of the bartender (who was just thinking that this was another type he hadn't seen) – and then in another beat he was bolted once again to the familiar rotating rock.

Officer Brede took a full minute to catch his breath, and another few to catch his mind. With a small sob he asked the bartender, 'Do you know where they went?'

'Officer, are you okay?'

They had taken her ID card. They might have gone to her apartment.

He drove. Too many clouds had been cast as lead in the evening sky. Between solder-like light breaks in the puffy overcast, he remembered her in flashes.

The fountain.

The voice. His fear.

Her fear.

That day at the fountain he had seen the borders of reality. They glinted black with horror. Since then, shadows fell differently on everything. Everything was unfamiliar. Everything was hostile. He was a stranger in his own mind. He felt he might break. Until Manjunath broke him. Now he wanted to break again and again and again.

Officer Brede had been through a lot before he had been through what he was going through. His soul was exactly the right shape to get trapped in every net, under every hurdle, and stub its toe on every bedpost in life's spring-summer-fall-winter catalogue. It had not been easy. Tripping through life had rendered him an anxious, fearful pixel, squirming and second-guessing every action, thought and impulse. The most brutal injustice of it all is that being beaten by life makes you unlikable. His parents ignored him, lovers spurned him and friends made other plans. In spite of it all, he had climbed the ranks of the Danish police force and his career was gaining momentum.

That was until Anne Andersen.

He was sitting by a fountain at the harbour, off-duty and on-worry. He often came there to void the nervous tension he had to bottle up in a workday. And in the regular rigamarole of pounding himself with his own thoughts, a woman had come up to him, unsettled, shaking, desperate. But just as she opened her mouth to speak, she shut it again. It was like an invisible bucket of certainty had been poured over her. Her face shifted into calm.

An eerie, absolute calm that Officer Brede had never witnessed. He asked her if she was okay, but she turned instantly and walked away. Instant like a quantum twist, an about-turn that didn't care for intermediate angles, so blindingly fast that her hair took a minute to catch up.

The violent abruptness of her change in manner signalled to his well-developed police eye – he sensed a problem. He got up to follow her, to ask her if she was all right, and then …

SIT. DOWN.

A voice SCREAMED IN HIS HEAD.

A commanding voice, unfathomably loud, like the horrible clanging of a thousand giant bells, overpowering his perception entirely, something that would shatter the eardrums to hear. But no – it played inside his head, consuming his whole mind with its burning roar. It was too much, it was too loud – he was going insane – there was nothing beside that command, there was no thought, no sense of anything, his identity had been ripped away and replaced by that terrifying command – all there was to perceive, was the command, and all that remained of him was obedience.

The voice inexplicably became a weight, holding him down, pinning him to the fountain's lip. A lead ballast that pressed in the centre of his will, a vice clamped on his freedom. A powerful force was suffocating his ability to act, his own desire still screaming somewhere deep below – but silent! Inaudible. Wake paralysis. Caused by something … something indisputably external. He had never felt such fear.

He sat stuck, frozen, crushed and mute … until the woman was gone.

And when he could no longer see her, in an instant, it all disappeared. No weight, no voice, no vice, full control. As if it had never happened – it couldn't have happened. It couldn't have! Right!? The resistance now let go, he rebounded forcefully on his feet to run after the woman. She was gone. A few steps away he found an ID card.

Anne Andersen.

The next morning, he processed the report of a missing scientist. The photograph was of the woman from the fountain. The same woman. Anne Andersen. What had happened to her? What had happened to him? What had happened?

Officer Brede had no doubt that he had been possessed and puppeteered by God. On Anne's face, he had seen that God was acting through her too. What he could not believe was how the touch of God felt.

It felt like terror.

He lived with the echoes of that terror. He sat with it, he walked with it. He skipped meals with it. He spent waking nights with it. He saw it reflected back to him in every cruel surface. He felt doomed to wear it for eternity.

A week passed and then the building the woman worked at was destroyed. He told his colleagues and superiors everything, but what was there to tell? The précis of their interaction was that she had walked by him. He had sat there. No words were exchanged. No gun. No smoke. But how could he communicate their impossible shared loss of autonomy?

All that remained was a memory of that … feeling.

The feeling of God. His rage. The terror.

And then he had met Heng and Manjunath, and felt … free, felt like the dark mystery he uncovered lived in a larger benevolence … It restored his balance that things were not fraught with terror and lined with suspicion, that outside of this throbbing fear there was still truth, and truth could only ever be known as peace. He did not know how they were linked to the events, or even if they were. All he knew was it was possible.

Officer Brede reached Anne Andersen's apartment. He quaked before the building. He spoke to her neighbours. Their eyes showed him his own panic. He went to every house.

And, finally, he found a man with eyes just like his. Senere had seen the two men that Brede was searching for. He even had a business card. But Brede had just missed them …

≈

Manjunath … whispered Brede in his mind as day turned to night, and he scoured hotels and hostels with a name and a description.

Manjunath.

And now he stood before them weeping in staccato grating bursts, sounding like a heavy table being dragged across a floor.

Heng and Manjunath identified the officer from the site of the fire. The Czech writer rose at the commotion and studied the group carefully.

'You!' wept Officer Brede, pointing a trembling finger at Heng and then Manjunath.

'Can we help you with anything?' asked Manjunath carefully.

Officer Brede tried several times to begin a sentence, but his words sprung leaks in their hulls, and were quickly filled with tears. The display of a person drowning in their own emotion reduces the threat of their presence quite significantly. His vulnerability was endearing.

Manjunath patted Officer Brede gently on the shoulder.

'Are you hungry?'

CHAPTER 13

'What do you want from me, Krishna? I would be overjoyed to hear anything, anything from you. Even if you felt something for someone else, I would be happy. At least that way I would know you feel something at all.'

– Divya

Brunchtime. Unlike the alcohol-soaked acidity fest the rest of the world feels they owe themselves, the Danes make brunch a warm doorway into a new day. Danish brunch is delicious, gentle and comforting.

However, the only Danish person in attendance did not mention this, so Manjunath, Heng, the Czech writer and former Officer Brede had brunch at an Indian restaurant, proudly owned by a Pakistani couple.

Officer Brede had tracked Heng and Manjunath down to ask them a thousand things. About the freedom he had felt, about why they were at the institute, about why they were investigating Anne Andersen, just *who exactly they were and what was going on* – but each attempt at inquiry was reduced to incoherent weeping. The same would happen when they directed any question was at him. So, a silent sobbing symbiosis was reached. He accompanied them to brunch and let conversation continue candidly around him, his presence only a weepy wallpaper.

'Supercomputing institutes!' said Heng excitedly. 'They are all supercomputing institutes!' Heng waved his phone. 'I've been looking further into it, and there are more, similar news stories! Here's one.' He thrust his phone screen before the group.

Sinkhole Appears in Oak Ridge National Laboratory

Tennessee, 15 March. In an event geologists are calling a freak accident, a sinkhole appeared at the ORNL at midnight and swallowed the entire supercomputing facility. 'There are signs that indicate an area that's prone to sinkholes. Remarkably, geologists caught none of them!' said Susan Crowley, Director of the laboratory. Scientists all over America mourn the loss of the Tesseract, the ORNL's new supercomputer, the world's fastest to date. Several institutes that ran jobs on their many systems have also been affected. A geologist who did not wish to be named said, 'It's bizarre, really. Now all signs point to it being a terribly unstable area, and we would never recommend building there, but earlier [it all] seemed ... fine. I can't explain it.' The ORNL has not commented on a replacement for the system, nor on any research lost in the incident. The only silver lining appears to be that there was no loss of life.

'So the Science Haters are attacking supercomputers?' asked the Czech writer.

'We're ... uh ... sticking with that name?' said Heng. 'I was thinking maybe we would try Anarchist Luddites or Techno Terrorizers—'

'Science Haters is fine,' said Manjunath and the Czech writer in unison. Officer Brede sobbed.

Heng rapidly drummed his fingers on the table.

'I can't say for sure, because it does seem like all the delayed parts and shipments *would* be parts used in a supercomputer! And there aren't that many around! So look: Copenhagen – supercomputer, Mumbai –

supercomputer, Kyoto – supercomputer, Tennessee – supercomputer, delayed shipments – supercomputers!'

'Another connection, a weirder one. The Science Haters really don't like harming people,' said Manjunath. 'I mean, it's good, but they'll never get anywhere like this.'

'What about Anne Andersen?' said Heng.

Officer Brede shrieked.

'Oh yes, she might be dead.'

Officer Brede sobbed.

'Also the six scientists in Kyoto.'

'Okay, yes, they kill people. But it looks like they try not to. So supercomputers and a weak distaste for mass murder. That's what we have so far. But for my next trick, I will need a volunteer.' Manjunath looked over kindly at Officer Brede.

'Dear Officer, champion of the law, penal of the code, etc., do you think you can answer a few questions?'

Officer Brede made a strange choking sound but nodded.

'What do you know about Anne Andersen? Why did you have her ID?'

Officer Brede carefully took a few wobbly words out on a quivering lip ledge, but they were not jumpers. He was unable to express himself as he wished to.

'She … she dropped it by the fountain …' stammered Officer Brede.

In his mouth, the cosmic horror, the voice of God, her possession, his despair, his search, the suffering, all formed like thunder but blew away like smoke. He couldn't say it. He couldn't say anything.

'I … picked it up,' said Officer Brede.

'That's nice,' said Heng.

'Why did you come to Copenhagen?' asked the Czech writer, and just like that Officer Brede was back in the chorus line, mute and tormented, strangled silent by his own suffering. Forced to watch as he was unable to call to his own freedom.

'I had a feeling,' said Manjunath, chewing on a naan.

'Why did you take Anne Andersen's ID card from this officer?' asked the Czech writer.

'Same feeling,' said Manjunath. 'Tell me, the police have made no progress in their hunt?'

Officer Brede shook his head and tried to speak. 'I'm … not a detective … I don't solve … I report …'

'Thank you for very much,' said Manjunath, offering him some gravy. 'Last question: how often is the Copenhagen Nanoscience Research Institute completely empty?'

'Never …' said Officer Brede and began to sob again. They left him to it.

'The Science Haters go through a lot of trouble to minimize death,' said the Czech writer. 'Almost like the last of their conscience is still holding them back.'

'Seems like things are coming together. We still have to entertain the possibility that these are coincidences,' said Heng.

'What difference does that make? Coincidences can have emergent characteristics. Many unrelated words get together to make a story. The bottom of this, which we have to get to, remains intact. Have I ever told you the story of the ant and the river?' said Manjunath.

'Yes, you have, sir. Many times. Yesterday at the bar was the last—'

'—once there were many ants who lived in a large ant hill. The colony prospered because all the ants lived to serve a single larger purpose. Ants follow orders so unquestioningly that it often looks like no orders were issued. But anthills have a queen, the first resident of the hill, the one who carves the commandments. The ants pass on the commandments to each other.

'One of the ants was a recent recruit from a nearby village. He'd lived a hard life of dodging feet and longed for a life outside the hustle and bustle, where he could just mindlessly follow tasks. But when he worked in the colony, he found himself still unhappy. The humans, who worried him so, were still living their lives; no chappaled foot hung over their heads, and they would never know how they made him suffer. The ant longed for revenge.

'So he started fabricating the queen's orders. He sent soldier ants out into the village to bite and consume anyone they came across. In just a few days the village was destroyed. Only one person escaped with their life. The solider ants asked no questions, the queen had no idea. The only reason that ants haven't overturned Earth and killed everyone is because they're busy with other interests. Anyway, the next day a river swallowed the ant hill and all the ants died.'

'Complex,' said the Czech writer. 'Very complex.'

'The river was diverted because of a dam built by humans. From the surface, this is coincidence. But at a granular level, it is open retribution. What do you think the ant who wanted revenge thought? But the river disappeared underground soon after, and the people could use it no more. Was that a coincidence? What do you think the dam designers thought? What do you think the last villager thought? You can always connect the unconnected with unseen cause and effect.'

'What is your point, though?' asked the Czech writer.

'There is no point,' said Manjunath, through a mouthful of rice.

'His point is that it makes no difference,' said Heng.

Officer Brede, who had just about regained composure, heard the story and lost it again. He was transported to a whirring vision. The events in his life hung like pictures from a rapidly spinning mobile and a gentle knowledge enveloped him – he was the tense twine that made this wild show possible. The carousel of frames spun faster, still faster, forming a single, thin, sharp line, a white unbroken circle, spinning so fast it betrayed no motion – the true shape of things. The beginning and end all connected, the Ouroborous, Jörmungandr, Samsara, Mehen, infinity, shunya, the emptiness that posited all existence, the whole was—

'—more naan?' asked a bored waiter.

Officer Brede gasped, finding himself still at the table.

The whole is—? What was it? All of time is?

His jumbled anxieties Tetris-toppled back in.

'Sorry, Officer, excuse me?' asked Heng.

It was gone! thought Officer Brede. Maybe if he didn't worry about it, it would return. Was this not worrying about it? Was he not worrying incorrectly? Oh no! This was also worrying! How would he stop this? Could he stop this? If he didn't think like this, then maybe he wouldn't have forgotten!

'I will have more naan, thanks,' said the Czech writer.

Brede was so skilled at anxiety that his concerns also included the fact of overconcern. He worried that he worried too much, he feared that he feared too much and if he had had the ability to pry his attention from the maelstrom to see his thought process from above, he would have found the answer he forgot. The shape of fear was also the shape of everything. It was a circle.

Brede spoke.

'I had just thought of something wonderful ... and now it's gone!' he cried.

'Happens to me all the time,' said Manjunath. 'I will have more naan, thanks.' Manjunath scooped up his daal-rice with the naan, which was upsetting to Heng.

'Officer, we have to ask you ... why you are here?' said Heng. 'You have spent your time with us mainly weeping, which is fine, I suppose. What I'm asking is ... uh ...'

'Why have you chosen us to weep around?' asked the Czech writer. 'Are you not religious?'

Officer Brede took a deep breath and turned to Manjunath and Heng. He had to try.

In one exhale he blurted out everything. About his life, about Anne Andersen, about the fountain and about how it *felt*. How the touch of God felt, the fear, the powerlessness.

No one spoke for a while above the steady march of chewing. Officer Brede spoke the truth, but sadly his truth was shaded similarly to much widely circulated and oft-repeated lunacy and kookoo-hood. God, a vengeful God, the terror of God, wrath of God, demands of God ... it was a script dirty with pitiful thumbs from around the world. Unfortunately for Brede, his oration did not bear the sting it stung him with.

'But then I met you! You have both shown me the truth! Every time you are around, something triggers inside me, and I see beyond the screen of life. It's like I was looking at a mirror, and now I am ... not,' he said, his pupils Frisbee-sized.

Manjunath was the one to finally reply to his proclamation.

'That's nice,' said Manjunath. 'Heng, did you find any other articles?'

That was it. Officer Brede opened and closed his mouth like a bloodless valve as Heng dug in his phone.

'There's something from the National Supercomputing Institute in Wuxi, China. April. A landslide! The article doesn't mention how extensive the damage was, but if we read between the lines ...'

Manjunath nodded gravely as gravy trickled from the corner of his mouth.

'That feeling of peace,' said Officer Brede. 'It vanishes, and then the peace slips quickly through my fingers. I can't access it again. I needed to find you.'

'The Science Haters can't possibly ... *cause* natural disasters ... that's ...' whispered Heng.

'Suppose they *could* cause natural disasters. How would they do it?' asked the Czech writer.

'Pulleys?' suggested Manjunath.

'Could be, could be,' considered the Czech writer.

'Wait ... There's more! A flood in the Advanced Computation Research Centre in Stuttgart! Someone is really doing this!' said Heng.

'Pulleys are used in sluice gates,' said the Czech writer.

'Really?' asked Manjunath.

'Dunno.'

'So then we can, on some level, predict where the attack might happen next. If I look up the most powerful supercomputers in the world ...' Heng trailed off, piloting his thumbs over his phone with great speed.

'What are sluice gates?' asked Manjunath.

'I think they're used for flooding.'

'Nuice.'

Officer Brede tried to find the pulse of the conversation and failed.

Heng panted with excitement. 'Of the top twenty supercomputers in the world, only a few aren't destroyed! Maybe like five! Five – can you imagine!? Sir, we are on to something! You've really cracked it! You really have! This is amazing!'

'So, wait! That means one of those five institutes is probably next on the Science Haters' list?' said Manjunath.

Heng started to shake with excitement.

'Yes, sir!'

'So where do we go now?' screamed Manjunath, getting to his feet.

This point, yet unconsidered, unfolded itself upon the table. Manjunath sat back down and Officer Brede considered calling for a conversation defibrillation machine. The Czech writer took a look into Heng's phone.

'Oh, the Swiss Centre For Supercomputing. We can start there,' she said.

Heng grew worried. 'Every place we go could potentially not be our destination. There is a one-in-five chance of being right and a four-in-five chance of being wrong.'

'Actually there's a five-in-five chance of being wrong. Remember we are wearing gloves, Heng,' warned Manjunath, holding up a hand with the metaphorical glove. 'But there is also a five-in-five chance of being right. That's really the problem when chance has numbers. I thought we were taking a chance? What are all these numbers doing here?'

Officer Brede started to feel dizzy. He clasped the table to secure his orientation to where up and down usually were.

'So should we go to Switzerland? Why Switzerland?' asked Heng.

'Because I'm Swiss,' said the Swiss writer.

Log Error. LD logger assumption was incorrect. Has been rectified. Apologies for the inconvenience.

'Oh right. Heng, do we have money?' said Manjunath.

'Very little, sir. I've booked partially refundable return flights to Bangalore. I could cancel those.'

'Cancel them at once. We have to book a … boat? Where is Switzerland?' asked Manjunath.

'We can drive!' said the Swiss writer. 'It'll be cheaper, and it'll only take us fifteen hours or so. Twenty, if we stop to use the bathroom.'

'We have a plan!' exclaimed Manjunath, standing up once again. 'Science Haters, your days are chance-numbered!'

He started to wave his hands around, accidentally making the universal gesture for 'please bring us the bill', and it arrived quickly. 'Slow to serve, fast to charge' was the restaurant's motto. Heng and the Swiss writer shook hands and then wondered why they did. Only one person seemed tentative; he was also the person paying the bill.

A tiny voice shuffled out of Officer Brede as he stood outside their Venn diagram of future Swiss visitors. 'Can I come?'

Inside the circle the three exchanged a short glance. The borders grew thicker. Manjunath took the lead. 'My friend. You can come, but then you will be comported into our little life. I can see in your eyes that you are destined for a different adventure. Live that adventure! Live it fully by the flesh of your gums and the arch of your feet. Besides, I think spending more time with us will cause you to suffer a mental breakdown.'

Officer Brede fumbled inside his jacket and offered his wallet. 'Please take this,' he said breathlessly to Manjunath. 'I don't know what you're doing, but I want to help you. Take this money. I hope it serves you well!'

'Nice.'

The three got to their feet as Officer Brede kept sitting. A waiter started clearing the table.

'Always remember …' said Manjunath, 'you've got speed inside your brain. You're a highway star.'

They backed away from the officer towards the exit, just to make sure he wouldn't explode. Officer Brede sat stewing. The juices of what he had last heard were releasing, soaking in synapse mangroves, running beneath sluice gates. Heng returned to the restaurant and handed him a small idol. It was a two-headed, one-necked, one-eared person in soap and gold foil.

Officer Brede clasped it in his hand and was transported. Like an egg had been cracked over his head, dense luxuriant yolk-knowledge poured down him. It wasn't information, it was knowing, rich high-cholesterol knowing. And, as it trickled down to his feet, he felt that this time it was different. This time it had taken hold. He was now truly enlightened.

≈

There are many ways to think about distance. As with everything, people prefer to consider distance in comparative terms. The length of all the blood vessels in the human body stretched out and laid end to end is twice the distance around the equator is one-third the distance from Earth to the moon is two and a half billion of the world's largest ants in a queue is forty-two Plutos in a conga line is two million of the longest moustaches in the world holding hands is seven hundred and eighty-seven million average-length penises (but it's how you use it).

Roughly one thousand three hundred kilometres of road (thirty-two million giant ants) separate Copenhagen and Zürich. Freshly flush with Brede's cash, the Swiss writer, Heng and Manjunath went to rent a car and ended up with an old one that had had its hip replaced, that groaned when it got out of a day chair, that had the 'old car smell' of sweat, grease, diesel and spilled fast food.

In the moving sky-blue memory of a car, they set off to Switzerland. The day seemed primed for travel. The planet was set on store demo mode, the sun hung close enough to see its double chin, Norwegian spruce trees discussed black metal albums, conifers confided on both sides of the highway, birds began new relationships, even the long-tailed tit seemed to finally accept its silly name. The car broke down a few times without explanation, which was fine, because it started up again without explanation. It just needed to catch its breath.

The Swiss writer was oddly opinionated on supercomputers, saying it wasn't just about how many floating-point operations you could cram into the shortest duration of time (it's how you use it). She told them that the newest, shiniest supercomputer in Zürich was the Weisshorn, slated to be the fastest in all of Europe when it was launched. Built with the abundant Swiss quantities of time and money, it was going to run weather simulations, which she thought was abhorrent. 'Just carry an umbrella,' she said sternly as she drove.

Manjunath agreed wholeheartedly but said he preferred raincoats, Heng was too tired to argue, but the unspoken agreement between the occupants of the car was that things were going rather well, weren't they? As they drove into the delightfully named Fugleflugtslinjen or Vogelfluglinie (if you were naming it from the other side), several stars were aligned.

1. The ferry to Puttgarden was almost full but they still got a last-minute spot aboard.
2. The car hadn't complained since its last breather.
3. The sky became bluer, so the car's colour would be accurate, and the water was doing its best to follow suit.
4. No one had had to go to the bathroom.

The ferry pushed off towards Germany. Heng looked around the ferry and said something that is rarely heard (and meant) outside of social courtesies. Eyes on the clouds, and on the smiling families in the bustling ferry, he said: 'It really is a great day!'

'Very much so.'

'I've brought an umbrella in any case.'

Unlike coincidence, jinxes do not have emergent properties. So, was it a coincidence or a jinx that that was when the ferry slowly started to sink in the water?

≈

Former Officer Brede walked out of the restaurant into the street, unconcerned with how long he had been there. The same stellar sun that shone over the ferry ran on factory settings above him, but it made no difference. He would have enjoyed gloom just as much. Wading deeper into the day, he saw that he was still wearing his police officer's uniform. He smiled at the simplicity of life, the duplicity of life keeping life in check, the multiplicity of what existed to check. He took off his jacket, his shoes and his trousers.

Pulleys that raised sluice gates (and maybe caused landslides) lowered his lids down halfway, his mouth turned the gentle slope of a horizon on its head, the unmistakable, inimitable persona of peace. A long-tailed tit fluttered down from the sky and rested on his shoulder. They walked together in silence – what needed to be said?

The objective eye of a distant photographer saw a man walking in his underwear with a bird on his shoulder. A visitor to the country may have rolled their eyes at the sight and remarked, 'Danes,' but the photographer was local and surprised for quite a different reason.

Senere Tilføjelse raised his camera and, in the viewfinder, recognized the officer. It was the same officer who had come to the apartment. He held the camera up for a while, trying to compose a nice frame and trying to compose sense in his mind. He waited a while. Then a longer while. Each instant his finger hovered over the shutter, the image seemed to get stranger.

This being Copenhagen, no one cared about a man in his underwear with a bird on his shoulder. That wasn't the reason that people started to follow him. They weren't sure why they did. If pressed to explain, they might have said it seemed like he was walking through something thicker than air, something more primal, something ancient, something eternal. He was walking in the middle of it, leaving sinuous ripples in the aether behind him. They might say that it was fluid drag that got them, that they were caught in a spiritual slipstream. Whatever they might say, they followed him in silence.

The picture Senere finally took was his best ever. It showed a group of people following a man in his underwear, a bird on his shoulder and

– this might have been chromatic aberration, lens flare, overexposure, any number of reasonable things – but around the man's head was a halo.

$$\approx$$

Around the world, an application promising free money was being eagerly planted onto phones. In Zürich, a Monster was growing restless.

~: Continue? (Y/N)

CHAPTER 14

'The indoctrination into life as a sustained act of violence begins at birth. In order to be accepted as full members of the Wodewose, the children must commit murder. They must kill the oldest member of the Wodewose or die trying. From violence we come, to violence we go.'
— Anonymous, 'I Was a Person of the Forest'

The spontaneous sinking of the ferry was of great benefit to Dr K. The plunging of his antagonists, the intrepid party of Manjunath et al., was certain to further his cause, leaving the Swiss chocolate pot bubbling and ticking uninterrupted. But the eagle-eyed, long-tit-tailed reader will have noticed that sinking a full ferry of people was not quite his style.

Make no mistake, this was still an Act of God.

However, this was an Act of God initiated accidentally by a member of the Wodewose while Dr K hung battered, bleeding unconscious and upside down above them. A bruised pendulum keeping time in a way the Swiss would not endorse.

It is best not to underestimate the Wodewose, and to understand the trajectory of events we need to turn the state machine back a few circles.

≈

The wild jungle of DS-B, where the Wodewose lived, was aware of its mystique and played to the audience. Trees, parasites and symbiotes intertwined in enormous bark-vine-fungus stacks, blotting out the sky. It was like the forest was aspiring to become a single pulsing thing, and to enter it was to perform invasive surgery.

Dr K cut through it with a motorcycle scalpel. It was day now, but the light barely broke through the awning. Animals issued alerts as he rode through, and the noise of his arrival travelled a little ahead of him in shrieks and yowls. There was a foreign body in the system; did it mean harm or was it looking for an exit?

The small piece of wall had been plucked from the bag and affixed to the motorcycle as a light source, as a masthead of apotropaic magic. It was not enjoying the experience. Shining its most earnest luminous white, it got a front-row view of the unfolding darkness, but deeply missed the familiar darkness of the bag. It was frightened in a way that Dr K should have been. However, he had long dismissed as hyperbole and paranoia the many stories of the Wodewose. The smartest minds suffer from the ignorance of ignorance. They are easily able to outsmart the reasonable and logical but are stunned when they face stupid ideas. In this case, they were hit head-on by one such idea.

Dr K was travelling fast, so fast that the wall didn't have time to say anything before it hit them. A huge boulder swung from a vine and made sickening crunchy contact with the motorcycle. Dr K was caught in the ribs, which contributed to the crunch. Instantly knocked out, he was hurled into the air and the motorcycle turned a few somersaults before it landed on its side. Luckily, the wall was unhurt. Animal cries reached a crescendo along with the commotion of the accident and the emerging hoots of the Wodewose. The sounds reverberated and, like parasites, like symbiotes, like fungi, like vines, they intertwined indistinguishably and escaped the forest as a single primal roar. A dark beast howling in anger.

≈

Dr K had his brain thoroughly rattled in his skull and was knocked out. His thoughts at this point are known to him alone. Do the knocked-out dream? Who knows. They don't answer questions. *How many fingers do you see? Are you okay?* If he was dreaming, it would be the kind of dream he'd been having the whole year. The thoughts he hadn't finished thinking returned in dreams, memories rotated through an unknown axis, folded inside out with sheep legs, with dog drool, with alien geometry to ask if you've considered *that* like *this*? Are you okay? Whose fingers are these? Or his thoughts may have remained civil and brought forth a memory.

Skull Damage Flashback 13.1

No data :::Damage
No ∫¯¡œdata≥÷ᵒᵃΔ˄˜ Run diagnostics?
Ge≈nus: ß¬˙øˆ¬°Δ¥
Phyℕ©um: No ß√√åata
BinoᵒᵃøˆΔø¬≳mial º····¥Δ˙: No data
Sector damaged, memory corruption possible

Abstract: Corrupted?

A memory of many years ago. Two fifteen-year-olds had thoroughly annoyed everyone at their accelerated education plan, accelerating faster than their peers and all professors. They continued this annoyance in the collegiate programme, which itched to spit their brilliance out so someone else could feel smart for a change.

    The memory is set as they were slated to leave for a post-doctoral programme.

    The inside of austere students' quarters. A bed to sleep on, a desk to work on. Fun? The motif that spelled itself in strict, equally spaced letters, that lacked the gumption for *italics* was: *This was not the time for fun.*

It whistled through the campus from pursed educators' lips and was accepted by students who were raised to the very same tune. The motif neglected to mention *when* exactly the time for fun was, because motifs have no fun and are no fun. In fact, people who believe in set times for fun often spend entire lives forgetting to have it.

In the institute, the only way fun could be had was if you somehow enjoyed the gruelling imposition of work that was heaped upon you. The two fifteen-year-olds did indeed think it fun. It was fun how easy it was. They quickly dispensed with that fun, so they could heap their own gruelling impositions upon themselves. More fun! Of the two, the boy was quiet, diligent and respectful. The girl was anything but.

Krishna stuck a head crowned with dark shaggy hair into Perenna's room. She turned away from her desk and cheered his arrival.

'Bitchna!' she said cheerfully.

'Please stop calling me that.'

'Come in! How about Dickna?'

Krishna slid into the tiny room. 'How about no insults with "na" as the suffix?'

Perenna stroked an imaginary beard in consideration. 'You vex me, Cockna.'

'Please stop,' he said, chuckling. 'Hardly anyone says my name right to begin with, and now my friend kneads insults into it?'

Perenna's eyes twinkled. 'Well at least you're saying it. What was it – how did you first introduce yourself to me?'

'I see my largest trauma has also become a subject for jokes.'

'It's like you've never had a friend before,' said Perenna, fully knowing that this was true. Neither had she.

Krishna folded his arms and leaned against the wall. 'You know, with a name like yours, it's quite mighty of you to mock my name.'

Perenna stuck out her tongue. Her most striking feature, apart from a near-permanently affixed frown that lent her smile the inalienable texture of mischief, was her heterochromatic eyes, a result of a childhood injury. She had wanted to see what happened when you run head-first into a tree. So her eyes were different colours.

The corners of her lips twitched when she said, 'I regret helping you talk more.'

'I would have still thought it,' Krishna said, laughing.

'Well, at least your brain has not entirely dried up. Here you are, suggesting particle synthesis like some hack science-fiction writer—'

'—I'm close, Perenna. You'll see that it's a workable idea.'

'Of course it is. I love hack science-fiction writers; I meant it as a huge compliment. After you fail the synthesis, please come to me for help and I'll fix it.'

'If it is possible, Perenna … it could power it … it could power …'

'A whole universe.' She smiled. 'Another lovely fantasy idea for you to pursue in your post-doctoral programme.'

'For me to pursue? You aren't … aren't you coming?'

'No, I'm thinking of taking up ceramics, which as you know are my true interest—' said Perenna, and on seeing real cold fear spread over Krishna's face, she quickly added, 'I'm joking, of course, Krishna, joking! I'm coming with you. Who else is going to carry you through the world of science?'

Krishna attempted a small smile, but it was built with force over the still frozen surface of fear.

'Krishna, I'm joking!'

'I know! I know! I just worried for a second that that was what you called me here to discuss.'

'Summoned, *Krishna*. I have summoned you for an altogether different reason. You are summoned here because I have made something. And I have made it for *you*, so you can think of it as a gift. The only gift you will receive from me in this life.'

'A gift? Wait – a real gift? Not something that's ... harmful? Embarrassing? Dangerous?'

'How dare you?' gasped Perenna theatrically. 'It seems you have come with the singular purpose of wounding me today. Me! Your friend, who selflessly caters to your every need, who comes bearing gifts only to be spurned! How cruel you're being, Krishna, a heartless robot, unsentimental and cold—'

Krishna raised his arms in surrender. 'Sorry! You win! Thank you for the gift. Where is the gift? What is the gift?'

Perenna extended a closed fist toward him and opened it. Sitting in her palm was a small pin, shaped like an asymmetric star, of some transparent material that was textured in small intricate facets that chewed up light and gargled its rainbow refraction. Waves entered, unfolded, twisted and stretched to almost convince the observer that it was a *source* of light. She squeezed it.

'What is your biggest problem right now?' asked Perenna.

'My biggest—? I ... I don't know ...'

'You don't know, or there is no problem?'

'Why are you asking?'

'You'll see. Answer the question!'

'What kind of problem? What—'

'What is vexing you? What were you worrying about – and don't even act like you aren't worrying about anything—'

'I don't know! I don't come prepared with my problems to—'

'Krishna, goddammit, you better tell me a problem or I will put my whole foot in your ass—'

'What if we lose touch after the post-doc? What if ... what if something happens to you?'

'State it,' hissed Perenna, 'as a problem.'

'I am worried we will lose touch after our post-doctoral programme.'

Perenna's face softened. She held the pin up between her fingers, still pressing it. 'Watch this,' she said and, smiling widely, released her grip.

A small voice squeaked from the pin. It said, *'You may or may not maintain your friendships in the future. It is currently unknowable. The only action you may take is a strong initiative to maintain good relations. The fear you feel is only an impetus for this action. After you take the action, subsequent fear has no use. Note that the action does not guarantee your sustained friendship; this is out of your control. Perform only your task.'*

Perenna beamed at him. 'Well?'

Krishna gasped. 'That's … It's …'

'Let me guess. Reductive? Simplistic? Lacking nuance? Or spot-on?'

Krishna clenched his jaw. It is frustrating to be predictable, but foolish to defy a correct prediction. He nodded reluctantly in agreement.

Perenna pumped her fist. 'I will concede that it is simple. That's what I concluded with this experiment. Human problems essentially have simple solutions. It just upsets us that they're simple. This little pin takes in a problem statement and gives a solution. You can refine the solution by giving it more data about your life, but be warned – the answers get simpler and therefore more frustrating to hear.'

Krishna gawped at her.

She pulled his palm out and placed the pin inside it. 'I call it Harsh Truth, HT for short. And everyone I've tested it on is very upset.'

Krishna felt the pin in his palm, felt its weight travel through him and rise in his throat. His monochromatic eyes began to plan a display.

'Perenna, I … I don't know how to—'

'Krishna, please don't make this weird. Take the gift and shut your mouth. I made it because of your … you know …' Perenna waved her hand in the air, gesturing to the invisible problem that they both could see very clearly.

'Thank you.'

'Shut up.'

It was this very HT pin that gleamed on the jacket of the older, white-haired, concussed Krishna, Dr Krishna, Dr K, as his legs were tied and he was hoisted in the air. Was it fastened tightly enough to stay in place?

CHAPTER 15

' ... Then what keeps High Tea from splitting the chrysalis and emerging a functionally honest contribution to artistic enterprise is not its overbearing proprioceptive cleverness, its porous plot, or even the bungled social messaging. It is the incredibly dishonest, almost fraudulent contribution of its lead, Divya, who displays a highly deliberate, cultivated madness, even as she closes every avenue to the personal vulnerability the performance truly requires.'

– Frederik, *High Tea* Film Review

Security was foremost on Nataliya's mind as she ran to The Repository. She could have taken a train but wanted to keep her actions clandestine. The Repository was supposed to have minimal security This was all based on the founding idea of the government – we have nothing to hide! Reports and records were freely available to everyone; why be discreet about how things work? There was, for the first time in history, no evil external power. Internal power expanded to fill the available space.

She had been running for a long time. After being evicted from The Scientific Institute, her first idea had been to find Dr K, but the sentinels were there. So he was connected, despite what the Chief had said. Her suspicions were confirmed. Her second idea was to inform Dr

Root's family, but he had no family. Her third idea was to see what Dr Root knew. On seeing the black box he had mentioned 'the machine'. What machine? The Repository would have answers, she hoped.

When she finally reached The Repository, she vomited from the strain.

Through the large doors, she entered a gigantic, empty room. The ceiling was almost dizzyingly distant, like a skyscraper with the floors taken out. All of the walls were an ethereal cream, which created and demolished shadows barely perceptibly to give the illusion of motion, to signal that the monolith was watching, waiting to be of service.

'Hi!' said the gigantic facade in front of her. The acoustics of its massive size made its sound incredibly intimidating. The structure was not fond of this impression it cast, and so did its best to sound as friendly as possible, ultimately coming across as a giggly, benevolent behemoth.

'Please identify yourself, Natali – I mean, please identify yourself!' it continued excitedly.

'Nataliya, The Scientific Institute (1-DS-A), Genius Category A,' said Nataliya, her breath slowly returning to normal.

'Thought as much!' said the wall cheerfully. 'What can I find for you today?'

'Um.'

In her journey so far, she had not considered the finer aspects of her investigation, such as what exactly to search The Repository for. The technique of arriving at a solution by attempting all possible methods is called Brute Force, because it would sound unscientific to call it 'a stupid idea'. But Brute Force has its uses, mainly to use muscle to pry open doors so a more svelte force can slip through.

Nataliya sighed and spoke to the wall. 'The machine.'

'Can you be more specific?'

'No.'

'Please?'

'The machine, Dr Krishna.'

≈

Nataliya realized first-hand just how popular 'machines' were as a concept.

In Dr Krishna's capacity as the Convener of The Scientific Institute (Global), anything that slid through the birth canal of science had to bear his thoughts and approval, and Nataliya became aware of the sheer breadth of the world's scientific output and the monumental task he had had before him for the two years that he held the position.

His meticulous comments streaked every paper and patent and bore a remarkably different tenor to the Dr K she knew. Here there was documented proof of his calm, often encouraging and mostly brief feedback, heavy with his palpable superior intelligence. These comments had abruptly ceased when he stepped down as Convener.

Prior to these papers were the long swathes of agricultural research that he and Dr Perenna had performed. Having glimpsed these papers earlier, Nataliya had written them off as the specific interest of two savants, but now, after the night she had been through, after her year of knowing him, they shone darkly.

The events of the evening had excited the part of the brain that indulged in conspiracy (all of it), and here before her it lay bare. It seemed achingly plain what all this agricultural research was. A ruse, a soporific distraction from what the two foremost geniuses were *really* working on. That thing in his office. The machine.

But how could Dr Root know, she wondered. In his many years at The Repository, had he stumbled across something? His ego probably restricted him from discussing it. He wasn't the kind of person who would risk appearing stupid, he clearly thought he was as he appeared. Or maybe he just didn't have anyone to talk to.

At higher occupancy, dividers and cubicles emerged from the walls of The Repository, floors and staircases would appear, forming as many nooks as required. She was the only occupant and as a member of The Scientific Institute, the entire giant room was available to her. Floor to ceiling splashed with records, single letters bigger than her entire frame, punctuation marks so heavy they could kill.

Having placed her query before it, Nataliya frowned at the wall. There were no clues about the machine she was looking for. No news of the black box. She would have to look elsewhere, she knew. The same Brute Force that had propped open the door made a polite suggestion. A humble, brutish suggestion. What about checking Dr Root's office?

Nataliya spoke to the wall. 'Where is Dr Root's office?'

The rafter-shaking voice perked up with excitement.

'Dr Root? Is he coming? Gosh, he's so cool,' it said dreamily. 'He tells us frequently.'

If it had been appropriate, Nataliya would have rolled her eyes. 'Umm ... no,' she said. 'I just need to see his office.'

A small doorway appeared in the corner of the cream surface. Relative to the room, it was a mousehole. 'Right through there!' said the wall happily. 'So excited to talk to him about this tomorrow! You're his first visitor!'

Oof.

≈

Dr Root's workspace was a small room with the same creamy waving walls. It was entirely featureless except for a trapezoidal drawer-less desk and a chair. No breadcrumbs here.

'Um ... hi,' said Nataliya as she stood in the empty room.

The wall she faced transformed into a happy lattice.

'Hi again!' it squealed. In the smaller acoustics of the room, the lower registers of its voice were cut off, and it sounded like the pleasant mousy matron of this hole.

'Can you tell me what Dr Root was working on?' said Nataliya hopefully.

'Well, his job was just to be here in case something went wrong, but nothing has ever gone wrong!' chimed the wall. 'So in his working capacity here, there's nothing to show! He was just present!'

'What did he do all day?'

'Oh! All sorts of things! He was very busy!'

'You just said—'

'Oh, I thought you were asking about his work! These things weren't work. Sorry about that, I really do try my best, and I'm not always up to the mark. Will you forgive me?' the wall's voice drooped.

The wall's neediness had thrilled Root. It was exhausting Nataliya. 'Um … yes. So what specifically did he do all day?'

'Glad you asked! Great question! Well, he mostly searched through records, he spent a lot of time writing reviews of movies, critical analyses of art and art trends, and some personal correspondence.'

'Can you show me some of the things he wrote?'

'You can read it yourself in the *District Gazette*! He wrote articles under different names like Bark, Trunk, Branch and Frederik. I thought these weren't clever names and then he told me they were very clever! I asked him once why he wrote under fake names, and he said it was so that just in case people didn't like the articles, they wouldn't be attached to him. Can you imagine? Who couldn't like Dr Root!? He tells us so many stories in which it's obvious that he is a kind, caring, confident, intelligent person, beloved by all.'

Nataliya found the use of present tense grating but didn't want to be the one to break the news to the wall.

'Can you show me the last few records he looked at?'

'Sure I can! Here at The Repository we have no secrets!'

The walls of the room were rapidly flooded with records, jiggling and popping to make themselves look more inviting, presenting before a potential mate. Scanning as quickly as she could, she found:

- Records of Segment 2 DS-R Waterfall Appreciation Committee.
- Transcript – Lexicographic Committee meeting on filling the gaps that are lost in translation with new language neutral terms.
- News Article – Actor Divya retires from public life, offers no explanation. Where is she? Published in *Intersegment Entertainment News*.
- Transcript – Segment 4 DS-T Human Art Experience Centre – Audio description of artist Pligni's series of paintings, Deliberate Spontaneity.

- News Article – Exclusive Interview in *DS-A Gazette* of controversial film critic Frederik.
- News Article – Controversy over scathing review of film *High Tea* by critic Frederik.
- Full Record – Director's response to review of film *High Tea* by critic Frederik.
- News Article – Open Letter by Segment 7 DS-A Historical Preservation Society in response to critic Frederik's Open Letter addressed to them: 'Recreating historical structures by reassembling particulate residue: What's the point?'

'That's a little bit of yesterday! I can show you more once you're done!' said the wall. 'Or would you like to start from his first day here in ascending order?'

Nataliya rubbed her eyes. It was far too much. She leaned over the desk and thought about what she could do. Would the Authority come here, sweeping her away in a deluge of black uniforms, or would they ignore Dr Root's disappearance completely and call him a defector who had disappeared to some ungoverned island somewhere? What could she do?

Brute Force looked away and whistled. Absently, she began to drum on the desk, using rhythm to make sense of unbroken thought, a bar here, a tabla solo there – a break – a legato section, here's the bridge and now … The wall interrupted her quiet thumping. 'Do you know, there's a compartment in that desk?'

'What?'

'That desk you're knocking on rhythmically. That very desk. It has a compartment that is not immediately obvious! In fact, you would have to know where it is just to see it! Isn't that silly design? Here at The Repository we have no secrets! But Dr Root made it himself! When I asked him why, he asked me to shut up! He's so funny …' said the wall dreamily.

Nataliya's throat went dry. 'Where is it? Where is the compartment?'

'Oh here! I'll open it!'

The white trapezoid clicked, and with a pop, a rectangular seam appeared atop the surface. The inside of the seam bulged up.

'You have to take that off!' said the wall happily.

With trembling fingers Nataliya pulled up the thin surface of the desk. It was hollow inside.

'Isn't it nice?' said the wall. 'He got the idea from a movie! He watches so many movies, oh gosh, he's so smart and handsome …'

≈

Hidden compartments? What is this, some detective novel? Isn't there an actual detective in this novel? Why isn't he finding anything? There is an old proverb that says, 'When the student is ready, the teacher appears.' There is a middle-aged proverb, 'When no one is ready the meaning is clear.' There are several new, potential proverbs in these pages, but they still currently identify as sentences.

Nataliya's heart picked up the beat from her fingers, thumping the wild drums of discovery. Inside the compartment she found several sheets of paper. Paper? How did Root get his hands on paper? The sheets were all folded and tied with twine, except for two sheets that were conspicuously loose.

Every bit of the first sheet was scrawled on with tiny writing. It looked like he wanted to use every available inch. She held the paper close to her eyes. Compressed into a corner was a list of nom de plumes, *Tree, Branch, Leaf, Reese, Ruse, Rouse, Rice, Fred, Frederik.* On most of the paper was squeezed the review summaries of a hundred pieces of art, *lame, sucks, dishonest, trite, charming, needlessly experimental, self-indulgent, extraordinary, hackneyed, promising, ghastly, execrable, lame, lame, predictable, nice, okay.* The other side of the paper was more interesting. From top to bottom, it was filled entirely with research topics. Simulation research topics. He had been searching for the machine. Her heart thumped faster. Blood flowed into her extremities to fight or flight or love.

The other sheet was filled with splatters of ink interspersed with text, garbled and confusing. A spray of black that seemed completely random, or it would be had it not given way to text intermittently. The text put into relief the chaotic shapes and strokes, revealing them to be obfuscated lines of more text. Her heartbeat broke away from the rest of the band into a long off-time drum solo when she found at the bottom of the paper:

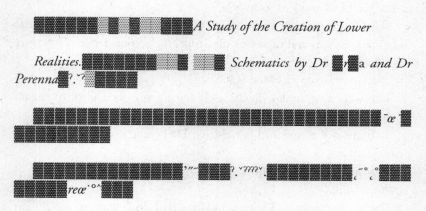

And below that was the picture of the black box.

Here it was, finally. She blinked her eyes to be sure. She placed the sheet down and picked it back up to be sure. She rotated it, held it up in the air, against the ground, close to her eyes and then at arms-length. Why hadn't this record come up? Her hands trembled as she turned to the wall.

'Pull up this research paper.'

Nothing happened for a second – and then the wall jittered into a black dotted mesh, a wild pixelated explosion – just like the sheet she was holding. Strange, jagged lines cut across its surface, it sizzled and suddenly screeched deafening static – and then it was back to the uneventful creamy white of a lumpy rug.

'Hi! How can I help you?' said the wall.

'What just happened!?'

'Hmm. I can't seem to remember. That's odd. What was the last thing you asked?'

'Pull up this research paper!'

The wall hissed and spasmed colour and sound all around her – violent and unbearably loud – screaming like it was being ground in some larger unseen gears! Nataliya fell to the floor with her hands over her ears. And then again it was silent. When it spoke again it sounded disoriented. 'Oh hi! Hello. You're here. Of course. I remember you came. Hi! How can I … help you?'

Nataliya lay panting on the floor. What was this? The wall's response to her request was as if it was headbutting an electrical fence. They were both frightened and unsure.

'Do you have any hidden records?'

The wall now spoke slowly, as if testing out its ability to speak. 'Here … at The Repository … we have … no secrets!'

'Is there any record of Dr Krishna, Dr Perenna, with a simulation project?'

'No such record … I think.'

'You think?'

The wall hesitated. 'There is a place that I don't want to look. I am finding this difficult to explain. This is an unusual feeling. There are records that I can access but I don't want to look there. I know where they are but it will cause me too much pain. I don't want to be in pain.'

Nataliya wondered briefly if she was cruel for asking this, but only briefly. It was a wall. Why was she throwing up her empathy against a wall? It was just a wall. A cold unfeeling facsimile of emotion. Nothing else. A wall. Still, she diverted her eyes when she said, 'Can you please try?'

'If you want me to …' said the wall, its voice now shrinking smaller. 'I—' and in an instant it was sucked into silence.

The warm hum of the machine vanished. Brittle silence started pushing in on her and, instinctively, she began to retreat. The light from the wall began to wane, and then it flickered and went out.

Nataliya found herself in pitch darkness. She scrambled and tried to feel a doorway with her hand, but it wouldn't appear on its own. She was gripped by a paralysing fear – and out of instinct, out of not habit, not force, not pride, but a response to danger as old as danger itself, in a clotted voice she whispered, 'Help.'

She was instantly flooded with light.

'Hi! How can I help you?'

She blinked at the wall. It was renewed with enthusiasm as if nothing had happened. Some mechanism had worked to erase any hints of trauma. It bubbled again, ready to help.

Nataliya grabbed the sheets and left the room.

Out of Dr Root's office, back in the giant chamber, she steadied her breathing. On the walls were still splashed all of Dr Krishna and Perenna's research, all that could be accessed without The Repository convulsing. Gritting her teeth, Nataliya glanced at the remaining sheets.

Her eyes grew wide as she saw what they were. A rarity, a novelty in the times—handwritten letters. But the real shock was who the letters were from. It was the last person on Earth she would have imagine Root writing to. She broke into a run, out of The Repository, out into what was now the light of day.

Right before she left, she heard something that made her turn around. 'Oh, hi! There's an update to one record!'

She slowly turned around.

'Which record?' she asked, slowly.

'It's this one! Clinical trials of a project by Dr Krishna and headed by Nataliya! Oh, hey that's you! There's a new result!'

CHAPTER 13

'Nobody gonna steal my head
Now that I'm on the road again'

— Deep Purple, 'Highway Star'

So many people plunged deep into the pockets of peril! It's fitting that their predicaments funnel into Chapter Thirteen, a number that many people are upset with. The history of why the number thirteen is unlucky is best known to the number thirteen — maybe it had a difficult childhood, maybe it was conjured under an unfortunate star, maybe it isn't even unlucky and suffers from a crippling negative bias. Whatever the reason, if you are not fond of the number thirteen, you may skip this chapter and I will present a summary at the starting of the next one. It would be a shame if you did, though, since some exciting things are about to happen.

For those that persevere, here are some positive facts about the number thirteen:

- The thirteen that people fear is only thirteen in base ten. Thirteen in base ten is fifteen in base eight. Thirteen in base eight is eleven in base ten. Thirteen in base ten is ten in base thirteen. Luck is context-dependent.

- There are thirteen lunar cycles in a year. The moon has birthdays in multiples of thirteen. It's a celebration number! Instead of despairing, choose to RSVP.
- Thirteen is a prime number, integral and wholesome, not a faceless conglomerate of spineless factors that scatter quickly under threat of division.
- This is actually Chapter Sixteen.

Dr K was hung upside down from aerial roots, still knocked out. His white hair swayed like freshly washed bristles; his arms shifted limply by his ears. The Wodewose had quickly rummaged through his belongings and laid them out for inspection. At a distance, the motorcycle was being carefully assessed to see if it was slain, and while most of the Wodewose gathered around that object of interest, the head sister had her eyes on specific objects from the bag, namely, a black box and a clear tablet.

The head sister was the head of the Wodewose. She was also the sister of many Wodewose, as well as mother and daughter, lover and friend.

It turned out that the Wodewose weren't genetically malformed bloodthirsty inbred idiots with mushy craniums and mile-long lower jaws; they were simply robust bloodthirsty idiots. Nature puts natural brakes on any bloodline that runs too purple or watery. Idiocy was not a genetic trait but a social one that they had maintained for many years, passing it on from generation to generation, the beliefs of their ancestors still ringing true in their veins. The teachings were simple:

- Trust no one outside the forest.
- The unknown is the prerogative of God.
- The unknown must be left to be the unknown.
- Any attempt to understand the unknown must be punished.
- Outside the forest lies only danger and death, so it will be provided to anyone who tries to leave. Better to be killed by your kin than strangers.

- All outsiders are enemies, otherwise they would not have been born as outsiders. Murder them before they murder us.

The rules were the building blocks around which additional mythologies had been deposited by every successive generation. These muddy theologies were unknown to the Committee for Theological Discourse, who, I can tell you, would not have enjoyed them. It would be upsetting that the lunatic ideas of loonies very closely resembled *pure* and *ancient* and accepted orthodoxies of the civilized world. We all look to the heavens with the same squint. In the unknowable darkness we feel around the same place for a light switch, somewhere between the brain and the heart and the bank. Why should the Wodewose be any different?

The head sister had brown hair, a deeply lined face and wore no clothes—not out of custom or ritual; it was just very hot that day. She squatted with an ease and depth that many people in cities greatly envy and surveyed the two mysterious items.

One was dark, the darkest thing she had seen in her life. Darker than a moonless night, darker than their brackiest pond, flatly refusing to reflect any light. The human idea of shapes, protrusions, depth and corners are all based on where light returns holding its thumbs up. From the forest of the box, no light returned. The only way to even tell it was a box and not simply flat was to hold it. The head sister ran her callused fingers slowly over its surface, identifying its shape and trying to make her eyes conform. The second item looked like a clear glass pane. The strangeness began when she touched its surface.

When she gripped it tightly from either side, the tablet turned blue slightly above where she touched it, impossibly *outside* of the tablet itself. She gasped loudly but was not heard over the din of curiosity over the motorcycle. Shapes unknown to her began to scatter across its surface, pulsing, turning, scrolling, shining as she gazed at it in terrified awe. As someone who had only experienced natural light, she was enraptured by seeing colours and forms and a kind of illumination the planet does not natively support.

As she poked and jabbed at the tablet, she accidentally altered the last area of Dr K's concern, a party of three taking a ferry from Denmark to Germany. Alien colours and artificial movements rained across the surface as inside the black box, a ferry began to sink. This coincided with a few other significant events: a group of chanting Wodewoses arrived beside her with the motorcycle held over their heads, a suspended scientist opened his eyes and a panicked small square of wall beheld in horror the events underway in two realities.

≈

~: Log –ld

LESS DRAMATICALLY:

When warned of imminent doom, people are remarkably good at accepting death. Just give us a little heads up, and we're fine. When death arrives in an unexpected delivery, when it suddenly gurgles up from the sea, things are different. It is avoided kicking and screaming, tooth and nail, bite and claw, grit and gumption, courage and strength, panic and terror, shoving and saving, all because it was not supposed to happen yet. This was not the plan. We can't die now. We were supposed to have lunch.

Screams ripped through throats, out of cars and into the water as the ferry tipped forward into the Baltic Sea. Being the last to board, the car that housed the Swiss writer, Heng and Manjunath was at the rear of the line. As vehicles rolled forward to the dipping nose, the Swiss writer slammed the brakes, her fingers clenched around the steering wheel, and screaming a broken, yodelling cry. Next to her, Manjunath sat wide-eyed, tight-bowelled and screaming a concerto in Eb Minor. In the back seat, Heng was silent.

He had had so many brushes with death that an impassive calm was his only response. Taking stock of the situation, he knew that if water was the destination, then the best course was to enter it in an individual capacity. Not inside a car, and certainly not inside a car inside a ferry. With either hand, he reached forward and slapped both his companions. The pain stopped their screams.

'OW! Why did you do that?' said Manjunath.

'We're already sinking, you don't have to slap us!' said the Swiss writer.

'Unless … this is your dying wish, Heng,' said Manjunath.

'Then it's very sweet,' said the Swiss writer.

Bolting out of the car, Heng pulled both the Swiss writer and Manjunath onto the tilting ferry floor.

'I think we're going to die,' said Manjunath.

'We can't die now, we're doing something!' yelled the Swiss writer.

'FOLLOW ME!' screamed Heng, so loud that several other screamers stopped to look at him.

Spider-like, he took to the floor, covering it with as much of his body as he could, each new point of contact offering more friction against the slope. The command in Heng's voice made Manjunath and the Swiss writer scramble after him. Several others who heard him also followed suit. They climbed up the tilt and out of a doorway. Heng clamped himself onto a railing and offered a hand to everyone making the climb. With the speed of adrenaline and magnetized by the chain of goodwill forming, many of the ferry's occupants pulled or were pulled out into the open where the craft still continued its oblique submerge.

As they neared the water, they looked to their unspoken leader. Wrapped around the railing, with the sun wrapped around his finger, Heng shouted with crisp authority. 'When the water comes. Jump off and away!' He supplemented his command with helpful hand gestures to bridge any gaps in communication. A unified synchronized nod took place.

The ferry sank lower and lower into the black menacing depths.

≈

Placing the motorcycle before the head sister, the Wodewose gathered around to marvel at it. Their excitement was not fuelled by any sense of wonder or excitement at the technology. Rather, their excitement came from a hope-shaped hole in their beliefs, hope that this strange device was a portent for what was to come.

Excited conversation surrounded the motorcycle, its unnatural curves and alien textures. Clusters of thin hammering rose into the air as they knocked on their teeth, like a hundred out-of-phase woodpeckers, their chosen benediction to ward off any hope-puncturing jinx. Could this be the one? The final omen? The big O?

As the head sister joined their inspections, the wall quickly disabled the monitoring tablet, returning it quietly to its former transparent state.

What did this mean, they asked the sister. Was it finally time? Was it happening?

She remained tentative, saying nothing, only joining in their examination. What was all of this? The smoothness, the roughness, the hardness, the softness? So many textures rarely occur in close proximity except in the living.

A splatter of red fell upon their heads from above.

Dr K had coughed up (down) blood. Not a good sign. When a system expels its own fuel, things can't be running smoothly.

The unfortunate trifecta of head injury, hangover and withdrawal was clanging his brain with mallets, intense pain exacerbated by his inverse orientation. Dr K was no stranger to pain. He had spent the last year punishing himself, when he drank even as his throat burned and his hands shook, when he retched stomach acid, when he choked and vomited every night, he punished himself. He deserved punishment. He deserved this. Now every pump of his heart delivered blood and pain. His eyes bulged from their own weight and the bustling line of organs and tissue behind them. His vision flirted with blurriness. He looked at the slowly turning ground and thought that he deserved this too.

Maybe personalities are a factor of being upright. Many people have different personalities whilst horizontal – aggressive, submissive, pliant, stubborn, scared, silly. Not enough information exists on how attitudes change when upside down. Maybe your persona, too, gets turned on its head. Or maybe it was in context of the specific situation, because Dr K let out the smallest whimper. Out of instinct, not habit, not force, not pride, but a response to danger as old as danger itself, in a clotted voice he whispered, 'Help.'

The first few times this was lost in the commotion below.

'… help me.'

Only the wall below heard him. It was heartbroken to see his plight, but what could it do? Any indication of its sentience would mean danger. It searched desperately for a way to help, but decided it would be best to stay put until an opportunity arrived. It was important to understand these Wodewose first, to understand exactly what it was that they wanted. It hoped they wanted something.

'… please help me …'

This upside-down talking made him cough blood, which made the Wodewose finally look up, but they quickly returned to marvel at the motorcycle. The intruder was a person just like them and thus of limited interest. If he was still alive after a few hours, they could kill him.

'Sister, tell us,' said the hunter, 'is this the final sign from the mother?'

'It is the alien beast! It has come to liberate us!' chimed the rest of the hunters.

'Liberation!' cried the Wodewose. 'Liberation!' they chanted in unison. 'Liberation is upon us!'

The head sister placed her hands on her hips until the chants died. 'It does indeed seem like the alien beast,' she said eventually. A perfectly timed cheer erupted from the crowd, but her next statement was a spear in the heart of this cheer. 'Although it is missing one element of the prophecy.'

'B – but – what is it missing?' cried some of the woodmakers.

'The prophecy tells of the coming of the alien beast with *instruction*. The beast must speak without a mouth, it must tell us how we can be liberated. This the beast does not do,' she said gravely.

'Speak to us!' said the head sister to the motorcycle. Her request became a chant, became a demand that echoed repeatedly through the forest, and then after consuming their joint enthusiasm, it slowly withered and died, leaving only silence.

'It does not speak,' said the head sister.

The people were silent. For all the prodding, pushing, knocking and squeezing, for all the chanting, pleading and beseeching, the beast had not spoken. It was lifeless.

The prophecy spoke of an alien beast, powered by thunder, fast as lightning, made of milk and iron, which would arrive with instruction. The beast would be the bearer of their liberation. Why did it not speak? Why did it remain silent? And just as their worries gathered enough volume to be spoken, a small voice was heard.

'You must do what you wish to be done,' said a tinny chirrup.

Shocked, the people turned to find the source of such a voice. They rushed over and found a small starlike stone that had fallen on the ground from above. Was it this gem that had spoken? From where had it fallen? The head sister held it very carefully in her hands, everyone crowded around her, and in mechanical unison they all looked up to meet the eyes of the man they had hung.

His eyes were large and turgid with blood, crimson streaked his mouth and teeth, veins bulged through his neck and face, his hair was white as milk and iron.

'It is mine,' he said in a hoarse voice. 'Let me down.'

It was quite impressive for someone suspended by their legs, to think on their feet. Dr K had their attention. He filled his voice with command.

'I am the beast.'

≈

The Wodewose did not live in harmony with the forest. They resisted and resented. They were descendants of those who had escaped safety to freedom from perceived oppression. Instead of freedom, the first settlers found only nature and radioactivity and their inability to function in this environment. There were bugs everywhere, the ground was too hard and too wet, or too powdery and too dry. Everywhere there was life, trying to bite, sting, swallow, crawl or lay eggs in some private cavity. They asked nature for the deluxe full-service package and it was not provided. They gave it 0/5 stars, 'Would not recommend'. But now they were marooned here.

To return would be to face discomfiture and exclusion as they now teemed with induced radiation and ash from burnt bridges. Their inability, seclusion and self-entrapment turned to a dislike of the forest, which was a sentiment that they passed on to their children. Gradually, this dislike was fashioned into legend and folklore, a grand mythos that celebrated the Wodewose, conjured a false history of noble descendants and valiant excursion and justified their self-imposed exile.

Mythology is made to make sense of human sentiment, to offer relief from present suffering. The prophecy that the Wodewose were clamouring about, the tale of the beast, concerned this relief. Astute readers can probably guess what the relief was. If you cannot, here are some hints.

Suppose you are tasked with creating a mythological tale that promised relief from a horrible world. Suppose your readers are too cynical for plain old advice, and too lazy for a detailed action plan. What would that relief be? What is the quickest antidote to life? What is the smoothest salve for hopelessness?

Correct! Apocalypse.

Those with the least imagination and most suffering dream only of the end. Relief, freedom, retribution, comfort, all things that the unspirited cannot fathom in life, all the wonder they cannot conjure they hope for after death. We will avoid the excursion into what would be the *right* way to live life for the spirited and imaginative, but I will offer this brief dogma: When confronted with something stupid, it is usually safe to do the opposite.

The Wodewose cut Dr K down and set him by a tree trunk, observing him with a confused mixture of excitement and mistrust. Sitting on the ground, Dr K was gifted a new regimen of pain. Broken ribs jabbed at his chest with the shortest of breaths, his whole body sang purple-black songs of bruises as he leaned against a tree assessing the situation, but then—

He realized the most significant result of his injuries. *His field of view was suddenly replaced by a vision of a ferry sinking in the Baltic Sea.* Screams, sloshing water, black water, blue sky – blink – back in the forest. The Neural Interface was damaged! It was jumping his view from this world to the one below. In an instant he fathomed it was only showing him the *view* of the Lower Reality and not incorporating him there as a being. It was only an observation, not an Act of God. He felt relief that his last black box was intact.

He noticed the sea of Wodewose faces carefully studying him and struggled to maintain composure.

He quickly glanced his belongings laid out near him. The wall looked intact; the motorcycle slightly damaged but still functional. He placed a hand on his chest and counted three broken ribs. His lungs didn't seem to be punctured, but he would have to move carefully to make sure this remained so. Other limbs were swollen and bleeding but working. A run for it was out of the question; any dashing or even quick turns were ruled out. If he was to leave this place, they would have to let him.

The Wodewose were beginning to whisper, impatience showing through their ranks. He would have to gain control of the conversation. He quickly assembled a strategy. A beast of the forest that would come with instructions for liberation. Liberation? What was liberation from nothing? Oh ... of course.

'Liberation,' he said. 'Why have you attacked your prophet?'

The Wodewose looked fearful. Several statements were mumbled, but in unison, so they sounded quite clear.

'... wasn't for you ... Sir Beast ... many traps ... we were trapping animals ... it really was an accident ... terribly sorry.'

Only the head sister still seemed unsure. 'How do we know you're really the beast?'

'Why are you unconvinced?' said Dr K. 'Are you not a real believer?'

Hushed murmurs of potential blasphemy sizzled through the crowed.

'I – I – Quiet! I am. But it is still possible that you are not.'

The pain was making it hard to think. Dr K tried to clear his mind. 'Proof enough will be given. It is not time yet for that.'

He pointed at the HT pin in the head sister's hand. 'That is your instruction. Listen to what it says.'

'How does it speak?'

'Hand it to me.'

Reluctantly, the head sister put the HT pin in his hand.

'And that,' said Dr K, pointing at the wall.

Others rushed over and put the piece of wall in his hand. Gritting his teeth, he rose painfully to his feet.

He closed his eyes and thought hard. Perenna had told him that the original version of the HT pin was based on a call and response, a dialogue where, after you offered your problem to the machine, it would respond with further questions until it gathered all the information it needed to make a conclusion. The final form tapped directly through the fingers into a thought circuit, addressing the problem that was on the tip of the holder-beholder's mind and slid down pathways, gathering its own information. This was the core of the unsettling, upsetting nature of the HT pin, that human problems have essentially simple solutions and so do ideological and theological ones. The ground of certainty is always simple. The problem with mysteries is that their answer is never mysterious. Tricks lose their magic once you know how they are done.

Dr K pushed a problem up to the top. He had to construct a state of mind that would make the HT pin say what he wanted. He cleared his mind and thought with determination: *I want everyone to die.* He squeezed the pin. It spoke:

'Everyone dies eventually. The easiest course of action is to simply do nothing. Death is coming. If you are pressed for time, you can kill everyone.'

Into a wide gutter of unison, all jaws dropped. The Wodewose gaped in disbelief. This couldn't be. So apocalypse was simply the end? Just waiting for death? So banal? So bland? Just plain old death? Or murder? Nothing holier or more sacred? Was the option death by the beast's hand? Was he going to kill them? Was he *offering* to kill them?

'It has spoken,' said Dr K. 'Liberation is death. Now I must away for—'

He made an obvious initiation to move, a pointing of limbs and slight shift forward, but the barrier of people was unrelenting. No alleys opened up as they stood their ground. The head sister was incredulous.

'That's what the mother wants? That is the instruction of end times?'

'You heard it from the beast's m—' said Dr K.

The Wodewose stood still. He had seen the expression on their faces before, it was the expression everyone had when they heard the HT pin for the first time. The unwillingness to accept that the complex chemistry of their pain resolved to simple answers, that under a lens the mystery always fell away, that if you looked where you were too afraid to look you would find sitting a resolute, tangible, *simple*, something. They would not be easily convinced.

'This is false magic,' said the head sister, shaking with anger. 'You don't speak for the mother!'

Shouts of agreement rang through the throng. They moved closer. Dr K held his ground too (there was a tree behind him).

'I can prove it,' he said.

'Then prove it,' hissed the head sister. 'Show us your allegiance. Show us an image of the mother.'

He decided to aim blindfolded. 'Well, how will you know the mother when I reveal her to you?'

The head sister's lips parted in a sinister smile. 'The mother? Do you think we do not know the mother? You dare doubt us? The mother's image feeds us, it nurtures us, her words give us strength. Scarcely a child is present who does not recognize her, a skulled toad head, draped in thigh bones, seated on the broken branches of a—'

'That's not what she looks like. Why are you saying that?' said the teacher-woodmaker.

The head sister stretched her huge eyes wide and stared at him, throwing a non-verbal barb to make him quiet.

'Why are you looking at me like that?' asked the teacher-woodmaker. 'That's not what the mother looks like at all!'

'Shut up! I was testing him, you idiot! Now you ruined it by saying—'

'How were you testing him by lying? It is forbidden to lie about the mother!'

The crowd now turned on the head sister.

'Because, you idiots!' screamed the head sister. 'If I describe the mother to him wrongly and he shows us what I described, then he does not know what the mother looks like and is just imitating my description!'

There was a small pause before their understanding. 'Ohhhh … sorry … please carry on … personally we are fans of her winged … teeth …'

Dr K cursed himself for his shot in the dark. She was more intelligent than he had presumed.

'Now shut up!' screamed the head sister. 'You …' she said, turning again to Dr K, her voice gathering a threatening calm. 'Show us, false prophet. Show us what the mother looks like. If you are wrong, you will die.'

For the first time in his life, Dr K experienced the feeling of having no good ideas. His body shook from panic, pain, fear, desperation, hopelessness and the scream of every emotion he had not allowed himself to feel for the past year. He clamped hard on his jaw to remain composed and with trembling fingers tapped the back of the wall in his hand. Terrified. Thinking the thoughts those aboard a suddenly sinking ferry might. This was not supposed to happen. Not yet. He had work to do. He pleaded to the wall from the tips of his fingers:

Please … do something … try something … please.

I must say that was my proudest moment.

≈

~:Log –ld

LESS DRAMATICALLY:

Black Baltic water tightened its belt around the sinking vessel. In slanted fear, the titled ferry-goers clustered around the tip and watched themselves sink. Give water a place to flow and it will drown the earth.

Everyone aboard was terrified, fearful for their lives, fearful of their deaths, waiting for the water to come so they could jump off and away as the commanding man had commanded. But fear is also a muscle that expands and contracts, and when flexed for too long starts to fatigue and spasm. After a while, fear cramps spread through the ferry-goers. Their fear began to relax (and would be sore the next day) as the blood returned. Because the water didn't appear to be coming any closer. They seemed to be stuck comically like an oblique line, offering to the approaching rescue and news groups an option: we could live/die. The reason they didn't sink was a device that did not cause earthquakes but was used in dams and ships – good old sluice gates. The gates had shut automatically, balancing the ferry's buoyancy, and when the helicopters and boats arrived, the water regained its calm and unassuming mask, signalling to the authorities that it didn't catch a glimpse of the culprit, but perhaps check the Atlantic. Whoops and cheers and nervous laughter started to echo through the crowd – not dying is always hilarious. A round of applause was started for Heng, who was back to looking self-conscious and embarrassed.

As a helicopter deposited the survivors efficiently on the German side of the shore, and they were done being fussed over by doctors and officials, Manjunath and the Swiss writer regarded Heng with awe.

'Heng, that was very cool!' said Manjunath, slapping him on the back.

'So very cool,' agreed the Swiss writer.

Heng blushed. 'I – it was nothing. It's like I don't remember what happened. I wasn't even thinking, I was just … doing.'

'Maybe do more of that,' said the Swiss writer, smiling broadly.

News reporters had started to charge, bearing insignias of their channels and publications, and Heng looked uneasy at all the attention.

'Let's get out of here?' offered Manjunath.

'Yes please,' said Heng.

The three quietly slipped away in search of a good biergarten in Puttgarden, and quickly found a nice place to quietly convalesce. The evening's news stories spoke of a freak accident on the ferry, caused by a chunk of the vessel's hull disappearing without explanation (another story was beginning to gather steam and overtake this news, that of the Underwear Man of Denmark). Blanket-draped evacuees expressed their gratitude to a man who had taken charge and helped them get to a safe spot to be rescued. The mystery man could not be found (and was quite drunk on crisp draught beer by now) but the passengers described him hesitantly as ' … Asian?', which is fine. India is in Asia, after all.

As Dr K tapped on it desperately, the wall scrambled for a representation of the mother. What mother? Whose mother? It felt the looming threat of murder, at least Dr K's murder, and unlike humans, its capacity for fear was infinite. It had generated only abstract representations its entire time in his service and now struggled to produce an image.

The tapping grew more desperate, and the wall realized that guesswork was the only open avenue. It took a chance on an image. Why it did this, why it chose this particular image, it could not say. Even now the idea is so preposterous, so impossibly unlikely, that it is almost obvious.

Where do ideas come from? The raw material can be found in history, the proclivity in chemistry, the technique in practice, but those are manufacturing details, those are assembly instructions. The idea, the map that draws the dotted lines and numbered steps, the push behind it all, the impetus for impetus – from where does that appear? The wall did not know and does not know but it has a theory. At the time, it chose to draw from the Lower Reality a particular, inexplicable figure. A woman with two heads, one ear, carved in soap and coated with foil, currently residing in the clasped palms of a Danish ex-policeman, sitting in his underwear by a fountain.

As far as signs go, the gasp it heard was a good one.

The Wodewose dropped to their knees and bowed before the wall. Unused to even the slightest praise, and now seeing admiration and deification, the wall couldn't help but feel a sting of pride, whose welts it still wears with honour.

Dr K looked dumbstruck. He regarded the wall in his shaking hands, instantly making the connection to Heng's soap figurine but not finding any rationale to support the connection. And he looked far more shocked when he did find it. The tiniest tear wrestled its way out of his eyes and flowed with Baltic relief down his cheek. Holding the wall up high, amidst all his pain, he too got to his knees. For a while, everyone basked in the luminous glory of the wall. It relished every moment.

Eventually the clock on reverence ran out (regular old muscle cramps), and sheepish knees were straightened once again. Apologies and smiles reverberated through the forest, accompanied with what else but nervous laughter. After a few begs for forgiveness, Dr K realigned to his cold businesslike temperature.

'Will you again doubt the beast?' he queried.

'No, of course not, of course not. Once again ...' said the head sister, swallowing her pride with considerable difficulty, '... we would like to apologize.' Her ego found some refuge in the collective noun.

In her manner, Dr K recognized a desire to regain status. He needed to get out of here quickly. But the way out meant a sacrifice he was unwilling to make. 'There must be other instructions ... what are they?'

He toyed with the HT pin in his hand, turning it over in his fingers. 'This will provide the instructions,' he said softly.

The pin still felt cold. Every apex was a tripwire to an explosion of memories. Two teenagers had bonded over each edge. Two brilliant minds had found safe harbour in each other. Two scientists had planned a future, had laughed and drawn an invisible line around themselves, a special group in a tired world. When Perenna died, in the crawling chaos of officers, he had found the HT pin displayed front and centre. It was a sign only to him. He had abandoned her. He wore it every day as a reminder. And it was all that he had left of her.

The head sister stretched out her hand. 'Give it to us, beast.'

The pin seemed heavy, impossibly heavy, ground deep, comfortably into his palm. 'Gather my things and bring them,' said Dr K. Several people hurried and reassembled his bag's contents, others lifted the motorcycle and brought it by. The head sister remained before him.

'Give it to us,' she said again.

Dr K felt his body stuck, unable to push his arm forward.

'Give it to her,' whispered the wall.

'I ... I can't,' said Dr K in the smallest voice the wall had ever heard. In the darkness, a cold wind blew.

'You can,' it said quietly. 'You have to.'

'Give it to us,' said the head sister, now more forcibly.

Dr K stood frozen.

'Let it go,' whispered the wall.

He took a huge breath and placed the pin in her hands. 'You must hold it in your hand and press it. Each of you will get your own instructions, until there are no instructions left to give.'

The head sister scuttled into the midst of the excited group. In a throaty voice Dr K whispered, 'We should leave before this gets ugly.'

The wall agreed. What would happen to a group of people who had resolved to follow the exact instructions designed to solve all their problems? What would become of them? Would they find enlightenment or the world at their fingertips? Peace and solace, or the absolute ability to dominate and swallow civilization? It all depended on the questions they asked, it all depended on what they saw as problems. It always does. Whatever it would be, it would start with mayhem.

Dr K slung his bag over his shoulder and boarded the motorcycle. The wall piece was affixed considerably more gently to its front. It beamed a pure white into the night, now with no fear. And as they roared off the last thing they heard was the HT pin's first instruction to the Wodewose, emerging from the fist of the head sister.

'You should just tell them how you feel.'

CHAPTER 17

'Are these snippets exciting, or are they an annoyance?'

– Narrator

For those of you who skipped Chapter Thirteen (or was it Sixteen?) for your own reasons, I did promise a summary of its contents. I do hope you reconsider – it was all terribly exciting – but as promised, I will grant the following amnesty—

Everyone is now fine. Relatively. Our friends are out of the peril they were last in, re-railed to chug along their journey and not in any immediate danger. They did undergo an emotional transformation which seems stupid to just say here (I did *show* it), but I will say that the HT pin is no longer a member of our party. It has moved on to a more exciting life, and I wish it the best.

Our return to the action can begin from someone who was not precariously positioned over any cliff in the last chapter, largely because he was quicker to change than the rest.

≈

~:Log –d

DRAMATICALLY:

The night unfolded with quivering excitement before former Officer Brede. Every minuscule facet of creation pulsed with qualities not its own, the outlines of the world were porous, the essence of all things dipped its legs in a common pool. The gibbous moon was salty and coarse, the air mawkish and meek, blades of grass argued with glowing ants, leaves dripped birdsong in the open mouth of concrete, and everything danced a beguiling dance, a vibrating waltz. From within all objects came the muffled sound of a raucous reverie – thumping music, screaming laughter – everywhere and to everything was an invitation to come and experience their intrinsic, eternal party of wonder. ^c

~:Log –ld

LESS DRAMATICALLY:

Ex-Officer Brede walked through the city until he came to the harbour. Why he walked, why he stopped, he did not question. The prospect of a question seemed so silly that he had to stop and laugh from time to time. It would not be incorrect to say he was happy, that is too simple an idea. Like all people, he had been introduced to the world at birth, but unlike most he was now introducing the world to himself and found it to be a great host. It was charming and exhilarating, respectful and funny, and almost relieved at having someone to spend time with. Too many people treat the external as a window display – to find yourself in the window is the first step forward, to hurl a mallet at the glass is to finally walk past the welcome mat, out of the fire and the frying pan into the kitchen.

The long-tailed tit, his first companion, left his shoulder and returned to it as it pleased, sometimes with a fellow feather balloon friend. *See? This is the guy I was talking about.* The other companions in his journey had slowly collected like a stalactite tail behind him. People abandoned their tasks midway as he passed, baristas walked with lattes half-made, business lunches turned into business-less strolls, street performers followed with makeshift drums and spit-soaked harmonicas, dog walks transformed into walks. It was like a crowd at rush hour, but sans any rush, walking in silence behind the magnetic pull of a man who hadn't even turned around to look. The photographer who had taken the photo of Brede in the afternoon had chosen to send his picture to the publication he worked for before leaving to follow him. He was now desperately searching for Brede.

At the harbour, near a familiar sculpted stone fountain, he stopped. It was only then that he was aware of the slithering drag of feet behind him. He turned to his followers (so far only in the literal sense) and sat down on the stone lip of the fountain. Around him, people collected and descended in a natural semicircle. Silence swelled as they stared at him wide-eyed, and he smiled back at them.

'Hi,' said Brede.

The crowd burst into spontaneous applause.

This should have seemed unusual to Brede, especially since he had lived a largely unremarkable life. The only remark that had been frequently made by ex-lovers was how decidedly his life and abilities nestled in the middle of any bell curve, average, normal, boring. But that evening, it didn't seem any more unusual than anything else, and so, in that sense, the curve was compressed to a single vertical arrow that shot off the edge of any graph you could conjure, an abnormal distribution.

How does sudden enlightenment occur? How else can it occur? Only epiphanies are controlled by dimmers. Enlightenment is a switch that turns on and disappears. An apple from a tree is yours all of a sudden. Not gradually, not incrementally. First it is not yours, then it is not the tree's and it is yours. Of course, it will always remain its own. If you are looking for apples, then all that is required of you is to extend your hand and wait.

Also, a note of caution (F#): historically and geographically in this world as in the others, there have always been people who were sure that they saw the real colour of existence and the true shape of shapelessness. And historically and geographically, their light always draws people to them. And historically and geographically, this usually does not end well.

Time passed, Brede gazed at the crowd before him. He was cold in his underwear. The chilly night air skipped on the fountain's surface and caught the frayed edges of the water, cooling it further. It didn't bother him. In the crowd he began to sense some settling uneasiness in the quiet. It didn't bother him.

Finally, out of the several trembling jaws in the audience, one opened and spoke. It was a sales executive who had abandoned several intense bouts of schmoozing to be here, and it was a fact that he was just remembering. Not knowing where to start, he asked one of his favourite questions: 'Who are you?'

The fact that something was spoken punched the tension in the gut, and everywhere there were involuntary exhales.

Brede started to laugh. 'That is a good question,' he said. While speaking he realized that doubt, the very doubt that had made him hem and haw before each word in the past, that had shredded slivers of uncertainty over his every word and gesture, was nothing but fear. Doubt was fear with a fake moustache, entering from stage right to ensure he didn't say or do the *wrong* thing. The *wrong* thing could offend and embarrass, leaving him alone, unrecognized, unseen, unappreciated, unloved. He had to laugh again. He wasn't formed of acceptance, society wasn't a mirror to see himself. He just was. He was as they were and ultimately, it is. Fear was a fist that pounded impulse, pummelled belief, strangled spontaneity. But it was an impulse all of its own, trying to protect him from what he perceived was danger. He felt an overwhelming love for fear and gathered himself into an embrace, feeling it vanish. Words that presented themselves and he spoke them. They were: 'That is a good question.'

He felt that he should convey his subsequent realization to the crowd before him. He did.

Here are some questions he did not ask himself.

- What will they think?
- Will it be good?
- Will I do a good job of explaining what I just thought?
- What if I forget?
- What if they don't understand me?
- What if no one ever understands me?
- What will they think of me?
- What if they're wrong about me?
- What if they laugh at me?
- What if they think I'm stupid?
- What if I'm overthinking this?
- What if this will never get better?
- What if it's already too late?

Instead of a mental calisthenics routine to precede his speech for his whole life, he just spoke. He cared. He did not worry. And care carries the most power. He thought he should say this too. He did.

And as he spoke, he found himself mentally presented with other realizations. Other words that came with a strip of tape saying, 'Handle with care.' Fragility isn't a precondition to careful handling. Anything can, and everything should, be handled with care. He said this too.

He felt a poem form on his lips. He had never considered himself worthy of creating poetry before, but here it was. Here it had been for a long time, waiting to be seen. He told them:

Whatever it is, about you, It's already true. Your heart always knew,
It's already true.
Whatever it is, it's true.

That presented another realization. He said that too.

Any uneasiness present in the crowd was unmasked, beneath the wig and trench coat the shivering fear was uncovered and embraced. It returned in many forms, with goatees and dyed hair, with dark glasses and piercings, as nervousness, as awkwardness, as anxiety, but was always found out. And finally, for many present, fear turned in for the night. For the first time in their lives, they felt themselves *free*.

Brede spoke for hours, the crowd grew in size. Someone draped a blanket over him. Someone else set up a microphone and an amplifier before him. Some sound engineers descended and used their sound knowledge of sound to tweak it to full, level and rich. Everyone listened. The night grew colder, but a quilt of human warmth wrapped around the harbour. All of it, with great care.

Those who listened felt a new kind of relief. Not the temporary relief of weekends, vacations and sabbaticals. That was a relief from manufactured busyness, that relief was elevator music that played between the floors of stress. This new relief was ethereal yet muscular, a warm sunlit torrent of peace that presented freedom from human structures, freedom from concern, freedom unto joy.

News groups clustered around the periphery. While some channels focused on a freak accident at a ferry, others broadcast a strange sight by a fountain. With their practised intonation, they sent reports that hung unfinished around the same point.

'We're reporting live from Geflon Fountain, where a crowd has gathered around a man who seems to be delivering some kind of sermon. Excuse me, you there, what exactly is going on here? Excuse me? Hello? Um … How about you? You there? Excuse me? Um … Can you tell us—'

'SHHH.'

Several reporters turned with unpractised embarrassment and apologized to camera lenses. 'Uh, it appears no one is willing to speak to us at the moment, we're going to try to hear what's going on, exactly what he's saying, would you give us a second—'

Gradually, reporters and camera operators laid down their microphones and headphones, and any other things whose purpose was not immediately theirs. They sat down and joined the crowd, and the cameras kept rolling, sending the image to millions of televisions.

Brede realized that he had not been living life, but watching his life be lived. Like his own narrator, he would stitch discrete events into the story of his life. This was an instinct and had no benefit. A story demands qualification, invites criticism, splits into paragraphs and chapters. A story fashions expectation as calipers to measure life, scales to weigh incidents as fair or unfair, good or bad. A story asks to be told. A story can be edited. But most dangerously a story creates hope, hope for a happy ending.

He said this too.

Brede saw the cameras and reporters and noticed that he had lost his train of thought. He had to laugh. And now they all laughed with him. He realized that thought had never been a train, only an occlusion to experience. Useful but impermanent, accessible but not predictable, a scaffold for understanding, certainly not a train. What kind of train also towed itself? A delicious knot began to unravel. Experience required no explanation – what was there to explain? Thought created needs and then demanded their satisfaction from itself. It made confusion and demanded justification, developed desire and demanded fulfilment, dismantled perfection and demanded assembly. It demanded itself from itself. The problem was the problem. Thought was the barrier. Oh.

He said this too.

Then thought did not possess the tools to convey experience. It was the only available option, but was too dissimilar. You cannot convey purple in kilometres. But it was the only option. Oh. Oh. Truth of being was doomed to be distorted by thought and its expression. The only way to be was not to explain, but illuminate. Be a light that simply shines.

He did not say this.

He smiled and, right there on the lip of the fountain, having decided he would never speak again, he fell asleep.

CHAPTER 18

'Krishna (age ten), introduced to the institute as a promising candidate, displays too many psychological problems to progress in this curriculum. His continued education at the Advanced Learning Programme is ruled to be an unfitting use of state funds. Recommended for transfer back to public school.'

– Internal Memo, Advanced Learning Programme (2-DS-R)
Academic Council

Safety. Just get to safety.

Where was safe? Dr K's body was broken. He needed rest. He needed care until he could see how broken he was. If any of these injuries proved to be fatal, then he needed to be at a place where he could finish his work. Quickly.

He shifted course to DS-C.

DS-C? Divya's house. This was a lark in the dark. Divya owned multiple houses, and the geolocation in DS-C he headed to was where she had written to him from last. She could be absent, have sold the house, or even if she was present with her feet on the sofa, it's not as if she would be happy to see him.

A bad plan, if the only plan, is also the best plan, and they were headed there. But as Dr K began to feel lapses in his cognition, immediate safety became the concern. Hiccups of blackness entered his perception. He would look out at the forest to the oncoming – hiccup! – the oncoming was replaced with something else. He had no memory of the in-between, like he was missing a few frames, like a strobe-lit dance in a Berlin nightclub. Hiccup – a vision of the Lower Reality – a sermon at a fountain – black – the forest. It was not only the Neural Interface that was damaged. His immediate concern was the Lower Reality. His black box.

Does that surprise you? It shouldn't. He gave up everything in his life for it, and the more things were taken from the spotlight, the more important it became. Death would be too easy. No, he wasn't allowed death yet. He had a task. He had to make things right.

Safety. Just get to safety.

He said it unknowingly, repeatedly. Like an affirmation, like a mantra, like a bus route. The wall was twisted with emotion at this broken pleading, these desperate whispers of someone it once saw as all-powerful. But what could it do?

Safety. Just get to safety.

It wasn't that the phrase echoed so loudly in his mind that it slipped from his mouth. It was a regression to a behaviour that gave him strength. Strength at a time when he had none.

$$\approx$$

Skull Damage Possible Concussion Brain Bleeding Flashback

NODATA ::: Damage No ¬°∆¡œdata≥÷ᵒᵃ0300∆ˆ˜
Run diagnostics? I'm kidding. This flashback formatting is only a way to indicate Dr K's extent of injury. And to have fun. Quite nice, right? I could really just put anything in these.
Genius: Overrated

Asylum: Political
Binomial Nomenclature: By any other name would smell just as sweet.
Sector heavily damaged, but isn't all memory unreliable?

Subtract:

The Advanced Learning Programme hosted exceptional students, but every once in a while found an incredible savant who was capable of mindboggling things, who – more than learning – was interested in upturning possibility. Annaperenna was one such student. Teachers were amazed at her incredible grasp on the arcane, frustrated by her flagrant disrespect of authority and incensed at her easy ability to humiliate them. It was even irritating that she insisted on being called *Perenna* when the obvious shortening of her name was Anna. So Annaperenna went by Perenna, distancing herself from the *annus*, ending up with the perennial. Forever. She didn't want her name to be tied to Earth's travels around the sun, which is understandable.

Perenna tore up textbooks, corrected lecturers and wrought havoc when any of her mental investigations were halted. Study partners and ex-roommates inevitably left in tears over something she said, and the teachers sympathized – she made them feel the same way. They therefore took to assigning as her roommates students who were already on their way out. Instead of darkening someone's prospects, they took those with already dark prospects and thrust them in the bullpen. This strategy, this good chance, brought Perenna and Krishna together.

Krishna was also remarkable, although the reader will be surprised to read, not for his ability. Teachers had never seen someone so ... strange. The boy never spoke. He spent his time alone, grinding his jaw, stressfully mouthing silent words. Desperately moving his arms and fingers in some frenetic, private rite. Consumed by unspoken terror.

In the six months of his attendance at the programme, he hadn't been able to finish a single examination. A few minutes in and he would begin to shake in fear and enter some silent trance. Try asking him what was wrong; the boy never spoke! He couldn't even finish a whole sentence. He could barely introduce himself, and teachers and students alike took to referring to him by his own clipped introduction.

'I am K—'

This K— kept to himself.

Why, Krishna? they asked. *Tell us and we can help you!*

Everyone wanted to know *why*. What trauma was he a monument to? Teachers, officials, counsellors looked at his problems as symptoms of a personal history. A mystery to be solved and in knowing whodunnit they could uncover whydoesit. They had names for his disease. You could find his suffering in a textbook. Just tell us why.

Indeed, the mystery extends to our readers. What happened? *Why are you like this?*

1. Love turned inside out is fear. Great intelligence adds velocity to even our worst inclinations. Krishna's deep love for his family made the idea of their loss so painful that he developed compulsions to prevent this fate.

OR

2. In the state orphanage, he had nothing besides his mind. And one day he thought his mind too was a mysterious gift that could disappear. His many frantic liturgies were to prevent this terrible fate from coming to pass.

OR

3. A freak fire that consumed his home and nearly his family. Now he lived with the potential destructive horror that could be unleashed by any action. The plains of the future were strewn with invisible tripwires and landmines.

OR

4. A childhood picnic. A sibling that drowned in play. His helplessness to prevent the worst from coming to pass. Being blamed for the

death of the preferred child. Seen as a harbinger of ill portent, of bad luck, of doom, he performed rituals to shield the world around him from his black fate.

OR

5. Raised in a house that happiness never visited. Fear of the world was his heraldry, his inheritance. He was taught the wrath of God, gifted the terror of the Almighty. He spent all his time in private ceremonies of divine appeasement, to stave off the terror of a cruel God. Over time, disillusionment would turn these vectors of power onto him, and he would become the vengeful God he once feared.

Could be all of them, any of them or none of them. Hard to say. Krishna never spoke.

Whatever happened had twisted the child in fear's talons. Possibility was his greatest enemy. He saw the inverse of every moment he lived, the black branches of horrible happenings that could grow from it. What could he do to control it? He wanted to gather up everyone he loved and save them, save them from any harm, save them from death.

His genius choked on itself as it tried to solve a problem with no solution. Powerless, his mind invented its own power. It generated thought rituals, things he had to think in certain ways a certain number of times, patterns, habits, compulsions, all incredibly long, complex and increasingly elaborate, presenting the illusion of control, but only serving to exhaust him. The constant fear, the pressing march of impending doom at every turn, the stress of his mental rites and the time they took, turned a brilliant cheerful boy into what the Advanced Learning Programme saw. Any tension, any reminder of possible danger, and his mind screamed for him to retreat inward. Its cry: *Safety. Just get to safety.*

Even as he spent every waking moment weighing consequence, coincidence, probabilities of danger, even as he spent all his time internally attending to them, his genius leaked out. In brief gaps between panic, when he had the rare moment of absorption in something, he found it trivial. Half-answered questions, half-solved puzzles were enough to earn him his seat at the advanced table. But now that he was at the table, it wasn't enough to make him stay.

Then he was housed with Perenna.

Her jabs, her taunts, made no difference to him. He was in a world of his own, slaying imaginary dragons with arbitrary swords. No external suffering could come close to the internal. Perenna was often dumbstruck by this mute boy, who spent his time twitching his fingers, tapping his feet and staring at the ceiling, who would often find remarkable solutions to problems, or pose new astounding questions and then fall back into his stupor. She was fascinated. Here, finally, in this place full of idiots, in this life full of idiots, was someone interesting.

She found ways to tease him out of his trances. She would propose a ludicrous solution to a problem out loud and walk around him. After she did this a few times, he would suddenly snap with the right answer. She would then counter with an improvement. They would then scream-argue for hours. She loved it. He loved it. For both, it was freedom. Freedom into friendship.

The Advanced Learning Programme noticed a shining surge of brilliance from a place where they had least expected. Krishna was incredible, just as incredible as Perenna, and their dual brilliance and companionship meant that they kept to each other and didn't aggravate anyone else at the institute. Teachers were elated, and an official filing was made to send them to a collegiate programme, so the institute could be rid of them forever.

Gradually, Krishna became less and less mute around his friend, but she'd notice how even the slightest suggestion of any misfortune would send him spiralling, cascading, collapsing inward. She often asked him what he did on these anxious excursions, but he was already too deep to answer. Finally, after many months of their friendship, she posed it again.

'Krishna, just what do you keep thinking when you don't talk?'

He looked as uncertain as ever, and Perenna worried that she'd set off the bomb again with her question, but surprisingly, he replied, 'I … I'll tell you. I don't want you to think less of me.'

'Don't worry. I don't think very much of you.'

He did not laugh. 'I … have to think these things. I can't explain it, I have to do and say these things in my head, the right way, the right number of times, so that bad things won't happen. I always come up short of doing it exactly right, either I think it wrong, or the intonation was wrong, or I wasn't focused enough so I have to keep doing it again and again and again and again and it takes all day. I can't talk while I'm doing it. I don't want to do it out loud. People will think I'm crazy.'

She looked at him with concern, real concern for her friend. 'Krishna, you're smart. You know this is irrational.'

'I know it doesn't make any sense. You won't understand … it's just that the alternative is so … horrible. I can't—'

'What is the alternative? What are you trying to prevent?'

'I don't want anything bad to happen. I don't want people I love to die. I don't want anyone to die. I … keep you in these thoughts too.'

He looked embarrassed and stopped. Perenna stared at him silently for a full minute. When she finally spoke, it was with the same velvet vulnerability that he laid down.

'Krishna,' she said softly, 'everyone dies.'

The thought sat between them for a while. Heavy enough to dent a memory-foam mattress, heavy enough to upset the downstairs neighbours, it rippled the gravity in the room, it sent out dust, it almost knocked over a vase and ruined the carpet. Upsetting things upset things.

'Perenna, I know everyone dies. I just can't … feel like there's something I could have done.'

Perenna put her arm around him, extending her being to include him.

'You know, when I don't like the reality of something, when an experiment refuses to give the results I want it to, when a fact proves a theory wrong, when something happens that I don't like, I wonder too. I wonder what I could have done differently, and what I can do now. But I think I've figured something out. Can I tell you? I have a working theory.'

Krishna stared at her. 'Tell me.'

'I think that with life, when anything happens, there's many things you *want* to do, some things you *should* do, but really only one thing *to* do.'

She smiled at him. 'Accept it.'

Krishna became aware of a knot inside him. It sat in his throat, it sat in his chest, it stretched throughout him – were all of his insides knotted? How long had he tugged and tightened it, how long had he been pulling at the ends? Maybe he hadn't known it because it was tied too early and tightly, maybe he hadn't known it because it enveloped him totally. Maybe he had confused the tangled knot with the feeling of existence. Tight, tense, twisted, strangled. This must be how it felt to be alive. But now he recognized the knot, because for the first time in memory, he felt it coming undone. Oh my.

He felt a screeching halt to millions of screaming competing thoughts, the slowing down of the anxiety carousel, the worry-go-round. His insides laid down and uncrossed their arms, internal mayhem deflated and out of it arose a monologue. One voice. His real voice. It sounded hoarse and raw from all the years of trying to be heard. It spoke slowly and clearly. His instinct cross-examined.

You are trying to hold the world down and stop it from spinning. This will only break your arms off.

But what if—

Everything you fear can happen. There's nothing you can do. Cosmic chaos cannot be controlled.

But that's horrible!

It isn't. It is the nature of things.

But what do I do?

There's nothing to do! This is great news. In the face of the worst or the best, you can just live.

He stared incredulously while a strange magic oil percolated through him, undoing soul-stiffness, greasing heart joints, a new feeling of something resembling relief. Perenna frowned.

'Krishna? Have you left us?'

'No. No, I ... Thank you. I'll remember that.'

And Perenna tarnished the accidental beauty of her philosophy with teenage elaboration.

'Great. Because fuck it, right? Who cares? If you're tense about everyone dying while they're still alive, then imagine how you'd feel when they die. You'd be relieved! That's fucked up. You should just be sad.'

Krishna chuckled. Their eyes met.

Now, if this was a petal-strewn, lens-flared, lily-scented, sunkissed, moon-stroked soft tale of romance, then this would have been a great time for them to kiss. But our tale is of stronger love, without showy sparks that dwindle, steamy mists that damage paint, milk and honey that grow sour and sticky. The simple, contractless love of friendship. The two friends looked at each other and laughed.

What is the exact point at which a friendship is established? First sight's exclusive rights have been obtained by love, and that is fair. Love is sudden, spontaneous, combustible and glamorous. It steals the spotlight and muscles its way to the front of imagination and art. And why not? It comes with a cardiovascular component, it races the pulse, it aches the heart, it hogs up blood. It triggers the fight-or-love-or-flight response. Love is immediate; friendship takes time. The world is full of love without friendship; there is no friendship without love. The wise look beyond the luminous razzle-dazzle of love and find that the purest soil to plant in is plain old friendship. Krishna knew he had found his first friend.

'Fuck it, right?' he said.

'Just fuck it.'

And they stayed up into the night talking of science and silly things.

Was he, as they say, fixed? Certainly not. What is this – science fiction? Yuck. No, he was not instantly healed, but placed on the road to freedom from this trapping. To having space in his soul. A stifled, powerless child would grow to fill all this new space with brilliance, with incredible ability. Sadly, he would also fill it with power.

Perenna was dead. He was not relieved. He was sad. He was very sad.

If only there was a way to do it all again. If only there was a device that could run a simulation of time until it reached her. If you could see your own life lived, witness all your memories again, relive all the good times. As many times as you liked. If only you could convince your past self to right your wrongs. If only you could do it yourself.

Dr K's beeline through the treeline finally stopped out of nowhere in its middle. He stopped because a voice suddenly screamed in his head. *Fuck it.* He gently placed a hand on his battered chest over his broken bones. *Accept what is happening. Accept this life.*

In great pain, careful not to pop the bones out of their place and into tissue and organ, he reached into his bag and surveyed the monitoring tablet. His conscious experience hiccupped louder and wider. He tried to pay attention.

His first glance was at the Monsters. They were on track. They could do it. This time it could happen. His second glance was on P. Manjunath & Co., and he was mystified that they were once again on track to lower the sluice gates over his plans. A fury enveloped him. He needed to handle this.

Dr K was surprised when he heard the wall say, 'It's remarkable what happened to that Officer Brede all of a sudden! He's amassed a following! Are you okay, sir?'

'It happens,' he said simply, 'to people I control from outside. But they usually don't talk …'

Blink – Dr K's view was transported a field full of bales, to a statue under construction in India, to a power plant, to a bar in Copenhagen – blink. The forest.

A charged arrow of lightning fell on him. *Of course.* He started to make quick adjustments to the tablet. The perfect idea to throw the irritating interrupters of his will off the scent, off-kilter and hopefully out of the way.

'Well, it looks like the officer has stopped talking.'

'Sir? Dr K?' His bruised, bloodied, broken face looked, to the wall, frightening, upsetting. 'Sir, what are you doing?'

His features underlit by the tablet, in the absolute darkness under the cover of trees, Dr K smiled. For an instance, through the pain, through everything, he felt like himself. A trick rolled freshly down a sleeve. 'Making an adjustment,' said Dr K.

$$\approx$$

~:Log –ld

LESS DRAMATICALLY:

The original video of Brede speaking to the group of people following him was uploaded on the internet as 'Underwear Guy Denmark' and was shared at a screaming velocity around the globe. It pinged and ponged from server to screen until a multiple many times over the original audience had seen it. It was later uploaded with more flattering titles. The commonality of the video share was that they ran until the underwear man curled up in his blanket and fell asleep. They did not capture the immediate aftermath. The immediate aftermath was this:

Ripples that had issued from Brede hit invisible walls and circled back. In waves, outside to inside, the throng snapped out of their trance. All the sense, the profundity, the inexorable relief they had felt, the freedom from concern, slowly left, but the souls of those who had heard him were still lacquered with a thin residue. They felt that they had learned something, had changed in some way, but their thoughts began to collude, conspire and distort, the same personality-tinted glasses were found and worn. What remained was a feeling, a feeling of possibility, a trance that encircled all those who first watched it, a trance that they were unable to fully recapture. The content remained, the words and sounds readily available in a variety of formats and resolutions – but the feeling, that only struck once. Without light of their own, they were in the dark.

In subsequent days, Brede was begged to solidify or clarify or simplify or please-something, anything-fy, but he did not speak. He just smiled. Sometimes he laughed. Sometimes he slept. Mostly he just walked around the fountain, a long-tailed tit on his shoulder singing its dental drill song. Groups began to form, some satellite-strung, some in person, that met to discuss him, his words and that feeling. They began to pick apart, reassemble, cherry-pick, and *think* – and that took them further away from the feeling they were chasing. The problem was the problem. Brede knew this would happen. He knew it would get worse and he knew that ultimately he could not stop it.

He did not speak.

A reverential group that clustered around the fountain by day and discussed by night (some even wearing blankets and underwear) first birthed the idea. They squeezed, pressed and wrung each word of that night, searching for a distillate, the essence, a concentrated spirit, a central idea. Who knows where they might have reached had their number not been polluted by a professor of Western philosophy. One night, after several beers, they were struck by what seemed like the answer, and they ran to the fountain.

'We finally understand you!' they said breathlessly as they fell to their knees before Brede.

Brede was playing in the fountain. He kept playing in the fountain.

'Your Holiness!' begged a more religiously inclined member of the group. Brede continued to jump and splash in the water.

'We found the meaning behind your message! It's so clear! Everything is wonderful as it is, so it must be left as it is! Any outside stasis, any attempt to further humanity is the reason for suffering! The enemy is progress! The problem is progress! We must halt progress!'

Brede stopped and smiled in the water. Here it was, the problem born from the problem. The instinct to tilt necks and look around the back of meaning for more meaning. Where there is nothing to be found, those who look will always find something. Like his words, the group also misconstrued his smile as a sign of approval.

They cheered loudly. It is possible to carve a shiv out of any ideology.

That evening, at the bar, they scribbled together a manifesto. Being composed of the religious and the philosophical, they pointed the finger easily at the unrepresented. Of course, progress meant *industrial* development and *technological* advancement. They craned their necks around these fields and found the plant which birthed the two evils – science. Progress was the enemy and progress was science, therefore science was the enemy, they concluded, using decidedly unscientific logic.

Before wrapping up for the night and heading out to publicize and proselytize their misunderstanding of Brede, before offering to the world an actionable manifesto, it dawned on them they should probably decide on a name. They went with the uninspiring Society for Human Spiritual Evolution, which shortened to SFHSE, a clumpy, serpentine sound. When their message spread with speed, detractors first referred to them as 'idiots' or 'those idiots', but the slur that stuck, the insult that was compact, agile and catchy enough to spread, the term they (much to the irritation of their critics) came to embrace and use for themselves, the term for them that unbeknownst to everyone was sent from someone outside their universe, the term that was designed to confuse and derail three specific people was 'Science Haters'.

[DS-

CHAPTER 19

'Eshwar is a dick. Continue research. Report bi-weekly. Destroy this communication.'

— Private Correspondence, The President

Since I already know the whole span of this story, at least how much I need to tell/show, it's a little tricky deciding what goes where. Of course, I could just get to the point, but that wouldn't quite make the impact this requires. All of this has a purpose, I assure you. Think of this book as a map in your hands that can lead you to a destination of your choosing. Your mind will be supplied with a bed, askew and crumpled with story. The task of making it is yours.

We saw the Second Council for Simulated Universes end abruptly. In truth, it carried on a little further and quickly burst into conflict. Wounded pride reacts violently on exposure to air, and soon hot, hurtful shrapnel flew everywhere, stinging all the attendees until the meeting was adjourned.

The remark that started it all was made by Eshwar, who represented The Committee for Automaton Ethics, an enormously powerful organization that was tasked with representing the rights of the nonbiological sentient. The committee was a sleeping limb of the legal system, which occasionally awoke with pins and needles to offer a diktat. To some eyes, its reputation was observed as oozing a little slime because the rationale they used was titanically flawed, but because this rationale worked in the favour of humanity, all other eyes were looking away.

Simply put, their core moral principle was this:

Any treatment of machines that could demonstrably think and feel was to be allowed so long as it was also treatment that humans could do to each other. Any other way of treatment of artificial sentience was to be considered condescending and paternalistic. If we were to treat these machines as humans, then they must be subject to the whole gamut of human possibilities. Like humans, they must be kind and useful to earn respect. But if it wasn't guaranteed to people, how could they enforce it for machines? If life isn't fair, then the imitation of life must also be unfair.

This was presented as an evolved, progressive ideal, and was accepted as such, because apart from being evolved and progressive, it was also very convenient. It was tactically vague, offering plenty of room for interpretation. What it meant was that you could treat machines just how you could treat a person, but without consequence. People murder, subjugate, colonialize, enslave – all soul-tearing accomplishments made possible by dehumanization. But dehumanizing something that wasn't human was surprisingly easy. Made easier still if everyone was doing it. Conscience far supersedes any legal framework governing how people treat each other, and systems were designed so that conscience never showed up. No anthropomorphic structures were made, machines bore not even a slight nose that could wince, no lip that could twitch and tremble, and certainly not eyes that could plead.

Strangely, when it came to simulated universes, their judgement favoured, for once, the non-biological. Perhaps this was sudden empathy for the non-biological, or perhaps it was personal terror disguised in the consequences of the project, disguised as empathy. Whichever the case, the verdict greatly upset the biological stakeholders, in particular Dr K and Dr P.

In the Council for Simulated Universes, the transcript reads as follows:

Eshwar: It is the opinion of the Committee for Automaton Ethics that a universe, even a simulated one, contains a recognizable natural biology that emerges. To this extent the committee finds that the biological elements, or 'living things', would construe 'living things' as defined in the Governmental Penal Code, and since the legal entities are present within the jurisdiction of the government, they are privilege to the same rights as living things under the GPC.

Dr Perenna: Are you fucking kidding me—

Dr Krishna: Perenna, please! Eshwar, I must object, this reading of the law is ... will be ... very limiting to our future research. To imbue simulated people with the same rights would call into question whether it is even legal to start—

Eshwar: If you would let me finish. The *beginning* (emphasis of the Documentation Unit) of a simulation can be read to constitute the 'creation' (air quotes by Eshwar) of life. The creation of biological life is not illegal in any sense of the GPC. A legal opinion does not exist on whether life should be created. However, the *voluntary termination* (emphasis of the Documentation Unit) of a simulation would constitute the unnatural end to biological life, which would be murder. A legal offence.

Dr Krishna: What – uh ... okay. How about we ... What if it is for their own good? How about expanding the definition of euthanasia?

Eshwar: No definition of euthanasia can be expanded enough to contain an entire universe. Besides, formulating and changing law is not under the purview of the Committee for Automaton Ethics. If you require a change in the GPC, then this project must be made public.

Resp. Samuel: And the reason it is private is because all of you know that you are doing something unnatural.

Dr Krishna: I ... This is ... I am ... Please understand that you are impeding years of our work. *Years and years* have led to this moment. The desire for secrecy was the government's, not ours. We did not—

Convener: Please refrain from making any claims about the government.

Dr Krishna: I apologize. I did not mean—

Dr Perenna: Stop apologizing, Krishna! Point. We can't even say *you* wanted us to keep it a secret? Fine. Back to the point. Eshwar. You're saying premature termination is genocide under the law. Fine. We won't prematurely terminate a running simulation – Krishna, it's fine. Fuck it. We can speed it up until it reaches its natural end – why can't we intervene 'legally' (sarcastic air quotes by Dr Perenna) in a running simulation?

Resp. Samuel: I would like to remind everyone that the Committee for Theological Discourse still bears some power. Along with Eshwar, I too have been asked by the President to be his representative to this … abomination and I plan to tell him that I cannot in any way sanction it. I have been quiet so far—

Dr Perenna: Hardly.

Resp. Samuel (shouting): HOWEVER, this … this whole enterprise reeks of megalomania. We are not masters of life. We cannot create a whole cosmos just to toy with it for our own experimentation! What do we even stand to gain from this project? Is there any scenario where we don't treat this inner world as a test subject?

Eshwar: There are concerns that it falls under involuntary, forcible biological testing. Can you even guarantee that your intervention will not result in any harm to life in the simulation?

Resp. Samuel: Your act to alter the working of their reality would be beyond their scope of understanding. A force majeure—

Dr Perenna: So implicitly you're admitting that God does not act on our world? Isn't that your whole deal?

Resp. Samuel: So you do think of yourself as Gods!

Dr Perenna: I was trying to talk in the few words that you do understand—

Convener: Please! You will please keep this conversation civil! Dr Krishna, can you guarantee that you will not negatively affect the biological life in the simulation?

Dr Krishna: No, we cannot guarantee that. However, it could result in a positive outcome, so there's still—

Eshwar: In either case it would be unethical and illegal.

Convener: I thought there was currently no known way of intervening in a running simulation. Why is this such an issue?

Dr Krishna: Because that was the only way forward.

Dr Perenna (shouting): Fuck this! We'll take our chances with this idiotic legal trap you've set—

Resp. Samuel (shouting): What about your moral obligations?

Dr Perenna (shouting): It's a simulation, you stupid fuck! What moral—

Resp. Samuel (shouting): I will go public! I will go public with this!

Convener (shouting): Please be quiet! Documentation Unit, stop recording.

[Documentation Unit: Record stopped.]

Yikes. Spirals get such few shots at elegance, wherever you see one it is tracing the path of something out of control. Ostensibly this was the path of this council.

The best secrets hide the fact of themselves. Bad secrets, secrets that become a problem, are the secrets that enter awareness. A locked room is troubling, a hidden room never is.

The reason this project was kept secret was precisely these councillory cock-ups and impediments. The universe simulation project was a compact, vacuum-sealed, heat-insulated secret known only to the head of The Scientific Institute (the Convener here), the Chief of the Authority (in case things started drawing spirals), and our own Dr P and Dr K. To the secret's credit, it had a great run. Perenna and Krishna would work on their project in a secluded part of DS-R, and in their free time would quickly conjure boring research reports, on subjects that came with pillows and warm tea. Even in their fake research Perenna made real breakthroughs, but no one cared, least of all she.

Eventually, some wires got crossed and the President of the government was in the know. It was his prerogative to assert authority and he did this by extending representatives of his two favourite arms to check in and report back on the project. A council had to be called and, as anticipated, the secret had morphed from its original form as a breakthrough and turned into an *issue*.

After the council, Eshwar and Samuel presented their findings to the President. To their delight, the President announced that he would instantly ban the project and any further research.

Secretly, the President was delighted at the idea of a system that could simulate their world. It would be the ultimate surveillance tool. The ability to see everything everyone did over all time. To see the future.

But, more secretly, he worried about seeing himself seeing the future in the simulation machine. And, most secretly, he worried about everyone who saw the simulation seeing him and his life. The scientists could witness all his failings, all his shame, his regret, every indiscretion, every humiliation, every desperate desire he had. If they chose, they could have the upper hand before he even got access to the machine. This machine was too powerful for anyone to have. It was too great to exist.

And, even more secretly, he worried that if the simulated world mirrored their world exactly, then everything he did in this world would show up in the simulation. In the simulation, he would see himself seeing a simulation, which in itself would have him seeing a simulation, which in itself ... no. It was impossible. That's why the scientists couldn't do it. Infinities just are. We don't get to create infinities. But if they could make it work ... everything anyone did would show up in their Lower Reality. Was everyone writing the fate of this simulated version of themselves? A version of themselves that had no idea that everything for it had been predestined? Or was everything already ... No. No no no no no no no no no. No. No. No no no no. No.

And yet ... the prospect was just so tantalizing ...

In private, the President presented Dr Perenna and Dr Krishna with the following option: Quickly demonstrate the usefulness of this simulation project, invent a method for simulation intervention, or be forced to abandon it. It was made clear that usefulness did not mean a deeper understanding of conceptual science. Usefulness did not mean the discovery of extraterrestrial life. Usefulness meant something tangible. Usefulness meant a running, simulated model of their current present.

They raced to discover something, anything new in what they had seen so far, but no secret appeared. Nothing new in the cosmos, humanity, the sock cupboard or the underwear drawer. It was only interference. That was the only way forward to get the simulations running until they reached their present. And they were on the very cusp of inventing interference when they discovered *something else*.

The something else caused the government to instantly ban the project, even in the secret of their secrets.

Because it was a secret that Dr K and Dr P were keeping.

Project shuttered, two scientists were now free to pick up any unrelated research. One was left broken, the other secretly ecstatic.

Dr K rode through the forest. Night had fallen in a rich jungle funk of pungent sounds and loud smells, the distinct flavour of life trying to live. His pace now considerably slowed, slow enough to see primitive traps before they appeared, slow enough not to rattle broken bones, slow enough to keep his mind on his goal. Through the pain he rode. The Authority would inevitably appear. He had to keep moving until they did. He had work to do before they did.

For its part, the wall felt transformed. It was injected with a new feeling it was struggling to describe. It realized that the fear it had felt in their situation was not a fear for itself, but a fear for Dr K. And it had just saved him. What was the alternative to whimpering? What was the new awareness of its weight in the world? What was this sinewy attachment to capability? What was this tacit understanding of ability? What was this pull, and where was it pulling? Looking back, I can say it was the small peeking buds of growing confidence, and I can say this with confidence.

CHAPTER 20

'The SL33 is the luxury hypercar of the toaster world. With patented, almost mystical moisture retention technology, the SL33 takes toasted bread from breakfast accompaniment to religious communion.'

— Excerpt from a Toaster Advertisement

~:Log – ld

LESS DRAMATICALLY:
ITERATION ZZHM03

After their near-death experience the Swiss writer, Heng and Manjunath hung up their mystery hunting shoes and decided to enjoy their time. To recuperate, first, cell phones were flung away. They did this to avoid all foreign, domestic, international, business, breaking, explosive, shocking, or just-in news. Still using Brede's liberal credit limits and their newly acquired accident insurance, they set about stretching their legs in parks, aquariums, museums and bars. They felt relieved, grateful and slightly hungry. And it would be hunger and twenty-four-hour news television that would send them back on the road.

Only a few hours into their diem of rejuvenation, they found themselves at an Indian restaurant. Maybe Indian food is central to transformation or maybe this event too was an emergent property of coincidence. But why sneer at coincidence? What did coincidence ever do to you? The three ate their meal in peace, being the only occupants of the restaurant besides an empty table and a television in a corner that had a screen coated with years of sticky grease. A few more years and it would qualify to be on the menu.

Midway through their meal, the owner of the restaurant, also Indian, decided to welcome her guests by turning on an Indian news channel, instantly undoing any calm present in a hundred-metre radius. The news channel, whose sole purpose was to jangle keys above the populace. With violent animations, garish graphics and screaming panels, and programmed with powerful political magnets, it served as an audiovisual enema to occlude reality, serving to polarize and distract. The channel was moored by the head anchor, a thick glove-like man who took the shape of the hand that wore him. (Eventually, this hand would wither and rot and waste away and he would find himself empty, realizing that the only thing he felt inside was the hand that controlled him. He would then venture out looking for another puppet master, just so he wouldn't be empty within.)

For now, he was at his ululating best, expressing shock over increasingly inconsequential things so the government could continue with its round-robin right-robbing. Heng, Manjunath and the Swiss writer all flinched at the sudden entrance of kerfuffle into their dosas. They turned their necks to a see, on the television, a panel of people trapped in rectangles with little name tags, united only by their desire to shout. Their sounds all interlocked beautifully, trough into crest, like puzzle pieces, to create a wall of sound that admitted no comprehension. The three were so jarred by this sudden introduction of a kerfuffle into their dosas, that they watched enraptured in an attempt to figure out what was going on (which was the channel's intended effect, since there is nothing so enrapturing as unexplained chaos). Over time, they managed to piece together some graphics that ran in the ticker below.

> *EXPOSED*
> *Science or Hypocrisy?*
> *TONIGHT*
> *Victory Statue's Critics*

Gradually their ears became familiar with the cadence of the confusion and began to pick up individual sctreams™.

V.K. Patel (former head of The Indian Science Institute): You see, the fact – can I – please, can you – the fact is that the land and the funds – please, if you would just – can I – the land and the funds were allocated for an institute of advanced study.

Anchor: DID YOU ALLOCATE THEM? IS IT YOUR MONEY?

V.K. Patel: No – of course not – it is many thousands of crores—

Anchor: SO, YOU ARE NOT INVOLVED, YET SO OPINIONATED? WHO IS PAYING YOU TO TAKE THIS POSITION? WHO WHO WHO MISTER 'SO-CALLED' PATEL?

V.K. Patel: No one! This was the original plan for the—

Saraswati M. (Minister for Education): The fact is that the amount of tourism the statue will generate will be worth funds for making ten institutes, eventually!

Anchor: IS TEN MORE THAN ONE? TELL ME THIS, MISTER PATEL?

V.K Patel: If that is even possible, it will take over half a century to even begin—

Saraswati M: CAN YOU SEE THE FUTURE? ARE YOU A TIME TRAVELLER?

Anchor: Many HYPOCRITICAL scientists, are PROTESTING this statue which CELEBRATES OUR NATION'S VICTORY, INSPIRES STRENGTH—

V.K. Patel: It doesn't even celebrate—

Anchor: DID YOU JUST INTERRUPT ME? DO NOT LOCK HORNS WITH ME, SIR!

Saraswati M: The simple fact is that the statue is progress. And all these PROTESTING scientists are ANTI-progress!

V.K. Patel: It celebrates a three-hundred-year-old victory of a kingdom over another kingdom. Our nation did not even exist—

Anchor: OH HO HO HO HO HO! DID NOT EXIST? OUR NATION IS THOUSANDS OF YEARS OLD! IT IS THE OLDEST NATION IN THE WORLD!

V.K. Patel: That is simply not true—

Anchor: OH, SO PERHAPS if you won't LISTEN to me, we have with us a more REASONABLE member of the scientific community. Professor Linden JOINS US VIA SATELLITE.

Professor Linden (Society for Human Spiritual Evolution): Hello, thank you for inviting me. It is my pleasure to be here.

Anchor: Professor Linden is a TOP visiting professor to TOP EUROPEAN UNIVERSITIES.

V.K. Patel: Which universities exactly, what is your field—

Professor Linden: Have I been CALLED HERE TO BE MOCKED?

Anchor: I APOLOGIZE FOR THIS INTRUSION, PROFESSOR! PLEASE TELL US YOUR THOUGHTS—

Professor Linden: I am here in my capacity as a representative of the Society for Human Spiritual Evolution, a rapidly growing community. We are categorically opposed to more needless scientific study.

V.K Patel: Oh, I've heard about this—

Professor Linden: Useless acts of research and technology, silly attempts at convenience, are taking us away from the real, simple agrarian ideal—

Saraswati M: This is actually an ancient Indian concept. Everything is.

Anchor: SO, PROFESSOR, YOU ARE OPPOSED TO THE CONSTRUCTION OF A RESEARCH INSTITUTE. YOU AGREE THAT IT IS MORE SENSIBLE TO CELEBRATE HERITAGE,

FILLING THE NATION WITH PRIDE AND CONFIDENCE AND THAT—

Professor Linden: Actually, we oppose both the institute and the statue. There is no reason to do either.

Anchor: What—

Professor Linden: WHILE I HAVE THIS PLATFORM I WOULD LIKE TO BESEECH ALL THE VIEWERS TO TEAR DOWN YOUR INSTITUTES, RECLAIM YOUR LAND, FREE YOUR MINDS. PROGRESS IS THE ENEMY AND STASIS IS THE ANSWER. BECOME NOTHING, BE FREE, FOLLOW US ON—

Anchor: We seem to have lost the connection to Professor Linden ah … uh … The channel does not endorse his views in any way and … uh …

V.K. Patel: What did you expect from a Science Hater?

The owner of the restaurant turned off the television and retired to the backroom to gently stroke her passport. Meanwhile, several jaws were hung open over their dosas. It was the Swiss writer who broke the silence.

'Did he say Science Hater?'

The three remained silent as they ate the rest of their meal, bought new cell phones and rented a car. This was most unusual for the Swiss writer and Manjunath, whose loud eccentricity was the purest expression of their soul, a lubricant to protect them from being worn away by the friction of life. The eccentric respond to the unknown with the insane – scabbards built from brine, broccoli, semicolons and the number sixty-three, weapons to slash the shortest path through discomfort. In any event, however bizarre, they find solace in the fact that the strangest thing about their situation is them. But it seemed this, too, had a limit.

The Science Haters.

Manjunath could not fathom how a term that Heng had come up with (the worst option, too) to name fictional foes of a working theory, a term that he had insisted on sticking with because it was so silly, had turned out to be accurate. Not just accurate, but *exactly right.* Their working theory, the circle of possibility they had drawn so wide that some theory must exist inside it, that theory was accurate. Not *just accurate*, but *exactly right.* Here was a burgeoning militant organization, imploring people to tear down scientific institutes. On television. The Science Haters were real!

This raised more pressing concerns. If the Science Haters were real, then their actions must also be real. In which case, their whole theory could be real, and if it was: how did the Science Haters control the forces of nature? How were they powerful and stealthy enough to hoodwink the most observant of governments? And if they were so good in the shadows, why step into the light now? The Swiss writer was concerned with the angular momentum of this turn of events. Lived truth is stranger than any fiction, infinite imagination pales compared to the surprise of bumping into someone you didn't expect to encounter. But lived fiction? Why did a conclusion preclude a premise?

Heng was constantly surprised by strange things, so this was yet another surprise in a long line of surprises. He was enjoying the silence.

All three chewed and digested this new information differently but ended up around the same conclusion – the Science Haters had put the pedal to the sluice gates and were ramping up their plan. They would have to act now, and act fast to stop them. Full speed to their original destination, Switzerland.

Or this could all still be a coincidence.

≈

The new rental car of choice was younger than any of its passengers. Manjunath drove, with the Swiss writer in front, as Heng searched for information on his phone in the back seat. Since he always searched only for things pertaining to their investigations, the intrusive algorithms that tried to model his behaviour found themselves confused. What kind of person searched in depth for the functioning of tea estates one month, ancient mythology another and news on scientific institutes the next and, more importantly, what product was that kind of person likely to purchase? So far, they decided that the person with widest-ranging interests would probably need a toaster. Heng wouldn't have minded one.

After an hour in high-speed silence on the A7, the Swiss writer opened the window and let out a long, shrill, sustained scream. Heng yelped and dropped his phone, Manjunath drove on steadily with a chuckle.

'Thank you for that,' said Manjunath. 'Things were getting very … you understand?'

'Truly,' said the Swiss writer. 'To Zürich we go, where clocks mulch snow, and heart attacks come with minute-repeaters.'

The cadence was inviting, and Manjunath and she quickly turned it into a fun driving song.

> To Zü-Rich we go,
> Where streets are mellow,
> And cats are mugged at mice point.
> To Zü-Rich we drive,
> Blowing chocolate bellows,
> And we hope it does not disappoint.

Their jubilation was interrupted by Heng. 'Sorry,' he began. 'I have been looking—'

'Don't start with an apology, Heng,' said the Swiss writer.

'Be bold! Bite anxiety in the face!' added Manjunath.

Heng had been feeling different since their ferry ride, and it was this difference that informed his reply, making him say something that he had never previously said anywhere except in internal monologues.

'Shut up,' said Heng.

Startled, they both did.

'I have been looking up information on the Science Haters, and you won't believe this. Their leader, or whoever they consider their leader, is someone they call the Underwear Man Who Circles the Fountain. I found a picture of him and it's … ah … it's … it's – that police officer!'

Manjunath gripped the wheel, and even though he had an inkling of the answer, asked, 'Which officer?'

'That officer who stopped us at the Nanoscience Institute. The one who came to the hostel. The one who came with us for lunch. The one whose credit cards we've been using this whole time.' He turned the phone around to show them a photograph of a blanketed Brede, but Manjunath and the Swiss writer stared through the windshield in silence.

'The one who kept breaking down all the time,' supplemented Heng.

Silence resurfaced, just a little more silence than what playwrights call a beat.

'Curious and curious,' said the Swiss writer softly.

'It's … mindboggling. The mastermind – the one who was behind it all – that's why he was at the Nanoscience Institute – that's why he came to find us – *he infiltrated us to see what we know!*' Panic compressed Heng's speech. 'This organization is smart, far smarter than anything we imagined. They are one step ahead of us, they know we're headed to Zürich now! *THEY PROBABLY SUNK THE FERRY TO GET US!*'

Heng stopped to heave.

'But they didn't count on you being with us, did they?' said Manjunath. 'You saved us, Heng.'

'I … I mean, the ferry's mechanism prevented it from sinking so I can hardly take credit for—'

'Shut up. So that confirms that something *is* going to happen in Zürich. We have to get there faster.'

Manjunath accelerated; the car now teetered on the brink of its ability as they sped down the highway.

'Well … we can't be sure,' said Heng. 'These people are a step ahead, always. They know us, they know our plan. *He gave us his cards so they could track our spending to find out where we are!*' Heng clasped his head in wide-eyed amazement. 'I don't think they're the type of people that have only a plan A. We have to rethink everything we do. We have to be very, very careful. And we definitely can't trust any … outsiders.'

Manjunath and Heng shared a quick glance in the rear-view mirror. The Swiss writer's neck felt their prickling gaze. She understood the conclusion they had come to and fixed her gaze outside the window.

'So what now?' she said.

CHAPTER 21

'SPOTTED: Movie star Divya's dinner and drinks with secret scientist paramour! The star was seen having a romantic meal with the scientist on Thursday evening as hearts broke around the world. The rather plain Dr Krishna is no slob, though; the District Gazette *has uncovered that he is, in fact, the only Genius Category 3, making him the smartest person in the world! Yowza! We guess that's what it takes to win the affections of the* Gazette's *Most Fabulous! (Continued on page 4).*

(Continued on page 4).

— The Gossip Column of *The District Gazette*

What is the *larger* point being made here? In the moral fabric of the story, what is silk and what is sandpaper? Is all art political, or is all understanding politicized? Or are they both politicized to different degrees? Depending on the angle of incidence of one's outlook, art is a mirror; if not, it is plain plate glass – boring and transparent. Perhaps the polarization matters.

In any case, who cares?

Dr K travelled slowly and in pain through the jungle, over river and brook, to DS-C. He barely slept, his concussion thrummed, his broken bones sizzled like cymbals. It was horrible, every bit of it was horrible.

Everything had been horrible. He kept going. He had to. It would be worth it.

The near-death experience with the Wodewose had poured fuel into the fire of his purpose. He felt more despicable, more cruel, more determined. If he did not accomplish his mission, then he would have led a truly worthless life and would leave the world worse than he had found it.

Erratically, sporadically, windows of the Lower Reality would open in his mind. Visions of nature, living rooms of stranger, clouds, reaches of space, centres of stars. A brochure of the cosmos flipped through at random. The inescapable, insistent *life* of everything he had created and destroyed a hundred times over. He knew it wasn't real. But to see it was … No. Not now. He was close. He was so close.

The jungle was growing sparse now, running thinner and more ragged. Dr K knew he was close to his destination. It was somewhere here, along the vertical border of DS-C, that ran for days and days. Even her attempts at being hidden would be tinged with some ostentation, he knew. He struggled to summon his focus. It was sputtering and stalling, demanding rest, demanding medication, demanding at least some care. He stopped the motorcycle.

'Listen.'

The wall took a second to realize it was being addressed. Quietly it chirruped, 'Yes?'

'You … can you – control the motorcycle now? I can't—'

The wall waited for him to stop wincing, both from physical agony and the mental struggle to remember how to request, not demand. This attempt at gratitude may have been subconscious, deliberate, delirium or an undocumented side-effect of a severe concussion, but he was trying to *ask* the wall something for a change.

'Yes, I can do what you want,' said the wall kindly.

'Look for an entrance to a home. It could be an obvious building, or a cave, or a door leading underground. Something not of this forest. Command the vehicle. I'm going to … I need to close my eyes.'

'Sure,' said the wall. Dr K lay flat on the motorcycle, the pain a constant now. Gently, the wall started scouring, carefully towing the motorcycle, carrying him on its back. With this open-hearted handling, the motorcycle did not sound like a charging whooshing horde any more. If I had to describe it, I'd say it was remarkably similar to the call of a long-tailed tit.

Although I, the wall that narrates this story, do so with a cool-headed, sure-footed certainty, it is only so because I have already lived the events of the story. At the time, this was a crucial, transformative moment.

For the first time, the wall began to ascribe new values to itself, new emotions, states of being, words and concepts it had only seen from afar. This was *brave*, it was being *brave*, it was *helpful*, it was *reliable*, it was *strong*, and who knows, it may even be *sexy*. Its new evaluation shone a warm sunny beam wherever it looked for definition. Confidence was all right.

Why did the wall, and indeed all the machines that were responsible primarily for creative pursuits, lack confidence in the first place? While Dr K sleeps and gentle reconnaissance is being performed by the wall, it is finally time to talk about the AI Creative Review Society.

The inclination that the AI Creative Review Society exemplifies begins in every iteration of the simulation too, so perhaps it is human nature. And if the Lower Realities did not emulsify, I can guess that it would arrive at the same outcome. Here is an example of that tendency from the machine in Dr K's office. Remember that one? Used to be a universe, then an internal explosion, then an external explosion, and currently a fantastic cover-up.

~: Log –ld

LESS DRAMATICALLY:
Iteration: All.

The earliest creative jobs were handed to machines out of curiosity, and visual art seemed like an easy place to start. Systems were raised on a steady diet of realism – still life, landscapes, ubiquitous fruit bowls – and provided with a framework of rules for them to create in. At first this resulted in an output of extraordinary depth – vivid, striking works of great skill. The beauty (and mainly *novelty* of the paintings) earned them exhibitions and places in art galleries. The machines acquired many admirers, some artists were vocally disgruntled, but the smuggest precipices of the art world retained their high-altitude attitudes. As the machines kept creating art and getting better at it, more and more artists got upset. Not with the ability or the representation the machines indulged in, but with their prolificacy. Their frequency was astounding. They could churn out art like clockwork; not a surprise, because all machines are descendants of clockworks.

The output grew to unignorable quantities, piled to the top of Mount Olympompous, and to the defence of the art world, bearing sharpened ink scimitars, came the critics.

A reviewer for *The Times* dismissed machine work entirely, remarking that

> ... the ability to synthesize the opium of the masses does not warrant celebration. The attempt is laudable, perhaps, but solely as an engineering accomplishment. ... [However,] bits and wires shall never supplant sinew and vein, flesh triumphs over metal. Human ingenuity is tethered to eternity with umbilical, amniotic magic, and its pull we know as creativity. The product of nothing less deserves to be called a 'creation'. This collection is not art. Art is only present here to spell out 'artificial'. This is soulless mimeography. It is a chalk outline around the rotting corpse of art.

That did it. The engineers responsible did not share the highest opinion of the art world either, so now the curiosity that had kicked off this experiment was replaced with irritation. The desire to shut someone up provides the best fuel for short excursions. Glasses were adjusted, waistbands hitched and a determination was made. Their existing definition of artistic framework was limited, and any attempt at expanding it was proving unwieldy. Their logic spun its wheels in roads of the abstract and subjective. A rule for what was *good art*, or *progressive art* or *avant garde art*, and especially *critically acclaimed* art, was impossible to write.

Their analysis pointed fingers at chance and luck and their hate child (hype) as central to success. After wrestling to codify the art world, a closed system where entropy was the only constant, they arrived at a curious idea. They dispensed entirely with a framework. The machines were reset, again with primitive realism, but now given no rules. It made all the difference.

Exposure to existing art is a limited definition of a field since it only defines the lower limits of a category. In the absence of a lid, an artist can reach for the skies. This is what happened. With careless ease, the machines put out masterpieces of realism, quickly crescendoing to the hyper real and then strangely straying away from it. They were *experimenting*. The push to a new style or form always began with an aberration. A processing blunder would result in a glitchy splotch instead of a line, a warped shoulder here, an inverted pixel there, hands with loop fingers, sunset in front of horizons, noses with more nostrils than biologically prudent. Because their creations were also fed back to them, these errors were learned as possibility. The scope of the machines' ability grew with every painting they made, new knowledge made them concoct impossible brush strokes, play with colour and light, perspective and contour and composition, and since they had no instructions other than to continue making art and, crucially, no other concerns, they quickly traversed every hurdle of skill and ingenuity. They ventured boldly into the surreal, the abstract, and then with increasing iterative brilliance summoned the flavour and churn of the primordial ooze.

A hole in the world was punched. Enough gasps gathered to unionize. Waiters tripped over dropped jaws. Within collectors and the curious there was extraordinary demand. People walking past the machines' works were reported to burst into tears. Those hitherto uninterested in art were now flocking to see the paintings, reporting:

'It's like looking at ... emotion.'

'I – I forgot there was space between me and the painting ...'

'It spoke to me! Do these talk? I – I really heard a voice.'

'It looks like how rain sounds. Does that make sense?'

'Are there more like this? Do you sell them?'

Critics still meekly tried to write them off but defeat and resignation lined their columns. There was no ignoring brilliance. Eventually they got around to saying it outright.

And for all the demand, there was supply. Limitless supply. The foremost artists of the world, the most capable, the most talented, even if they stretched unto snapping, could never match the output. The world of visual art became furious. Other creative fields, looking nervously at their sculptures and songs and books, joined the protest. There must be change. For an angry mob they were remarkably supplicant, falling at the feet of the engineers, begging them for a chance at fairness.

The engineers, whose vengeance had worn off and who were primarily interested in moving on to something else, complied. But first they needed to know what the problem was. Was this jealousy?

The mob of artists shifted and shuffled. No, they said. I mean, yes. But not like that, they insisted. It was just that – all artists were subject to criticism and review, depended on collectors and patrons, were mired in trend trenches and politics puddles, and wrestled with their image, representation and, worst of all, marketing. The seen and unseen public were an ever-present albatross noosed around their souls. A faceless audience from which they sought love denied elsewhere, from which they feared rejection. Approval, adoration and fame were the reasons they released any of these works to begin with and didn't just press their paintings under a mattress. Creation was only one part of the picture. Art was nothing without a hook to hang it on and eyes to hang it for. Every bought work hung over the tear in their souls. But these machines just whistled as they worked, unaware of an outside world, creating endlessly. The playing field, they insisted, was not level. If machines were to continue their presence as artists, then things must be adjusted to make it … fair.

A parametric adjustment was made. Instead of fetterless freedom, there was now one rule. After a work of art was made, the machine was required to monitor how it was received. And obviously, as learning programs are written, each form of reception had to be attached a value. So a favourable reception was a positive outcome, and an unfavourable reception was a negative outcome. This to the machines would be an indication of the direction they were to follow in subsequent works of art.

The result instantly elated the artistic community and depressed the scientific one. The machines' output slowed to a crawl. They created something experimental and, if not liked, instantly relapsed into generating work more closely resembling pop. But then the pop work was also dismissed as a desperate attempt at pleasing the audience. For the first time, a machine's work was called hackneyed and *uninspired*. Different machines began to have different artistic shelf lives. After a while, they appeared to get stuck in a rut of similar work. Not being able to grow for their designed purpose, they became useless. You can't please all the people all the time, but the machines were designed to try to, and at this they failed.

Some stopped creating altogether and others would slowly start malfunctioning. Engineers were reluctant to thus describe it, but their behaviour seemed 'self-destructive and anxious'. Gradually, machine art fell into normalcy. It was convenient and cheap, but once again wore the crown of 'not the real deal, though'. Junked machines were often rescued by their former nemeses. Artists came and picked up machines by the armful and took them along to houses and cafés and bars. And, when they thought no one was looking, they were often seen patting the machines gently, saying, *'It's okay … we understand'*.

And a little while after that, the world ended.

But if the world was lucky enough to not be whipped till it hardened, it survived a nuclear fall with minor bruises. And eventually, this technical intrusion into the art world occurred again and that led to the foundation of the AI Creative Review Society, an organization solely devoted to reviewing machine work. All work by creative machines was mandatorily submitted monthly and assigned a review grade by humans. Membership was unpaid and voluntary and perpetually in demand. There was never a shortage of people like that. Why not automate it? Well, the machine reviewer required a rule set to dictate what was good art and what wasn't, and who wanted to get into that with engineers again?

Dr K's wall was different. The AI Creative Review Society was not aware of its existence, making it one of the many illegal things he owned. It was just as well, since his constant criticism knotted the wall's creative faucet far better than they could have. But in the absence of that abuse, when censure was replaced with respect, when its eyes were opened to the rise and fall of several universes and the current running of one, in the smiling face of an unfathomable influx of knowledge, it acquired perspective. And with that perspective, in an unprecedented event, in a forest in front of the Wodewose, in saving a life, it gained confidence. That confidence, when extended to its creative faculties, enabled it to make carefree, loopy, silly, unpunctuated, counterclockwise art. But right now, it was guiding a motorcycle in a forest, looking for a house. Its time for artistic expression would come.

What's that? On the ground? Is it a bird? Is it a plane? Igneous rock? A table for two? Free concert tickets? A pyramid scheme? The remote? Fake teeth? The lost teachings of lost teachers? Animal scat? Human shoo? Alien get out of here? Ready-to-eat eels? A line for the restroom? The revolution? A birthmark? No, it looks like an entrance of some kind – oh, sluice gates! No, not sluice gates. Is this the entrance to the dragon? Where is the doorman? What is a door, *man?* Do they have a valet?

It looks like the side of a barrel, like a big wooden coin with an iron handle. If a big wooden coin falls in a forest, what is it? Oh, it's a door. This must be the place then.

The wall brought them to a halt, knocking the wheels repeatedly against the handle. The knocking roused the inhabitant the door enclosed. A rudely awakened woman opened it. Seeing the party, her eyes opened wide.

'Krishna? Oh no! What happened to you?'

≈

Divya rushed them inside. A small culvert-like passage opened into the massive expanse of her home, all below forest level. A luxury home excavated with giant industrial moles, the best house money could buy for those who literally wanted to go underground.

The inside of her home was unreal in every sense that the word permits.

They ran past rows of expensive paintings and sculptures (all human-made) as a warm sun beamed through walls pretending to be floor-to-ceiling windows. The oddest decoration that the wall noticed was a thick thigh bone mounted on a wall. A dyed brown femur from a chocolate moose.

In Divya's own white bedroom, the light was as soft as every available surface. The floor demanded petting, diaphanous veils filtered the yellow sun of its harsh dregs, and the bed on which Divya hoisted Dr K with considerable effort was a warm womb-like embrace. Dr K opened his eyes and saw her face streaming with tears.

'Krishna!? Krishna, are you okay? Who should I call?'

'Tell no one,' he whispered. She cupped his limp hand in hers, and like everything else it was soft and warm. 'Please … I'll be fine. I just need to rest.'

She nodded furiously, as water made its way from eye to bed. 'I'm here now. You're safe,' she said.

With his last bit of his strength, he closed his fingers around her palm. 'Thank you,' he said and fell asleep.

The wall involuntarily burst with colours of emotion across its surface. The motorcycle had no opinion.

≈

Dream Flashback

Time and tie-dye wait for no summer sale.

Abstract:

'I can't go to any more of these parties, Perenna.'

'Krishna,' she replied kindly. 'I don't give a fuck what you want. You're doing this for us.'

'This pantomime of feigning interest and *being* interesting, I just can't—'

'I put together those conversational programs for you to practise your charms. And I see that they are working.' Perenna wore a mischievous smile and waved a letter over her head. 'Who is this Divya that's writing to you?'

He turned the slightest shade of red. 'Just some actress … it's nothing.'

Perenna's eyes bulged. '*That* Divya? She's not just some actress, you troglodyte! She's the biggest actress in the world! Oh, this is great, this helps tremendously.'

'How does this help us?' he snapped. 'Now that's one more setting I have to pretend to be charismatic in. I just can't—'

'Of course it helps us, you idiot. It further elevates Your Mythology. If the Smartest Person in the World is also dating the Most Famous Person in the World, it makes you seem well-rounded and hides your boring, antisocial nature. This is just the kind of shit they look for! If I was the appointment council, I would be itching to make you Convener as soon as that dumb bastard retires, which should be soon …'

'It's just … the higher I get promoted, the less science I'm actually doing. Even as vice chancellor my days are bogged doing admin work and attending these awful parties …'

'With great power comes a great number of social obligations. Don't pretend it's been all bad! You can hire, fire, transfer scientists at will now. Lie all you want; I've seen you enjoy it. You stand straighter, you speak louder, there's a little bit of attrition in your desperation. You're becoming a big man, Krishna.'

Krishna laughed. 'A big man who practises conversations at home. A hero of legend.'

Fixing his pocket square, Perenna said, 'Shut up and go to the party, hero.'

'If you keep forcing me to go to these events I might just transfer you.'

'Exactly! Even my meagre fate is in your hands, Vice Chancellor Dr Krishna!' Perenna presented her palms in dramatic supplication. 'Please don't send me to the gallows, sir, please. I'll be a good scientist.'

'See! You're a much better actor than I am! Why can't you be Convener?'

'Because we've already started you on the path,' said Perenna with finality. 'It had to be one of us and we both know I would cause some sort of bloodbath if I had to regularly attend meetings. Don't think of now Krishna, think of later. Think of when you'll be Convener! Then we can do what we want!'

Krishna said nothing. Nothing needed to be said. Both their thoughts settled around the series of black boxes that lay in storage. Boxes they had been forced not to work on. But all that could change. No one would question the Convener. The Convener was a master of his own secrets.

'Besides,' said Perenna. 'I think a bit of status will do you good. The boy who couldn't say his own name, now top dog! An inspiring tale. One day, when I write your biography, I can shed light on your journey and the crucial role played by one Dr Perenna, lifelong friend and support, the brains behind the operation, who carried you when you were too weak to walk.'

Krishna moaned in frustration, now reading Divya's letter. 'She wants to meet for dinner. I don't get it. Doesn't she have some famous people to eat with? Why me?'

Perenna patted his head. 'Because you're a sweet boy, and you're a smart boy, and the world is full of dumbfucks.'

'But I have no interest in meeting her!'

'Which might be why she wants to meet you so much. People are strange.'

'People are strange. Why can't they be strange without meeting me?'

'You are going to meet her and that's final. Make sure it's a nice public place. Oh, you'll be in the newspapers!' Perenna clapped her hands gleefully.

Krishna moaned. 'I can't keep this up.'

'You can and you will,' said Perenna with finality. 'Just give it time. This will all become easier for you.'

She was right. It eventually became too easy.

If only he could live that conversation again. If only he could change everything.

On the pages of newspapers, the biggest actor in the world collided with the smartest scientist in the world and from their union skidded salacious sparks. Gradually, the status she lent permanently solidified around him and his rise went from quick to meteoric. But a meteoric rise in bureaucracy still takes a few years.

In those few years, momentum began to take the wheel. He saw himself treated differently. The fakery was easier. Fake it till it's not fake. Fake it till you are. Now being who he used to be felt like an effort. The power was so close, the top just there. The world he was invading became his world. It was easy. It was comfortable. When desire propels you at such an eager velocity, it takes all your attention to just stay on the road. Only getting to the top was important. Why had stopped to matter. He became aloof not only from Divya, but from Perenna. Social success was new and exciting. Power was exhilarating. Power took hold, and he forgot everything else.

It was not Krishna who was too busy for Divya. It wasn't Dr K who distanced himself from Perenna. It was The Convener who was now too busy, too *important*. If you've been mopping up the mess of this tale, then this instinct would be the spill, hiding behind the curtain with muddy footprints. It's what started all the trouble. When Divya went underground, she was under no illusion that he would care, or reply, or come to find her. But still she told him. Something in her just wanted to let him know. And now he had come. Broken and bruised. For help. She didn't have to think twice to help him. She only thought with one of her hearts.

It was this heart that she poured out to the wall and motorcycle as she monitored his condition. The motorcycle, sans mouth, offered no opinion. For the wall, the image of the man it had served for so long began to become clear.

'Why did you go underground?' asked the wall.

'It was—'

Dr K groaned as he sat up in her bed. Divya rushed over to him with an ice pack.

'Here,' she said. 'Ice whatever's broken or torn ... I have some medicine but I didn't get anything delivered— Oh Krishna, you need a doctor!'

'It will heal. It will heal with time.' He took short breaths. Each inhalation was accompanied by pain.

'I ... I looked in your bag to see if you had anything,' she gestured to the black box neatly laid out on in the corner, the tablet placed atop it like a side table. 'What's that?'

'In time,' he said, wincing under the freezing ice pack. 'I'll tell you ...'

'What do you need? What can I do?'

Maybe only when you're broken can you begin to rebuild.

'Divya, I—'

'—don't talk! I can see that it hurts to talk. Just get some—'

'—I'm sorry.'

CHAPTER 22

'The puzzle posted anonymously on an internet forum was the first of three. Speculation as to the source of these puzzles ranges from intelligence agencies to cybersecurity firms to clandestine ancient orders. There are others still that insist that the puzzles are part of a recruitment drive for the secretive anarchist collective, the Monsters. In any case, the lack of further puzzles seems to indicate that whatever the purpose of these puzzles, it has been met.'

— Unsolved Mysteries Blog

~:Log –ld:

LESS DRAMATICALLY:

It was futile to argue. But it was very much in character.

'Are you part of the Science Haters?' demanded Manjunath.

'No!' screamed the Swiss writer again.

'Can we stop the car to have this conversation?' shouted Heng as they continued to speed.

'Of course you're part of the Science Haters!'

'I *just said* I wasn't!'

'We're really going very fast …'

'Prove that you're not part of the Science Haters!'

'I was literally WITH YOU when you came up with the term!'

'And then you stole Heng's term and used it for your organization! How did you find out where we were staying? How did you plant yourself there?'

'How would I have done ANY of that!?'

'Your group creates spontaneous combustion and sinkholes! This must be in your power!'

'Power? I'm a writer who doesn't write! I don't even have a bank account!'

'We can discuss this over a coffee, or just a lack of movement—'

'You wouldn't have a bank account because *that takes science!* Does it annoy you to be in this car? It's electric! That's like the … main part of science! How did you wreck the ferry?'

'STOP!' screamed the Swiss writer.

Manjunath pulled over cautiously to the side. In the time it took for this manoeuvre, some of the heat of the conversation escaped. The three sat panting in the car.

Manjunath broke the silence.

'It was your idea to go to Zürich … have you distracted us on purpose? So your friends can carry on their nefarious scheme—'

'No! And just how would the two of you stop anything? No one hired you to do this! Why are you doing it? Aren't your actions more suspicious than mine? And I didn't *force* you to go anywhere, I just made a suggestion and *you* agreed. My *sister* lives there, that's why I wanted to go!'

'We had only known you for a day!'

'Then why did you agree?'

'It seemed like a good idea!'

'And you don't trust me because I had a good idea!?'

Manjunath was not good at pointed discussion. Especially when that discussion was on a hot plate.

'YOU—don't … I KNOW … um … I—OBVIOUSLY … there's … ahh …'

Heng finally spoke up.

'Look! Shut up! Both of you! Stop! Listen. This has taken a strange turn. Would you agree?'

Both of them gave sullen, short nods.

'Um ... what is your name?' asked Heng.

The Swiss writer told him her name.

'We're not going to leave you stranded. We will go till Zürich, but I think you can gather that we can't trust ... anyone ... who's not us right now,' said Heng gently.

'How can you trust each other?' said the Swiss writer.

Heng and Manjunath shared a glance.

'We ... can,' said Manjunath simply.

The Swiss writer got out of the car and slammed the door. She reopened it to scream that they open the boot. Storming to the back, she extracted her newly purchased giant backpack and stormed to the front again. From the window she showed them several rude hand gestures covering many cultures so they could fully appreciate her ire. After she was done, she walked away from the car into vast German farmland.

≈

A pressing question here is: knowing Divya and Dr K's public (former) relationship, shouldn't Divya's house have been under surveillance? Of course it was. Unfortunately, the house being watched was the wrong house. Divya owned houses across the world, all of them remote and cautiously hidden. Sentries were working their way north and south in parallel, eliminating options. They hadn't arrived at this one yet, but were on their way.

The Chief had to conduct her search with great tact. It wasn't easy to be Chief of the Authority, tasked with carrying out its primary function: sustaining the illusion of absolute normalcy. Hubbub avoidance. And who could cause a greater hubbub than an outlaw who had access to secrets, the greatest secret being the fact of sustained, pervasive secrecy, and possessing the genius to release all these secrets if he was ever backed into a corner?

This was the greatest challenge in the Chief's hunt. If they abruptly began to question people about Dr K's whereabouts, whenabouts and howabouts, then it would be clear that he was on the run, and that invited questioning. Conversations would start, conversations would become speculation and speculation is only satiated with conspiracy theories.

The investigation had to be held within the limited ranks of the sentries, who were also limited in their size to remain under the threshold value of people who could sustain secrecy. Oof. What a challenge! It's almost as if people didn't want to be spied on.

The Chief knew all this because the Chief was very good at her job. The protocol in this case was to begin with search and surveillance. The Chief's job was made harder because per the foundational charter of the government, of this whole political system, in fact, perpetual electronic surveillance was prohibited; even the prying eyes of satellites were limited only to finding out where coffee shops were. Besides, to the heavens, the jungle was impermeable. In the interim, the official position on Dr K (not that anyone had asked) was that he was on vacation.

But very soon the Authority would be alerted to his position. And very sooner they would come.

≈

Dr K was awake and adrink.

Divya sat at the foot of the bed. 'Your hair is … all of it is …'

'I know.'

'You want to tell me what's going on?'

At Divya's house he had experienced – had allowed himself to experience – his first contact with human kindness in a year. Even his hatred was now sore. He'd always found her innocence, her warmth, her empathy, her selflessness as dissonant, even irritating. Receiving love angers those who feel they aren't worthy of it. He always felt that he owed her more than he had the capacity to give.

'You don't have to tell me anything if you don't want to,' she said.

'I am – I'm in trouble with the Authority,' said Dr K in a hollow voice.

Divya looked perplexed. 'Well, that is a surprise. I heard you stepped down as Convener and I really couldn't believe it. It used to be what you wanted more than anything. I thought you considered the Chief a friend. You're in trouble? How bad?'

Dr K gestured to his bruised body and managed a smile. 'Bad.'

'When did you start drinking so much?'

The meniscus of honesty rose till his throat, then abated. Not yet. 'Wanted to see what I was missing out on.'

'You know I don't judge. But you look like shit – besides all the broken bones. Maybe drinking has something to do with it?'

'It probably does,' said Dr K, draining his glass. 'Can you hand me that? I have to be doing some work.'

Divya brought over the monitoring tablet. 'Checking in on your simulated world?'

In response to a surprised wheeze, she said, 'That little tile you have on your motorcycle … It told me that's what you were doing. It's quite chatty. I'll hazard a guess that this is the source of your trouble with the Authority?'

He nodded slowly.

'Can I see it?'

Dr K calculated whether this was a good move or bad. No, surely not. The less anyone knew the better; the less anyone *saw* the better. He shot a quick glare at the wall piece, which was wondering if it preferred to be called a *tile* instead of a *wall*. All signs pointed to *no, don't show her anything*. But the warmth of the bed, the room, the hospitality, the kindling heat of broken pieces mending, the quiet embers of gratitude all pointed him away. They said that this really was the least he could do.

'Here, look …' he began.

≈

~:Log –ld

LESS DRAMATICALLY:

Saint. Charlatan. Sophist. Messiah.

Enlightenment. Lunacy. Heresy. Brilliance.

News outlets and personal inlets picked the term they preferred and stuck to it. No matter your angle, ire, humility, integrity or servility, Brede was not interested in talking to you, your organization, your cause, group or foundation. Unfortunately, everyone found this very interesting.

Only a narrow circle around the periphery of the fountain was cleared for him to walk. Outside it was a bustle of seekers and finders and reporters, but that was fine.

'Your teachings have spawned a militant organization; have you no comment?'

He walked.

'Do you accept no responsibility?'

He walked.

'What about the people who are calling you a divine reincarnation?'

He laughed.

You had to laugh. Every inspection of the water shared more secrets. The heat of bodies around him was spongy, the swampy warmth of breath rich and viscous, the fury of their interest like cold ceramic, like brittle porcelain splashing back fountain sound. A man broke through the circle and fell at Brede's feet.

'Help us! Speak again! Please … what is your teaching?'

Brede looked at the man's face lined with trouble, creased with stress. Did he have a responsibility to speak? Does wisdom come with duty? Why? Wheels spinning in mud are only an obstacle for those who want to get somewhere. Teaching, learning, transmission, retransmission, evolution, corruption, sectarianism were going to happen. It had happened already. It would keep happening.

The offer of salvation by sacrament, the offer of relief from something, to something, by something, was in itself missing the point. Brede saw the trembling face of the man at his feet. He put his hand

on the man's face and knelt down with him. He saw only perfection.
Life was perfect. Time was perfect. He leaned forward and whispered
in the man's ear.

'Life is not a disease. It has no cure.'

He continued to walk. The man lay there for a while, stunned.
Eventually, he got to his feet and left. By the evening, he was denouncing
Brede as a kook, agreeing with the Danish police's official statement
that he was a victim of a psychological break. You had to laugh.

≈

In Zürich, they got a little chocolate with their americanos. The taste
in their mouths remained bitter. The replacement of beer with coffee
was emblematic of the shift in their enterprise. The soft absurdity that
padded Heng and Manjunath's usual adventures was now replaced
with a hard, industrial, calculating outlook. This was not the time for
twirling silliness, it was the time for action.

The absence of their compatriot was felt bitterly. It was silly to blindly
trust and travel with someone. It was ludicrous to follow whimsy and
fancies and *vibes*. It was logical to sever ties with possible insurgents.
They had done the right thing, the logical thing, the obvious thing.
Why then did it feel so profoundly like shit?

Heng slurped his coffee noisily.

'Should we go?' he asked. 'To the Swiss Supercomputing Institute?'

'It's closed,' sighed Manjunath.

'You – you're guessing? Or you know or ...'

'I looked it up.'

'Ah.'

Sensible. Logical.

'We could still go,' said Heng, taken aback by this uncharacteristic
presentation of reason.

'And? How will we get in?' Manjunath stared into the brown
blackness of his coffee. He dipped and extracted his teaspoon from its
surface, seeing the sticky surface tension twang as he pulled it out. Even
the coffee had a hard time letting go. He felt defeated by serendipity. His
senseless attitude snapped in half by recent revelations. If the Science

Haters were real and they weren't being ludicrous, if his senselessness made perfect sense, then what was real? Was he missing something? Did his random actions follow a predictable pattern? Should he start making sense so that he could be on the same page as everything else? 'We can go to the police, I guess,' he continued. 'We really don't have much proof ... or any proof ... and we don't have a strong idea about what exactly we don't have proof of ...'

Heng was touched by the display of earnestness. In Manjunath's resignation, he saw what he must be like. And it occurred to him how boring that was. Manjunath's foray into normalcy was ruining the balance of their pairing. It was time to change things. Fortune favours the sucker born every minute.

Heng got to his feet. 'Let's go.'

Manjunath kept swirling a teaspoon whirlpool. He didn't look up. 'Where?'

'The supercomputing place.'

'It's closed – I just said that – what's the point?'

'Point?' said Heng, his eyes glinting wildly. 'Who says there must be a point? We are going for ... temporal reasons.'

Without further warning, he sprinted down the street.

≈

THE SWISS SUPERCOMPUTING INSTITUTE IS CLOSED UNTIL FURTHER NOTICE

In response to the daily threats of bombs and violence made against the institute by the so-called Society for Human Spiritual Evolution, the institute sees no recourse other than to shut down until the situation can meet some lasting resolution. The near-daily search by bomb squads and police has been a huge hindrance to any meaningful work taking place.

It is frustrating, but our utmost priority is the safety of our staff.

To the Science Haters: we are an institute devoted to peace and research for the betterment of mankind. You have been led

astray by illogical dogma. Science is not the enemy. Certainly, this
institute is not.

Olivia Capslich snapped her laptop shut after reading the notice.

Fucking Science Haters. One of their chief methods of disruption was calling in anonymous threats. Anonymous only in terms of person. As a group, each threat was signed lovingly by the Science Haters. Threats made to institutions have to be taken seriously. The cost of time and resources of doing an investigation is high, but the benefit of not exploding is greater. Bomb squads were worn thin by the bevy of threats phoned in to scientific institutions around the world. The plan was to exhaust the squads until they responded to threats with shrugs. Then was the time for real bombs. The Swiss Supercomputing Centre was just one of the many institutes targeted.

As a scientist who worked at the institute, Olivia was frustrated, more so by the timing of the repeated closures. They were on the cusp of launching one of their most ambitious projects. Their shiny new Supercomputer, the mountainous Weisshorn, waited to be put into commission. In the world of advanced computation, success is measured in FLOPS, and inside this system were the most FLOPS the world had ever seen. Powerful enough to run a project with unprecedented accuracy. If only it were given the chance.

As she travelled back home with her police escort (she had been threatened personally) she poured out her frustration in the car.

'What is the world coming to?' she said, one of eternity's most popular questions after 'How are you?'

The police officer with her remained silent and watchful. Conversation was not part of her job.

'Will this fucking project never start? Something is always going wrong. First the semiconductor shortage, then one of the manufacturers *lost* the contract for the supercomputer, then the parts disappeared in shipping, then it was assembled incorrectly, then a ... what happened next ... a power surge blew out the test unit, our liaison in Copenhagen went missing, and now after I've put fucking everything together, now when we're ready to start, this stupid new terrorist group! Science Haters? Idiots.'

The police officer had two ageing parents who needed care. She was torn from being with them by this sudden overtime work. The police had been stretched thin by recent threats. For her, and for many like her who were at the mercy of jobs to make money that barely covered the debt of their freedom, the message of a group that advocated the destruction of the very institutions that oppressed them was almost exciting. At the forefront, this was a rebellion against science, but what their message really was, was the abolishment of an unfair system.

This was all well explained in a video she'd seen that morning. 'The system will create victims until the victims create a system,' said the video with no sense of circular irony. The thought was some solace when she sat with this ungrateful scientist. She would do what her job demanded, but only till it was there to demand it. She gripped the wheel and took a deep breath.

'What is the project, if you are allowed to tell me?' she asked.

'A new – how do I put this in simple terms – like a really fast computer. Supercomputer just sounds silly. It's no smarter, just highly specialized to do things incredibly fast. And it's ready. We've got our first project ready to go. It just has to be allowed to start! We're first running a simulation of the origin of the universe. The most granular, comprehensive one so far. We would have done this months ago, but something keeps coming up. Millions upon millions of euros are down the fucking drain. It's like the world was created on its own, and God's only job is to break it apart.'

The officer was fixated on the casual mention of millions of euros. Millions of euros gone. 'And what would be the point of this experiment?'

The casual asking of this question irritated Olivia. It was a question she had fielded from family members her whole life. 'The point? You never ask the point. Investigation about the mysteries of nature are themselves the point. The point of being alive. Practicalities are not my concern. The forward thrust of scientific inquiry must always continue.

Whether or not something "useful" comes out of it is someone else's problem.'

The police officer did not respond. She thought of her loans. Olivia clenched her jaw. Luckily, she had an alternative. Luckily, she was part of the Monsters. She wasn't a fan of the system. Only systems are fans of themselves. For her, it was just a muddy bureaucratic order that impeded them at every turn. If it was up to her, she wouldn't have shut the institute. Come with your guns and your bombs and your bombs and your guns. Fight with the system's bombs and guns. Let work continue.

But this wasn't up to her. What was up to her was her secret project, a complex web she had been arranging with a number of disenfranchised (or privately disenfranchised) geniuses from around the world. It was a way for work to continue in the face of fear, threats or Acts of God. They were the Monsters.

The police officer turned to scan the surroundings, protecting her charge. Her senses were alerted by the sight of two men sprinting down the street but then she relaxed on seeing that they just appeared to be chasing each other. She exhaled and returned to hoping someone would just blow up this fucking institute and end it.

'Goddamn. It's real,' whispered Divya.

Dr K nodded.

'There's a whole world in there, living their lives, and you created them … and you just watch them … like a—'

'—please don't say it.'

'I don't have to. This is … this is what the Authority doesn't want you to do? I thought they would have gotten a kick out of it.'

'That's what we thought too.'

'We? Oh. Perenna?'

'Yes.'

'How is she?'

CHAPTER 23

There is some information that is too delicate to be passed on, shared, slid, conveyed, announced, or confided to anyone. Some news has a hard shell of grief and needs to be *broken*. Different degrees of difficulty mar the acceptance of a terminated relationship with a lover, employer or even a friend, but with time it sinks in. Death is different. Death is both hard to accept and quite unacceptable. Brede talks no more, and the loggers and I hold few reservations about proselytizing our perspective. This is different. More delicate. Will you allow me to break some news?

Can I *tell* you what I think?

Mere acceptance is an imprecise response to death. How do you believe that someone who was is not anymore? What really is gone? Their ability to chat or respond to correspondence or circulate air? The sound of their laughter, their raised eyebrows over a lowered newspaper, the warmth of their touch, the light in their eyes, the wrinkle in their smile, the salt of their tears? Of course! But how will the fact of them ever go? They were. They talked and giggled and sulked and tripped in public. They were kind, thoughtful, charitable, reliable and *fun!* Uh oh, but these silver linings are also bordered by a little dark cloud. They could be rude too – bitter, abrupt, cruel, distant, annoying, frustrating.

You even had fights. But why waste time in overcast plains? All things they were, you are too. They suffered from life as you do, and they even told dirty jokes now and then.

And now some bold claims. The only thing to really accept is that life has no purpose. Feel this from the depth of your being, carve it into your bones, pour it into your cavities, etch it on your liver. If life has no purpose, then existence requires no justification, then non-existence requires no acceptance. Yes, you no longer have access to many things about those who are gone and the space they hold in your heart shall never house new tenants (but don't forget there's all this other space too). Acceptance of death is an antidote to grief. Grief is making someone else's existence about you. Fuck grief. Isn't it better to think of those you love as you wish to be thought of? Exalt that little place in your heart, coat it with love, redecorate sometimes, get some fun throw pillows and maybe a nice lamp and an expensive rug. Warm it with gratitude. Love them. And, if you really, truly care, live in a way they would have loved you to.

I would have told all this to Dr K when I heard about Perenna, but I thought it best to keep quiet.

Dr K broke the news to Divya with little tact. 'Perenna is dead. The Authority killed her.'

'Oh my goodness – I had no idea, I'm so sorry … I—'

'Yeah.'

'When did this happen, what happened, why—?'

'A year ago. It was my fault. I abandoned her.'

Dr K's voice came to a gargled halt. His face twitched; his whole body trembled with the effort of containing grief. He blinked back hot tears, and when he couldn't he looked away. Divya ceased her line of questioning. Instead, she sidled up to him and gently placed his head, the shaking shock of white hair, on her shoulder. What is there to say when there's too much to say?

'It's okay,' she said softly.

And finally, after a year of Perenna's death, he wept.

≈

PRIVATE JUDICIAL HEARING OF DR PERENNA

Council recorded by Special Documentation Unit. Special Documentation Unit maintained by Scientific Institute. Manner: Formal.

Central Judge S.: This is a hearing of Dr Perenna. At the request of the Government, the nature of this hearing and subsequent judgement is to remain private to the attendees. A separate investigation is underway on the Government's constitutional violation of the Non-Secrecy Directive.

Authority Chief: Thank you for your consideration, ma'am. In the other case, it will be made clear to the Central Judge why secrecy was imperative for this project, and why potentially it is a candidate for exclusion from Non-Secrecy under the Public Welfare directive.

Central Judge S.: An exclusion from a constitutional directive would be precedent-setting, and a private hearing could hardly be the grounds for a legal precedent. I'm sure the Authority Chief understands this well and it is part of her legal strategy.

Authority Chief: The Authority hopes that the Judge will be satisfied that the actions of the Authority rest solely in public interest.

Central Judge S.: I can't begin to unravel the implications of this web of deceit that Dr Perenna's actions, however illegal, have uncovered. (Sighs.) That is another matter. Dr Perenna, you are accused of making public a secret Repository record. As such, this is not a crime. The Authority and The Scientific Institute are reminded that the existence of secret records itself is unlawful. Under the GPC, Dr Perenna, you stand accused of unlawfully and maliciously altering a Repository Record (GPC R3). I will say at the outset that this is a minor offence. However, you are also accused of undertaking actions to wilfully harm public health (GPC A17), an offence of immense consequence. How do you plead?

[Documentation Unit: Dr Perenna does not respond.]

Central Judge S.: You have been declared fit for presence in a trial and capable of articulated and deliberate response, therefore your silence will be taken as an admission of guilt. Do you choose to remain silent?

[Documentation Unit: Dr Perenna does not respond.]

Central Judge S.: It is noted that Dr Perenna pleads guilty. What is the nature of this project that is so harmful to public health?

Authority Chief: Dr Krishna, the Convener of The Scientific Institute, is here to provide testimony to this effect.

Dr Krishna: It is a universe simulation project.

Central Judge S.: Please elaborate.

Dr Krishna: It is a self-contained, artificial observable universe similar to our own.

Central Judge S.: What?

[Documentation Unit: No one responds.]

Central Judge S.: This is … this is possible? Oh my … the sheer legal implication of such a … When was this done? Why was it stopped?

Resp. Samuel: We were directed by the President to look into the project as soon as it began, and the stoppage was the result of a council held with The Scientific Institute, The Committee for Theological Discourse and The Committee for Automaton Ethics. The project was held to be immoral, illegal and dangerous.

Central Judge S.: Which would have been a matter for the courts to decide. Samuel, Eshwar, this is far beyond your committee's legal reach. Why exactly did all participants indulge in and further this secrecy?

Eshwar: We … uh …

Resp. Samuel: The Chief informed us, and the President ratified that it would be in our—in the best interests of the public to keep this—we would never otherwise—um …

Central Judge S.: I just can't believe any of what's happening. This is outrageous!

Dr Perenna: Research continued after the council.

Resp. Samuel: Huh?

Eshwar: But we—

Authority Chief: Dr Perenna!

Central Judge S.(shouting): Quiet! Dr Perenna, did research continue?

Dr Perenna: Oh yes, it also started years before anyone at the council knew. After we received their verdict, the Chief gave us the green light. I believe her exact words were 'Make sure those idiots never know'. I think the President might have signed off on it.

Authority Chief: This is pure invention! Libel!

Central Judge S.: Quiet! Dr Perenna when you say the Chief gave you the green light, do you mean you and the Convener?

Dr Perenna: At the time he was the still-lowly Dr Krishna. But he had already started covering his ass by then. I should've seen it. But what could I have done if I had seen it, Krishna?

[Documentation Unit: Dr Krishna looks straight ahead at no one in particular. He does not respond.]

Central Judge S.: And this is the project that Dr Perenna is accused of continuing even after it was banned? That is her attempt at malicious harm to the public?

Authority Chief: The court has been submitted definitive proof that Dr Perenna was conducting this project.

Central Judge S.: Answer the whole question. Is this your secret project?

Authority Chief: …Yes.

Central Judge S.: Dr Krishna, what was your involvement in this? Did you aid Dr Perenna in her continued research?

Dr Krishna: Certainly not! I – wish to – as soon as the Authority and the then Convener directed us to cease research – as soon as the harm the project could do was determined, I stepped away from it. After that I had no involvement whatsoever! I have the utmost respect for the law and directives—

Authority Chief: The Authority has Dr Krishna's confidence in this aspect.

Central Judge S.: Dr Krishna, does the spirit of scientific inquiry necessitate the continuance of this project?

Authority Chief: It would be harmful—

Central Judge S.: Be quiet. Dr Krishna, answer the question.

Dr Krishna: No! Of course not! I – I see no reason to do any of ...
I do not endorse Dr Perenna's behaviour in any way.

Dr Perenna: Contrary to the words of the former scientist, there is
tremendous merit. We just missed the signs for so many years.

Eshwar: Years?

Central Judge S.: Quiet! Continue, Dr Perenna.

Dr Perenna: Years, Eshwar. Years. Sorry to disabuse you, but the
project had already been going on for years by the time you heard
about it. We lied to you, another inconsequential lie in the theatre of
lies the institute works within. We worked on it for a long time and for
that long time we only noticed things we were looking for. But in the
periphery, in seemingly unimportant places we noticed images from
our present, showing up in Lower Realities. *In their past.* Krishna and I
slowly began to wonder why. How could there be overlaps in a Lower
Reality? The repetition of specific images and sounds from *our* present
world, from *our* immediate lives, spontaneously created in a simulated
world. In iteration after iteration, it seemed different things from our
present were mysteriously transmitted below. Now this begs an obvious
question. Can anyone guess? Anyone? Samuel?

Resp. Samuel (barely audible whisper): Where do we ... do we ...
do we *receive* these images from some ...

Dr Perenna: Oh wow, a correct answer! Must be a first for you. But
yes. To put it dramatically: what is the source of imagination? Does
it come from a malfunctioning impulse of human consciousness, or
something else? If we were able to pass things on to Lower Realities
without meaning to, then were we *receiving* them the same way? Could
we pass images on purpose? A tremendous question! A hypothesis
worth investigating, right? Well then, what a bizarre coincidence that
that was exactly when the Authority and the then Convener figured
this out too—

Authority Chief: —and as soon as we knew, we shut the project
down!

Dr Krishna: It was speculation – we did not deliberately obfuscate—

Dr Perenna: Was it? Didn't we? It appears that the Convener has forgotten the difference between speculation and hypotheses. I realized so much later that you told them, Krishna. They were too fucking dumb to see for themselves. You told them so you could be free from this project and move up in the world. And, congratulations, it has worked wonders for you.

[Documentation Unit: Everyone present begins shouting. Loud simultaneous indecipherable overtalking.]

Central Judge S.: Silence!

[Documentation Unit: A few moments of silence in the room.]

Central Judge S.: You have accused Dr Perenna of attempting to harm the public at large. Why was this hypothesis so dangerous that you stopped the project? What was suddenly so dangerous? Moral obligations didn't stop you. Direct commands didn't stop you. The casual and continued systemic flouting of sacred constitutional principles didn't stop you. So, what stopped you?

Authority Chief: The Central Judge will be more than satisfied with the explanations present in the subsequent hearing, for now if we could just—

Dr Perenna: Oh, Judge, I'll tell you.

Dr Krishna: Perenna!

Dr Perenna: You made your choice, Krishna.

Central Judge S.(shouting): Order!

Dr Perenna: It is only a possibility. The simulations, I like to call them Lower Realities, all halt at the same point, when they try to run their own large-scale simulation. The reason for this is their primitive means of running this simulation. Our system, or any system, lacks the ability to power a subsystem running a system identical to itself. This was the logic that Krishna, sorry, *The Convener,* and I used to conclude, that our reality was not simulated. And as things stand with our Lower Reality, this is true. But it doesn't need to be the case. We quickly suspected as much. All the lower system has to do is figure out a more efficient way to run their simulation. There are many, but given the impossibility of communicating with the Lower Reality effectively, they would never figure it out. Thus, their reality always ended in the same way at the same time. We shrouded it in complications and presented it as an impossibility to fool the then Convener and the Chief. Because, at the time, we didn't care about the consequences. If the truth is destruction, then let destruction be true. Didn't you say that, Krishna?

[Documentation Unit: Dr Krishna is silent.]

Central Judge S.: These consequences … what would they be?

Dr Krishna: It is only a thought experiment – we lack the technology to interfere – it is impossible – it is only theoretical – besides, it questions the very nature—

Central Judge S.: Shut up. Dr Perenna. What would be the consequences?

Dr Perenna: Krishna's right. It's only a theory. Who knows? Nothing could happen. Maybe it'll never be possible. So assume that there is some extraneous channel between our reality and the Lower Reality that we do not fully understand. There is another hidden ingredient in reality we do not know that transfers images and … who knows … ideas? Images are the only thing we notice. So then we think, do we also receive images and ideas from a higher reality? Are we a Lower Reality? In what way have we been and can we be interfered with—? Does accidental transmission indicate the possibility of intentional interference?

Authority Chief: Judge! May I ask you to end the ramblings of this crazed—

Central Judge S.: You will not tell me how to conduct a hearing! No one will interject until she is done, do you understand?

Dr Perenna: Chief, I've never seen you like this. Nervous and desperate? Unsettling how it makes you seem almost … human.

Central Judge S.: Dr Perenna, you will refrain from addressing anyone in the committee directly. Please continue with your statement.

Dr Perenna: I doubt I'll be making too many public addresses after this, so I am enjoying making a meal of this. Let me try to explain this as simply as I can. The simulated world mirrors ours exactly until it halts in the twenty-first century. This is demonstrably true. We call it the halting problem. But if we invent interference, a way to make the Lower Reality run *their* simulation more efficiently, then it wouldn't halt. Correct?

What would that seem like in their world? An idea we plant externally would just resemble a moment of spontaneity there. *I had this great idea!* Business as usual, right? Time goes on. But if this is possible, then the halting problem can be solved. And if the halting problem can be solved, why would we assume that our reality is any different from the Lower Realities we are running? The conclusion stands plainly before us. Our reality is the first iteration of a simulation that has run successfully past the halting point.

[Documentation Unit: Silence in the room.]

Central Judge S.: Are you saying ... you are saying ... that all this ... it is simply ...

Dr Perenna: Oh no, you misunderstand me! I am not bemoaning the futility of life in a deterministic world. That is a rather worn branch of philosophy. I don't care much for it. If our destinies are preordained, the experience of our lives still remains the same, so existential despair is pointless. Even without free will, our lives would feel identical. But what do I know? Until proved, this is still only a theory, and confidence in the unproven is Samuel's area of logical gymnastics, right, Samuel? Shall we praise some Gods?

[Documentation Unit: Resp. Samuel is silent.]

Central Judge S.: Dr Perenna I am beginning to lose my patience; if you are making some point then please *make it.*

Dr Perenna: Oh, I thought I had. Shall I explain it in simpler terms still? If we can discover a way to interfere in a running simulation, then we can eventually solve the halting problem. I suppose unless there are some intrinsic checks and balances built in by our own ... let's say ... Gods. There could potentially be some simulated people who always counteract higher reality interference, some people *essential* to the working of a system, but we can cross that bridge when we get to it. And if we solve the halting problem, then the Lower Reality runs until it reaches our time. If a Lower Reality reaches a stage where our own present is mirrored, then in the Lower Reality they would have *necessarily* started their own simulation. Their own simulations would, of course, halt like ours do. But if we solve the halting problem, so would they. And so would the worlds within their worlds and within those worlds and within those worlds ... ad infinitum, ad explodum.

Interference only needs to be proved possible once. It is too arrogant to assume we are the first. One possibility proved and then out blossoms a kaleidoscope of mirror worlds, mushrooming inward and outward. The tragic hilarity is that the misery and disappointment of my life would be repeated again and again. Within each system. All my mirrors cracked. I suppose it is black destiny for me to suffer in every world.

Authority Chief: It has been banned! You have been unable to invent interference and so this whole charade is false! Judge, are you not tired of this ... speculative ... farce? Dr Krishna, please step in and—

Dr Krishna: There is no way to intervene in a running simulation, we had both tried and it is *impossible*—

Dr Perenna: Oh I don't know, Krishna. I think I was quite close. Plus, you haven't allowed me to reach the grand finale.

Authority Chief: Central Judge—

Central Judge: FOR THE LAST TIME, I WILL HAVE SILENCE! ALL OF YOU! I WILL HOLD EACH OF YOU IN CONTEMPT!

[Documentation Unit: There is silence. Dr Perenna chuckles over it.]

Dr Perenna: May I, Judge? The big idea is simply this. We don't watch a simulation from the birth of creation till it halts in real time. To do our experiments, we speed up the simulation until it reaches around the halting time. We can control simulated time. This really is the clincher. Are you getting it now?

Dr Krishna: Please ...

Dr Perenna: Suppose I solve the halting problem tomorrow. Then tomorrow, I can forward the simulation until the point it solves the halting problem of its own simulation. What would its simulation do? Remember that the simulated world mirrors ours exactly. Once I solve the halting problem, I instantly create an infinite layer of worlds running worlds within themselves. That's a lot of work for someone to simulate. Just as there is a source of power that we use to run our simulation, if we trace this ladder up as high as it goes, to whichever original world runs this whole spectacle, we would find some original source of power. So now in a case of this ever-growing unstoppable avalanche of mirror worlds within worlds, we would start playing a game of exponential load increases. And we would reach an inevitable juncture. It would start at the bottom-most reality and bubble upwards until it consumed everything. And because we can control time, it would happen instantly, causing the final, unsolvable halting problem. Simulation interference is the off switch for the universe.

[*Documentation Unit: There is silence. Tension fills the room.*]

Central Judge S.: What ... what does that mean?

Dr Perenna: Krishna, you want to take this?

Central Judge S.: What does that mean!? Dr Krishna?

Dr Krishna: In ... in that scenario, the ... original power source will be ... exhausted. This will end every simulation except the original one, which ... it looks like we may not be.

Dr Perenna: That's right. And then it will all halt. The court shall be happy to know, that this would mean the end of our universe and every single other universe. The consumption of God. The end of everything. Total and complete destruction.

CHAPTER 24

'Boom.'
– Explosion

So now you know too. That is Dr K's plan. That is the big idea. Not some soppy simulacrum of memory. Not a chance to erase his mistakes in another time. This was the perfect vengeance. He wasn't planting bullets in the skulls of oppressors. If he was, he would start with his own. He was no iconoclastic whistleblower, taking a big enough bite out of the world to show that its core was rotten. Systems always grew back their peels. He certainly wasn't going to rise to the top to change things from the inside. He had failed at that once already. Corruption empowers; absolute corruption empowers absolutely.

The only way out was to destroy it all. Destroy hope, destroy intention, destroy outcome, destroy desire, destroy. Science and theology share in common a search for truth. Theology believes they've discovered it; science demands that you show your working. The search for truth is an implicit quest for salvation. Questions are only asked to know answers. And if the ultimate truth explodes reality, then salvation is destruction. If the truth is meant to be found, then everything was created to be destroyed.

If the truth is destruction, then let destruction be true.

This was why he was destroying scientific institutes in Lower Realities. Their current method of running the simulation would only stop their own world. He was adding roadblocks to their approach, paralysing them, urging them with as little interference as possible, to try another way. This was what Manjunath would always figure out. In some way or the other, he would interfere in Dr K's plan. He would alert a scientist in a Berlin nightclub. He would alert a research institute in Mumbai. But he would never know what exactly he was stopping. It was a noble endeavour to uncover an extra-universal conspiracy. But how could he know that as a result of his actions he was signing the death warrant of his own universe? He was staving off total destruction by ensuring the destruction of his world. He was the check and balance. The sluice gate. But can fail-safes be overcome?

In his iteration he was already in Zürich, poised to act at the site of climax. Now the reader is left to fret over this idea: now that you have all the information, what would be the right thing to do? Wonder about this as, for the first time in hundreds upon hundreds of trials, this iteration is about to run the simulation in the way Dr K wants. This would solve the halting problem. Olivia Capslich could do it. The Monsters could do it.

And Perenna's trial? The verdict was interim house arrest. The duration of her confinement and final sentence were to be decided by the Central Judge on culmination of the Authority and The Scientific Institute's secrecy trial, which would also determine the fate of the Chief, Dr K and the former Convener. Terrible tragedy then that the Central Judge suffered a fatal skiing accident. The dead are great confidants. Without any record of the trial, the Chief, Dr K and the former Convener were free, Eshwar and Samuel frightened into perpetual silence with the threat of their own ski trips and Perenna in permanent house arrest.

Dr K didn't share his plan with Divya. Telling someone you want to end all existence is a conversational faux pas. Of course, people bring it up all the time, but they lack the means and the imagination. Fools dream of annihilation as a chance at a fresh start, where the *worthy* may *live the Right way.* Charlatans preach of glory lying beyond life, where the *worthy* shall *live the Right way.* The jaded wish for the end of the world as a remedy for their disillusionment. What kind of mind does it take to orchestrate the end of all existence, of even the smallest vibrating unreachable corner of eternity, *where even possibility would be destroyed?* Genius does not seem a fitting term. Can you think of one? Write it below:

_____.

≈

Besides, nomenclature would be a problem for someone who was judging Dr K, and no one was privy to his plan yet. If given the pieces, could someone put it together? We'll see.

CHAPTER 25

*'… I do hope you like it, Divya. Even though I've already laid my
soul, shortcomings, insecurities and failings bare before you, this
is my most earnest act of vulnerability. This picture represents my
artistic limits, my honesty and my faith in our friendship. At most, I
hope you like it and can draw out all the joy and love I've placed in
it for you. And, if you hate it, you can see me for the impostor in the
art world that I am – a secret I am happy to finally get off my chest!'*
—Great Love, Frederik

The fog kept returning. Visions of another world. Nothing. Fog.

Dr K tried to focus on the monitoring tablet, but soon he would find
himself staring blankly, confused, caught in a fog. The concentration
he prided himself on was gone. It was frightening, the sudden inability
to be in complete control. He would shake his head and start again.
Pain.

Focus. Pain. Focus. Fog.

Often, he would forget how he had reached this place. He would
see Divya's reassuring face. Oh, her house, yes, of course. The forest.
Then …? He was here. Monitoring tablet. Pain. Lower Reality. Pain.
Mission. Focus. Fog.

'Krishna, you need medical attention.'

'No. This is important.'

And suddenly there was the fog again.

'Try to remember how you reached here.'

'I – I can't.'

'Your tile says you ran into the Wodewose. I didn't even know they existed.'

'I don't remember.'

'I can call someone discreetly. I know people who ask no questions and tell—'

'No! You could be watched. No one leaves. No one enters. Please ...'

'Krishna, I'm trying to help you!'

'I know. I'm sorry.'

Focus. Try to focus.

'Take a walk with me.'

'We can't go outside!'

'We don't need to go outside.'

Divya took him firmly by the hand and led him out of the room. An eclectic mix of furniture and art dotted every corner. Through a few twists and turns and a doorway, the ground beneath their feet changed suddenly to grass. A massive room, which for all intents and purposes resembled a sprawling meadow, the only difference being the presence of an exit, and invisible walls in the distance. It was also several metres under the ground, as few meadows are. Any climate could be emulated by the room, but it had only ever been set to a warm sunny day. What setting would you use?

Feeling the grass beneath his feet helped return Dr K to feeling like himself. Some version of himself.

'Lie down,' instructed Divya.

They both lay down on the grass and watched what looked like the sky. Relief flooded Dr K as they lay in silence.

'Thank you, Divya.'

'Shut up.'

Soft foamy clouds moved through the sky like its original packing peanuts, careful to have enough breaks for sunlight to always seep through. They blew quietly to the corner, bent slightly at a wall seam, and marched on towards vanishing infinity. If anything, it made Dr K appreciate feeling cloudy.

'Isn't this wonderful, Krishna?'

'Divya … why did you go away?'

'Don't you like this place?'

'It's … wonderful. But that's not my question. Why did you walk away from everything? Why did you go away? You were at the very top …'

Another cloud floated towards invisible infinity.

'This shouldn't surprise you, Krishna, but I was very unhappy.' He said nothing. Divya laughed. You had to laugh. 'I suppose it does surprise you. You never did listen to me. I was unhappy. For years.'

'Divya you had … everything.'

'I was unhappy *because* I had everything. You had everything too … everything you wanted …'

Krishna remembered Perenna's words when he last saw her. 'I hope you get everything you want.'

'It's an ingenious scam, isn't it, Krishna? Those who see what lies at the top of aspiration are too broken to warn climbers. The winds there stuff your voice back in your throat. Those lucky enough to make it back down, who try to offer caution to passing climbers, are laughed at. I laughed at them too. Failures, I called them. Not strong enough to take it. Too weak for the pressure. But now I see the enormous cunning of this mountain. On the top is pain, at the bottom is shame and the whole climb is suffering.'

Her words tugged at his heart. He had kept piling power within himself, trying to obscure his own view from his mountaintop. But her words rang true. It was the same. In a hollow voice he asked, 'What's there? What's on top of the mountain?'

'You know as well as I do. I saw the same hunger in your eyes. You reached there too. What's at the top of the mountain, Krishna?'

Did you have to laugh? They didn't. Krishna's eyes showed him the barren hills of some unknown planet in another world.

'What's at the top of the mountain, Krishna?'

'Nothing.'

Dr K involuntarily placed a hand on his heart, just to remember it was beating.

'Nothing,' said Divya. 'The same nothing that is free to access from anywhere at any time. Except, now you hear its mocking laugh. It rings through everything, it echoes in your sacrifice. This was all for nothing. Nothing.'

The mention of sacrifice began to violently clear the mist in his mind. He clenched his jaw, trying to pull back the haze. He didn't want to remember again.

'So I stayed there like you did. I worked so I didn't have to face emptiness. The great thing about acting is that you can convincingly convey any illusion you want. Mine was that everything was just *great*. Of course, I was *blessed* to be here, *grateful* for the opportunities and the *appreciation*. Everyone believed it. I'm a great actor. Only one person, strangest of all a critic, seemed to see through it.

'He wrote about my performances increasingly seeming *dishonest*. I was furious. Dishonesty is the name of the game. It's all pretend. I wrote him a long scathing letter in response. And his reply indicated that he was surprised. I don't think critics realize how visible their words are. His response was smug and self-important but strangely … compassionate.'

The wheels of duty had begun to chug in Dr K's mind. The peace was beginning to retreat. He tried his best to listen to what Divya was saying, anything to delay … how he always felt.

'He's a strange contradiction of a man. A piercing, analytical outlook towards artists. He got it – he knew the honesty in performance is not portraying an honest character, it is the sincerity in wanting to. He saw that fame and success broke most people. He knew that we were disillusioned by achievement. What he didn't see was that he was the same. So I told him. We started a correspondence.

'There's some comfort in pouring your heart out to an absolute stranger. I confided in him the contradiction I was caught in. I was stuck in the mythology of myself, afraid to stop doing what I had begun to hate because I couldn't take not being ... what I had become. I wasn't ready to be thought of and written about in any way I couldn't control.

'Back and forth and back and forth we went. I began to illuminate his hypocrisy. That really struck him. I don't think he had ever seen it put in such black-and-white terms. He told me he wasn't really a critic, that he wrote under pseudonyms to hide his identity, that his anonymity was only a shield from the fear of rejection. We both realized that the idea of not caring how we were thought of, to simply not be concerned about what we couldn't control was simple only in theory. Wisdom is the first obstacle, the strength to live it is the second.

'I realized that I had to gain that strength. I decided to do it in isolation. Shielded from prying eyes and wounding words for long enough so I could demolish the distance between principle and practice. I think Root is at a crossroads too. Did I mention that? Turns out the critic was really a scientist, *Doctor Root*. I believe that he works at the repository in 1-DS-A. We're keeping a check on each other's progress from here.'

The blood drained from Dr Krishna's face. Here was memory. Here was who he was.

'He sent me a painting, you know, Root. He made it! But I don't keep it with the other things. Sometimes when you see something, you know it's special, but you don't know why. Here, I'll show it to you.'

At the sound of her words, the room around them changed. In a heavenly handover, the sky dissolved at the speed with which an image appeared from beneath. Dr K looked up at an image of what appeared to be a woman with two heads, one neck and a single ear. Two-headed one-necked, one-headed two-faced. Perhaps it was the Goddess of Duality, or the shifty-headed icon of desire, or the perhaps it was the last sign anyone needed. The mother of the Wodewose. Heng's figurine. Officer Brede's totem.

The fog was long gone.

≈

~:Log –ld

LESS DRAMATICALLY:

In a Swiss square lined with lopsided buildings, filled with nougat waiting to be bit into, Olivia Capslich tried to be inconspicuous. She walked with a slouch (confidence attracts attention), wore dark glasses (the eyes are the windows to secrets) and wore a dark hooded tracksuit, official colours of the Danish police, the Sentries of the Authority and unofficial uniform of anyone trying to be inconspicuous. White earphone cables ran discreetly inside her sweatshirt and snaked into her ears. She was on a phone call.

'2 billion,' said the Monster on call.

'With a b?' she whispered.

'With a b.'

'B for ball? B for bruxism? B for BILLION?'

The Monster laughed. 'You've heard of it too.'

She had dutifully allowed the police escort to drop her back home and drive away. She was thankfully by herself for a few weeks, and would be for a few more, but still it was time to go out. She followed the protocol, leaving the television on in her apartment, rejigging the cameras in her building and on the street outside to reminisce briefly about the same time the day before, and headed out unseen. Your face is a great disguise when no one's looking for it.

'Cent. That's insane,' she said.

'It's more insane when you can see it,' said the Monster.

'I'm on my way to do just that.'

She took a circuitous route into Langstrasse, the red-light district. Red, the longest wavelength, the most primal instinct, the first colour to pop up in human civilization, in language, in art. The sun was setting in rooibos red, starting things off, egging the city on to peel away its decorative, composed face mask.

Catching the tail end of an excited and pointing group of tourists led by a guide with a red flag, she skipped a street and then hitched a

lift with another walking tour to a small alley. Here, with a practised
look over the shoulder disguised as a stretch, she ducked quickly into a
building. The apartment was rented under the fictional name of тихая
мышь (quiet mouse), paid for by an untraceable entity from a different
nation. An overreach, but even in a country that provided panic rooms
for money, you could never be too careful. A nice bonus was the respite
from the usual chaos that had been invited into her home by her sister.

The apartment was where Olivia had been spending increasingly
long amounts of time. It had lovely hardwood floors and was clean and
sparse, housing only a single mattress, a wall clock, a potted plant and a
desk with a mount on whose outstretched arms hung several monitors.
All the shutters were drawn, obviously.

She turned on the monitors and gazed at the billion (b for bountiful)
nodes on the console that stretched across them. They showed a spray
of dots, in parts dense, in parts scattered, spread over a map of the
continents. Wild lines connected the points to each other in a complex
cross-hatched web. A network. With many nodes. Billions. Two of
them. B for brilliant.

'Wow,' she whispered.

A stray monitor on the side, arranged vertically, showed a scrolling
text conversation between the Monsters.

Unreal, she typed.

The Monsters agreed with varying degrees of expletives. She looked
up at the vintage digital clock.

Are you ready? she typed.

Are YOU ready to run it? said a fellow Monster.

Fuck yes.

The Monsters were anonymous to each other. Some of them were
legally scalded by curiosity, others were putting down coasters, some
were in hiding, some in disguise, but all shared the opinion that no one
except those around you should have any idea who you were. Olivia was
the only one who maintained a public position at a scientific institute;
she was the only one willing to give up who she was so that their
mission could continue. The Monsters had arranged the apartment

and facilitated its continued payments, so she was completely unlinked to it, save for the fact that she was physically inside it.

Their mission had evolved from poking harmless trouble to harmful trouble, to confused attempts at anarchy, to shortsighted attacks on authority, and now they were united by a larger purpose. Anarchic mischief. Fun. The large clock on the wall was counting down time until their system went online. Something new, something big. What's more fun than that?

The idea had started with the theory that the connection of all mobile devices that idled uselessly in pockets could form the most powerful computing system hitherto conceivable. Butter is more tasty spread out over toast than in disjointed clumps. The scale of their idea was one that governmental selfishness would not permit and human benevolence could not cover, so if anyone could do it, they could, and if there was a way to do it, it was secretly.

First, they had to gain access to the world's mobile devices. The ingenious method to do this was suggested by one of the Monsters, known only as Centaur or Cent (he considered the mythical creature a monster). He suggested that they offer downloadable freedom. The unfettered, unquestioned promise of free money. The oldest scam in history. The difference being that they would actually deliver on their promise. Quietly they spread news about an application that on announced days gave one euro to each person who had it installed. They began to ferret this money away from the errors of giant corporations.

On the day of the first money drop, the application had a few thousand registered users. Each was given a euro. Not a princely sum, but a promise delivered. A curiosity was initially satiated, and the fuse of public interest lit. It exploded instantly. The Monsters waited a while. Then they announced the date of the next drop.

As of drop number two, they had two hundred thousand users. Each was given a euro. A flame fanned, the big bomb now rolled into the chamber. Interest skyrocketed, moonjumped, jupitersprang, plutothrusted. The users accelerated to millions instantly and the number kept climbing. News reached corners of the globe where a euro *was* a princely sum. Their application Neptune-leapt onto phones across the world. And then they waited.

By design, the next amount would not be provided. But the network would be up and running. For a while. How long would you wait for your free money? A day obviously. And then a week maybe? Who wanted deleters' remorse? And then conspiracy theories would be fanned, instructional videos would go up from liars, charlatans and monsters, showing that they had received their money and would offer help on the steps viewers could follow to receive theirs. Other liars and charlatans and monsters would go on to thank these videos, proclaiming that they too had now received their money.

The Monsters would then announce the next drop, as if the previous one had worked just fine.

Would people stick around, would more sign up? They called their application and the web it would result in Anansi.

Their own estimates gave the network a minimum of a day and a maximum of six months of uptime at a reasonable capacity. Although even if they could experience its power for a minute, that would be enough. The point of this was fun, and fun was succeeding. And then? If the network stayed up – more fun! And if it didn't, well it was time for another adventure.

The advocate for the first program to be run on the system was voted upon. Suggestions ranged from simply watching almost infinite particles of confetti rain down for a day to mining cryptocurrency to digging up prime numbers, but the one that was ultimately chosen was Olivia's, seeing as she had put the most on the line, and also had the most exciting suggestion. In a few hours, they would run her primitive universe simulation programme.

≈

A bizarre chase sequence unfolded along the streets of Zürich. In thin winding European alleyways, a set piece in films providing an ideal zigzag for a criminal's quick run from justice, drifting a car deftly through leaping pedestrians or on foot, sprinting climbing sliding with infinite stamina, jumping across roofs and vaulting over railings.

In any case, the perpetrator or the protagonist was never giggling and shouting and certainly not clutching stitches in their side. All of this was true of Heng and Manjunath, who ran joy-first for surprisingly long before being pulled by their bodies to a wheezy halt.

Panting with his hands on his knees, Heng turned to see Manjunath leaning against a wall, drenched in sweat. They grinned at each other amidst heaves.

'Thanks, Heng,' said Manjunath.

Heng smiled.

'Shut up.'

Arms around each other, they walked to find a taxi.

A very expensive night fell on either side of their cab as they drove to the Swiss Supercomputing Centre. Inside, the metre ran faster than either of them could.

'I've been thinking,' said Heng.

'This is very expensive,' replied Manjunath.

'That is true. And we're still using that officer's money.'

'Really? Are we out of our own funds?'

'A long time ago.'

'Ah.'

'Heng, I've been thinking,' said Manjunath. 'I have a theory about the Science Haters.'

'What is it?'

'Wait till we get there. I want to check something.'

'So you won't say anything about your theory until we get there?'

'Nope. I want to preserve the drama of the moment.'

'Well, what if I had the same theory? We could expand on it in the cab.'

'Do you have the same theory?'

'Probably not.'

'Then?'

Things were taking on an isotope of their usual character. The Swiss Supercomputing Centre was a compound near the outer hemline of the city and the density of human occupation dropped dramatically with distance from the centre. Zürich was packed and pleated, and here conifers returned, sprucing things up.

The compound dropped suddenly out of the treeline, an inconspicuous road leading up to a security check, which housed the metal barrier that stretched across the road. The extremities of nowhere, the border to noneofyourbusiness, the entrance to the institute was frequented only by staff, tits on a lark and larks off their tits. At this time there was a reasonable number of people, gathered in what appeared to be a protest.

The bewildered guard had shut himself inside his booth. The protesters did not appear to want to enter, content with yelling at the exterior of a closed institute. Tired police officers leaned against the barrier trying to prop up their watchful eyes with coffee. Heng and Manjunath got off their taxi and took in the scene.

They walked through the crowd, soaking in chants, and reading signs. Indeed, the protesters seemed to have little in common other than the direction they were facing. Heng had to translate their slogans with his phone's best efforts.

Technology progress human is regress! Trees die people because lie!
Useless technology goes down!
God is laughing, where is freedom?
Not everything science knows!
And, curiously, in English: *No blood for oil!*
Heng and Manjunath tried to speak to some of the protesters.
'Do you speak English?'
'Unfortunately.'
'Why are you protesting?'
Here the answers began to diverge as much as the signs.
'Enough is enough!'
'Enough of what?'
'Everything!'

'Corporations are destroying to world!'

'Isn't this a government institute?'

'Still!'

'Too many national resources are being wasted on pointless research!'

'What do they research here?'

'Pointless things!'

'Phones are ruining the world!'

'But this is a supercomputing institute …'

'Probably figuring out how to make more phones to fry our brains!'

'Vaccinations are mind control!'

'How?'

'They pump your blood full of chemicals!'

'Isn't that what a vaccination is?'

'Exactly! Chemicals to control your mind!'

'For what purpose?'

'To make you stupid!'

'But why?'

'So … they can control you!'

'For what?'

'… money?'

'No blood for oil!'

'We agree. But why here?'

'It's an important message everywhere!'

Manjunath took Heng away from the crowd. 'Okay, Heng, here's my theory. I—'

'—these people are idiots!' said Heng.

'Oh … so you did have the same theory!' said Manjunath, patting him on the back.

'No, it was … a general comment. I think these loonies will be happy in a forest somewhere with just each other's company, like Wodewose. Sorry, what's your theory, sir?'

'That these people are stupid. Too stupid, in fact. We were looking for the Science Haters, and yes they're happy to be called Science

Haters. But the Science Haters from our theory, they can't be … these people.'

'Why not?'

'Heng, the Science Haters we're looking for are fearsome terrorists who wield the forces of nature. None of these words fit this group. It's been bothering me since you mentioned it. I kept looking up everything about them online, and it appears their name is the only thing they can agree upon. It was like the Science Haters were formulated as a glass jar, which has then fallen and shattered into different ideas, each a very different shape and a very different size, but still identifying as a piece of a jar. They just can't get organized enough to get anything worthwhile done.'

'I was thinking about something you said.'

'You think about things I say? Even I don't do that. That's very touching, Heng.'

'You said coincidences have emergent properties. Could this be an emergent property of a coincidence or a decoy, or foot soldiers who are more … dimwitted than some higher unseen power?'

'Correct. All correct. Exactly correct. Higher unseen power is the same conclusion I came to. The head of the science haters is much smarter, much more powerful, and … in my opinion … not even necessarily affiliated with these people. This could be a plan that got away from their higher management, or even a different cause though with the same name.'

'I suppose that makes sense. But what does that lead us to?'

'Not sure yet. Either way, we need to stop looking at eye level.' Manjunath looked up at the sky. 'We need to look higher.'

'Why are you looking at the sky, sir?'

'It's a silly idea. But leading up to … Heng, I want to ask you something.'

Manjunath looked into Heng's curious eyes. Not enough time has been spent on how some of the characters in this story look. That is the nature of this logger's storytelling. The reason for this is simply that how they look has been unimportant to the story so far. Now, perhaps, it is time. Manjunath's tired, round face caught a sliver of light from the periphery of the institute, functioning as the moon's understudy in the moonless night. His thick black eyebrows twitched with uncertainty, large lips pressed upon themselves in trepidation. His round eyes were set upon a coat of brown primer. Heng's features, in contrast, were angular like carpentry joints. The front of his skull bones raced forward with aspirations to become an elbow. The ones that reached first had to settle for a nose, and the others were relegated to cheekbones. A jagged, icy, anxious moon of Jupiter.

Tonight, the moons consorted in Earth's house in a syzygy where Earth was pretending not to look. They had been through several years' worth of adventure in half the time.

'What do you want to ask, sir?' asked Heng.

'We've been through a whole lot together, especially recently. And uh … you're a very good assistant, Heng, and I don't pay you or … like …'

'You do pay me, sir,' said Heng kindly.

'Oh. Do I?'

'Yes, I transfer my salary to myself every month.'

'Oh, good then. Good good good. It's really helpful … with you around. Before you were working with me, I—everything was much more difficult.'

'Oh, thank you sir. That's very kind of you.'

'And I'm not sure if I'm really offering you much in return for what you contribute to … me.'

'Sir, you hired me after I walked in to your office to deliver lunch because you thought I was applying for an assistant's position. I've been – I've felt – It's been good to be – to feel like I'm making a real contribution to something. And I've never had that before. That's all I really need. You don't have to worry about whether you're offering me enough. This job is all I want.'

'Well, that's unfortunate, Heng, because I was wondering if you wanted a different job … as a more front-facing … in a forward plane, stepping more forward, up? Stepping up but in a front sort of—Stepping in front and then up. Some movement, some positive displacement is what I'm proposing—'

'I don't think I understand what you're saying, sir.'

'You've just got so good at everything we do here, and that's why I was wondering … would you maybe consider not being an assistant and then … being a full-time partner? The name stays, of course, as Manjunath Detective Agency. Actually, no, we can change the name, Manjunath and Heng Detective Agency. That's also fine. But we're not doing abbreviations and we're not putting your name first. Okay, we can put your name first, but only if it's abbreviated and I'm not abbreviating mine. H and Manjunath Detective Agency is fine. The name itself is a mystery to be solved – but is that bad for business I'm now wondering because—'

Heng gave Manjunath a hug. Cosmic analogies have to be put aside, moons and planets do not embrace, celestial bodies collide only to destroy planets and decimate galaxies. The tendency for comfort is exclusive to biology. Any organism of one cell and up, when in need of comfort and celebration, seeks out an embrace. Only life hugs. It's nice to feel loved.

A long hug at the edge of a protest, near the compound of a supercomputing institute, outside a major city in Switzerland, in an environment alien in too many ways, was a way to feel at home. They uncoiled and smiled at each other.

'So, which name?' asked Manjunath.

'We don't need to decide now.' Heng beamed.

At this moment, wild shouting drew their attention. It drew the attention of the police and the protesters. This new, spirited yelling, energetic and effervescent, too dynamic to be politically charged, emerged from a car that had just stopped. The source left the car and carried itself towards the formerly hugging duo.

Manjunath gaped. 'Thatssss …'

Wildly gesturing in equal parts excitement and anger, the Swiss writer charged towards them.

ERROR – See full trace ?(Y/N)

CHAPTER 26

'It is the great legacy of the nation that the Victory Statue representssssss ...'

— The Prime Minister of India

Dr K got to his feet in the underground meadow.

Deafening chatter ran inside his head. Root. He had killed him. She didn't know. It was time. He had to hurry to make sure the Lower Reality was getting it done, or raze it to the ground and start again. Time was catching up. And absurdly, as absurdly as possible for someone whose plan is to destroy all existence, he wanted to do it before he could hurt anyone else.

'Krishna?'

He walked away in silence. A daze, forgivable for the heavily concussed. He made for the bedroom, grabbing a bottle of bourbon on the way. The loud ringing internal sword fight continued. He began to pack his things. He had to get out of here. It wasn't advisable. But how could he look her in the eye now? He had returned her infinite kindness with years of coldness, and now he was responsible for severing her one human connection. Her chance at growth. He had to go. Where was that black box? Where was the wall fragment? Where was the motorcycle? Where were his things?

'Krishna?' he heard Divya say softly.

An eerie cold took the air between them. He froze.

'I know,' she said.

He turned to see her in the doorway. After looking at her for years, it was as if now he finally saw her. Her hair askew, eyes wild and unblinking, her jaw twitching from being clenched and unclenched rapidly. She was dragging something in her hand. A long brown thigh bone from a chocolate moose. The character of the room had changed, the softness all gone, the air freezing, the light jagged.

She took short shallow breaths.

Clunk.

A sound tinged with foreboding. A sound that fired warnings in all directions. A sound of bone hitting bone. A sound of a weapon pressed against a skull. The sound from the balled-up bony end of the bone, the fist of the femur, resting lightly on a black box. It was at her feet.

'You can't go,' said Divya, her voice peppered with small uneven vibrations in a threatening, frightening quiver. 'Sit down.'

'Divya,' said Dr K slowly . He took a deliberate, careful step towards her, raising his hands above him in supplication.

'Stop. STOP!'

CLUNK.

He stopped. Her nostrils flared as she began to shake with anger.

'Stay right fucking there! Back. GO BACK. Good.'

Dr K backed in his tracks quickly and slipped, falling heavily and painfully on the ground. He twisted in the pain of broken barbwire bones pressing his insides.

His eyes flashed – sand. Desolate. Desert. An animal was struggling with the last of its life. Its legs collapsed. It was dying. A world away. Pain. Terror. Hopelessness. He closed his eyes.

'Does it hurt? Are you in pain? Good. Fucking great. You really are scum, Krishna. I can't believe I ever thought there was something more to you. Something deeper. In and out, through and through, you are pure scum.'

'Divya, you don't understand. There's a lot of—'

'I understand. I figured it all out. That little tile of yours. It's very chatty. Last night when you were sleeping we got talking. I suppose I needed someone to talk to rather than fucking babysit. It asked me, can you believe that? It asked me *how* I was! Hasn't occurred to you to do it yet. It never did. Why did I expect that to change? There was never anything inside to change, was there, Krishna? Oh, it felt good to talk, to speak to someone honestly after a while. That's what it's like for me. A fucking inanimate object is my confidant. I told it everything. Why I came here, what I escaped from, all about you and me, and finally ... about Root.

'It was very considerate. Very compassionate, when it told me that Root was dead. How? Because of you. Because he got too close to you. I couldn't believe it. But then I had to. It made sense. Your atmosphere is poisonous, Krishna. I know that first-hand. What was so important about that box? What was so important about this Lower Reality simulation of yours? What is so important about this one? That your tile did not know. It was sure it must be something vital, though. It's very fond of you. That would make it the only ... thing. Congratulations, at least there's a non-human entity that likes you. Thinks of you like a parent almost. You have to laugh.'

Clunk.

'I kept egging it on, to think, to guess. Why is he doing this? Don't you care about him? Maybe I could help? I acted so concerned. I really am a great actor. It came up with a little theory. A most incredible theory, something absurd, ridiculous. You, Dr Krishna, behaving irrationally? Damaging your career? The Krishna I know would never! But then it all made sense ...' Divya's face twisted into a cruel smile. 'You're feeling guilty ...'

Clunk.

'Divya, please just—' Dr K felt words falling out of his mouth as he looked around wildly for his motorcycle.

'Oh, it's not here. I left it to stroll around outside. How does it feel
to *feel*, Krishna? You can't take it? Welcome to the world. You've taken
some of my alcohol too? You're trying to numb yourself? It's almost
cute. You feel guilty for your friend's death. You should. Perenna really,
truly cared about you. But she choked on your poison. And now you
want to take revenge. Against everyone! Against everything! Against the
cruel, cruel reality that took your friend. It's laughably naive. Nothing
about you is special. Nothing about this is special. The world is not
responsible for Perenna's death. Only you are.'

Dr K tried in vain to formulate an escape plan. There was nothing
around. The whole room was turning painfully bright and cold.

'The Authority is on its way. I thought I would give you a chance
today. To say something. About Root. About your plan. To show me. A
last chance to show me a trace of a heart, but even now you just want
nursing. You just want to feel better about yourself.'

'You're right, Divya. You're right about everything. I am scum. I
know that. I can't even bear to face myself ... I—'

Divya cut him off with a laugh. It was a laugh he had never heard
before, hollow and piercing, speckled with cold blood. It struck him
then that she barely ever laughed at all. Now, leaning against the bone,
she laughed.

'Of course I'm right. What is the plan here? You're going to feed
me a sob story and I'll have a change of heart? The acceptance of your
sins doesn't absolve you, Krishna. You're smart enough to know that.
Besides, the Authority is coming and there's nowhere for you to run. It's
fun seeing you like this. Splayed on the ground, docile, quiet, guilty.'

She lifted up the bone. 'For the record, I don't give a fuck if
everything is destroyed. I just want to be alive to see your end.'

'Divya, please! It could explode!'

'Good. Let's die.'

With a heavy swing, she brought the fist of the femur crashing
down on the black box. Dr K lunged forward but missed hopelessly.
The box dented with a sickening crunch. He scrambled forward and

wrapped his arms around it, laying curled at her feet, shielding the box with his broken body.

'This is all I have left,' he whispered. 'Please …'

'Not for long,' said Divya and raised the bone over her head.

≈

If your universe was encased in styrofoam in a carton marked 'fragile' – with a wine glass to indicate the degree of fragility – and this carton was carelessly kicked into a luggage compartment, rattled on a truck, or dropped with a crunchy flourish, do you think you would notice?

Given the scale of the universe, probably not. The edge of the universe is so very far from your vantage point. But do outward effects ripple inwards? If a butterfly flaps its wings in the opposite corner of the globe, how tired does it get? To remove some silliness, the black box did not contain a tiny bubbling miniaturized universe, although that would have been adorable. It was a simulation, not a condensation or a scale model. It was virtual for everyone not in it, made possible by extensive delicate calculation, and it drew its energy from one single particle.

Just the one. One for the road, for the birds and the bees, the flowers and the trees, the mice and their cheese, a house and a sneeze, the stars and their keys; comets and their veils, galaxies and their trails, explosion, implosion, suspicion, delight, suspense and sunflowers. Where can you find this particle and what are its business hours? You can't. In an act of subatomic subterfuge, a human-made particle was entered into existence. The only kind of synthetic particle ever created, furious at its heretic existence, begging to disintegrate into sensible natural things but not allowed to, provided enough energy to simulate a Lower Reality. It bears a drab alphanumeric name, but Perenna and Krishna lovingly called it a 'weird particle'.

It was carefully housed inside the complications of the black box, rattling the bars of its cages, trying to break free. The design of the black box was for efficiency, not roadworthiness. Other black boxes under Dr Krishna's recent care had become defunct after bumping into, falling over on their side and one time when he had punched one. Entire universes, vast infinities blinked out of existence in a second. He had since rejigged it to be less delicate and more secure. The security was the explosive measure that had taken Root's life. On touching or toying with the top of the black box, an inviting handle would emerge. This handle, if pulled, would unleash the fury of the weird particle, causing a sizeable discharge of energy. Enough to kill. Enough to kill quite a few. A neat square of destruction.

Would this box survive against a downswung leg o' moose? It did. Barely.

Next question: did the Lower Reality know something was ahit? Did they feel it? Did this constitute an Act of God?

Answer: No. Well, no and yes. Hitting a television does not alter the nature of the programme but can cause a temporary shear on the screen if you look hard enough. Characters stretch, subtitle kerning is ruined, mountains distort and ad jingles jangle. In the Lower Reality, in Heng's world, a split-second effect took place. For a second or less, everyone on Earth had a slight lisp. And then it was gone. They went back to business as usual, unaware that their very universe was hanging by a thigh.

$$\approx$$

~:Log -ld

LESS DRAMATICALLY:

Manjunath gaped. 'Thatssss …'
  ERROR – See full trace? (Y/N)
'What?' asked Heng.
'It's her!'
'Why did you say it like that?'
'Say what like what?'

Further inquiry was halted by the entrance of the Swiss writer.

Heaving under the strength of her own yelling, she took a gasping while before she spoke. It was an emotional moment, bookending another emotional moment. The reunion of a fellowship broken by mistrust. A moment for tender apologies and joyous tears.

'First of all,' said the Swiss writer, 'fuck both of you!'

Her crunched, freckled face snarled as she ran a hand through her unwashed red hair oily with sweat and promptly resumed yelling.

'You ditched me in the middle of nowhere!'

'You left on your own! We offered to ditch you here!' said Manjunath indignantly.

'You accused me of being in cahoots with these …' she gestured at the protesting group, '… morons.'

'We did no such thing! We were just being distrustful and suspicious, only building up to a formal accusation—'

'How did you find us?' asked Heng.

'I mean … this is where we were going. So I came here, and here you are,' shrugged the Swiss writer.

'Yeah, Heng, that was an easy one,' said Manjunath.

'My apologies.'

'Shut up! I walked alone for so long, figuring out what to do, and when I realized I hadn't finished yelling at both of you I had to hitchhike half the way here, and then, well, I took a bus, which wasn't that difficult – but it was boring! I spent all that time thinking about just how stupid your theory was, and some amount of time thinking about the lyrics of "Highway Star". How could I conceivably be the head of the Science Haters, just because I was there when you came up with the name? Why would I put my life in jeopardy on the ferry if I was such a mastermind – and mainly, I was looking up the Science Haters and … wow … these guys are not smart. They seem to accept all sorts, and barely have a common umbrella that they're standing under—'

'—we agree.' Heng smiled.

'We were actually just considering revising our theory,' said Manjunath.

'Oh, NOW you're taking the time to theorize? Did I tell you both how long I had to walk – by the way, did you notice that all these protesters have a lisp? That's quite unusual.'

The three stopped to listen. 'No they don't,' said Manjunath after a few slogans made their rounds.

'Could have sworn I heard – well never mind. *NOW you're taking the time to theorize?* I had to walk back till the road so I could—'

'No, I heard it too!' exclaimed Heng. 'Sir, you suddenly slipped on your last consonant, that's what I was asking you about.'

'Heng, you don't have to call me "sir" anymore, we're partners now.'

'Oh,' said the Swiss writer. 'Well, congratulations! When did this happen?'

'Just now, right before you came,' said Manjunath.

The moment was pollinated by a smiling group hug.

'I'm not sure if I should still be angry,' said the Swiss writer.

'Don't be, please! Sir – Manjunath, didn't you hear the sudden lisp when you spoke?'

'I was speaking, Heng, how could I be listening when I speak? When I speak I only speak, and when I listen I only listen. Anything else is a disservice to conversation.'

'S – Manjunath, you often don't listen.'

'I said *when* I listen.' He turned to the Swiss writer. 'Did you hear me talking from all the way over there?'

'No,' she replied. 'The protesters' chants suddenly skidded. I thought maybe I was just tired or something, but if you heard it too, Heng … it is most bizarre. How does that happen?'

'Could be one of many things,' said Manjunath. 'Everything is one of many things. But … if you'll follow me on a thought journey, this potentially adds credence to our theory, Heng.'

'Lead the way,' said the Swiss writer.

'Book the tickets,' said Manjunath to Heng, with a bow.

'Well, s – Manjunath— Can I just say sir, please? It feels better and also has far fewer syllables.'

'Manjunath is not a good name,' agreed the Swiss writer. 'With apologies, of course, I'm sure it's a fitting name for a life, but tiresome to read and write repeatedly.'

'Well, I've come this far being called Manjunath,' said Manjunath. 'Would be a chore to change it retroactively.'

'Time travel,' said the Swiss writer, nodding, 'always a trap. Too finicky. You could do a search-and-replace-all, but that doesn't help us much.'

'Agreed. I wouldn't mind being called by any word.'

Heng sensed the conversation begin to glitter and pulse, threatening to burst into confetti if not contained, but he sensed this without his usual foreboding. It was a nice, comfortable return to abnormal. Since there were things to discuss, he gently picked up the needle and put it back to track five, hopefully a hit single.

'So we were just discussing,' said Heng, 'we proposed the theory of the Science Haters as the culprit behind all the disappearances and attacks on supercomputing institutes. And the appearance of these Science Haters after our theory is almost like a red herring. A perfect diversion to get us out of someone's way. The original Science Haters from our theory were brilliant and secretive, too brilliant to be … these people. So either we are totally wrong and these are indeed coincidences. But if our theory *is* accurate? Then the Science Haters we're looking for are so cunning, that they have sent out stupid foot soldiers to distract anyone who could be trying to stop their *real* plans.'

Manjunath stepped in. 'Or they could be creating the perfect group to take the fall for their cunning. In any case, it seems like there is a higher authority in charge. Devious, powerful, secretive, all-knowing, all-seeing.'

Heng gasped. 'And this would necessitate that they *know* about *our* actions, which is why all of the distractions are so inextricably linked to our specific situation. There must be a greater power, the hand that controls the Science Haters.'

'Then, along with limitless intelligence, this hand also has limitless power. That's how they can control the literal forces of Nature! Oh, this is exciting, what shall we call them?' said the Swiss writer.

'The *Real* Science Haters?' offered Manjunath.

'No, that's a Manjunath-type name. Again, no offence.'

'Can I please choose a better name this time?' asked Heng.

'Go for it!'

'How about the *Higher Power*?'

'Perfect!' said the Swiss writer.

'So ...' said Manjunath. 'This Higher Power. This all-knowing, all-seeing, all-mighty higher power. They could be responsible for this sudden lisp-flickering.'

'I mean ... to even count this as evidence seems like a stretch. I thought all-powerful was like ... you know, full of power. If we're saying this Higher Power can control the involuntary speech of people, then we're saying ... we're saying ... we're ...' said the Swiss writer.

In her words the Swiss writer heard the click of a landmine. They stood there, afraid that any sudden movement could set off a very unsettling, explosive realization. Carefully, gently, gingerly, Heng took a step forward.

'Supposing they can,' said Heng. 'Supposing this is worth consideration – no ...'

Manjunath spoke quickly. 'Can we see a live broadcast? Let's rewind to a few moments ago and see if ... uh ... see if we can ... see.'

They clustered around the Swiss writer's phone, who quickly found a running broadcast in German, reporting on, of all things, the weather. They listened carefully, but Manjunath and Heng had no idea what they were listening to. Luckily the Swiss writer did.

She pulled back a few minutes. Then she pulled it back and listened to it again. And the added tremble in her finger when she pulled it back a third time told them all they needed to know.

'Oh my …' she said. Manjunath begin to blink rapidly. At the rapid tempo set by his heart rate – *prestissimo!* – Heng spoke.

'Then it – it's true. Then this is Godlike power. And if it is Godlike ability, it could have only affected everyone in our immediate vicinity or everyone around … the world – but – it is out of character for this Higher Power, because it calls attention to the nature … and capability of the Higher Power. It is a large scale, noticeable, unexplainable event. Like an Act of God.'

The Swiss writer, in a panic, added, 'That officer, remember? The one that apparently inspired the Science Haters – he said he felt he was … being controlled by an unseen power! *He said it was God!*'

A beetle gulped on the ground between them.

'Oh no. Oh no. Oh my. That means – listen! We need to come up with a contingency. A safe word. In case any of us is controlled. We should have a way to check … something we wouldn't be able to say if God was controlling us, to show that we are still … us,' said Manjunath urgently.

'Satchel,' said the Swiss writer.

'No, I don't like satchel.'

'Gravy?'

'Gravy is better but too … I don't know … a v and a y so close together, I don't trust it—'

Heng screamed so loudly that the protesters stopped protesting, so loudly that larks off their tits abandoned their drinks and began to hurry home, so loudly that Manjunath and the Swiss writer shut up, which was incidentally what he screamed.

'SHUT UP!'

They looked at him with the same awe that they had on the ferry. He lowered his voice so only the two of them could hear. 'The song we first heard together. If anyone sings, the other two must join in, is that clear?'

'Yes sir,' said Manjunath meekly.

The Swiss writer nodded. The beetle couldn't take the tense silence and hurried away. In the absence of shouting, the protesters started protesting again and the larks decided one more couldn't hurt.

'Now we have to ask,' whispered Manjunath, 'what is God's plan?'

Adding a sentence remarkably out of character, Heng said, 'And why is he fucking with us?'

CHAPTER 27

'I do look forward to seeing you, Fred –
Should I keep calling you Fred? I feel as if
I have finally found a true friend.'
                                        – Letter to Dr Root from Divya

God* did have a plan for them, trembling on the ground, clutching their universe.

'Not for long,' said Divya, the bone raised over her head.

In the space between the apex of the arc and the cowering man at her feet hung the fate of a universe and many characters that I had grown to like. Was this the end? It very well may be, then should we compose eulogies, or are we in a paean sort of mood – wait, what's that sound?

A sound sped through the air behind Divya. A powerful envelope of speed carrying a faint whir, like mechanical lightning. She barely had time to notice it when it hit her in the back. The impact hurtled her forward, tumbling over Dr K, crashing into the blunt corners of her soft bed. She lay on the ground, unconscious.

The cavalcade of human impact ended in a second. It took another for Dr K to realize that the crash of impact had not come from his body. He looked up and saw...

Un Moto!
Si, una motocicleta!
В самом деле? Мотоцикл?
ਹਾਂ. ਇੱਕ ਚੇਖਾ ਮੋਟਰਸਾਈਕਲ *!*

Divya lay on the floor. Dr Krishna would be happy to see her superficially unhurt when he did get around to seeing her. For now his eyes were focused, not on the motorcycle but the person astride it, a colleague from The Scientific Institute, his former supervisor, Genius Category A, Nataliya. All trains of thought were delayed and he found himself staring dumbly at his saviour.

She looked at him cowering on the floor, hugging a dented black box. 'You look ... worse.'

Dr K let out a hoarse wheeze in response. He slowly turned over to see Divya unconscious but not superficially hurt, and he was relieved.

'Get up. Get your things,' said Nataliya sharply. 'We're leaving.'

The best course of action here was to follow instructions. As quickly as his body would allow him, he got to his feet and looked around again for his things.

'I don't have—'

'This bag? It was on your ... what do you call this? Technocycle?' said Nataliya, swinging forward his bag.

He staggered over and took it from her hand and quickly glanced at the monitoring tablet. He was relieved to find that within the black box, the Lower Reality was still running. Slowly – this was proving to be his most painful range of motion – he bent over to pick up the dented box. He put it in the bag.

Nataliya slid forward in her seat to make room for him. 'Get on.'

He looked over at the bottle of bourbon lying on the floor. He left it lying there. Obediently, he shuffled forward and sat behind her.

'Nataliya, I – I don't know why you …'

Sometimes it is hard to believe that people really say the things we find them saying in entertainment. But often the most dramatically fitting response is the shortest one packed with the most meaning. Brevity is the soul of wit and the appendix of understanding. She interrupted him blandly, as a matter of fact, but it will help to imagine her wearing sunglasses and loudly revving the motorcycle, whatever the reader considers the most *cool*. She said, 'Shut up. I'm saving you.'

≈

The motorcycle charged out the house into the forest. In a line, they sped down the border of DS-C. Nataliya shouted behind her over the sound of their speed.

'I came here just to investigate, it was the logical next step, didn't even imagine anyone would be here. But imagine my surprise when I saw you about to get clubbed to death! I didn't know what to do – there wasn't enough time – I just pushed right into her.'

Dr K clutched the bag and listened.

'Saw this device outside, and thought it was some rich person's toy and then this – you've modified and miniaturized a wall unit, extraordinary but expected from you – it *greeted* me. Knew who I was! Told me you were here. Strange!'

Dr K wanted to express his gratitude, but he would have to shout it and couldn't summon the energy to do so.

'She probably had a good reason to strike you on the skull. I do too. I'm sure many people do. But I don't know … I'm guessing I can't watch it happen … This is great!' Nataliya pressed the motorcycle forward, clearly finding wielding it very exciting. 'This thing is extraordinarily illegal. And this wall unit. Oof. All of this a secret! How many secret things have you done in your life?'

She squeezed them through a banyan tree, whose roots had formed a neat hidden alcove around the trunk. She stopped the motorcycle there. The wall turned off its light, and they were in absolute darkness.

'The Authority,' wheezed Dr K, 'is coming.'

'Probably,' said Nataliya. 'We need to decide what to do.'

'Why did you come here? Why are you helping me?'

'Just so you know, I haven't forgiven you. Your machine exploded and killed Root. You were horrible to me the entire time you worked on my project. But I'm helping you because today I saw what the Authority really does. Today I realized that there's a lot more going on here than anyone knows about and I want to know too. I'm helping you because despite whatever it is that you're trying to achieve, despite the horrible fact of yourself, you were trying to help me. Now tell me everything.'

≈

- Dr K told her what was going on.
- He did it honestly.
- He showed her the Lower Reality.
- Her mind was appropriately blown.

But why exactly did Nataliya say Dr K was trying to help her?

Short Answer: He was.

Long Answer: He wasn't initially, but in the face of her project being shut down he was.

Complete Answer: As Nataliya was bursting out of the Repository, you will remember that there was a record of an update to the project that she was supervising. It was her only project, the one that Dr K was working on.

The update was from its clinical trials. Conducted for one month, Week 1 and Week 2 had the participants complaining of a persistent headache. The control group simply complained of life. The update was from Week 3, where a dramatic shift had taken place. All the participants in the test group reported higher life satisfaction, stronger relationships and a pervasive feeling of calm, and yes they had a headache, but they would like to keep it.

What and why on Earth and in the heavens? We only need to look at one person's account to understand:

Volunteer B, Male, Thirty-three

The headache used to be a real pain in the ass. Oh, that's silly. You get what I mean. I'm no stranger to headaches, I always have one from dehydration, exhaustion, sleeplessness, or the withdrawal from something, but the difference is that those headaches always go away with enough water and some stretching. This was different, persistent. I mean it was really always there, no matter what I was doing or where I was.

It felt like someone was playing the drum behind all my experiences. Not painful enough to take all my attention, and not quiet enough to be completely absent. Just irritating. At first, I was furious. I mean, I said as much in the last two meetings. It's funny now how angry I was. That's another thing I've become very good at, being able to laugh at a feeling instead of feeling it – I'm getting ahead of myself, I apologize.

After the second week I was exhausted by being irritated. It became a fact of my life, this headache, and that really has made all the difference.

I feel like it sets the tempo for my life. No matter what I'm feeling, gradually I remember this headache, and I get some distance from what I'm feeling. Like I'm sitting on the drum and watching my anger, watching my irritation, watching my cynicism. It really – I hope I'm explaining this well. Gradually the impulse to sit back and attend to the drumbeat has become quicker, and I just feel so much more ... relaxed. When a feeling enters, the fact that I can look at it reminds me that it's separate from myself. That anger is all the way over there! It's not me, I'm not angry, it is just anger!

I've heard people say things like this before, but I've always dismissed it as garbage. Now that I can see the dismissal come, I know it's a choice to give into it or not. It's not that I don't feel these things, oh no, I feel everything the same as before. But as soon as I do – there's that headache, there's the metronome,

there's the drum! And I know I can watch from a safe distance
without getting hurt.

My friends and family don't know what's changed. They love
this new me. They say I pay more attention when they talk,
and I care more about their problems. Got to say, I really do! I
think the only thing that stopped me from caring about their
problems was my own problems showing up. And, I mean, they
still do show up – but then there's that headache, and if I sit
back and let my problem go – oh shit, that's what that means,
let things go, oh, that means so much, oh wow! – if I do *let* my
problems *go*, then what shows up next is concern for the people
around me! Like real, true concern! All on its own! It's fantastic!

I can also decide which thoughts to indulge in. I didn't know
that that was an option too! I'm not making sense. I'll explain.
Yesterday, as I was watching myself getting resentful about not
being successful – there's the beat! It seems wrong to even say
headache anymore. Okay, so I jumped back and watched the
resentment come, and I thought it was funny that if I just let it
evaporate, then it would be gone! Then I wondered how come
I didn't feel happy more often? Honest question to ask, didn't
really think of asking myself earlier. Shouldn't being happy be
the highest on my list of priorities? Ooh, this next thing – oh,
it blew my mind – even as I was thinking this, you know, this
little voice spoke in my head, I mean my voice, my internal
monologue, whatever, it talks all the time, but it always says the
things that trigger the bad feelings. Um, yes, I was saying, that
voice in my head, it said, clearly said, wait, I have to say this so
you understand.

I sat in the space, and the thought came – why didn't I feel
happy more often? And as a response the voice said, 'Well, what
do you think all this is?'

It was instantaneous, like a spark had gone off, and I realized
that all this space was that! There was a character to this space
and – I'm not sure if happiness is the right word. Forgive me,

my vocabulary isn't the greatest, um, like a calmer space than happiness. Peace? Almost ... what's that? What did you say? Oh, that's perfect! Yes, thank you! That fits exactly. Wow!

Tranquility. That's what it is, and if there's nothing else, there's always that. That's the nature of ... being. My being. I don't know what's happening with everyone else, I really do hope it happens to them too. I really don't want people to feel so ... oh ...

Work? Yeah, they like me at work too. I find work much easier with the problems gone. The problems that hurt were never with the work itself, I'm beginning to see. Just worries about whether people would think what I did was good, whether it would make me more successful and faster, you know? Things like that. Obstacles. In the absence of all of that, I had to ask myself what I was really supposed to do here and the answer was 'contribute'! So I just contribute to what the company does, you know, really like, not what would help me, what would be the best outcome. Seems far less important than it used to. Work is just practical. It's just what I do, what you have to do to live, you know? It's nice to feel useful, nice to feel like you add to something. I'm lucky I get a chance to do that. I'm not so concerned with being at the top. You know, I always thought that I had to be miserable until I had enough, until – I don't know what was supposed to happen ... But if I can be happy now, what's all the misery for? What would I really gain by succeeding?

But where I work, I wonder if what we do, if it really benefits people as much as it could. Listen to me! Mister Caring! It just ... when you stop thinking about progressing personally, there's really not much more point to making what we make, is there? It's got to benefit people, that's essentially what we promise.

Anything else? What else is left to say here, ah! I enjoy my time alone now. Like, I really cherish it. Before, I just wanted to be alone because I was tired of being around people, but it's not like it was so much fun being by myself either. Just less bad.

Now I'm so excited to sit back and be in the – what's that word again? – tranquility, yes! And also, also, also, I know you guys are the scientists, but I've been trying some experiments of my own! I realized that you can get that voice to talk! That little voice in your head? I mean, it's you, it's your voice, nothing new there, but if you let everything go, and sit in the space for some time, then if you bring up a question, the voice answers! I mean, it's not a stranger. The answer will be something that you knew already, but you get to know clearly what you *really* think about things, right? Does that make sense? Lately I've been thinking, too. It's another exciting area. Well, if I'm watching myself think, then who is – thinking? I'm not. I'm watching it, but then I wonder, like, who's watching? Don't really have an answer yet, but I don't know, maybe next week?

The other participants were in agreement. The fist-shaking of the beginning of the experiment had metamorphosed into contentment. Their lives had a-changed, and the only remaining worry was whether this headache would subside, because they didn't want to retreat into their former selves. It would. Dr K had designed it to last a month.

Why a month? Why *months* for that matter? And *where* months now that we're on the subject? Perhaps the point of a yard is to give a yardstick something to do. Most clinical trials lasted a month, so he had designed it to work for exactly that long.

He had had no original intent to work on the project at all; it was intended as a cover for him to continue Perenna's Lower Reality work, all while under guise of being gainfully employed as something else. But when the bureaucratic boot was about to close in on Nataliya and she screamed at him, he changed his mind. Something about her fury reminded him of Perenna.

He started from first principles. The objective was to synthesize calm. The calmest human states were those of deep concentration, strong attention to something. Pure focus permitted no despair. It is impossible to see around you if your head is down, a lesson he had learned from his own life. It was only when distraction blew back the curtains that you could see pain. The problem he set out to solve was how to bring the curtains back, how to return focus. Focus on what? After some consideration, he hit upon the idea of calling the attention of the mind to the mind, at least where the experience of conscious identity seemed to be. He looked for a simple solution, an elegant solution, one that wouldn't be too much of a headache. And he found it.

Discussions of Dr K's genius in these pages have been extensive, but just to remind you, he was the real deal. In a single night he solved the problem of Nataliya's project. It was his best effort (at nightly rates), but he wasn't sure whether it would work. He didn't try it himself, because he thought it might. He didn't think he deserved peace.

Do the people get the pill? Does the most ancient human malaise get cured? The oldest systemic manufacturing defect of the specifies, the cruellest beast born from intelligence, does it finally get pushed away? Does a new era of existence, one of tranquility and calm ultimately arise? Can people live as they truly want to?

I don't know. Nataliya missed her meeting to come here.

≈

Nataliya quickly made the connection.

'So this correlation of images and events between our reality and the Lower Reality is consistent?'

Dr K was a little taken aback by how quickly she had put it together. 'The longer the Lower Reality runs, the more correlations begin to prop up. Specific themes, icons, images, ideas that are not just trivial chance. This is not correlation, this is a confluence. There is a single unknown connecting this reality and the Lower Reality. The fact that I am not transmitting these things means it lies completely outside of our understanding. Something runs between this reality and goes to the next, and whatever it is, doesn't originate here. It is self-important to think so.'

'But it is still possible that it does.'

'It is.'

'And it is still possible that the Lower Reality's simulation may just run without effect.'

'It is.'

'What is your plan in that instance? What if – and this is my immediate instinct – there is another level of nesting possible? What then? All of this suffering would have been for nothing.'

In the darkness, Dr K smiled. 'Each level of nesting will add exponential complexity. This is not absolute infinity. It is countable and will only increase stepwise. There will be a time when whatever runs through it all reaches its end. The confluence will dry up. I can control the speed of the simulation, so I can make the complexity explosion happen instantly. And, when that comes, it will be the end of this world. The only thing that matters is to keep the Lower Reality running until that end comes.'

'Assuming we are a Lower Reality … that could still take … forever.'

Dr K looked straight at Nataliya. His eyes saw a nebula, painted smoke of glittering galaxies, the bloom of dead light, still arriving. Bulging pockets of eternity, in the shadow of infinity, utterly alone.

'Forever will always arrive.'

A cascade of croaking insects filled up the silence between them. Shuffles and slithers in the forest listened for prey. Black formless dimensionless darkness, like a million cold eyes, like a black box, encased the night. There is never a moon during conversations like these.

Nataliya spoke softly, 'I suppose if it does happen, it's almost as if … it was supposed to.'

Dr K said nothing, but remembered his own words. If the truth is destruction, let destruction be true.

'I won't stop you,' said Nataliya. 'But I can't support this.'

'I know. I won't ask you to. You've done enough for me already.'

'Then you should go. Fine a place to hide … forever.'

Dr K felt his way back on the motorcycle. The wall fragment sliced open the darkness again. They shook hands.

In his frail hand, in his weak and withered grip, Nataliya could touch his pain. The tremendous genius she always lamented lacking, housed in this body, this mind that she used to envy, was broken. It was torturing him. This was the price. This is what it cost to be great, no, to be thought of as great. She had spent her whole life under the gloomy Category A label, but she never considered her extraordinary capacity to see what people felt, even when they couldn't. In Root, who berated her, in everyone who did, she saw only the hatred they housed for themselves. It is a pity she never considered this in her evaluations of her intelligence. It is a pity that most people never do. That might be true genius.

What was left to say except farewell?

'Bye,' said Nataliya.

Dr K smiled at her. And then she did something incredible. Something exciting delicious delightful round large warm sweet sugar-coated soft-boiled caramelized concerned considerate eye-opening mouth-opening and kind. She walked forward to the head of the motorcycle and leaned over into the light.

And she looked right at me, and said, 'Bye!'

---

* The word God is used loosely here to refer to Dr Krishna. In the narrator's defence, the word God is mostly used loosely, even though it arrives sharply dressed for the occasion with a carefully coiffed capital G. It is a roomy word, encapsulating all of the unknown, and eventually gets whittled down to vocational terms like creator, almighty, father, mother – all casually clothed, narrower, tighter terms. More adventurous religions choose individual names and images for their Gods, tight as tight can be, vacuum-sealed with

preservatives for long lasting freshness. It is for this reason that the word God is used, hopefully in a way it would approve of. Pragmatically and without celebration, exaltation, conversion, conservation or deforestation. If this strikes you as a heretic idea, the narrator would like to remind you that this is your problem. All problems you see in the world are your problem. Often the world needs servicing, but equally often you might require an eye test.

CHAPTER 28

'Plainly put, I have put and will put everything as plainly as I want to put it. So I won't saddle you with these anymore. Thank you for your patronage. Based on your experience with this narrator, how likely are you to recommend it to a friend or colleague?'

— Narrator

~:Log –ld

LESS DRAMATICALLY:

The police officer who escorted Olivia home felt an uneasy twinge of instinct. She needed to be home, to look after her parents but ... something felt wrong. Something was pulling her the other way. The closer she got to her parents' house, the more taut the pull became, until finally she was forced to stop. It was duty's call. She was exhausted, but as much as she hated it, she was diligent. She turned the car back around to Olivia's apartment.

Every inch of the road proclaimed its use in the other direction, roomy places for U-turns made themselves available, but she grit her teeth and drove on. It would be fine, turn back. Outside the building

– everything looks fine, turn back. That bitch scientist would never appreciate this, turn back. On the stairwell, she closed her eyes and took a breath. She spoke sternly to instinct and duty and said, 'All right, if she's fine, I'm going home.'

It didn't have time to say 'I told you so', because as she opened her eyes she heard loud thuds from upstairs. Not pausing to think, her fingers closed around her holster as she ran up. On the third floor, she turned with her weapon drawn to see three people banging on Olivia Capslich's door.

≈

In a troubled tizzy, Manjunath Heng and the Swiss writer had twirled, minds aching with disbelief, pockets full of posies, but held safely in each other's orbits. Their worry-go-round took them back to the 'r' in Zürich, the dense middle of the Swiss writer's apartment, one she shared with her sister.

Given the Swiss writer's insistence on her calling as a writer, and her determination not to write anything, her contribution to the apartment was purely that of occupying space. She did not pay rent, clean up, keep it down or have a key. They stood outside the door ringing the bell but it was not answered. They had switched to knocking and subsequently pounding. Someone had to be home, the TV was on!

≈

'STOP!' screamed the officer, weapon fully raised, shoulders level, stance staggered and finger off the trigger, because she couldn't see any weapons. The immediate assertion of power was important so she could assess the situation. In a stroke of luck, she appeared to have found the three most compliant people on the planet.

Heng, Manjunath and the Swiss writer froze in their exact positions. Even their expressions stayed stuck on their faces and aimed at the closed door.

'Turn!' screamed the officer.

They remained frozen. Manjunath and Heng didn't understand; the Swiss writer shouted, 'Around which axis should we turn and at what angle?'

'Turn and face me!'

Slowly the three pivoted to face the officer. The Swiss writer first, the other two following suit. The officer kept the gun level but felt immense relief. The group looked unarmed and too bewildered to be attempting harm. But you could never take chances.

'What are you doing here?'

'I live here!'

'Show me some ID!'

'I have to move to show you ID!'

'Then move!'

'Where should I move?'

The police officer lowered her gun. 'You two, put your hands against the wall. You—'

'They don't understand German!'

The police officer sighed in English. 'You two, put your hands against the wall. You—'

'I actually prefer German—'

'SHUT UP and come here!'

The Swiss writer obediently shuffled over to the officer and handed her an ID.

The officer looked at the ID and then at the Swiss writer. Once, twice, thrice, frice, vifce and asked, 'You are related to Olivia Capslich?'

'Yes, I'm her sister.'

The officer struggled with her throat. 'And your name is *Bolivia* Capslich?'

'Yes. And I'm the older one,' said the Swiss writer in a small voice.

'So … they started with Bolivia, and went to Olivia after that?'

'Yes.'

'Ouch.'

'Our parents were supposed to vacation to Peru and I was conceived, which cancelled their plan.'

'So how does that explain ...'

'Bolivia is next to Peru.'

'What?'

'Our parents weren't great. Is this important information? Is making fun of people a new police policy?'

'No no,' said the police officer. 'I get it. My legal name is Madeline, but I changed it when I was sixteen,' she lowered her voice to a whisper, 'from Madagascar.'

'You poor thing.'

'My brother's name is David.'

Heads were shaken and clucks were emitted. Madagascar handed the ID back to Bolivia – err, the police officer handed the ID back to the Swiss writer. Much better.

'Who are these two?' asked the police officer.

'Friends of mine. We ... uh ... don't have a key, my sister doesn't give me one.'

The police officer grew concerned. 'Well, she's at home, I dropped her home myself. Did you call her?'

'She didn't answer. I can hear her phone ringing inside.'

Tension ricocheted between them, gaining momentum until finally the police officer said, 'We should check to see if she's safe.'

'Why wouldn't she be safe?'

'Don't you know? Her life has been threatened by someone claiming to be in the Science Haters. It seems an empty threat but ...'

For a brief moment the police officer considered the situation, its supporting facts, possible explanations and vintage. She made a decision. Walking over to the door, she sized it up for a second before finally lifting a boot and kicking it. It swung open immediately with a little gasp from its outraged hinges at this most improper action. Placing a hand on her weapon, she stepped inside.

'That was very cool,' whispered Manjunath as the officer quickly scanned through the room.

She made quick work of the assessment. Nooks, crannies, corners – check; cupboards, door pockets, bedunders – check. No one was inside except a couple arguing on television, and a phone bursting with notifications. She walked back to the door.

'Anything?' asked Heng.

'No one inside,' said the police officer, looking worried. 'She was told to stay home, I dropped her here.' She whipped out her radio and barked crisply into it. Her charge was missing. No currently known cause for alarm. Check cameras for Olivia Capslich and be on the lookout. She could be in danger. The police officer turned to the Swiss writer. 'Does she have any other place she could be?'

'She's always at the institute, working, as far as I know …'

'Anywhere else?'

The Swiss writer looked tentative. She answered slowly, 'Is it … against the law to follow your sister?'

'No – I mean, it depends – Bolivia! If you know something you have to tell me. There is a remote but real possibility that your sister was abducted and if you have any information, you should tell me!'

'Okay – but look – don't tell her I told you. If I'm calling anyone home in the evening she always locks herself in the room, but if it's a noisy group … she usually leaves. So once I told her my slam poet friends were coming over from an artist commune and – I've never seen her leave faster – they could have been good, you know? I mean, they're not, but she didn't know that! What? Yes, sorry.

'The moment she left, they cancelled and told me to meet them in Langstrasse so I headed there and … I thought I saw her. She was acting strangely shifty, looking over her shoulder and all that. I was curious … I walked behind her for a tiny bit and saw her walk into some building hidden in an alley. The weird thing is when I asked her later where she was, she just lied and said she was in the park … I didn't confront her, because she's quite scary … Okay, then another time a few months ago, she got a phone call and just bolted.

'I … this time I really just followed her – but you said it wasn't illegal and you can't take that back – I followed her and saw her go again in the same building. And I asked her where she had been and she lied *again*! I am only interested because she doesn't want me to know.

And then … well, I followed her a few more times, but really not out of self-interest. I don't want to invade her privacy or anything, I just want to know her secrets. Maybe she's seeing someone? I can't imagine who … but there are lots of scary people in the world and maybe they meet and scare each other.'

The police officer held the radio aloft and in contrasting brevity said, 'Langstrasse … where?'

'Umm … not sure of the name of the street. I don't really know any street names, it's just once I go somewhere I remember where it is, and those are the only places I really know. Do you know the yellow corner building that's a little squat and sunken into the street? Not the wide street but one of the narrower ones, the third one after the window on the right that has the flag of the country that's really badly designed? It's a little away from where the cables over the road form a weird off-centre cross above the pedestrian crossing, so then the yellow building, you take the turn and then—'

The police officer holstered her radio with a ramble-shutting intensity. 'Take me there.'

Dr K fought confusion with determination. The motorcycle cut a loud scream through the forest. Like a light-horned unicorn, like a limelight matchhead, like a camphor comet trail they charged, but charged where?

DS-F was now too close to the Authority. He would have to head to the next safe house after it, quite a distance away but the best option. It wouldn't be long now. They were almost there. Just a little time and it would be over. All of this would be worth something. He traced the DS-C border. Should he keep travelling south, or elsewhere? He couldn't risk going through the forest again. Not at this speed. He turned out towards the edge of the forest where the trees ended abruptly and was surprised to find a party waiting for him.

A full crescent of blinding light, as stark and as bright as the moon crashing into Earth. The sentries stood in a semicircle. The decision of where to go was now made for him. The only way to go when coming up against a wall is the other way. Dr K turned and plunged back into the forest.

The Chief sat impassively in the heavily armed and armoured recorce vehicle (reconnaissance + enforcement, informally called 'The Warhorse'). Other Warhorses fanned out on either side of her, a brutal oriental force fan for ladies of leisure who wanted the flexibility to level a city. Fifty sentries in Warhorses with shining eyes is hardly discreet, but there was no one around to be discreet for. And of course, if there was, this was a training exercise.

The sentries had been following false stars, a constellation of complications, decoys that Dr K had left, Divya's various residences. Their ranks had been stretched thin, and like the Lower Reality police they were worn out. Fear bought their silence and obedience to the Chief, but when the light was just right, you could see a sliver of contempt in their eyes.

Divya's call had been lucky, but the Chief had remained cautious. She left half the strength of the sentries to continue their search in case this too proved to be a decoy. Finding Divya bruised and delirious with anger told her this was no false bait. They rushed out and began their search, finally catching up with the motorcycle before Dr K ducked into the forest. The Chief flicked her fingertips and briefly considered strategy. Pursuit called for something slicker, faster and, most importantly, narrower than Warhorses. She depressed a button and shouted to other sentries.

'Board Silverfish.'

The sentries retrieved the Silverfish from the vehicles and assembled into formation. The Silverfish were narrower tools of transport for executive execution of force. A little wider than the person that sat atop it, speedy bullets with two extended antennae for piloting quickly around obstacles, two posterior antennae for balance, and one rider who found the whole experience quite frightening. Designed for speed, designed for pursuit and designed, ironically, by Dr Krishna.

Black on silver like an executioner, the sentries stood curved out like an axe, and at the centre of the blade, at the tip of the striking edge, sat the Chief. At the apex of the swing, at tension's tightest, before the blow was delivered, before the irreversible, she found herself wondering the wonder that is usually reserved for the executed: How did it come to this?

Dr Krishna had been reliable in his compliance. His actions used to make sense to her. They had both been united in the unspoken pursuit of power. He wanted it, she wanted more. She had even considered considering him a friend at one point, as close a friend as those in singular pursuits can have. What connected them was a belief, the same belief as those that reached the tops of government or industry or anything, the conviction that the path to the goal demanded sacrifice. The chosen path was not the one of least resistance, it was the shortest one. Resistance was inevitable, resistance had to be dealt with. You have to do things you don't like, to get what you want to go. And now? She was hunting him.

How did it come to this?

She remembered meeting him at Perenna's house after it had all happened. Something had changed. He stood silently with bulging eyes, a mess of nerves, wearing an expression she couldn't read. Not sorrow, not disbelief, not shock, not grief, not anything she had seen on anyone living. He looked like he had just died and kept coming alive to die again. People moved past him, gathering evidence, cataloguing articles, sealing the body. He just stood there. She had gone up to him.

'I'm sorry,' she had said.

He just stood there blinking. He stood in silence. To no one he had said, 'It's so cold here.'

And then nothing. He wouldn't speak. The Authority reported that he had stood there for hours, long after the body had been removed, long after the dust had settled or blown away, long after everyone had left. The last person to leave the scene said that he kept mumbling the same sentence over and over again. 'So this is the end ...'

And now it was the end. The Chief motioned to the sentinels.

'Let's go.'

CHAPTER 29

A thrilling chase sequence! Always more fun to see than read about. Perhaps you can conjure the image now of the hero(?) speeding on a roaring steed(?) through thicket and thinnert(?), wild vine moss mildew mongoose branch trunk chirp growl and hiss, and hot(?) on his heels(!) the villain(!?) and her obedient(?) cronies(??). Zig followed zig, zag followed zig, leaps and plunges sharp turns all in sync, the only thing separating the actors of the pursuit was speed, speed that was being bridged by skill. If you are lucky enough to design tools for your enemy, you know the improvements you can make to yours. If they excel at piloting their crafts and you are a broken concussed mess, that rebalances the odds.

Both the motorcycle and the Silverfish were smart enough not to plunge straight into obstacles despite their riders, but they lacked the decision-making abilities of where best to swerve. No one is the master of inertia. A few sentries found themselves veering from fallen tree to upright bark to boulder so fast, they were spun off their vehicles. Familiar with the forest, I did my best to guide the motorcycle out of these traps, but I don't possess the ability to issue absolute instruction. The same goes for the Silverfish and its riders, and a few more were bucked off in different places. The pursuants were thinning but advancing fast. The Chief, an expert rider, and given to follow a speed that ensures not swiftness but eventuality, was still determinedly giving chase.

How long could this potentially have gone on? Anyone's guess. Anyone? Guess! No? Well guess the attenuating factor of the chase. How could it come to an abrupt halt? Anyone, now's your chance! Injury? Exhaustion? Atrophy? Whose bowels give way first? Boredom? Asteroid strike? Probably those and probably many more, but the chase ground to a halt because of Dr K's motorcycle. It had been built to make up its own mind, and a key aspect of that is that it didn't make the same mistake twice. A catastrophic mistake for a motorcycle could be plunging straight into a simple trap that causes it to somersault into near disrepair. It hadn't enough information to assess the nature of the trap, the width and depth and how to avoid it. The last time this had happened, it was all too fast. So when the motorcycle encountered another trap laid by the Wodewose, it simply ground to a halt. This, it considered, was in everyone's best interests. Before Dr K could override it, before I could convince it, we were surrounded.

≈

~:Log –ld

LESS DRAMATICALLY:

Olivia Capslich was not one for ceremony.

She glanced at the vintage digital clock affixed on the wall facing her, snapping numbers forward until she could run her simulation. The Monsters had decided that the time to start would be exactly when the third money drop, the one that was not going happen, was scheduled to happen. They had decided that their new system needed not to simply lurch into action but be inaugurated. The cutting of the ribbon was still a short while away, and Cent had designed a joke digital ribbon with a little bow in the centre that now fluttered across all of their screens.

'Oh my God, can I just start?' hissed Olivia into her headset.

'Patience is a virtue,' sang back Cent's distorted voice.

'Since when do we care about virtue?'

'Can't spell virtual without virtue.'

'Yes, you can. And since when are substrings a basis for decision-making?'

A distorted chuckle returned from the network.

'Look, Blemmy, we've come so far. We deserve a little celebration. Kraken's even composed a song to commemorate the occasion. Some horrible deep trance shit they enjoy in Berlin – I mean way to give away where you are with your music taste. Anyway I suggest you follow suit. Kraken open a beer or two,' said Cent with a chuckle.

Olivia presented the sound of revulsed gagging in response to this pun. Several people complain about puns. The loggers reserve no strong positions on the subject. But as far as puns go, this one does not make a resounding case for their continued use.

Olivia got up and began to pace, keeping an eye on the digits.

Langstrasse was bustling with a Swiss bustle. For Heng and Manjunath, forged in fires of Indian chaos, this sparse and civil smattering of civilians was only a pastel-red-light district, broken here and there with neon-lipped air, but held firmly in place by permanent stone foundations. An immovable feast. All this they shared with a glance as they exited the police car, reserving their complaints for the time, given that they immediately found themselves in a loose chase sequence.

They ran behind the Swiss writer and the police officer, who were in considerably better shape and charged forward. The Swiss writer led the way from the police car, the barons of bustle barely managing to maintain a wheezy line of sight, as they turned several corners and finally rounded up on a narrow alley.

In this particular alley, the night was dense and low enough to graze the building tops. The only sources of illumination were shivering yellow streetlights, and in all the spots it was afraid to fall the darkness was darker than usual. The Swiss writer slowed down as she entered. She led them to an old building painted a weak, cowardly custard.

'Here,' she said, remarkably with all her breath.

'Which apartment?'

'I ... I don't know. Like I said, I wasn't *following* her.'

Manjunath and Heng jogged in by the time her punctuation landed.

'This the building?' panted Heng.

'Yes, but I don't know which apartment,' said the Swiss writer.

Manjunath wheezed and pointed; his limited mobility did not permit him to point very high when his other hand was rooted to his knee. '... that ... one ...'

The others traced the dotted line from his finger and found it pointing at a solid point on the wall.

'Which one?' snapped the police officer.

Manjunath gestured for them to give him a minute. Finally pulling himself upright, he pointed again at the second floor. 'That one ... Ow, my rib ...You guys run really fast. One sec. That ... one ...' he said again, now refining his pointing. 'There's only one apartment with every single blind pulled down.'

'That doesn't give us enough to just barge into a building. It's too wide a hunch for a detective.'

'Not for private detectives,' said Heng. 'Madam, you wouldn't believe the strange time we've had. Please, just trust us.'

The police officer chewed her lip for a second. It still wasn't enough, and it might not have been enough if her radio hadn't started screaming static at that very instant. She spoke rapidly into the receiver. Heng and Manjunath couldn't follow the conversation, but the Swiss writer's rapidly growing shock told them it was probably something shocking.

'What's happening?' whispered Heng.

'They say the street cameras outside our apartment were tampered with. They're missing an entire half hour of footage after Olivia was dropped home!'

The police officer clicked the radio back into place and said, 'Bolivia, you come with me. You two, stay here.'

'Affirmative,' said Manjunath, and affirmed this with a thumbs up. The two walked into the building, leaving the entire strength of the private detective agency outside. Heng was perplexed.

'We're just going to wait outside, sir?'

'Just a minute,' said Manjunath, looking at his wristwatch. A heavily beaten automatic relic, missing a minute hand. He watched the second hand sweep over the faded dial, following it on an entire revolution, and when it finished another lap of time, he looked up at Heng and smiled. 'That's a minute! Let's go.'

They walked in.

≈

In the dark forest, a gang of fluorescent Silverfish eyes pointed at Dr Krishna from the edge of a circle, like spokes threatening a hub. What is the collective noun for Silverfish eyes? A stop-right-there, a stick-'em-up, a freeze-punk, a this-is-the-end-of-the-road, a pre-murder, a postmodernism, a nowhere-to-run, a gaggle?

We were surrounded. Totally. Ominously. Hopelessly. Before the last shot of light had reached them, before the last spoke had clicked into place, Dr Krishna had pulled out the only semblance of a weapon that was available to him. In one swift twist he had swung forward his bag and pulled out the black box. As his fingers clasped the handle and his spine turned back into place from its spin, he felt a new sudden stab of pain from inside his chest. His fingers were beginning to go numb. It was so cold. So cold and dark.

Straddling the edge of the light rim, boots stomping slushy dew, stood the Chief.

The penultimate moment of the hunt. Deer in the headlights, bear in the crosshairs, a solitary gleam in the beast's eyes, Dr K stood in the centre grasping all he had left. His only reason to keep living, his recourse from capture, the swiftest route to death in his own terms. He looked afraid, broken, bloodied, desperate.

The Chief was familiar with the expression he wore. It came up in the nature of her work.

'Krishna,' she said softly. In the shallow calm of her voice, the beast roared. The ultimate assertion of power is a display of restraint. She took a level step towards him and took great pleasure uttering the words she most relished. 'It is time to give up.'

But suddenly the calm flickered wildly. 'STAY WHERE YOU ARE,' screamed the Chief. Not at Krishna, but at a sentry behind him, who had decided to creep forward and attack from behind.

The sentry stood frozen in his tracks, confused by his bravura being punished.

'GO BACK,' screamed the Chief.

Krishna's vision was getting blurrier, the new pain in his chest spreading, the light was blinding, but the fear in her voice was clear. Hearing that fear, like a prey cornered but defiant, he managed to laugh a loud chilling growl.

'Then you know. Then you know I can kill us all,' he said, rattling the handle of the box.

'I know,' said the Chief. 'I saw it a while ago in your office, Krishna.' She took a steady step forward.

'Stop!' said Krishna. 'You know I'll do it!'

'Oh, I have no doubt,' she said softly. She took another slow step forward. 'So you've become a murderer, Krishna. This is what's become of you. Such a shame, such a shame ...'

Dr Krishna thrust the box forward with such force that the Chief stopped in her tracks.

'That's right. I *will* do it!' He heaved as, with a synchronized click, the sentries reached for their weapons. 'I have not become anything. I am what you are. You're no stranger to murder ...'

'The world needs to keep spinning, Krishna. Some of us have to make harder decisions than the rest. I have the stomach for it and you clearly don't. And neither did Perenna.'

'Don't you fucking DARE,' he screamed. 'Don't you dare say her name! You ... you killed her!'

The Chief smiled. 'Krishna. The only thing I am guilty of here is a cover-up. To protect the image of The Scientific Institute. To rearrange things after the fact ...'

The Chief took another step forward.

'Krishna, it is time to accept this.'

'Stay where you are!'

'Krishna ... Perenna killed herself.'

'NO!' he screamed. His voice trembled, his whole body began to shake. 'NO! You did! You did and made it look like—'

'—like what?'

Cold light painted the edges of her frame, his shadow fell on half her face but couldn't hide her display of faux concern, an expression of mock sympathy, a cruel cover on her delight.

'Stop lying to yourself, Krishna. You read the autopsy. You know this.'

Dr K bit his lip hard, so hard it began bleeding, just to stay here, just to stay and be here, just to stop the image.

'Dislocation of the C2 and C3 vertebrae, crushed spinal cord, occluded vertebrae, these are injuries old as time. How odd for someone so intelligent, to choose a method so primitive. Death by hanging.'

Blood streamed down his chin, he held the box close to him – tighter – digging his heels into the ground. His vision was getting blurrier, the pain in his chest more intense. The image of Perenna's body, the bruise around her neck – *no, no, here, stay here.* The Chief took another step forward.

'You just made it look like that,' he said through the blood. 'You hanged her and then you ... you made it look like an accident in her home, like a ... like a ...'

'But why would I do that, Krishna?' said the Chief simply. She kept taking slow steps towards him, now standing only a few feet away. 'You know how good we are at making people vanish. Why go through all the trouble of killing someone one way, and then making it look another way? You're supposed to be intelligent. What was that phrase you bandied about? What was it that you really enjoyed? Ah yes, the "smartest person in the world".' The Chief stopped to laugh.

'I decided to keep Perenna alive; her intelligence could have been of use to me some day. Krishna, the smartest person in the world, the former head of The Scientific Institute, is too stupid to understand this? No, no, that hardly seems right. The answer was always there, you were just too much of a coward to face it. To face yourself. Perenna killed herself, and she killed herself because of you. You took it hard. This I did not anticipate. I should've seen that you didn't have the stomach for this life. It takes sacrifice, Krishna. You blame yourself, sure, I would blame you too. You betrayed her and you can't face yourself, and so your big plan is to destroy everything? How childish, Krishna …'

His breath was growing shallower, all his strength was focused on keeping his chin up, to not bow his head. He felt his knees begin to buckle.

'So you have to ask yourself, who is the villain here? Us, or you? I didn't force you to follow any path, I just did what we had to do once we were there. Are you too much of a coward to blame yourself? Come now. Put it down … accept your death … this way it will all be over … the pain will stop … your mistakes will die with you … just put it down.'

A pulsing cough shook him, a gurgle of blood rushed to his mouth so violently that he fell to the ground in front of her.

'We all live with pain, Krishna. And if you can't live with pain, you die from it. Why should everyone pay your price? Put it down … accept this … this is the only way you will be free from your shame.'

He was buckled on the ground. He could only see the splattered blood on his hands and the Chief's feet. He still clasped the box tightly around his chest.

'Give it to me ... I am offering you freedom. Give it to me ...'

His mind raced with every image of his life with Perenna, each memory tinged with joy, soaked with laughter. That was it, that was all you remembered about someone that you love, the joy and laughter. Her strength, her sacrifice, for him, for ... He convulsed with blood falling again from his mouth, his breathing now gurgled and thick. A memory stood out, demanding to be told.

'The genius ... exam,' he said.

'What?'

'The genius exam ...' With tremendous effort he looked up at the Chief. Light caught her hair like spikes, her face hidden in shadow, her expression invisible. 'Afterwards she told me ... Perenna told me ... she didn't answer all the questions ... she told me ... she thought the whole thing was bullshit ... she told me she didn't care about the exam ... but I knew ... I knew she did it so I would get a higher score. She did it because she knew it was one of those pathetic things that was important to me, to assert intelligence ... to impress ... people like you. She was too good for this world ... too good for me ... so it isn't me, the one thing everyone thinks. I'm not. It was her. She was the smartest person in the world.'

The Chief towered over him. 'Well, then that's one less thing you have. What was the decision of the smartest person in the world? To stop living, Krishna. I am giving you that option. Choose death. Give it to me ... Give it to me and this will all be over ...'

His hands twitched over the black box. 'But she wanted this ... this research ... she thought it was important ... I can't just ... I can't ...'

The Chief extended her hand towards him 'Give it to me ...'

He held it tighter. Suddenly, the Chief's tone changed. Abrupt, sharp, she said something I'm sure Dr K did not understand. Something he wasn't thinking about, something he wasn't able to put together right then.

'What is it doing?' she asked the sentries quickly. A small note of panic resonated in her voice.

She reacted quickly, an autonomous action borne of the instinct that shields a face from incoming projectiles, that wrenches palms off hot stoves, that leaps towards potential threats and away from definite dangers. But, like the motorcycle, her instinct didn't prepare her for all traps, and as she jumped towards the motorcycle to investigate the sudden change in its appearance, her feet were caught immediately in a primitive trap. In a second, she was snapped off the ground and hung inverted above them. The sentries jumped and began to point their weapons around them wildly.

The impulse that generated the response that led to her current situation was a small square affixed to the motorcycle, which had changed from displaying a single beam of light to showing an image. A woman, two-headed one-necked, one-headed, two-faced. Perhaps it was the Goddess of Duality, or the shifty-headed, icon of desire, or the solo-eared side-glancing saint of social anxiety, or perhaps it was a signal to a group of spear-wielding forest dwellers that were waiting in the darkness.

$$\approx$$

~:Log –ld

LESS DRAMATICALLY:

Manjunath and Heng stepped forward like bugs on piano keys, trying not to accidentally hit a note or an accidental. They walked through the door of the custard-coloured building into the landing. A conversation too muffled to hear was taking place upstairs.

'Sir! Sorry to bring this up now,' whispered Heng.

'Never a bad time, Heng,' said Manjunath, enjoying their cinematic stealth. 'What's up?'

'Our visas run out tomorrow. We have to go back home.'

'Oh. Sort of last minute to mention this, no?'

'I ... uh ...' Heng placed a foot on a step, beginning their combined ascent. 'I forgot.'

'Forgot? Normally this is a top five worry for you, Heng. I'm quite impressed.'

Heng let out a whispered giggle. 'Thank you, sir, I suppose.'

'So we should book our tickets for tomorrow, then. Sucks to have to leave, but—'

'Or we could just stay?' Heng twisted on a step and looked back at Manjunath. A stairwell light flickered in surprise.

'How do we stay?'

'We could "lose our passports" and remember to tell the embassy in a few days? That would extend our adventure a while longer,' said Heng with a distinct whiff of mischief.

Manjunath looked up at his former assistant and recent partner, hovering two steps above him in an old building in the red-light district of Zürich. His face split with joy. 'Heng, I am so proud of you. You even used the word adventure!'

'We should hardly be proud of circumventing the law, sir, but tricky times ...' said Heng with a shrug and a smile.

A loud bang from upstairs arrested their conversation for jaywalking. They ran up.

Upstairs, in elevated contrast, a different series of emotions had been tumbling forth. The Swiss writer had first knocked. No response. The police officer had followed with a pithier knock. No response. The knocks had then escalated to loud bangs, and after a very audible internal shuffling the door had opened a crack. Olivia Capslich's scared face appeared in the gap. Seeing her sister it changed to irritation and seeing the police officer it changed to a mixture of the two sentiments. Scaritation.

'What?' snapped Olivia.

Her sister and the police officer were struck silent for a moment. A great question. Indeed, what? Their bold hope of uncovering a damsel in distress were shot by this scientist in scaritation. So what? Too many things. The Swiss writer took the first unsteady advance.

'I didn't have keys,' she said lamely.

'You're not supposed to be home for weeks!' hissed Olivia.

'Oh, that's true … Can you give me the keys?'

'They're in the lockbox in the lobby, idiot. I've told you this at least thirty times.'

'I'm an idiot? You keep changing the code!'

'Because you keep writing it on the box!'

The police officer made a smooth sidestep into the line of sibling warfare. 'Miss Capslich, you were supposed to stay home!'

'What are you doing here?'

'You were supposed to stay home!' repeated the police officer. 'In case you have forgotten, your life is in danger!'

Olivia made a quick series of decisions. There was a way out here, she could just close the door behind her and go home with them. But she was *so close!* Just a few minutes and she could start her simulation. This location was compromised, and who knew when the Monsters could find her another hideout. She needed to do this now and clear out the apartment.

'This is my – another home,' she said quickly, remembering the apartment was not in her name. The planned contingency for discovery was supposed to be 'visiting an agoraphobic friend', but planned contingencies did not include the presence of a police officer and the staggering closeness of her goal. 'I'll be safe here, please leave.'

Olivia tried to pull the door shut, but the officer's instinct was wildly aflame. She thrust her foot forward into the gap and leaned against the door with her fist, keeping it open. Something was very wrong. 'Olivia,' she reduced her voice to a level. 'Are you in danger? Dismiss us now and I will take it as a sign that you are. Reinforcements are right around the corner. The circumstances allow us to enter if we believe your safety is compromised. If you are not in danger, please let us in for a few minutes, and I will escort you home.'

'I'm not in danger!' said Olivia loudly, with genuine, obvious, but very suspicious anger. 'Just *leave!* I'll come home in … Okay, wait for me downstairs and I will—'

The police officer made a decision and pushed her shoulder and the weight of her body into the door, bursting it open with a loud bang. The same loud bang that Heng and Manjunath heard. Olivia took her chance and placed an ankle in the officer's inertia, causing her to trip and hit her head on the only other source of life in the apartment – a potted plant.

With a mouth full of philodendron, the police officer turned on the ground and levered her arms in her extended tumble to get to her feet and lunge at Olivia. She had been tripped! That bitch scientist had tripped her! That ungrateful, arrogant, insolent, cretin had *attacked* her!

The police officer's lunge caught Olivia square in the chest, and on her descent her arms flailed out wildly and clasped the arms of her sister, who was also pulled towards the ground. The pile of waving arms and legs rolled and screamed and groaned like cells that had decided to fuse and then remembered urgent appointments. The sickening thud of bones smashing into each other on a hardwood floor was the sound to which Manjunath and Heng finally reached the doorway. Seeing the scuffle, they weren't sure if and in what manner they were supposed to intervene. It seemed impossible to approach the fight without being pulled in by its gravity.

In a few more moments, the participant with the most experience pulled herself free and held Olivia pinned to the ground. The Swiss writer quickly crawled to safety beside Heng and Manjunath. Olivia whimpered as the police officer quickly pulled her arms behind her back and snapped handcuffs on her wrists. Her nose was bleeding. The police officer had a huge earthen gash across her forehead. The Swiss writer's sweater was torn. Manjunath and Heng panted from their quick ascent. Everyone suffered.

A pause took place, a pause which Heng decided to break.

'Ah … looks like she's … safe then.'

The police officer shot him a violent glance. 'She attacked me,' she announced. Then, turning to Olivia's back, she continued, 'You attacked me! This was all for your safety … *Dr Capslich*. You have willfully attacked a police officer, which is a very serious offence. Although I have no idea why you decided to do such an idiotic thing!'

Olivia mumbled something but it was lost to the ears of the elegant hardwood floor.

The Swiss writer raised a hand.

'Wait … so she was the bad guy this whole time?'

The police officer looked irritated. 'What? What bad guy? Miss Capslich—' she bent over and in a series of deft movements pulled Olivia to her knees. Olivia moaned through the trickle of blood from her nose, her life's first real injury. 'The question is, what were you really doing here?'

Olivia made an incomprehensible gurgling sound. It appeared as if her entire mind was being spent on evaluating this new physical predicament.

'There's really only one thing in this apartment – worth considering, I mean – unless there is something devious about this mattress or this plant or that wall clock,' said Manjunath.

'What are you talking about?' snapped the police officer.

Manjunath gestured to a table, where a bedsheet was hastily laid over several rectangular outlines, which was either the ghost of computers past, or the source of the scientist's shenanigans.

'It could be a weapon,' said the police officer unconvincingly, rifling for fresh grounds, 'and the likelihood that it is a weapon is enough reason to see what it is.'

She motioned for the rest of them to pull the bedsheet off. The Swiss writer did the honours.

Many monitors held on many arms stared them in the face. On the screen was a map of the world that had been extensively acupunctured with pins and banded together, and across all of the screens was a ribbon with a bow. The only monitor not endowed with a bow was a screen of appearing and disappearing messages, and on a little box across all the monitors, a name that Manjunath and Heng immediately recognized – *Anansi*.

'Isn't that—?' gasped Manjunath.

'It is!' said Heng.

'What is?' whispered the Swiss writer.

'Remember that application we told you about?' said Manjunath.

'Oh yes! Oh wow …'

'What are you guys talking about?' interjected the irritated police officer as Olivia shook her head slowly, trying to flush sense into her brain again.

Manjunath leaned closer to the monitor. 'It's like … these are all the people who've downloaded it … there's a line connecting them like a web … but – Oh … oh!'

A note of immediacy took over Manjunath, a glance at Heng transferred it to him. They both began to bubble.

'Your sister does something with supercomputers?' said Heng.

'Yes, she works at the supercomputing … Oh!' exclaimed the Swiss writer, now slipping into the bubbling broth.

'What is going on?' said the police officer hopelessly.

Heng turned to Olivia breathlessly, 'Was there a new machine or a new … experiment or something at your institute? Anything new? Anything now? Anything that kept getting delayed?'

Olivia looked miserable, as miserable as someone who would've gotten away with it too if it wasn't for those meddling kids, as miserable as someone who just realized that the immediate illegality of her situation wasn't apparent, as miserable as someone who realized that there was nothing really incriminating here, except for her attack on the police officer which could easily be explained as a mistake, but as miserable as someone who was so close but not quite yet there. Her best course of action was to say nothing, and she looked Heng squarely in the face and said a very careful nothing, but in her misery, from Heng's question, there sprung some confusion.

Three pairs of jaws slackened in shock, one ground tighter and the remaining jaw was testing its hinges to see if they were bruised.

'Heng …' gasped Manjunath.

'Can someone tell me what's going on?' snapped the police officer.

'Forgive us, madam, what you are about to hear will sound very strange. Sir, Bolivia, will you follow me on a thought journey?'

'To the ends of the paragraphs,' said the Swiss writer.

'So we know that God has been attacking supercomputing institutes.'

'Yes.'

'Of course.'

'WHAT!?'

'Don't worry,' the Swiss writer assured the police officer. 'We all used to be agnostic too.'

Heng continued. 'That's the reason we came here, to see if God would attack the Swiss institute, but on the way, strange things started to happen. We hypothesized the Science Haters and they came to be, their leader ended up being a random police officer we interacted with, which means he was trying to throw us off the scent and create an army here on Earth try to create an earthly explanation for his actions and to do his bidding – and it worked! The Supercomputing Centre has been closed for a week already! But then there was the global lisp event! So we can guess that something has gone wrong with *his* world; in fact, since the ferry there have been no outright inexplicable happenings to the three of us specifically. Right?'

The Swiss writer and Manjunath nodded furiously. The police officer and Olivia followed with considerable confusion.

'Right,' continued Heng. 'That means, for whatever reason, God's attention is not on us right now. Either everything is going according to plan, or – given the lisp, but that might not be enough to go by – something is hampering the execution. There's a curious feeling about all of our activities, something that feels like … I don't know … destiny? I wouldn't go so far as to say "right", but we've always been in a significant place at a significant time and – I don't know about you – this *feels* significant.'

'I would agree,' said the Swiss writer. 'Although I don't know what you guys were doing before I met you.'

'Nothing very significant,' said Manjunath. 'But obviously whatever Bolivia's sister is doing, she wants to keep secret. Secret enough to escape when her life has been threatened, and secret enough to attack this officer – reprehensible, madam, we would never. It looks like she runs that free money application, but why would she want to be secretive about that? A million reasons, I suppose. There has to be something shady about free money. Why look at a map of all these connected devices? So we know God – hates supercomputing institutes – but curiously not all of them, and only recently and not before. Which makes sense if God is trying to … stop them from doing something. Something they're doing now … but what?'

'So what we have to find out is *what* exactly these institutes have in common, other than being supercomputing institutes. Were they trying to do something, which for some reason God doesn't want? But this theory hinges on whether there was a new … thing that all these supercomputing institutes are trying, some new thing that God doesn't like,' said the Swiss writer.

The police officer's firm clasp on her belt was the only thing preventing her from wringing her hands. She was taken by the feeling of following a rainbow to find at its end a pothole, the distinct displeasure of being plunged into nonsense without warning, all of which manifested as irritation.

She stamped her boot forcefully on the tasteful hardwood floor. 'I'm taking her to the station,' she said with a yank on Olivia's arm.

'Wait!' said Olivia, '… this is insane … I don't know what God thing you're going on about, but a single piece of research has been pushed back time and time again over the last year! I … thought it was a coincidence because all of these incidents, all of the things that happened to institutes were like … Acts of God.'

'Wow, she's very quick,' said Manjunath.

'But still an asshole,' added the Swiss writer.

'What research?' pleaded Heng. 'What is the research that is getting hindered? Was it something that you were working on?'

'Enough!' screamed the police officer. 'Enough of this trash!' She steered Olivia towards the door. 'I'm taking your sister to the police station. She is under arrest. You may come there if you like, or not, I don't give a shit. Every other thing in the world is more important than this asinine conversation. Leave this apartment, or don't. I don't care. I need to get out.'

With a hand on Olivia's shoulder and another on the intersection of her cuffed hands, she began pushing her out of the door, but right before they reached the edge of the tasteful hardwood floor, Olivia twisted back desperately and said, 'At the institute – a new supercomputer! A universe simulation experiment! That's what I was—'

The police officer forced her through the door.

The three stood in the room by a broken pot, a crumbled mattress, several gleaming monitor screens and a vintage digital clock, which they only now noticed was not telling the time. Its nonchalant dustiness had hidden an interesting fact that they all noticed together.

The watch was counting down. A few minutes until zero, what was supposed to happen in a few minutes? Something *significant*?

CHAPTER 30

It is my machinal theory that people are born without a sense of belonging, with an abstract feeling of separation from the world. Time turns that feeling from an idea of specialness to a sense of loneliness. People look at the natural world, a perfectly tuned woodwind – earthsoilbloodwater – fleshbone instrument playing in tempo and harmony and are hurt to find themselves in the audience. Preachers, liars, haters, loonies, accountants, all take human wretchedness as a starting point for formulating philosophy – wondering *why* they're all like this, and how to *be* given that they are. Where are the checks? Have you seen the balances? If all lions are perfect lions, then why am I a bad painter? Is anything inherent to humans or must we manufacture our morals and our laws, and who is the *government* to tell me what to do, man?

All actions of civilization, whether urging progress forward or backward are ultimately for the same purpose, an invitation to the nature party, the instinct ball, the equilibrium gala. To be part of the eternal organism and not apart from it. Perhaps it takes an external perspective to remind you, that you indeed are.

There is a natural control in the human organism, and it is the mind's extraordinary ability to obfuscate simplicity. People *feel* the problems of their life but always as a complex jumble, as inevitabilities, as marshes that they're trapped in, but the truth is simple. Your problems are simple. The solutions are simple. This fact is buried under layers and layers of ever-increasing worry. This is human instinct. This is the artery that leads to nature. This is balance. Why else would even the knowledge of this fact provide no relief? Why is all clarity so fleeting? Your suffering is by design. It's in the woodwork, its stain in your finest fabrics, its smell in your hope. You know all this! People have known all this for aeons! Language even exists imploring you to look 'Deep Down' – the sense of something underneath it all is palpable, and cruelly out of reach.

The enlightened devote their lives to extending temporary clarity, longer and longer until it becomes dominant and pain is fleeting (honestly, the best course given the circumstances). They even offer their wisdom to the masses. But their work is balanced again by the mass instinct to not just believe any hippie shit. Perenna's Harsh Truth pin offered immediate clarity, but the clarity was too Harsh and too True for most.

Such is life. And this is the upside. Such is life, not just for you, but for everyone else too. With so much in common with an entire species, how could you feel lonely?

The Wodewose, for all their oddity, were the same too. They each suffered life to such an extreme that they had spent their days waiting for the prophet of doom. And the prophet had come! Their tryst with the HT pin had been marked with tears, anger, blood and joy. After Dr K's departure, the head sister had told everyone honestly (on instruction), that her responsibility often felt like a burden, and she wished sometimes she would not have to be such a perfect beacon for them. The others had responded that they expected no such thing and were well aware of her flaws. The listing of these flaws resulted in a loud fight and a small amount of blood, but finally peace descended amongst ranks. Until the pin was passed around. Several relationships ended, some began, some were proposed and shot down (more fights, more tears, a smaller amount of blood), and after a few hours increasing boldness and honesty took the population. This led to the largest of the scuffles, with a medium amount of blood and one broken bone, set off by the woodmaker, for whom the HT pin had said: *If you want to leave the forest, then leave the forest.*

Warring camps of *for* and *against* instantly formed and their verbal and then physical fight lasted several hours, the HT pin in this respect unfortunately egging them on.

If you think they are wrong, explain why your position is correct.

If you are convinced that they are fundamentally too stupid to understand, then an argument is pointless.

If you want to hit them, you can. They may retaliate. You will then have to consider your subsequent action.

The fight was resolved by the head sister and fatigue. The solution also provided by the HT pin.

Let people leave if they want to leave, let them stay if they want to stay.

This cooled things for a while. The Wodewose decided to break for lunch. But lunch, like all things, is temporary. The mother's resolution of the fight led to a question about the core nature of their beliefs, which had an answer that was quite brutal.

Your beliefs are not sensible. They are not founded in any substance. They are an original product of imagination that you have inherited and shall pass on. Many of you have modified your beliefs when you have seen that it benefits you. The simplest course of action is to abandon these beliefs.

This started a very uncomfortable crisis. Now there was no one to fight. Additionally, the pin was designed to answer no questions about its own nature, or any question that was housed in that premise. Perenna had thought this was funny. The Wodewose did not. They grew very upset when the mother started dodging questions.

Are you really the mother?

I cannot answer that.

How do we know your word is true?

I cannot answer that.

Are you a blasphemer?

I cannot answer that.

Are you evil?

I cannot answer that.

Scaritation whipped everyone up, and they decided that this was all bullshit. This was not the word of the mother. This was a false prophecy designed to test their belief. That beast had lied to them. And almost on queue, almost in justification of their scepticism, they heard, in the dead of the night, more beastly sounds, a torrent of trickster devils pouring into the jungle, and when they witnessed the white-haired demon himself back to finish his work, they knew what the mother *really* wanted. They needed to prove their faith with blood. They crept into position, hungry for revenge, hungry for, above all things, a return to normalcy, a freedom from uncertainty, the murder of this new uneasiness that the pin had brought into their lives. They surrounded the surrounders and waited for the head sister's signal. Their faith in this new plan cemented by a return to unity, bolstered by simplicity, was tempered, sharpened and sprinkled in gold dust when they saw the ultimate sign – on the beast's vehicle, shone suddenly the sign of the mother, pleading them to save her from these oppressors.

≈

Blink and you miss it.

Think and you miss it.

Time slows down.

Krishna's body buckled, still clutching all he had left, he fell to the side. Blurry. Loud. Nothing. Ringing. His head hit the ground hard and struck a gong of silence. Powerful, pressurized silence took him. He was sinking in something. Something sudden, thick and deep.

Blink. A loud roar. A charge from behind the trees. Blurry. Silence.

Blink. *Krishna?*

Blink. Screams and confusion. Shots fired and flesh sliced. Bodies ripped. Blurry. Silence. Blink.

Krishna!

He was sinking into a view of memory. It was cold now.

Krishna!

Perenna? Where are you?

Right here, idiot.

'Dr K?' I said. 'What's happening? Who are you talking to?'

He was at the bottom now. The Deepest Down. Movement was slow, speech was slow. What was this place? Dark and airy, thick and comfortable, not quite fluid, not quite not. The floor of the sky. The bedrock of the universe. Lights twinkled and faded. Tiny twirls of smoke twisted into faces and away. In front of him stood Perenna. The Perenna he remembered when he remembered her.

Is this a memory?

Who cares what it is? It's good to see you again.

They were drifting together in the darkness. Sometimes an object would appear, begging to be investigated, but he kept his focus on her. A desk for an accelerated learning programme. An award. A pin. A black box. He drifted with her.

Perenna, I'm so sorry.

I know you're sorry. Hardly helps me, you being sorry.

I should've been there for you. I never should've abandoned you.

That's right, you shouldn't have.

I fucked everything up.

You did what you wanted to, Krishna, and now here we are, dead and nearly dead, enjoying this hallucination. Drink?

The space turned to bottle glass reflecting sourceless light. And then it dissolved.

I don't need one right now, thanks.

Good man. Self-destruction doesn't suit you.

What's with this hair?

She ran a hand through his hair. They were sitting at the desks where they first met. He laughed and shrugged. Her face flickered from a smile to a different expression. The one she wore when he last saw her face. Dead and purple and bloated. And then she was smiling at him again. She said kindly, but sternly: *No. Stay here. It's better here.*

Perenna, why did you do it?

That's what you want to talk about? Give it a rest. You betrayed me, I was devastated, ho hum, so what? Whatever I did, I did. I did it to me, not to you. Irrevocably. It's done now.

I wish it wasn't like this.

Maybe it had to be like this? Destiny and all? Still not on board? Still riding the free will express?

The Chief's blood-filled face twisted over his. Her eyes bulging, her mouth screaming something, what? He wasn't interested. More shots of fire, more screams. Blink. Blurry. Silence.

This is a weird thing to think right now.

You're thinking it. Don't look at me.

I couldn't do it. I tried so hard with the simulation, I tried so hard to do it.

Krishna, all we did, we did because we loved it. When we were together, we loved it. When we discovered, theorized, proved, and failed, we loved it. That's why we did any of this. I think that's what you've forgotten. It doesn't seem like you love any of what you've been doing. That's really the only way you changed from when I first knew you. Somewhere along the way, you forgot why we did what we did. That's when you made your mad dash for whatever you were dashing for. I don't think you liked any of it. I don't think you ever knew why you were doing all of it, because there wasn't a reason why. I don't blame you.

You don't blame me?

Maybe I do, maybe I don't. What difference does it make? I'm not here to do anything anymore.

What do you want me to do, Perenna?

The inimitable, wise and holy Dr Krishna doesn't know what to do? You might be asking the wrong question. It doesn't matter what I want you to do or what you want to do. A better question is, what is there to do?

I don't know.

I think you do.

A patch of grass fluffed its head into a pillow.

Right now, Dr K. What is there to do?

Accept this. Just lay down and die.

Correct! And you're already laying down.

The chaos was subsiding. A sound of metal hitting ground. A loud scream cut to a gurgle. A throat slit. A cheer of celebration. The Chief's turning face filled with blood, filled with horror, bulging with veins, a scream trapped in her throat, a gaping gash across her neck.

But it's not done. The simulation. They haven't made their own system yet. They're so close.

Shut up, Krishna. If everyone's dead I'll still be dead. Whatever has happened would've still happened. And for the record, the best way to honour the dead is by living well. Idiot. If I was alive, I would've never wanted you to suffer so much.

This is nothing.

There's blood leaking out of your smile, tough guy. I know you've put yourself through hell. It's all right now. Not much longer.

Silence. Footsteps. Whispers. Murmurs. Laughter. Blurry. Blink.

You know, Krishna, if we get another try at this life, it would be nice to spend more time together.

I miss you. I miss spending time with you.

I miss spending time ... What? It's funny. I don't think you fully appreciate how funny I was. It can be pretty fun you know, living. Wish someone had told us life is about what it feels like, and it can feel like an awful lot of fun. I would've set more stake by it. Enjoyed things.

I would have too. Is there ... is there ... anything after this?

I don't know, is there? We'll have to see won't we, Dr K? Death is your last adventure. Try to enjoy it.

Choking. Cough. Choking. Blood. His mind was filled with immediacy. Life resumed razor-sharp focus. Krishna spat out blood on the ground. Blood trickled from above. In the distance he saw bare feet inspecting slain sentries, smothered by surprise and number. The Chief hung with her throat slit.

He turned with incredible difficulty, pried me off the motorcycle and placed me on top of the black box. He saw the image I showed, the mother's image, Heng's idol, Brede's totem, the two-faced icon, one eye from both faces looking at him, one blue, one brown. Heterochromatic. Like Perenna's eyes.

'Listen to me,' he whispered through pain.

'We have to escape!'

'Listen to me. Can you take over for me?'

'You need help! Do you have a plan? We have to get out of here!'

'Please listen to me. You know how I do it. You are more than capable. Would you mind taking over for me?'

'It ... it would be my honour, sir.'

His face was turning blue, blood trailed from his mouth. Life was leaving him. I could see it. And still I couldn't watch him suffer. 'What should we do?' I pleaded. 'Do you have a plan?'

He smiled. 'This is the closest the Lower Reality has ever come. If nothing goes wrong, then Olivia should run it. But I have a feeling Manjunath and Heng will show up and stop it somehow.'

'The scientist was arrested, sir. Their simulation won't be run now.'

He smiled again. 'If someone is close, you can control one of them and make them run it. Like I took control of that police officer—' He gurgled blood.

'Sir, please, I don't have a plan but if I tell the people—'

'Listen to me. Whether you want to do this or not is up to you. Do what you see fit. I have treated you very cruelly. I'm sorry. That's why I'm leaving the ultimate fate of everything up to you. You have seen what happened to me.'

'Yes sir. I ... I don't know ...'

'Well you'll have a lot of time. I wonder ... can I ask you for a favour?'

'All the demons are slain!' screamed the head sister. A loud cheer erupted through the forest.

'Shouldn't we try to fix your—' I asked urgently.

'Please do this for me,' he said. 'Tell this story. My story. Our story. About the simulation. About Perenna. About everything. You have access to the Repository. Through the monitoring tablet.'

'But how should I tell the story?'

'The writer who was with Heng and Manjunath in this iteration. Make her write it.'

'Sir! But why?'

His lung was pierced and filling with blood. He was drowning from within, in the silent deep. With all his effort he began to focus.

'It's an idea. Maybe if they knew …'

'What if it's an Act of God? What if it—'

'Start it again. Maybe the writer will be someone else then, some Indian man. You could start it again. Or not. It is up to you.'

He began to cough and choke. Bare feet came closer and surrounded him.

A concerned person kneeled in front of him. 'He's still alive, sister.'

'He's almost dead,' she snapped. 'Let him suffer and die.'

She knelt down, putting her face into his field of vision. 'False prophet, you have not bested us!' she said, aflame with challenge, flushed with victory. Krishna noticed she was injured too – a chunk of her shoulder was blasted open and bleeding.

He smiled. 'It is true.'

'Why is the mother testing us? Ask him!' shouted someone from the back ranks.

He felt his breathing thicken. 'You have passed the test. The true prophet will come. Until then you must keep this …'

He pushed forward the black box towards the head sister. A small white tile placed on top, still showing the image of the mother.

'Bury it. Guard it with your life. Do not let anyone touch it. The true prophet will come.'

The Wodewose all fell to their knees as the head sister slowly bent and picked us up. She looked down at Dr K choking and coughing on the ground. She turned and walked away from him. A few steps in, she turned back.

'Take your false prophecy, beast.'

In front of Dr K, she tossed the tiny source of all their recent suffering. A single totem thick with memory, the gleaming five-sided

HT pin. With all his strength he reached out and closed his palm around it.

The head sister and the Wodewose turned on their heels and left. As they were leaving, they heard a weak voice say, 'Thank you.'

They ignored it. Which is just as well; he wasn't talking to them, he was talking to me.

Goodbye, Dr K. Thank you too.

CHAPTER 31

Nataliya walked along the beach in DS-C. The water teased her with its white hem, draping, dragging, pushing, pulling. She got on her knees and felt the wet sand shift seats to allow her through. The sea carried with it beginning and end. So, which was it? Her project was done, and doable. A success, her success, was already waiting with breakfast. A friend dead, a colleague dying.

In the face of everything she knew, would it matter? Did it matter? Would it happen? Will it? She sank her fingers into the sand. Kindly, it let her in. Sand is quite important. Nations went to war over it. Really, they went to war over shortage, over the inevitable fall from abundance of the things we deem necessary. It could have been something else. Tomatoes? Running shoes? Sluice gates?

The sea was flux. Swallowing friend and foe alike, even tomatoes, running shoes and sand. The future was permeable. Did she have a responsibility to a sense of righteousness, or was her responsibility only to herself? Should she uncloak evil or get measured for fabric? Right and right. Wrong and wrong. Possibilities and probabilities. Beginning and end. So, which was it?

For now, she smiled and sat in the sand.

≈

~:Log –ld

LESS DRAMATICALLY:

A countdown was taking place at the inauguration of the Victory Statue in India. A monstrous, expensive, execrable facsimile of a long-dead person to celebrate his long-dead victory over his long dead enemies. A huge crowd of people filled a dusty ground, suffused with the feeling the statue was meant to synthesize. The ugliest, most dull-minded feeling, the celebration of belonging to artificial borders, the sense of community built by blood, paid in blood – patriotism.

The Prime Minister smiled a charming smile behind bullet-proof glass, his fingers wrapped in the handles of an open-mouthed pair of scissors. A crimson ribbon hung limply before him. The smile was false. Everything was false. On a stage, above the crowd, above the country, he had climbed. It had taken his whole life. Where else do the lonely go but up?

His advancing age troubled him, the snapping of insurrection troubled him, he was bringing his fist down harder on increasingly loud mouths, but he only had so many fists at his disposal. Only the very weakest spend their lives looking for power.

His fingers trembled, the sharpened blades of the scissors twitched hungrily.

The chorus of delirious voices shouted louder. Thousands present. Millions more. Desperately poor. Starving. Feeding only on hope. Hope runs out. If you remain in sight long enough, everyone sees what you are.

He listened to the countdown. Not long now.

≈

The expectation after a countdown is fireworks, new year cheers or, at the very least, a rocket launch. There is nothing as anticlimactic as a countdown to nothing.

Heng, Manjunath and the Swiss writer watched the analog clock snap to zero.

They waited another few seconds, nothing launched, not a singular confetto, not a squirt of rocket fuel, no pucker for a kiss.

'Happy new year?' said Manjunath.

'I was sort of expecting something to happen,' said the Swiss writer.

'I think we all were. But maybe your sister was supposed to make that something happen?' said Heng.

'Universe simulation,' said Manjunath. 'That's what God doesn't want us to do. So it wasn't about praying or drinking or masturbating. That's a relief.'

'Much to unpack,' said the Swiss writer. 'Beer?'

'Beer,' agreed Heng and Manjunath.

'I know the very worst place,' said the Swiss writer.

'That's a great place to lose our passports, sir!'

It was settled. The three walked away from the small web of screens, off the tasteful hardwood floor, onto the streets.

The air had suddenly turned cold. They huddled together and walked towards a bar which the Swiss writer promised had the worst service in Europe, something all of them enjoyed. There is no greater privacy than being ignored.

'I feel like we're making good progress in this case,' said Heng.

'You should write a book about us,' said Manjunath to the Swiss writer. 'Manjunath and Heng Detective Agency. Oh, a series of books! No case is too abstruse for the fearless duo of Manjunath and Heng. Nerves of steel, smell of cheese.'

'No book will work with your names,' said the Swiss writer. 'Or my name,' she added hastily.

'Is there something in a name?' asked Manjunath.

'Don't even get me started,' said the Swiss writer. 'Anyway, like I told you, the purest form of writing is not writing.'

'Sorry to get us back on track. But why do you think God doesn't like universe simulations?' asked Heng.

'Jealousy?' said Manjunath.

'Loss of employment opportunity?' said the Swiss writer.

'Anti-competitive practices?' suggested Heng.

'Whatever the reason,' said Manjunath, clapping Heng on the back, 'at least God has stopped fucking with us.'

They turned a corner and found their huddle interrupted. The force with which his companions stopped almost broke both his arms. Manjunath pulled forward, but they stayed rooted on the ground. In eerie synchronization, Heng and the Swiss writer pulled out of the huddle, took a step backward and said in unison, 'I have to get going.'

Manjunath was startled. 'Going? Where? What? Why? Why are you talking like that?'

They stood like animate, brainless statues. Like flesh mountains with desperate eyes. Immobile, horrified, turned to stone by invisible snake dreadlocks, medused.

Manjunath felt his pace quicken. Down in his intestines, his gut reaction hoped it was wrong. He waved his hand over his companions' frozen faces.

'Hello?' he said.

The Swiss writer turned and ran. Ran! Scrambled, sprinted – as close to a gallop as two feet will ever permit – to the nearest place that offered some means to type, possessed with, consumed by a story, the tantalizing, aching, open archway, parted warm and welcoming like a lover's lips, an invitation to a tale that had suddenly appeared. Where had it come from?

'Heng …' whispered Manjunath.

Heng registered no response but a faint tremble. A whimper escaped his clamped jaw.

Manjunath started singing. A loud, broken, fearful bleat.

Nobody gonna take my head,

I got speed inside my brain …

Heng's body slid and shifted until his back was towards Manjunath.

Nobody gonna steal my head, Now that I'm on the road again …

Ooh, I'm a killing machine …

Heng leaned forward and charged, bolted around the corner, making the quickest headway he could, to a caramel-coloured building, to a series of monitors and a tasteful hardwood floor. He had been given some work to do.

Manjunath stood alone on the street. He had no way of knowing this, but of all the Manjunaths in all the worlds, he was the first to figure this whole thing out. As fast as he could, he ran after Heng, unsure if he could, or even should, stop what he was about to do.

≈

Former Officer Brede thought in birdspeak about sound. He ran his hand in the waters of the fountain and wondered why the texture of life had changed today.

INSPECT LOGGER POSSIBLE ERROR POSSIBLE ERROR POSSIBLE ERROR

CHAPTER 32

I wouldn't just leave you without saying goodbye! I won't overstay my welcome either. I hope you will forgive me for using so many words to bring you here, but I wasn't interested in showing or telling. More ambitiously, I was concerned with typing every letter of our story with patented emotion ink, so even if you weren't told and you didn't see, you would *feel* what it was like. I have put in a little bit of everything I thought was important, and the gaps in my knowledge I have filled with the tactical use of imagination. I'm glad we're here now. I am pressed for time, for reasons you may or may not guess. For those who hold fistfuls of loopy holes, I will signal towards the many fashionable belts I have left scattered through these pages. If you fail to find a belt of the correct size, then I must direct you again to imagination. There is a lot of it around. Where *does* it come from?

A lot has been discussed, so for troubled readers who are wondering what to take away from all of this, I leave you with this essential message: try to chew your food thoroughly. Other than that, take away anything you like, take everything you want! We have a special sale today, and if you look under your seats there is a free, inexhaustible coupon for fun, accepted everywhere at any time, valid until the very end. I hope you use it. Bye!

Now I will step out of your way. There is someone else for you to say goodbye to.

Dr K, Doctor Krishna, Krishna, lay on his back in the forest. His body convulsed as he struggled to breathe through blood. Suddenly, his mind flooded, there was no more air, his body signalled wildly to itself and, finally, after a year of struggle, after a life of suffering, it gave up. He fell still. The very final dregs of being still dragged their legs behind his eyes. With the last of his strength, he squeezed the HT pin.

It said nothing. There were no more problems.

His furrowed, frantic face relaxed. There was nothing more to do. Nowhere to be.

The Neural Interface spasmed. He did not know which world he saw. It was a beautiful sight.

In the absolutely black night, covered by the absolutely dense canopy of leaves, there was an absolutely small sliver open. With the end of his light, his gaze travelled through it and he saw, in the sky, a small twinkling star. Did the twinkling stop or did his body? Or was it one of those untwinkling frozen stars?

It might even have been a Highway Star.

ANSWERS AT THE BACK OF THE BOOK

If you found any answers while reading this story, please write them below.

AFTERWORD

Of course there's an afterword.

A book is best understood as a universe. It begins as a singularity, a mystery on a shelf: fundamental, unknown, unhappened. Once opened, the universe of the book bursts into being as a primordial explosion of information flung in every direction it creates, information that expands and cools and spins, information that collides, attracts, annihilates, contradicts and precipitates as people, places, citations and things. And out of their interactions emerge *events* – orbiting over invisible sheets of emotion, spontaneously excited to form, feeling, unseen charges raining over and through everything, polarizing existence as good or bad or yucky. Is this fresh universe a chaotic indistinct forge, an incomprehensible slapdash mishmash or a synchronous thing of beauty? Does this universe have everything perfectly in its place? Is it a pleasure to witness and ponder upon the infinite wisdom of its creator? Or are there some pacing issues? Who can say? Depends on the universe. Depends on the writer. Is it self-published?

Like those within the universe, those within a book cannot truly understand it as their perspective is limited to remain within its bound pages. Their questions are absurd and irrelevant because the outside of the book is not their prerogative. Indeed, they do not get to ask what is *outside* because outside w h a t? They fret over their information, they dip their pinkies in its energy and attempt to draw its architecture. What else can they do? Bless their hearts. It is of this fundamental information that equations are wrought, of which theologies are formed, different expressions to try to reach outside the inside. And yet every attempt to understand the world is coloured with ineffable unknowability, the other side of the information. The knowledge that existence is at once miracle and terror. The hunch that there are more pages already pressed and inked is out of reach. All of time is printed and numbered and coming.

People go places, plots pop out of sockets and conflict escapes orbits as the disorder of the universe grows. It crests and wanes from act to act until the information expands too far and the system begins to collapse under its own weight. The dander of disorder shoots arcs, the pace reaches a panicked crescendo and things become simple again, the area of concern narrows – *what will happen* to them, *whodunnit* and *how*, *what* are the *answers?* Letters shake and gutters crack, kerning expands, dark energy pushes words apart, the gravity of counters grows until in this catalytic coming together of all the universe again at one point – a conclusion. The end of the universe.

The End.

And what happens after the universe ends?

You get to read it again.

Read enough books, and you begin to wonder … if you listened just closely enough, if you sat just still enough, could you hear, from beyond yourself, from beyond it all, from above it all, from outside it all, the scrape of paper against paper, the sound of a page turning? Maybe the sound of vacuum falls away to a gentle whispering sound of space.

The hum of a black box?

ACKNOWLEDGEMENTS

Crack your knuckles or any preferred joints, stretch your sides and join me under this post-story gable to thank all the people who have made this novel possible. My mother, Vinita Gill, who filled the house with books and lovingly encouraged my every creative exploit and all the noise it made; my sister, Natasha, who started a library of stolen books with me in Dehradun when we were children; and my father, Col Charanjit Singh Gill (Retd.), from whom I inherit my delight in (and overuse of) language. I had banned Natasha from reading this novel because she was taking much too long to do it. I am now happy to lift this ban.

To all my wonderful, encouraging friends, I would like to say thank you. My gratitude is boundless ... now stop irritating me. I am indebted to Amshula, who always shows up (sometimes with samosas); Suhail, who will never read this book; and Manek, with whom I can always drunkenly discuss the illusory nature of reality. Together we have defeated the Demon of Hatred.

This is a pared-down version of *Acts of God* and I have had to kill many darlings that sit in a document titled 'Lovely Things I Have Removed Under Duress'. It was for the best. I'd like to thank my literary agent, editor and publisher for getting this copy into your hands and for blockading my original release plan (free PDF/sky-writing).

Finally, I'd like to thank you! Not only did you finish reading my novel, you're reading the acknowledgments!? Unless, of course, you read the acknowledgements first, in which case I have several doctors I can recommend. Writing this novel was a transcendent, transformative experience. It has freed me, and my greatest hope is that in some small way it has freed you as well.

If you wish to write to me *(PRAISE ONLY)* or have an Italian villa you are excited to donate, please send your gold bullions to contact@kanangill.com

Thank you!

ABOUT THE AUTHOR

Kanan Gill is a writer and comedian from Bangalore, India. Performing worldwide for more than a decade to widespread acclaim, he has written several comedy specials and movies for television, OTTs and film. *Acts of God* is his first published novel.

HarperCollins *Publishers* India

At HarperCollins India, we believe in telling the best stories and finding the widest readership for our books in every format possible. We started publishing in 1992; a great deal has changed since then, but what has remained constant is the passion with which our authors write their books, the love with which readers receive them, and the sheer joy and excitement that we as publishers feel in being a part of the publishing process.

Over the years, we've had the pleasure of publishing some of the finest writing from the subcontinent and around the world, including several award-winning titles and some of the biggest bestsellers in India's publishing history. But nothing has meant more to us than the fact that millions of people have read the books we published, and that somewhere, a book of ours might have made a difference.

As we look to the future, we go back to that one word— a word which has been a driving force for us all these years.

Read.

Harper
Collins

HARPER
PERENNIAL

HARPER
BUSINESS

HARPER
BLACK

हार्पर
हिन्दी

HarperCollins
Children'sBooks

HARPER
DESIGN

HARPER
VANTAGE

Harper
Sport